RONAN'S REVENGE

Also by James Bibby

Ronan the Barbarian
Ronan's Rescue

RONAN'S REVENGE

Painfully translated
from the original Gibberish by
James Bibby

MILLENNIUM
An Orion Book
London

The right of James Bibby to be identified as the author of
this work has been asserted by him in accordance with
the Copyright, Designs and Patents Act 1988.

First published
in Great Britain in 1997 by
Orion Books Ltd
Orion House, 5 Upper St Martin's Lane
London WC2H 9EA

A CIP catalogue record for this book
is available from the British Library

ISBN: (Csd) 1 85798 526 5

Typeset at The Spartan Press Ltd,
Lymington, Hants
Printed and bound in Great Britain by
Clays Ltd, St Ives plc

IN MEMORY OF JAMIE ROBERTS

Acknowledgements

Thanks to my editor, Caroline, and my agent, Tony, for help, guidance, support, and belief. And huge thanks to Collette for everything, but in particular for coping with Pavlov's gag-writer and dog-hair.

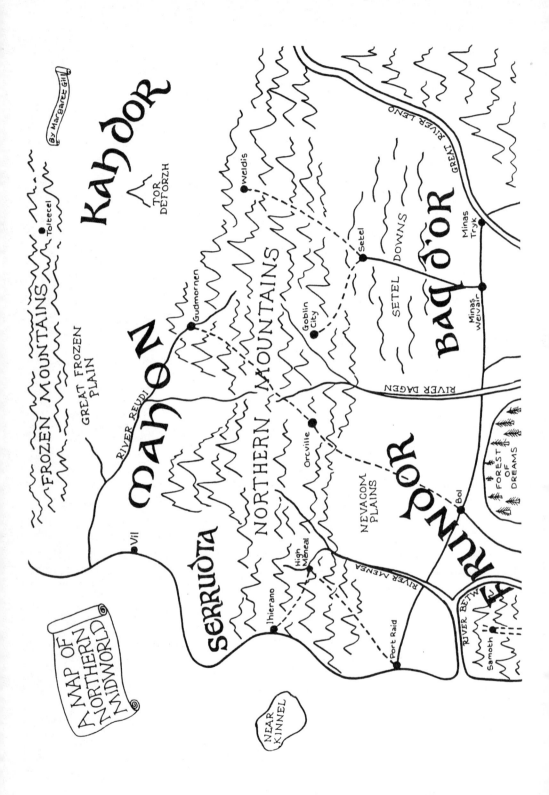

The tradition of myths and story-telling can, according to elvish folklore, be traced back to the very beginning of the world . . .

According to Progenitin, the Father of All Elves, when he chanced upon Midworld during his travels through the celestial sphere, it was a place of bare, barren rock, without living creatures of any kind. And thus did he tarry a while, creating the animals, the rivers, plants and trees using his powerful cosmic magic, and so many different species did he create that he was twelve whole days in the doing.

And when he had finished, he looked upon the world and saw that it was fair. And then did he return to his home in the heavens, where dwelt his wife, Welbrian the Fair. But Welbrian spoke to him angrily, saying, Where the hell have you been? Your dinner's ruined!

And so he told her of all that he had created in the twelve days, of plains of grass and forests of trees, of herds of deer and rivers full of fish, of trolls and dragons, and of elves and men and dwarves. A mighty tale he told, and five hours was he in the telling. And when he had finished, she looked on him and smiled scornfully, saying, You expect me to believe that? Bollocks! You've been down the pub with your mates again!

And so did Progenitin become known as the Great Father of All Story-tellers, as well as one or two other pithier names that Welbrian gave him before flinging his celestial dinner at his mighty head . . .

The Pink Book of Ulay

Ronan's Revenge follows closely in this classical tradition of story-telling. In fact, it's a right load of old myth . . .

PROLOGUE

... but the father of Midworldian Genetics is generally accepted to be Martel the Holy, a monk from Ilex, who postulated his Theory of Genetic Inheritance in Year 1027. In fact, hampered as he was by a sheltered and completely innocent upbringing, he postulated three different theories. Martel's First Theory stated that an individual would inherit fifty per cent of their genetic make-up from their mother, and fifty per cent from the gooseberry bush beneath which they had been found. Martel's Second Theory stated that this latter fifty per cent was in fact inherited from the stork which had brought them. It was only after an extremely close encounter with a nun from the Holy Sisterhood of Carnal Enlightenment (an off-shoot of the Seventh Day Hedonists) that he postulated his Third Theory, and this time he got it right. However, he also discovered that sex was an awful lot more fun than doing a load of crappy experiments with fruit-flies, and abandoned genetics for a life devoted to the pleasures of the flesh. He died, white-haired, stooped and almost blind, at the age of twenty-seven.

Encyclopedia Midworldia[1]

The explosion was only a comparatively minor one, but it shook the subterranean laboratory complex like a small earthquake. Reágin, Chief Scientist of the Dwarven Research Establishment of Deforzh, clutched the edge of his desk and shut his eyes as the blast of air blew his notes whirling about his office and sent his long, white, plaited beard thrashing around his face. Dust billowed through the bare stone archway, setting him coughing, and as the echoes of the blast faded he could hear the sounds of running feet and dwarvish swearing.

Oh, not again, he thought. *Klatting* troll research assistants! Always screwing up! This was the trouble with being a scientist in a

[1] All quotations from the *Encyclopedia Midworldia* are taken without the publisher's permission, but the author flaming well insisted, so please don't come round and trash our offices again as it's not our fault, honest.

world where most people thought of science as some strange and arcane variety of magic. You just couldn't get the staff.

Shaking his head, he hauled his short, bulky frame off his chair and stomped out into the bare stone passageway that was carved from the living rock beneath the mountain. Other dwarves were scurrying about worriedly, but in line with his position as Chief Scientist Reágin refused to panic. Calmly he strode along the passage, his feet leaving prints in the settling dust, until he came to the stone archway on the left that led into the main Alchemic Research Laboratory, and the small crowd of nervously muttering dwarves that had gathered across the doorway parted to let him through.

Inside, the smoke and dust was beginning to clear. The floor was littered with splintered remnants of wooden benches and tables, and broken glass fragments of vials and test-tubes crunched underfoot. A couple of dazed and bleeding dwarf scientists were dragging themselves towards the door, and in the centre of the floor a pair of troll technicians lay still, their white lab coats ripped and green-stained with blood. On the far side of the lab, next to a gaping hole that had been blasted through the solid rock wall, lay a single scaly, taloned foot that ended in a six-inch stump of torn, blood-stained, scabrous leg – the last visible remnant of the troll who had inadvertently caused the blast.

Gesturing to those behind him to help the injured, Reágin picked his way gingerly across to the hole in the wall and moodily booted the troll's foot through into the large and previously undiscovered cavern that had appeared on the other side. He supposed it was really his fault, employing such lame-brains as trolls, but in truth, he'd had no choice in the matter. The level of scientific research had been hugely stepped up in recent years, and his dwarven rulers were demanding quicker and better results. He just couldn't find enough people of his own race to fill all the available posts.

He sighed, and absently brushed a few gobbets of steaming troll flesh off the top of the first-aid box fixed to the wall near the hole. He'd have to stop using trolls. Admittedly they were cheap, plentiful and keen, but their idea of delicate scientific investigation was to hit things with large clubs, and in a laboratory whose contents included saltpetre and trinitrotoluene they didn't usually last very long. And, unfortunately, neither did the lab.

The problem was that no other races made good technicians. Elves flatly refused to work underground. Orcs had looked promising, as they seemed keen and eager to learn, but Reágin had discovered that within three days they had invariably stolen all the best lab equipment and set up complicated stills devoted to the large-scale and rapid production of concentrated ethyl alcohol, which was then drunk at laboratory parties that were inevitably more destructive and life-threatening than an enthusiastic group of trolls investigating nitroglycerine. And as for humans! They lazed about, argued, took time off pretending to be sick, demanded more pay, fewer hours and extra holidays, and when they eventually did turn up at the lab they did bugger-all work and just drank tea all day long.

Maybe he had better go back to using slave labour, but he was a little worried about doing that. Slaves could be surly and resentful, and you couldn't trust them. A few months before, one had suddenly grabbed a Petri dish of acid and hurled it in Reágin's face. Luckily it had been lysergic acid diethylamide and so it hadn't hurt, but some of the stuff had flown down his throat and he had spent the next three days locked in his bedroom, yammering in fear at a series of horrifically vivid hallucinations. No, slaves were out – that is, unless the Genetics Department had come up with anything in the past few months. Mitosin and Meiosin, the two brothers who ran it, had been slyly hinting at all sorts of advances in eugenics and genetic engineering recently. Perhaps he had better go and see what they were up to.

Pausing only to have a brief and sympathetic word with the disappointed Viscerin from Vivisection (who had come bustling in to see if he could get his hands on any seriously wounded trolls for his experiments), Reágin left the ruined laboratory and stomped off along the passage that led to Genetics, the newest research department, housed in a system of caverns that burrowed deeper and further into the heart of the mountain than any other. Reágin very seldom ventured there, partly because as a traditionalist he gave very little credence to all these new-fangled notions about genes and chromosomes and what-not, and partly because Mitosin and Meiosin had made it very obvious that they wanted to be left alone to get on with their work.

That wasn't unusual, of course. The traditional dwarvish method of research was to allow scientists to tinker aimlessly around, just to satisfy their curiosity, and if they came up with something useful, particularly in the field of gold-mining, so much the better. But recently the emphasis had changed, and the Chief Scientist was finding it a little worrying.

Take trinitrotoluene, or TNT, for example. They had known about its explosive qualities for quite a while, and Reágin himself had carried out a few interesting experiments with it, such as tying a couple of orcs to the top of a large block of the stuff and then detonating it, just to see what happened. (He'd discovered that this was only a good idea if you wanted a laboratory ceiling decorated with interesting shades of fragmented orc intestine.) He had eventually decided that the chemical could be used to blast away large quantities of rock if you were in a hurry to get at the gold ore behind it, but apart from mining, it appeared to have no discernible use. But now word had come down from above for Reágin to start examining its potential as a weapon of war. Ridiculous! How were you meant to persuade your enemies to sit on top of a block of dangerously explosive chemical while you detonated it? The Chief Scientist shook his head in exasperation. The problem with these people back home was that they just didn't have a scientific mind.

It was the same in every department now. All of a sudden his superiors were only interested in results, and the quicker, the better. Admittedly they had promised a vast increase in funding, but Reágin had heard a rumour just the other day that most of this was earmarked for genetic research. Yes, it was definitely time that he found out exactly what Mitosin and Meiosin were up to.

Coming to the solid metal door that sealed off the department, the Chief Scientist unlocked it with his pass key and eased it open. Immediately a cacophony of moans, howls and screams met his ears, and his nostrils were assailed by the rank, excremental stench from the creature pens. Most of the labyrinthine system of caverns that made up the Genetics Department had been turned into holding cages for the unfortunate animals that were the subjects of the experiments in selective breeding or the magically induced mutations produced by the new science of magenetics.[2]

Closing and locking the heavy door behind him, Reágin advanced cautiously. Flickering torches lined the walls of the stone passageway, but through the doorways on either side he could see that the laboratories were dark and deserted. No one seemed to be about. Ahead of him two side passages branched off, and the open lab doorways were replaced by the solid metal doors of the creature pens. The stench was almost overpowering now, and the noise from the captive creatures was continuous. Swallowing, Reágin crept along apprehensively. He had good reason to be nervous.

[2] For information on magenetics (and other Midworldian oddities) see Appendix One.

Initially, the two brothers' experiments had seemed harmless enough. Indeed, once or twice he had needed to reprimand them for their casual, almost irreverent attitudes. For example, there had been the time when they had successfully crossed an Ilectian Cavy (a small, pig-like creature) with an Irridic Mountain Grunt (a lethal giant wild boar). The resulting offspring had been harmless enough, but Reágin had been forced to step in and insist that they call it a Gravy. Mitosin's suggested name for the creature was, to say the least, unseemly, and had raised serious doubts in Reágin's mind about his suitability for such a responsible scientific post.

In recent years, however, the whole aspect of their experiments had changed, and they had come up with all sorts of strange and frightening crosses, some of which had been quite terrifying. And then they had produced the *cobrats* . . .

Reágin paused, and eased a finger around the inside of a collar that had suddenly become a size too small. All at once his face was damp with sweat. The *cobrats* were bred from *lenkats*, the sleek and lethal predators from the Azure Mountains, but with a lot of orc blood and a smattering of Cydorian Cobra thrown in for good luck. The result was a carnivore with sleek, glossy fur and razor-sharp, venomous teeth. It was more than six feet fall, moved on its hind legs, was lethally fast and had a fierce intelligence. And Mitosin and Meiosin had bred seven of the buggers!

Just how intelligent and dangerous they were had been amply demonstrated by the fact that, although incarcerated in securely locked creature pens, they had managed to escape on two separate occasions. And each time they had massacred and fed off the lab staff on duty in the Genetics Department. Reágin shuddered. He could still see the torn and mangled bodies, or what was left of them. After the second escape they had never found the slightest trace of Purin, the duty scientist, or his two sons, Adenin and Guanin. He sometimes wondered if he was the only person who found it suspicious that both Mitosin and Meiosin, who normally never left the laboratories, had been absent on both occasions.

Moving almost on tiptoe, Reágin followed the passage as it curved to the right, sloping gradually downwards into the heart of the mountain. The wall torches were less frequent here and the passage was darker, but then it bent sharply back to the left and ended abruptly. A single torch flickered in a rock-hewn sconce on the end wall, illuminating a thick metal door on the right-hand side of the passage – a stoutly locked and bolted door that Reágin knew to be six inches thick. The door that was the only access to the *cobrats'* high-security pen.

Hardly daring to breathe, the Chief Scientist crept up to the door and, ever so gently, eased aside the tiny spy-hole cover. Then very, very carefully he held his eye to the hole and peered through into the pen beyond. For a few seconds he stood there, motionless, and then he fell back with a gasp. The pen was empty! By the beard of Palin! Surely they hadn't escaped a third time? He thrust his eye back to the spy-hole again, desperately praying that he was somehow mistaken, and then light flared from behind him and he spun round gasping and fell back against the metal, his heart hammering with fear.

A small door on the other side of the passage had opened, and a dwarf was leaning nonchalantly against the lintel, framed in the candlelight that shone forth from within. Behind him Reágin could see a small table that appeared to be covered in bars of gold, gleaming and glinting dully in the light.

'Can I help you?' the dwarf drawled coldly.

'Meiosin!' Reágin gasped with relief, and steadied himself against the wall with one hand, trying to pull himself together. The other dwarf said nothing, but merely stroked his dark beard, reflectively.

'The *cobrats*!' continued Reágin. 'They're not in their pen!'

'No,' agreed Meiosin.

'But why not? Where are they?'

'They've . . . gone. We had a . . . client who was very interested in our work, and particularly in the *cobrats*. We sent him one, on approval. He was very impressed, and asked for the other six, as well. He was quite grateful . . .' Meiosin glanced back at the gold-laden table, and a small smile played about his lips. 'Remarkably grateful, in fact,' he continued. 'And he wishes to fund a lot more of our research.'

'Why wasn't I told?'

'The client was most concerned with secrecy.'

'But . . . but . . . those things are killers! Completely and utterly lethal! We can't let creatures like them loose upon the world!'

The other dwarf shrugged.

'We only made them,' he answered indifferently. 'It's up to the client now. It's not our problem any more.'

'But what on earth does he want with them?'

'I haven't the faintest idea,' answered Meiosin. 'But I'll tell you this much. I would feel extremely sorry for anyone who gets on the wrong side of him!'

And grinning sardonically, the dwarf stepped smartly backwards and shut the door deliberately in the Chief Scientist's face.

With a slightly apprehensive expression and a large bucket of fresh water in one hand, Wayta, the chairman of the board of the Orcbane Sword Corporation, strolled across the scorching-hot sunlit court-yard of his country residence and paused outside the heavily bolted storeroom door to wipe his sweating forehead with the back of his hand. From inside came the sound of rustling and a hissing that made the hairs on the back of his neck stand up. With his hand on the topmost bolt he paused and swallowed nervously. *Come on*, he told himself. *You're the one man in all of Midworld who has nothing to fear from this creature . . .*

Thrusting back the bolts, he pushed the door open. Light flooded into the windowless stone room, and at the sight of the tall, lithe creature that stood balanced on its hind legs, looking down at him, Wayta once again felt the unfamiliar thrill of fear. Its dark, oily fur gleamed in the light and the very tip of its long, sinuous tail twitched from side to side as it watched him quizzically, its head delicately tilted to one side. Its red eyes seemed to glow, as though on fire, but the lethal six-inch claws remained sheathed and the razor-sharp teeth stayed hidden.

Wayta put down the bucket of fresh water and picked up the empty one that was lying on its side by the door. He peered round, but apart from a few white and splintered bones protruding from the straw that covered the floor, there was no sign of the drunken old vagrant whom he had bundled through the door two days before, and he shivered. Meiosin had been right! The *cobrat* was absolutely lethal! But, as the dwarf had promised, it now regarded Wayta as its master, and it was genetically programmed to obey him, even unto death. All the same, he felt extremely and frighteningly vulnerable in its presence.

The *cobrat* stooped and sniffed delicately at the water, then straightened and stared at him, its eyes whirling a deeper, blood-like red.

'Massssster?' it hissed. 'Food?'

'You must hunt for food,' he told it. 'Tonight, I will send you out. But you are to track somebody down for me.'

The *cobrat* hissed excitedly, and with a frisson of fear Wayta watched the very tips of the creature's talons slide out from the sheaths of the front paws.

9

'He is staying in a hotel on the coast, north-west of here,' he continued. 'He is a guest.'

'Guessst!'

'Find him and kill him.'

'Ssssssssss!'

The *cobrat*'s mouth opened, and the rows of razor-sharp teeth grinned at Wayta as it hissed with excitement. A waft of hot breath blasted past him, and all at once he realised that it was heavy with the sweet smell of the vagrant's blood . . .

Hastily he stepped backwards, dragging the door shut and slamming home the bolts with hands that shook uncontrollably. For a short while he leant with his back against it, breathing heavily, fighting to control the panic that had all but overwhelmed him. In his years as chairman of the Orcbane Sword Corporation he had been responsible for many deaths, but always indirectly, through others. Such a dangerously close association with violent, painful death was not an experience that he was enjoying, and he would be glad when the creature had been programmed with an image of its intended target and was well away from here.

Sighing, he straightened up and recrossed the courtyard towards the broad stone keep. He was a busy man, and the *cobrat* wasn't the only killer that he was due to see that day.

Wayta liked to describe himself as the classic rags-to-riches story, although no one knew very much about his background. He claimed that he was the son of eastern barbarians, and that he had run away from home at the age of ten when his psychopathically cruel father had beaten him black and blue just for feeding the hamster. In fact, his parents had been extremely kind and enlightened folk for barbarians, and his father had merely smacked him when he had fed the hamster. And that was only because he had fed it to the cat. But Wayta had developed a fascination with wealth and power from an early age, and the truth was that he despised his parents, who were simple farming folk and quite happy with their lot.

Wherever he had spent the intervening months, Wayta had eventually surfaced in the city of Ged at the age of thirteen, and was soon successfully trading in farming produce, although rumour had said that the produce was stolen. Whatever the truth was, by the age of fifteen he had become a merchant, earning his living in more legal, if scarcely more moral, ways. It was at this time that he had discovered that money didn't buy him respect. The other merchants had looked down on him, laughing at his crude manners and his ignorant, barbarian ways, and had treated him with barely veiled contempt.

The turning point had come on the day that he first attended a Merchants' Guild dinner. It had also been his first time in a proper restaurant, and he had become convinced that people at every table kept calling out his name. He had grown angrier and angrier, and it was only after he had caused something of a scene that he had discovered they were merely trying to attract the attention of the serving staff. The other merchants had found the whole thing hilarious, and Wayta had become an object of open derision. It was then that the pursuit of wealth and power, which had so far been a mere crusade, became an obsession.

A few months later, he had been offered a seat on the board of the Orcbane Sword Corporation, a long-established but financially shaky family company that was looking for new ideas in a desperate attempt to stave off bankruptcy. His first move had been to bring on to the board his assistant and only friend, a plump and extremely devious eighteen-year-old called Grole. Within six months they had appointed to the board four other financial whiz-kids, who shared three things in common. They were young, they were financially astute, and they were ruthlessly eager to acquire both wealth and power. The original board members, sad old men burdened down with outmoded notions of honour and fair play, had gradually been elbowed aside and put out to grass, and the six men had set out to make what was then a comparatively small business into a success story.

As the business had grown, so had their power and ambition. They had expanded rapidly from their base in Ged, taking over and absorbing other arms manufacturers in other countries, until they had held a virtual monopoly throughout Midworld. Bribery and corruption had always been an integral part of their strategy, but it was no longer customs officials or rival sales personnel that they had bought, but councillors and politicians, and sometimes whole governments.

They had long known that, as a company which dealt exclusively in arms, the one thing guaranteed to increase the Orcbane turnover was a good war. Prolonged periods of peace always caused their profit margins to shrink alarmingly, and so when Wayta, by then the new chairman, had suggested that it might be a financially risky business to wait for another war to turn up when they were quite capable of fomenting one themselves, the other five went along with his suggestions without a second thought.

11

They had spent a lot of time and money in planning and setting up what was meant to have been the biggest major conflict of modern times. Central to their strategy had been two figures: the barbarian warrior-mage Nekros the Black, and the powerful young wizard Anthrax. But just as they were setting the whole process in motion, a young upstart of a warrior named Ronan had appeared from nowhere, caused Anthrax to defect and killed Nekros. The board had countered with the enlistment of Shikara, an extremely powerful but unstable sorceress. To their horror, they had discovered that they were out of their depth and could not control her. She had taken over their painstakingly assembled armies and had led them on a trail of death and destruction that had cut a swathe through the heart of Midworld,[3] before being defeated in battle by this same Ronan and his allies, and meeting her death at the hands of Tyson, Ronan's warrior girlfriend.

Having uncovered the board's role in these affairs, Ronan had sworn vengeance. He had acquired some powerful friends, and the board had realised that they were in real danger. Unnerved by their experience at the hands of Shikara and made uncomfortably aware of their own mortality, they had decided to lie low for a while, and had vanished to their own personal estates. But that had been two months ago, and since then nothing had happened.

In the meantime, the Chairman had set in motion a number of in-depth enquiries about Ronan. The Orcbane Sword Corporation's Personnel Department had been working overtime, and experts in warcraft, psychology and the arcane had delivered their reports. They made uncomfortable reading. Their assessment was that the warrior was the sort of sad, deluded human being who believed in Right and Wrong, and who would not be deflected by fear, bribery or any of Orcbane's other regular methods from doing what he believed to be the Decent Thing. He also had a number of powerful friends and allies, some of whom were magic-users of unusual ability, and one of whom (Anthrax the Wizard) had a detailed knowledge of the board's activities and methods. The reports went on to estimate that there was a ninety per cent probability that Ronan would kill at least one of the six board members if left unchecked, and that his most likely target would be the Chairman himself.

However, Wayta had no intention of leaving such a deluded, moralistic and, above all, dangerous meddler unchecked. A firm

3 See *Ronan the Barbarian* and *Ronan's Rescue* for these exploits.

believer in the tenet that attack is the best form of defence, he had already made his plans, and the release of the first *cobrat* was just the initial move.

He paused at the top of the broad stone steps that led to the solid wooden door of the keep and looked back over his shoulder. From here he could see over the top of the curtain walls and right across the acres of vineyards covering the south-facing ground that sloped down to the Maremma, the vast, swampy estuary of the Brannan River. Beyond it, the Maelvanta Sea was a distant golden sparkle in the noonday sunshine.

Turning, Wayta pushed open the stout oaken door and entered the cool shade of the stone-flagged hallway. Despite the scorching outside temperatures this far south, the three-feet-thick walls of the keep meant that it was always comfortably cool inside. As he closed the door behind him, Bownedd, his secretary/bodyguard, leapt up from the bench where he had been sitting, and made a deeply reverent, albeit ungainly, bow.

'Sir!' he boomed. 'The Guild Representative has arrived, and I have had further messages from our agents . . .'

He waved a small sheaf of parchments that were clutched in one mighty hand. Bownedd was a great hulk of a man, powerful and strong, yet intelligent too. Although his main work was secretarial, he came in useful in moments of danger, as he was lethal both with a sword and with his bare hands. Wayta had also found that he was invaluable whenever anyone needed to be persuaded about any-thing, as he was very good at breaking things and frightening people. In his spare time, by way of a change, he apparently liked to collect frightening things and enjoyed breaking people.

Wayta clicked his fingers.

'Tell me,' he ordered.

'Ronan and Tyson are still at the hotel.'

'Good! We'll release the first *cobrat* tonight. Anything else urgent?'

'Acquisitions have informed us that the takeover of the shield-making company, Brooke Brothers, is complete.'

'Excellent. I've wanted to get my hands on Brooke Shields for a long time. Is that it?'

'Er, well, no, not quite. It seems that in the wake of Shikara's rampage through Behan and Cydor, sales of Orcbane products in those two countries have risen by, er . . .' Bownedd plucked a parchment from the sheaf and consulted it. 'Um, eighty-seven per cent in the past two weeks. However, sales in western Iduin have plummeted, mainly because of the activities of a new company.'

'Unimportant.' Wayta dismissed this with a wave of his hand. 'Buy them out or frighten them off.'

'Could be difficult. It's a company called Tarltrad Inc. Deals in second-hand weapons, and it's run by that little piss-head who hangs around with Ronan . . .'

Wayta sighed and rubbed his eyes with his finger and thumb for a moment. This Ronan and his shabby little friends were rapidly becoming a major irritant.

'Right,' he muttered, vexedly. 'That settles it. I've had enough. We send out the other *cobrats* as soon as they get here. And send the Assassins' Guild Representative straight in to see me.'

He turned and marched through the door that led to his office, slamming it behind him. Crossing to the single window of the oak-panelled room, he stared out. The window was set facing eastwards in the outside wall of the keep, and had extensive views across Wayta's estate, which ran all the way to the distant wriggling line that was the Atro-to-Ged road.

This is not to be borne, he thought. *To be in danger of losing all this because of some upstart do-gooder of a warrior!*

The door opened, and a small, thin-faced man sidled in like oil creeping across the floor. He was dressed in the black and silver that was traditional Assassin's garb, and looked rather like a rat with a dash of *lenkat* blood in him. As Wayta turned to face him he gave the slightest of bows, as equal to equal.

'How may the Guild be of service?' he asked, in tones as cold and clipped as ice cracking.

'I want someone dead,' Wayta hissed. 'I want it done quickly, and I want no mistakes. I want to know that he is as surely dead as if I had just cut his head off myself . . .'

The Assassin stared at him levelly.

'It will be done. Who is the target?'

'A warrior called Ronan.'

'Ronan?' The Assassin drew in his breath sharply. 'A worthy foe, indeed. Then I think this errand had best be given to Slanved.'

For the first time in a long while, Wayta laughed out loud, and then he sat down in his chair and leant back, his arms behind his head.

'Slanved, eh?' he drawled. 'Wonderful! Do you know, I almost begin to feel sorry for that poor, deluded fool of a warrior . . .'

CHAPTER ONE

Aldis, a town to the south-east of Perplec, in northern Iduin, was originally the centre of an area of rich farming estates, and was ruled by a group of indolent, degenerate nobles, the Board of Aldis. However, the downtrodden serfs who tended the land arose in the revolt of AD 994 and seized power, forming a new ruling board from amongst their own, and thus was this new government known as the Serf Board . . .

The Pink Book of Ulay

As Tarl walked out through the town gates of Aldis with Puss the donkey trotting beside him, he could feel his spirits soaring like a vulture on a thermal. As he strode out along the dusty road that wound north-west towards Perplec, he thought that he had never before been so glad to leave a place behind. He glanced back over his shoulder towards the slender, pale stone walls and the graceful towers of the small town. What a *klatting* dump, he thought.

Oh, the business side of his trip had gone well enough. He'd made a few contacts, rented a stall in the local market, and had found an honest local boy to look after the stall and sell his weapons for him. Tarltrad Inc. had yet another retail outlet. No, it was the social side that was killing him. Quite frankly, Aldis didn't have one. Despite the sheer beauty of the town, it was probably the most boring place Tarl had been since the time he had spent four days locked in a prison cell with a Jehovah's Witless[4] who had spent the entire time trying to convert him to religion.

Apparently the inhabitants of Aldis had had a lot of problems in the past with drunken tourists, and so the puritan town council had passed a law forbidding the use of alcohol within the town walls and making it an imprisonable offence to be inebriated. As Tarl was a guy who regarded it as an offence to be sober, he and the town did not get on, and it was only thanks to Puss that he had avoided being seized

---

[4] A rather lazy religious sect which specifically targets the intellectually challenged, on the grounds that they tend to believe anything they are told, and are thus much easier to convert.

and arraigned by the Drunkfinder General. Still, that was one advantage of having as a friend a donkey which, thanks to a powerful wizard, could now speak, and was the owner of a mind as devious as something extremely devious indeed.

It had been his first night in town. Tarl had been dozing in a doorway with his head resting on a nearly empty wine-sac when the Drunkfinder had come marching up, peered at him closely, sniffed the air and had then started yelling out accusations. But Puss had intervened, and within a minute had convinced the man that, as he was having a conversation with a small brown donkey, he must be as pissed as a *vart*. The Drunkfinder had at first protested that he hadn't touched a drop of the stuff, but Puss had pointed out that memory loss was a frequent symptom of extreme drunkenness, and that as Drunkfinder General it was his job to arrest himself. The bemused man had wandered off towards the town Bridewell, and the donkey had shepherded Tarl out through the town gates to safety.

Robbed of his favourite pastime, Tarl would usually have headed for one of the few nightclubs and chanced his luck on the dance-floor. He tended to be far more successful with women than someone small, balding and seedy had a right to be, although Puss had pointed out that the sort of women he attracted tended to be like the nightclubs he frequented – loud, sweaty and with a couple of large bouncers at the front. But two months previously he had met Guebral, a member of the Dead Boys (a group of young and persecuted magic-users who lived rough on the streets of the city of Yai'El). Naive but street-wise, and with more natural magical ability than anyone Tarl had ever met, she had seen the goodness buried deep inside him, and they had become lovers. After the death of Shikara at the Battle of Grey Sea Fields she had returned to Yai'El with the surviving Dead Boys in an attempt to make their peace with a populace that had previously persecuted them. Tarl, having managed to acquire most of the weapons that had belonged to the dead or defeated at the battle, had spent the past two months touring towns and cities in south Cydor and west Iduin, setting up second-hand weapon franchises, and though fidelity was something he usually associated with orc mage-deck sound-systems, he was determined not to let Guebral down. So womanising was out.

That had left gambling. After much sniffing about, Tarl had heard rumours of a card-school, but when he had eventually tracked it down, it had turned out to be a room behind a knitting-supplies shop, where an old lady was teaching nine other old ladies how to play canasta. He had spent the worst evening of his life being flirted with by a couple of eighty-year-olds. And he'd lost five bronze *tablons* as well; the old dears cheated outrageously. No, as far as Tarl was concerned, Aldis was marginally less fun than standing in the middle of a desert watching a cactus grow.

But now he was free of the place! The franchise was arranged, the initial payment had been made and the delivery of weapons had arrived. Now he could take some time off. A few days with Ronan and Tyson at their hotel beckoned, followed by a lengthy sojourn with Guebral in Yai'El. Tarl strode on happily, Puss trotting contentedly beside him, and the sun beat down and warmed his scrawny shoulders through the thin leather vest.

The road wound on through the arid hills, and then after a while began to slope downwards, shimmering in the heat. Tarl wiped his brow with the back of his hand, and then unscrewed his water bottle and drained it. He was just trying to decide whether his first cocktail that night should be an Elf's Pecker or a Dol Dupp Daiquiri when suddenly there was a bang like a personalised thunderbolt and a blast of hot air sent him sprawling sideways.

For a few moments he lay there in the dust at the side of the road, shaking his dazed head to try and clear it, and then he realised that an image of Guebral's face was floating above the road and peering blankly towards him.

'Gueb!' he gasped.

'Tarl!' the image said urgently. 'Listen to me. Things have gone wrong here! The city has turned against us once more, virtually overnight. We're okay, but we're trapped in the warehouse again, and there are magic-users out there manipulating the mob. I can't leave the others. Someone has planned this, and I can feel the hand of the Orcbane board behind it. Warn Ronan and Tyson that the board are active again. You could all be in danger. Get to them quickly!'

And then the image was gone, and he found himself staring into the cynical eyes of the little brown donkey.

'Typical,' muttered Puss. 'Your friends are in danger, and you decide to have forty winks at the side of the road. Selfish, some would call it.'

Biting back an angry retort, Tarl grabbed the donkey's moth-eaten ears and hauled himself upright.

'Come on, carrot-breath, we'd better get moving. Last one there's a foul-smelling quadruped.'

And with that the two of them were trotting along the road as it bent away to the west, heading down through the hills towards the hidden hotels and villas that lined the shores of the Perplec coastline.

Ronan lay motionless as the scorching heat seared into his back, and pondered the choices that were open to him. There were only two, really, but deciding was difficult. Should he lie here in the sun a little longer, or wander down the beach and join Tyson, who was swimming in the sea. Tricky. Decisions, decisions. He rolled over and sat up, shielding his eyes against the glaring Iduinian sun and squinting out over the ocean. Out of the corner of his eye he saw a flash of brilliant red as a *fire-skink* scuttled hastily across the burning sand into the shade of a rock.

Halfway out towards the coral reef, Tyson was swimming on her back, her arms lazily windmilling in and out of the warm water, but seeing Ronan watching her she turned and swam towards the beach in a fast, effortless crawl. Standing, she waded through the surf that was drowsily lapping at the edge of the sand and walked slowly up the slope of the beach. She was naked, and her muscles moved smoothly under the skin of her super-fit body, the legacy of years of warrior training. Two months in the Perplec climate had tanned her a dark brown, and her short hair had bleached almost blonde.

Ronan watched her with a happy smile on his face. It was past noon now, time for them to wander back to the shade of the hotel patio bar in search of a bite to eat and a long, cool drink, followed by an hour or two together in the privacy of their hotel bedroom. During the past few weeks they had gorged themselves on food, drink and lovemaking, experimenting with recipes, cocktails and sexual positions that Ronan had never even dreamt of before. Merely thinking about it all gave him a warm glow inside. He had discovered the joys of a Screwdriver, a Rusty Nail and a Harvey Wallbanger. And they were just the sexual positions . . .

Reaching him, Tyson grinned down and then combed her hair back with the fingers of one hand and flicked sea-water at his face. A few drops fell in his open mouth, and the faint salt tang suddenly made him realise how thirsty he was.

'The water's just beautiful for swimming,' she said, reaching down for her cropped leather halter-top. 'You should come in more.'

Ronan shook his head doubtfully. He loved the feeling of being immersed in the warm blue-green sea, but he'd read far too many books about sea monsters as an impressionable child, and couldn't spend more than ten minutes in the water before becoming uncomfortably certain that something horrible was about to grab him and drag him under. He stood up and began to haul on the garishly patterned beach shorts that he had bought in Perplec market.

'I'm happy just working up a thirst on the beach,' he answered. 'Let's get to the bar. I'm dying for a drink.'

'Me too. I fancy a Southern Kiss today.'

'Is that when I . . .'

'Cool it, buster, it's the name of a cocktail.'

'Shame.'

'Talking of drink, did Tarl say when he'd be back?'

'Tonight, he hoped, if all goes well. Why?'

Tyson sighed and looked up at him with a serious expression on her face.

'Because we need to get everyone together soon, babe. Tarl, Guebral and the Dead Boys, maybe even Anthrax. We need to get after the board of the Orcbane Sword Corporation. We can't stay here for ever.'

'Ah, those sad old men?' said Ronan, waving a dismissive hand. 'They can wait a while. They'll all be hidden away somewhere, shivering with fear. We don't need to worry yet.'

And with that sadly inaccurate forecast, he turned and led the way through the palm trees towards the half-hidden white-stone hotel complex.

The manager of Thongs ('Iduin's Premier Beach Hotel') was a little perturbed. He had spent the past half-hour trying to pacify the cleaning staff, who had rebelled after being asked to clean up the mess left by a group of barbarian tribesmen on a package holiday who had all insisted on keeping their horses in their bedrooms. And now, just when he was looking forward to a sandwich and a cup of tea in his office, he'd found that there was no one in reception. The place was deserted.

He gazed around the cool, shady, marble-floored entrance hall, almost as if he was expecting the receptionist to leap out from behind one of the large, bushy pot-plants that lined the white-stone walls, but nothing stirred. Typical, he thought. You just can't get the staff. Mind you, it wasn't surprising, the way the barbarians had treated them. Used to being waited on by slaves, they had assumed that the staff were dispensable, and so every time they got bored they would kill a waiter, just to liven things up a bit. He had tried employing ex-warriors as waiters, but that had nearly backfired, and he had been forced to drum home to the new staff that you *never*, no matter how severe the provocation, massacre the clientele.

No, it wasn't easy running a luxury hotel in a world where most people thought luxury meant not having to live in the same room as the pigs. They were more trouble than they were worth, those northern tribesmen. Take their attitude to water. If there was a lot of it, they thought you sailed on it. If there was just a little, you drank from it (which had caused consternation in the toilets). If there was a medium amount, you drowned people in it or pissed in it (or sometimes both). They hadn't half made a mess of the hotel swimming pool. The manager shook his head tiredly. They had been the worst set of guests since that wizards' convention, three years previously, and he still had nightmares about that. The top storey of the hotel still hadn't reappeared, and they had never found a way of changing the assistant manager back from a ginger tom-cat. Mind you, he did keep the mice down . . .

The manager glanced over to the reception desk. It looked as though someone had left a pink hosepipe draped across the polished wooden top. Tutting to himself at such untidiness, he strode across the marble floor, but then slewed to a halt. A foot was sticking out from behind the desk, a foot that looked remarkably like that of the duty receptionist . . .

All at once the realisation hit him. He could see now that the 'hosepipe' was gleaming moistly, and had oozed a familiar red stain where it touched the wooden surface. Gagging, he inched forwards and peered over the top of the desk. An awful lot more of the stuff had flopped out on to the floor from the torn and empty stomach cavity of the dead receptionist. Horror-struck, he backed away and then turned to run for help, only to be confronted by three more eviscerated bodies draped across the back of the couch which stood in the alcove under the stairs that had once led to the first floor. Guests, probably, to judge by the garish clothes, but they were so ripped and blood-stained that it was almost impossible to recognise them. For a long time he stared at them blankly, rooted to the spot by shock, and then the door that led to the restaurant opened and a creature stalked through.

20

It was well over six feet tall and moved on its hind legs in a crouched posture. Dark, greasy fur covered it from head to foot, and a long, sinuous tail flicked from side to side behind it. A pair of cold red eyes gleamed across at the manager from deep recesses on either side of a short snout. Its head moved jerkily as it seemed to sniff the air, and then its vast mouth parted in a humourless grin, and a green, scaly tongue flicked out from behind rows of razor-sharp teeth.

'Guessst?' it hissed quizzically, and then started to pace smoothly towards him.

The manager turned to run, but before he had gone three paces he was grabbed from behind and hauled bodily into the air. The creature held him suspended from one wickedly taloned paw and seemed to be inspecting him. He was horrified to see that the fur round its mouth and down its chest was soaked and matted with blood.

'Guessst?' it enquired again in a voice that was high-pitched, slurred and reptilian. It sounded rather like a crocodile that had had several drinks too many, and he might even have found it comical if he hadn't been so frightened. But then it reached out the other paw and raked its vicious talons across his stomach, and the manager began to scream.

Ronan and Tyson strolled hand in hand up the steps and through the open door of the hotel. They were so wrapped up in each other that they were halfway across the lobby before a faint hiss attracted their attention, and they swung round and saw the creature that was standing by the reception desk. It was holding the manager up with one forepaw, and despite the fact that his innards had become his outards and were sagging from his abdomen like pleated red curtains, they could see he was still alive. His chest heaved in and out in agonised little jerks, and one blood-soaked hand was scrabbling weakly and ineffectually at his tormentor's furry throat.

The creature peered interestedly at them, and seemed almost to smile.

'Aah!' it hissed. 'Guessst!' Then it lifted the manager's arm in its other paw and opened its mouth wide. They watched, horrified, as a pair of long fangs hinged downwards to jut out past the rows of teeth, and gently, almost lovingly, it bit the arm. For a few seconds nothing happened, and then a purple coloration infused the flesh, spreading rapidly outwards from the puncture marks, and the arm seemed to swell up to twice its size. The manager twitched spasmodically and began to thresh about, a thin, agonised wailing coming from his

F/0148329

mouth. For what seemed like an age he twisted and jerked about like a child's puppet, then suddenly every muscle in his body gave one last huge convulsion, and he was hanging motionless like so much dead meat. For a few seconds the creature stared at him curiously, its head on one side, as though it still expected him to make a break for it, and then it dropped him carelessly into a lifeless heap on the floor.

Ronan swallowed. Whatever that venom was, it acted lethally fast. Then he realised that the creature had switched its gaze to him.

'Guessst!' it hissed again, and began to pace purposefully forwards, its eyes fixed on Ronan and Tyson. Warily the two of them backed away, their hands reaching for their swords, and the horrifying realisation hit them both at exactly the same moment. They glanced at each other, and each could see the panic in the other's eyes.

The relaxed and carefree beach lifestyle had caused them to forget one of the most basic tenets of the warrior code, and they were both completely and totally unarmed.

CHAPTER TWO

*Of the many unpleasant flora found in the western lands,
surely one of the foulest must be the Brannian Deathbush. This
semi-intelligent, carnivorous shrub-like tree has mobile
tendrils, on the end of which are conical mouth-shaped leaves
lined with sharp spines. These the shrub thrusts towards any
mobile living creature that comes within reach in an attempt
to take bites out of their flesh, and although the leaves are only
small, the resulting nips can be quite painful. Far more
dangerous is the tree's bark, which exudes a toxic sap so deadly
that contact with human skin causes death in seconds.*

*The Deathbush is often used as a hedge by rich house-owners
who wish to ensure a little privacy for themselves, and it is the
only Midworldian organism of which it can accurately be said
that its bark truly is worse than its bite . . .*

Maxon the Small, Vita Horribilorum

Tarl had only been running for about thirty minutes, but to judge by
the dull ache in his legs and the savage stitch in his side it could have
been three days. As he liked to tell people, the nearest he ever got to
keeping fit was running up a large tab in his local wine bar. If the gods
had meant him to exercise, he'd always said, they would have given
him some muscles, but as they hadn't, he didn't. Now, as his
labouring lungs seemed about to explode inside his chest, he was
regretting it. But he didn't dare to stop. Since getting Guebral's
message he had become strangely convinced that Ronan and Tyson
were in some horrible danger, and he felt a desperate compulsion to
get to them and warn them. And so he ignored the insistent little
voice in the back of his mind that kept suggesting that he would be
better off sitting at the side of the road to get his breath back for a
while, and trotted on with Puss at his side.

Still, there wasn't far to go now. Ahead, the road wound down the
hill to the hotel complex half hidden in the palm trees below, and
beyond it, the sea glittered and shimmered in the heat-haze. Up here
the air was cooler, and the on-shore breeze provided some small

relief from the searing sun. On either side of the road, tall Deathbush hedges screened off the sprawling white-stone villas that were the summer residences of Iduin's rich and famous: top gladiators from the Cumanceum such as Nuddo the Talkative, singing stars like Elven Stardust and Elvish Costello, or successful actors such as James the Mason and Stanley the Baker. Somewhere behind the thick hedge on the left was the mansion belonging to Jack, the son of Nichol, a hell-raising actor who reputedly threw some of the wildest parties in Midworld, and peeping out from the trees to the right was the roof of the distinctive pink villa belonging to Rock, the son of Hud.

Tarl let the slope carry him down to the foot of the hill and then stopped. The track curved off to the right, disappearing into the palm trees, and ahead of him lay the arched gateway and the paved drive that led to the Thongs holiday complex. Bending forwards, he rested with his hands on his knees, his head hanging down and his chest heaving, and then retched noisily.

The donkey watched him sadly and shook its head.

'I've seen month-old corpses that were in better condition than you are, mate,' it muttered, before wandering across to the gate.

Tarl didn't bother replying. He was too busy struggling to get his breath back. Then something odd struck him, and he lifted his head. There was no movement anywhere, no people to be seen, no sound of holidaymakers enjoying themselves. The only noise he could hear was the rasping of his own breath and the occasional disdainful snort from Puss. Nothing else, not even birdsong.

Puzzled, he looked across to where the little donkey was sniffing at a crumpled bundle of clothing piled against the left-hand gate. Straightening, he opened his mouth to make a sarcastic remark, but the words died in his throat and he lurched across to stand beside the donkey and stared down, horror-struck.

The crumpled bundle of clothing was the gate security guard, an experienced warrior from Velos whom Tarl had met on his way down to Aldis. Or at least, Tarl assumed it was the gate guard. It was a little difficult to be sure. The body and the blood-stained clothes looked familiar, but there weren't any other distinguishing features for him to go by. In fact, there weren't many features of any description. Something large, powerful and hungry had bitten the man's face clean off.

Usually, when faced with sudden danger, Ronan's warrior training took over and he intuitively selected the most favourable course of action from the many possibilities that presented themselves. This time, however, there weren't too many options available. Weaponless, and facing a massive but agile creature with more teeth than a convention of dentists that was seemingly intent on turning both him and Tyson into dragon-sized portions of chitterlings, his paralysed mind could only come up with one plan of action. Get the *klat* out of here, fast!

Grabbing Tyson's hand, Ronan yanked open a door in the wall behind them and dragged her through, and then slamming it shut he thrust home the bolt and turned to run. That was when he found that he had locked them inside a windowless office that contained a large desk, a padded chair, several pot-plants and a small wooden cocktail cabinet, but was desperately short of other doors.

'Oh,' he said.

Tyson gazed quickly around as a resounding crash against the other side of the door nearly ripped it from its hinges, but there was no way out. Ronan looked down at her.

'We're trapped,' he added, a little guiltily.

'Looks like it.'

'How much longer do you think the door will hold?'

Crash!

'About three seconds.'

'Getting drunk is out, then.'

'Looks like it.' Tyson strode across to the desk and lifted one side of it. 'Here, help me to move this across. If we can wedge . . .'

CRASH!! The door burst away from its hinges, sagging tiredly to one side, and the creature strode through. For a moment it paused, its gaze flicking from Ronan to Tyson and back again, its breath coming in menacing hisses, and the cloying smell of the blood that matted the thick fur of its chest filled the room. Then its glittering red eyes fixed on Ronan, and it gave a humourless grin that looked like a couple of man-traps mating.

'Kill guessst!' it hissed, and then nodded happily, as though agreeing with itself that this would be a good move.

Ronan dropped into the balanced crouch used by warriors for unarmed combat and readied himself for an attack, but he was totally unprepared for the speed at which the creature moved. It seemed to blur, and before he could so much as blink, the curving claws of one lethal forepaw had closed around his neck, and he was thrust backwards so forcefully that his head smashed violently against the wall, half stunning him. Feebly he punched and clawed at the fearsome head that swam in front of his eyes, but his blows just skidded harmlessly off the thick, greasy fur, and he watched helplessly in mounting horror as the jaws opened and the two curved, venomous fangs hinged smoothly forwards into position.

Yelling with rage, Tyson flung herself at the creature's flank, but without even looking at her it lashed out sideways with its free paw and sent her flying backwards across the room to land on the cluttered desktop and go skidding on to the floor beyond in a welter of stationery. For a moment the creature peered at her as she lay there dazed, and its long tail flicked from side to side. Then it hissed with satisfaction, and its evil red eyes glittered malevolently as it turned its attention back to Ronan, took hold of his right arm and opened wide its jaws.

In the brief time it took them to cover the few hundred yards of the hotel driveway, Tarl and Puss found eight hotel guests, all of whom were extremely dead, and all of whom seemed to have been under the impression that entrails were being worn externally this year. As they came to the steps that led up to reception, they could see the legs of a ninth poking out of the bushes that screened the swimming pool. Tarl swallowed and looked shakily down at the little donkey.

'What the *klat* has happened to this place?' he whispered, but before Puss could answer the silence was shattered by a loud and furious yell from inside the hotel.

'That's Tyson's voice!' snapped Puss.

Together, the two of them raced up the steps and through the front door, skidding to a halt in the cool of the reception area. At first glance the place looked like the inside of an orcish butcher's shop, with dead humans seemingly everywhere. The only sign of life was ahead of them to the right, where through the shattered remnants of a door they could see that a tall, furry creature like a bipedal *lenkat* had Ronan pinned against the wall and appeared to be about to take a bite out of his arm.

Cursing, Tarl fired off a quick blast of magic, but fear and panic caused him to stutter and stumble over the words, and instead of a bolt of lightning, a small iced bun materialised out of nowhere and fizzed through the air to bounce harmlessly off the back of the creature's head. It glanced back at them for an instant, alert to this new challenge, but seeing only a small unarmed human and an

26

even smaller moth-eaten donkey it seemed to dismiss them as a threat, and turned back to Ronan.

With a furious bray that echoed around the reception hall, Puss lowered its head and charged. As the creature bared its fangs and lifted Ronan's arm to strike, the donkey burst through the door behind it and clamped its teeth on to the twitching tail with a snap like a rat-trap closing. The creature yowled in pain, and Ronan only just managed to jerk his arm free as it involuntarily clamped its jaws closed. Its eyes blazed like molten metal, and snarling, it swiped backwards with its free paw, but the little donkey ducked as the lethal claws whistled by inches above its flattened ears, and with its teeth still firmly clenched in the greasy fur of the creature's tail it shook its head violently from side to side. The creature snarled again and lashed backwards with its hind paw. This time it connected, and the donkey went hurtling backwards through the door and crashed into Tarl, knocking him head-first against the reception desk. There was a sound like two blocks of wood being smashed together, and Tarl went down as though pole-axed.

Tyson shook her head and sat up just in time to see Puss go sailing out of the door. Her left leg was throbbing painfully, and she could feel blood trickling down her thigh. Looking down, she saw that her leg was impaled on a stationery spindle. Its foot-long metal spike was sticking out of the flesh on the inside of her thigh, a few inches above her knee, and her blood was staining the thick sheaf of invoices and bills sandwiched between her leg and the spindle's round wooden base. Holding her thigh with one hand, she grabbed the spindle by the base, gritted her teeth and pulled.

The creature had turned its attention back to Ronan, and he was staring virtually paralysed with horror at the two venomous fangs that hovered hypnotically mere inches in front of his face when Tyson's scream of agony jerked him back to his senses. Distantly he heard her call his name, and realised that she was throwing something to him. Stretching out his left hand he caught the spindle by its wooden base, and in the same movement whirled it round in an arc, thrusting it upwards to send the point slamming home into the blood-soaked furry throat. The creature hissed in agony, and hot spittle blew out from the scaly lips into Ronan's face. Beneath its jaw the bills and invoices stuck out like some ludicrous home-made ruff. For a few seconds it stared unbelievingly at him, and then it laboriously dragged open its mouth, which had been slammed almost shut by the power of Ronan's blow, and he could see the blood-coated spindle stretching up through the green tongue into the roof of its mouth.

But then slowly, almost imperceptibly, the paw that held his throat relaxed its grip and began to slip down his chest, the claws leaving a trail of four parallel scratches behind them. The red eyes gradually lost their lustre, like the embers of a dying fire, and then the great head sagged forwards and the creature slumped lifeless to the floor.

Ronan looked down at it for a while, and prodded it with his foot. He looked across to where Tyson was sitting with her back against the wall, white-faced and cursing, tying someone's spare clean white shirt round her bleeding thigh. He looked out through the door to where Tarl lay slumped against the reception desk on the white marble floor, and where the donkey was painfully picking itself up and mumbling bitterly about people who think they can lob a bit of confectionery about and then doze off in the middle of a pitched battle. He looked back down at the creature again, and then he held up a shaking hand and examined it for a moment before slumping tiredly back against the wall.

'Well, I suppose it could have been worse,' he muttered to himself. 'At least there was only one of them!'

It was a silent, sore and dispirited group of friends who trooped back into the reception area an hour later, after searching the hotel and grounds. They had found a total of twenty-three dead bodies, both staff and guests, and the only survivor they had come across was the assistant manager, who had been curled up in a linen cupboard, asleep. They had left him in the kitchen with a saucer of milk, purring contentedly, and having decided that they needed something a good deal stronger, they were now heading for the bar.

Ronan led the way, stepping gingerly over the remains of the manager and flicking a nervous glance sideways at the furry body in the office. To his relief it was still dead, although after the events of the past six months he wouldn't have been at all surprised if the *klatting* thing had stood up and attacked him again. He pushed open the door in the far corner of the silent hallway, and held it ajar as the others filed past him into the cool, shaded elegance of the Vnaya Cocktail Lounge. *Fitting name,* he thought, surveying the mixture of bandages, lumps and bruises. *We look like a group of* vnaya-*fruit gatherers.*

Tyson limped across to a padded armchair and slumped into it, while the donkey trudged over to a hessian couch by the wide-open patio doors and climbed on to the plump cushions with a sigh, before draping its head over one arm and staring blankly out at the glimmering ocean behind the palm trees lining the patio. Tarl hobbled wearily behind the bar and started examining the myriad bottles and optics. Ronan let the door swing shut behind them, and then moodily began hacking individual leaves off a large pot-plant in the corner with a sword that he had found underneath the dead gate guard.

As he rummaged around behind the bar Tarl could feel his spirits beginning to lift. The familiar names and smells were starting to work their old magic. By the time he had got six different bottles lined up on the bar in front of him, and had found the seventh one he needed in a cupboard under the sink, he felt almost as good as new. True, he had a lump the size of a *vnaya*-fruit on the back of his skull and a pounding headache, but he had woken up so many times in the morning with the latter that he almost regarded it as normality. He glanced at his three friends, who were looking about as happy as people who have just woken from some wonderful, sexy dream and found that in reality they are tied to stakes in the arena of the Cumanceum, and that some bugger has just let the *lenkats* in. Well, he knew just what to do about that.

Hauling a large cocktail shaker down from the top shelf, he began to slosh in rough measures from the various bottles, and then after shaking it as much as his headache would allow he unscrewed the top and poured the resulting muddy-purple mixture into three highball glasses and a clean ashtray.

'Okay, guys,' he invited. 'These will help with your aches and pains. Come and get 'em.'

The others slouched across with all the enthusiasm of young orcs on their way to their yearly bath. Tarl pushed a couple of glasses forward, put the ashtray on the floor in front of Puss, and then raised his own glass high.

'Goodbye sadness, goodbye woe, goodbye breakfast, here we go!' he intoned, using the words of an old orcish toast, and then he threw back the cocktail, and the others reluctantly followed suit.

For several seconds there was no reaction at all. (Tyson later decided that this was probably because the cocktail instantly overloaded every single taste bud before they could register even the slightest sensation.) Then Ronan gasped (Tarl could have sworn he felt a great blast of burning-hot air waft past him) and began to cough violently. Tyson would have thumped him on the back if she could have seen him properly, but all of a sudden her eyes had gone completely out of focus, and anyway she was too busy trying to cope with a throat that felt as though someone had set fire to it. The overall sensation, she decided, was like drinking molten lead whilst being hit repeatedly on the back of the skull with a large lump-hammer.

'*Klat*, Tarl!' she managed to gasp. 'What the hell is in this drink?'

'It's a little cracker, isn't it?' beamed Tarl, who was busy with the cocktail shaker again. 'It's a recipe I picked up when I worked in the Blue Balrog Club, in Orcville. It's called a Stiff Shifter. The Cydorian brandy gives it body. The Razindi bitters add bite. The Troll Roger champagne gives it sparkle, and the cleaning fluid adds a certain insouciance . . . Orcs use it as a pick-me-up when they're feeling low or hungover.'

Tyson was just about to tell him that rather than a pick-me-up it was more like a knock-me-down-and-kick-me-in-the-slats when she realised that, to her surprise, her spirits had inexplicably lifted. The lump-hammer effect had stopped and the burning sensation had lessened, leaving a warm, fiery glow in her stomach, rather as though a small but contented dragon was nesting there. She glanced sideways at Ronan, who was wearing the surprised look of a warrior who has been unexpectedly attacked from the inside, but as she watched him the tension began to drain out of his muscles as he visibly relaxed. A slow smile spread across his face and he gave a great sigh.

'That was a bit close, before,' he said.

Tyson nodded and reached out a hand to stroke his cheek.

'I've never seen anything like that creature,' she said. 'Where do you suppose it came from?'

'I don't know,' muttered Ronan, shaking his head.

'I do,' interjected Tarl, pouring something green and viscous from the cocktail shaker into their empty glasses. 'Guebral says that the Orcbane board are up to their old tricks again.' He drained the last drops from the shaker into his own glass with a flourish, and then looked at Tyson. 'You said you got the impression that the creature was specifically hunting for Ronan. It just has to be them; who else would bother to send such a high-grade, top-of-the-range killing machine? But for Ronan they would be in control of half of Midworld by now. We should have been expecting something like this. I mean, they're not going to be sending him a box of chocolates and an invitation to afternoon tea, are they?'

Tyson nodded. 'It makes sense,' she mused. 'We're gonna have to do something about those sad old men, and quickly.'

'Dead right!' agreed Ronan. He picked up his glass and studied the new cocktail dubiously. It was giving off faint wisps of emerald vapour, and looked about as innocuous as strychnine. Still, to balk at drinking one of Tarl's concoctions seemed a little on the timid side after the events of the afternoon, and so he closed his eyes and knocked it back in one go. To his surprise, it was much milder than the first one, and he breathed a sigh of relief.

'So what are you going to do?' asked Tarl, over his shoulder. He had already finished his second drink and was working on the next, furiously chopping up a load of fruit that he had found in a cold-cupboard under the bar.

'That's easy. Kill them. But I'm not so sure how we're going to do it.'

'We could get Tarl to mix them a few cocktails,' suggested the donkey. It was lying spread-eagled on the floor, the ashtray between its front legs.

'I reckon we should head home to Welbug,' said Tyson. 'We need to talk to Anthrax. He used to be on the Orcbane payroll, and he has more magical power than anyone else around at the moment. If anyone knows how to get to the board, he does.'

'Good idea. We can set off at first light tomorrow. And then if we . . .' Ronan stopped dead as what appeared to be a small volcano suddenly erupted in his stomach. For a few moments it felt as though red-hot lava was coursing round his abdomen, and he wouldn't have been surprised to see smoke pouring out of his mouth. To judge by the startled expression on Tyson's face and the way her eyebrows had nearly disappeared over the top of her skull, she was suffering exactly the same sensations.

'It's another little beauty, isn't it?' grinned Tarl. 'I discovered it in Boozy Sue's, on the Vendai Strip. They call it a Delayed Action.'

'Good name. Says it all, really,' gasped Ronan. He hauled breath into lungs that had momentarily gone on strike, and watched apprehensively as Tarl poured out the third cocktail from a large glass jug. It was brownish-yellow, and seemed to be full of little chunks of fruit.

'What's this one?'

'It's a Yesterday's Lunch. Invented by Scorpion Joe, head barman at The Thirsty Works in Goblin City. Whisky, arrack, soda water, ice flakes, as much fruit as you can lay your hands on, and a shot of

Yellow Brannadine on top. Tastes one hell of a lot better than it looks.'

'It would have to,' muttered Tyson, throwing Ronan a what-the-hell-have-we-let-ourselves-in-for sort of glance. They picked up their glasses and sipped at the concoction within, but to their mutual surprise the cocktail was smooth, cool and completely delicious.

'*Klat!* You really know your stuff,' exclaimed Ronan. 'This is good!'

'You guys stick with me and you'll learn a thing or two,' beamed Tarl.

'We've heard,' answered Tyson. 'Puss told us that an evening out with you was a real education.'

'Yeah,' interjected the donkey, 'you get the three Rs. Rat-arsed, wrecked and regurgitating.'

Tarl smiled and turned back to the vast collection of bottles that lined the rear of the bar.

'If we're heading off tomorrow on another one of these *klatting* quests of yours,' he said, 'then I reckon we should have a bit of a send-off tonight. Oh, now, what have we here?'

Slowly and carefully he pulled a large bottle out from behind the others, and stared at it with the reverent expression of a High Elf studying a large block of the very best Razindi Gold. The bottle was heavy and translucent, and was made not from glass but from carved quartz. About the thick neck was wrapped a faded black label, on which were scrawled a few characters of ugly orcish script, and inside it a dark, syrupy liquid undulated slowly to and fro.

'Look at this!' he enthused. 'A bottle of twenty-year-old, matured-in-the-crystal *vlatzhkan gûl*! And it's nearly full!'

'*Vlatzhkan* what?'

'*Gûl. Vlatzhkan gûl.* Roughly translated, it means something like "removes-lining-of-stomach-in-seconds". It's an orcish liqueur, fermented from . . . er, well, I won't tell you what it's fermented from, because if I did you wouldn't touch it with a thirty-foot large-pole,[5] but take it from me, it's the nearest you can get to heaven without dying.'

Ronan looked at the bottle suspiciously.

[5] A long, pointed stick kept in the guard-rooms next to the main gates of Iduinian cities, and used from the safety of the city walls by the gate guards to poke and prod undesirables such as lepers, plague-carriers or double-glazing salesmen until they go away.

'Are you absolutely sure about the not dying bit?' he asked.

'Positive. But you may well wish you had, tomorrow morning,' Tarl replied, and then reaching up to a long, narrow shelf above the bar he brought down three small, delicate glasses. 'I haven't drunk this stuff in ages,' he continued, as he carefully poured out three measures. 'Not since I was last in Spiny Viney's, on Upper Flensing Street in Orcville. Boy, did I get drunk. Embarrassingly so. In fact, I peed all over my shoes.'

'That's not so embarrassing. We all aim badly when we've had a few drinks.'

'No, you don't understand. I wasn't wearing them at the time. I'd taken them off and put them on a shelf over the bar.' Tarl shook his head and smiled at the memory, then bent down and poured a few drops of the orcish liqueur into the donkey's ashtray. For a moment he watched fondly as Puss lapped them up, and then straightening, he raised his glass in a toast.

'*Nagûl klaatu rikbal*, as the orcs say. Or, even more roughly translated, may you never be sober.'

Ronan and Tyson picked up their glasses and looked at each other doubtfully.

'Listen,' said Tyson. 'We'll have a few drinks and relax, but we're not going to overdo it, right? We need to be up and away nice and early in the morning. Okay?'

'Okay,' agreed Tarl, and the three of them smiled at each other, clinked glasses and knocked back their drinks as one.

It was an extremely quiet and fragile group that set off at one o'clock the following afternoon. The little donkey led the way, ambling slowly along with its ears folded forward in an unsuccessful attempt to keep the bright sunlight out of eyes that were horribly bloodshot. Next came Tarl, pale of face, shaky of hand and with a dull headache, symptoms which for him made it just another day. Behind him, Ronan stumbled along with eyes nearly closed and one hand clamped tightly around a forehead that pounded like a hammer on an anvil. His black skin was an unhealthy grey colour, and although the day was no hotter than usual, sweat stood out on his brow. And finally came Tyson, her face ashen, her hair bedraggled and plastered to her scalp, her stomach threatening to revolt yet again.

They made their way painfully up the hot, dusty track, and in the minds of three of them was a single thought. *Never again . . . I swear it, never again . . .* Behind them they left a charnel-house that had once been a hotel full of happy, holidaying people, a necropolis of disembowelled, putrefying bodies that bore witness to the ferocity and the power of the wilfully mutated abomination that was the *cobrat*.

In the early evening of the next day, the assistant manager was stalking a mouse through the undergrowth near the swimming pool when a rustling in the bushes nearby gave the first warning of imminent danger. He froze, pointed ears alert and listening, amber eyes searching ahead, and the fur on his back stood on end. For a few seconds he crouched motionless, then he hissed a warning and turned to scramble rapidly up a tall palm tree nearby.

Safely ensconced in the branches some fifty feet up, he watched unblinkingly as six of the massive, fur-covered killers crept out of the bushes and slunk rapidly in through the front door of the hotel. Patiently he waited, and when they eventually emerged he growled a few feline threats, but softly, deep in his throat, so as not to be heard. He watched motionless as the six deadly creatures cast about the grounds, searching for a scent. After a while they seemed to find what they were looking for and loped off in a pack up the dusty track that wound up the hill, and as he watched them leave he growled again, defiantly. But it was a long, long time after they had vanished into the distance before he dared come down to prowl nervously around the domain that now was his alone.

CHAPTER THREE

It was a hard life being a jester working the variety clubs in those days. The orcish drinking dens were the worst. If you went down really well, they let you live. Oh, yes. But the dwarven nightclubs were nearly as bad. I toured them several times. We used to call them the short circuit . . .

The Sad Life of Tarbuk the Ancient

'But do you know who really annoys me? I'll tell you. The undead, that's who. Always moping and wailing about the place. I mean, get a life, guys! I've got this friend, Billy, who's a wraith, right? He was complaining that he never gets any time to himself, because of the kids wanting things, and his sisters calling round, and his mother-in-law is always on his back . . . I said to him, you want to go to the wraith relations board!'

Tarbuk the Jester paused out of habit and waited for the laugh, but as he'd expected, there wasn't one. Not even a titter. Unperturbed, he ploughed on.

'His brother Ralph is a cacodaemon. We were sat in the tavern one night, and someone trod on Ralph's tail. Snapped it clean off! I said to the landlord, can you give us a hand to stick this back on? He said, sorry gents, I'm not allowed to re-tail spirits! Huh-ho!'

He smiled chirpily around the cavern that was the dwarvish nightclub the Seam of Gold, and row upon row of stern dwarven faces stared icily back. Someone near the back coughed, and the sound echoed off the vast carved-stone walls, emphasising the silence. Tarbuk realised he was dying on his feet. Still, it was what he had expected. He'd done dwarven clubs before. Getting laughs was like pulling teeth, but at least they paid well, and you always got out alive.

'Apparently this place has been having trouble with a wraith, too. The manager told me that the spectre of an ancient king of the elves has been complaining about the standards of hygiene. Still, it's not the first time they've had problems with the Elfin Spectre.'

He paused again. This was one of his best gags and he would

normally have expected some sort of reaction, even from dwarves, but once more he was met with a wall of silence. He peered nervously out past the two large torches that guttered smokily in brackets on either side of the small stone stage. Somehow he was getting the impression that, this time, it wasn't his fault. The audience didn't even seem to be listening, save for one young dwarf in a front seat who was staring earnestly at him and taking notes. There were several hundred dwarvish scientists out there, sitting round tables clutching foaming mugs of Low In Brow and ostensibly celebrating their Founder's Day, yet to judge by the amount of sheer hilarity going on you'd think it was a funeral. They were clustered in two groups, and were taking great draughts of the ale and occasionally staring sullenly across at the other group. There was trouble brewing, if he was any judge. Maybe it was time he got the hell out of there.

'Okay, folks, you've been a lovely audience, but you've suffered enough so it's time to close the show. Thank you for listening, my name's Tarbuk the Jester, good night!'

From his position in the audience, Reágin watched as the ageing comedian shuffled off the stage, but his thoughts were elsewhere, and he hadn't taken in a single word of the jester's routine. Absent-mindedly he began to clap, and the group clustered about him followed his lead. The resulting brief and half-hearted round of applause was probably the best reception Tarbuk had ever got (and would later appear in his sadly inaccurate autobiography as a standing ovation). As the applause stuttered to a halt Reágin stared across the room at the rival group of scientists clustered around their leader, Meiosin, and frowned worriedly.

The Chief Scientist was very concerned, and with good reason. Since his unpleasant visit to the Genetics Department a couple of weeks before, he had begun to hear rumours that his superiors, back in their home city of Toltecel under the Frozen Mountains of the far north, were considering relieving him of his duties as head of the underground research establishment here at Deforzh and replacing him with Meiosin, from Genetics. Other rumours suggested that Meiosin was intending a leadership challenge of his own and, after supplanting Reágin, was intending to make the research institute an independent concern, his own little fiefdom. Whatever the truth was, the entire scientific staff had polarised into two distrustful groups of supporters, and as far as Reágin was concerned, the most worrying thing of all was that his support had been ebbing away in the past few days, deserting him in ones or twos to line up behind Meiosin. Initially he'd had the vast majority of scientists supporting him, but now there were almost as many dwarves clustered around his rival, who was currently seated at a table on the far side of the room, smugly supping his ale.

Reágin began to count surreptitiously. With the exception of Meiosin's brother, Mitosin, every scientist was here in the Seam of Gold to celebrate the anniversary of the foundation of their research centre many years ago by Kelvin, son of Ketin, and father of the science of Praecipitinfelicitology. Now that the dreadful comedian had finished, a hum of conversation had begun and the dwarves were milling around, ordering drinks from the long stone bar that lined the rear of the cave, or moving to neighbouring tables to converse with friends and colleagues. It all made counting a little difficult, but Reágin was pretty sure that he had counted accurately, and the result was extremely depressing. He appeared to have a majority of four. Allowing for Mitosin, that meant three. If just two of his followers changed sides, he would no longer have a majority, and if Meiosin challenged his leadership, as he was allowed to do under their laws, there would be a new chief scientist.

Gripping his flagon of ale tightly enough to strangle the life out of it, Reágin stared bitterly across at his rival, and as though sensing this, Meiosin looked up and met his gaze. For a few seconds the geneticist stared blankly, and then a small smile quivered about his lips. Standing, he made a bow in Reágin's direction that was so ironically deep and sincere it was a complete wind-up, and then he turned and strode out of the cave.

Fury flooded through Reágin and he surged to his feet. Ale slopped out of his mug and splashed on to the smooth stone surface of the table, but blinded by a red mist of anger, he didn't notice. How *dare* Meiosin treat him like that? How DARE he? Reágin was still chief scientist, and by the beard of Palin, he was going to stay in that position! He would follow Meiosin and confront him, challenge him to come out into the open instead of scheming in the shadows. They could put it to the vote tonight! Forthright action like this should be enough to make sure that he held on to his remaining followers, and Meiosin wouldn't be able to challenge him again for months. That would show him!

Slamming down his mug, Reágin strode through the throng after Meiosin. There was no sign of him in the high passageway outside, but Reágin knew that he would only have gone back to his beloved

37

Genetics Department, and so turning right he scurried off towards the stairs that led down to the laboratories. There were other dwarves going about their business here in the living areas – non-scientists, members of the lesser castes, who bowed deeply and reverently as the Chief Scientist scurried past them – but he ignored them in his haste.

Coming to the main hall, he strode past the plain blackstone pillars that lined either side, stretching up to the roof high above. At the northern end of the hall a wide, well-worn flight of marble stairs led downwards beneath an ornate archway, burrowing as straight as an arrow to the Research Levels beneath the very heart of the mountain. Every few yards guttering torches were fixed in brackets on the smoothly cut walls of the staircase, and they flickered in the draught of his passing. Here there was no one else to be seen, and his lonely footsteps echoed behind him eerily.

At the bottom of the stairs he came to the Lecture Room, a vast, high-vaulted cavern filled with rows of benches and chairs. On either side, arched passageways led off to the older departments; Alchemy, Physicks, and Machines and Contrivances on the left, Necromancy, Medicaments, and Biology on the right. Ahead lay the passageway leading to the newest: Genetics.

Muttering to himself excitedly, the Chief Scientist strode along until he came to the stout iron door that was the only entrance to the department. Unlocking it, he strode through and paced along the corridor, searching the dark, quiescent laboratories on either side for the two brothers, but all were deserted.

Coming to the first of the solid metal doors that sealed off the creature pens, he was startled to find it standing wide open. The pen was deserted, its bare stone floor scrubbed clean, and Reágin suddenly realised that this time there was no background cacophony of screams and howls from the captive animals, no overpowering excremental stench, but a silence that was broken only by his own tread, and a faint, musty odour clinging to the stone like a fading memory.

He followed the passage as it sloped gradually downwards, but every pen he passed was empty, every room deserted. If it hadn't been for the infrequent wall-torches flickering in their rock-hewn sconces, the whole department would have given the impression that it had been closed down and abandoned weeks ago.

Reágin felt baffled and, somehow, a little betrayed, Mitosin and Meiosin wouldn't have just closed their research down like that. But they couldn't have moved to another area, not without him knowing. Could they? What were they up to?

All at once the bafflement was replaced by a sure and certain feeling that something very unpleasant indeed was going on. Coming to the final left-hand bend, Reágin broke into an ungainly run, skidding to a halt at the very end of the passage beside the six-inch-thick door on the right that led to the *cobrats'* old pen. The door was open, like all the others, and the pen was still deserted.

Turning, he took a couple of quick steps across the passage to the small door on the other side and thrust it open, but what had been Meiosin's private office was also completely empty. There wasn't a stick of furniture or a shred of paper left. The room was just a bare rectangular cavern hewn out of the rock, with only a few footprints in the carpet of dust to show that it had ever been in use before.

Reágin shook his head slowly, puzzled, and then paused, his head on one side. He could hear a distant rhythmic humming, a low, almost inaudible sound that could be felt as much as heard. It seemed to be coming from the wall on his right, and so placing his ear against the smooth, cold surface he listened hard. He could hear it better now, a pulsing, throbbing noise that sounded as though a gigantic bee had been entombed in the living rock. And as he listened, fascinated, staring absently out through the doorway with his left ear pressed to the stone, he noticed that the torch fixed beside the door opposite was casting a shadow on the end wall of the passage. It was a thin, straight, vertical line, too straight to be caused by a flaw in the rock, and, intrigued, Reágin straightened up and walked out to have a closer look.

To his complete and utter amazement, he found he was staring at the outline of a door. It was the tiniest fraction ajar, and but for that it would have been such a close fit within its portals that it would have been all but invisible. Indeed, last time he had been down here he hadn't noticed it at all.

But what was it doing here? Reágin had seen the plans when the Genetics Department was first being excavated, and there were no other rooms beyond this wall! True, there were many natural caverns and tunnels under the mountain that were as yet unaccessed and unexplored, but they could not have been utilised without the permission or knowledge of the Chief Scientist. Could they?

He stretched out an apprehensive hand, and at his touch the door swung smoothly and silently back. Although of solid stone a foot thick, it was so well balanced on hidden hinges that no effort was needed to move it. Beyond was a square passage some sixty feet long, with wooden doors on either side and a solid metal door at the far end. There were no wall-torches or candles to be seen, but an eerie bluish light seemed to seep out of the very stone of the walls, giving them a metallic sheen.

Nervously, half convinced that he was dreaming, Reágin crept along the passage. The first door on the right was ajar, and gave on to another deserted laboratory, but this one seemed to be full of gleaming equipment. The marble worktops were crowded with bubbling glass vials and retorts, and rune-covered papers and open notebooks were strewn around them. The sinks were stacked with piles of dirty Petri dishes and test-tubes, and the air was heavy with the bitter, ammoniac stench typical of a busy laboratory.

The door facing, on the opposite side of the passage, however, was closed. Reágin gripped the handle, and listened. The humming noise was much louder here, and seemed to be coming from the other side of the door. For a moment he paused, and then, taking a deep breath, he thrust the door open.

Inside, the room was bare save for a single large machine seated on a stone plinth. It was humming loudly to itself, and a steel shaft that ran from the machine to disappear through a hole in the back wall glinted in the dim light as it spun almost too quickly for the eye to see. Two stout copper wires as thick as a dwarf's arm were bolted to metal bars at the top of the machine, looping across under the stone ceiling to vanish into ducts in the right-hand wall.

The whole thing was like a massive version of the machine which Electrin from the Physicks Department had built and demonstrated a couple of years previously. Although only as long as a forearm, that one had produced quite a sizeable amount of the mysterious force which Electrin had rather vainly named Electrycks. They had tried a few minor experiments with this force, and had found that if you connected the wires to an orc and cranked the machine, the orc's hair stood on end and it leapt around a lot, shouting. If you cranked the machine really fast, there was a crackling sound and a smell of burning, the orc shouted even louder, and smoke started to come out of its ears. It had all seemed quite dangerous, and Reágin had ordered an end to the experiments. He dreaded to think what damage the huge machine in front of him could do.

He watched it for a while, fascinated despite himself. The air in the room was slightly hazy, and seemed to itch and prickle at his skin as though alive, and all of a sudden he shivered, then jerked the door closed and stood there in the passage, trembling with a mixture of anger and apprehension. Mitosin and Meiosin must have been pursuing their own course in secret for years! They couldn't have built this extension to Genetics without the help and knowledge of the rest of the department staff. How dare they undermine his authority like this! Well, it was going to stop right now! Just wait until he got hold of them!

His anger stoked right to boiling point, Reágin strode down the corridor in search of the two targets of his wrath. He rattled the handle of the next door on the left but found it was locked, and after kicking it a couple of times in frustration he tried the door opposite. It swung open, and he found himself staring into a brightly lit and clinically clean laboratory. Like the first one it was deserted, but instead of workbenches crammed with test-tubes and retorts, this one contained gleaming metal dissecting tables, large white-stone sluices and rack upon rack of shiny, sharp-edged instruments that glinted in the light: knives, scalpels, saws, bistouries and cleavers, and other curiously shaped implements whose purpose Reágin could only guess at. The distinctive tang of formaldehyde was in the air, heavy and cloying, almost masking another smell, a sweet, familiar odour which at first he couldn't place. Then his eye was caught by an instrument lying on the side of a sluice near the door. It had a very, very slim, razor-sharp blade barely an inch long, and a thin, rod-shaped handle the length of his forearm, and looked as though it was meant to be inserted into something . . . And then the sweet smell clicked neatly into place in his brain. It was freshly spilt blood.

Reágin took two quick steps backwards and closed the door sharply behind him. He stood there clutching the handle, his breath coming rapidly, his eyes tightly shut. What was going *on* down here? Shaking his head, he turned and strode purposefully up the corridor. The last pair of wooden doors on either side were locked, but the solid, matt-black iron one at the end of the passage unlatched easily and swung open before him. The passage continued beyond it for a mere ten feet, ending in another similar door, and as he laid his hand on the latch of this second one, the first swung shut behind him with a clang like a battleaxe hitting an orc's helm. Reágin flinched and scowled back at it, and then hauling open the second one he strode through. And then he stopped and stared, so stunned by the sight that met his eyes that he didn't even notice when the second door slammed shut as well.

He was standing in a vast underground cavern, but from the view before him he could have been outside in the open air. The roof of the cave was somewhere far, far above, and was hidden by a bright, diffuse light that shone down from some concealed source, giving the impression of a cloudy summer's day. He was standing on soft, lush grass, and maybe fifty yards ahead of him a forest of trees and shrubs stretched right across from one side of the cavern to the other. Birds sang in the branches, insects buzzed lazily, butterflies floated past and a stream chuckled its way across in front of the nearest trees.

Unable to believe his eyes, Reágin stepped hesitantly forward into this subterranean parkland, and then bending down he plucked a blade of grass and rubbed it between his fingers and sniffed it. This was no mirage: he could smell it, and the bruised leaf had left a smear of green chlorophyll on his thumb. Then something rocketed out of the long grass on his left and shot past his feet so fast that it was a blur, disappearing into some shrubbery on his right and leaving a little whirlwind of dust behind it. He leapt back, startled, and strange, disembodied laughter rang out from behind him.

He twisted round to find Mitosin and Meiosin watching from the safety of a small enclosed observation booth hollowed out of the rock wall a few feet to the right of the door. They were sealed off from the cavern by a thick glass window, and Meiosin's laughter was emanating, somewhat disconcertingly, from a small speaking tube that emerged a good six feet above this window.

'Don't be scared of our *spiducks*,' Meiosin's voice boomed tinnily. 'They won't harm you.'

'Your what?'

'Our *spiducks*. One of our early failures, I'm afraid. Wild Brannian flightless ducks with a few arachnid genes added.'

Reágin leapt to one side as another blur rocketed past his feet. He caught a brief glimpse of something feathered, and then it was gone.

'Why was it a failure?' he asked, intrigued despite himself.

'Well, as you know, wild flightless ducks are something of a gourmet treat. The legs are delectable, although the breast meat tends to be tough and stringy. So we bred ducks with eight legs, expecting to make a fortune from them.'

'What went wrong? Don't they taste good?'

'We don't know,' answered Meiosin, and a frown crossed his face. 'So far we haven't been able to catch one.'

He lapsed into silence, staring broodingly at Reágin through the thick glass and stroking his dark beard, and the Chief Scientist looked away and tried to pull himself together. He knew that he should be interrogating the two brothers about all these secret goings-on, that he should be reaffirming his position as chief scientist and demanding explanations from a pair of dwarves who were, when all was said and done, his subordinates, but he was too shocked and shaken by events to think straight. He felt strangely vulnerable, as well. Mitosin and Meiosin were watching him with avid interest, almost as though he was some sort of specimen in a glass jar . . .

Reágin shuddered. That analogy was altogether a little too accurate for his liking. The brothers hadn't created this vast subterranean nature reserve just because they wanted a nice place to have a picnic. The whole thing was some gigantic experiment, and he was stuck in the middle of it! He looked nervously back at the forest behind him. To judge by the noises coming from the thick undergrowth, it was well populated with animal life. Who knew what nightmarish creatures the geneticists might have created by now? And what if there was a *cobrat* loose in here?

All of a sudden, he felt a surge of panic welling up inside him that threatened to take him over completely. Turning, he ran for the door, only to find that, on this side, it was a smooth, blank metal surface without a handle to be seen. It was shut fast, and he was trapped. With a blinding flash of insight, he realised that Meiosin had lured him down here, leaving the secret door ajar so that he could find it. They wanted him here, and it wasn't just to show him a few trees. He was in danger, and he'd better get out, fast!

He stared frantically round, searching for another exit. There was no way into the observation chamber from out here, and no evidence of a second door, but now he looked closely he could see a small wooden bridge crossing the steam over on the right, and beyond it a path ran into the edge of the trees. He began to stride determinedly towards it across the turf, aware of the two pairs of eyes watching him from behind, and suppressing the urge to break into a frightened, undignified run.

'But I'm forgetting my manners,' boomed Meiosin's voice from the speaking tube. 'Please allow us to welcome you to the Vivarium, a controlled environment constructed by the Genetics Department – without, I'm afraid, your knowledge or permission – to allow us to study the interaction of the creatures we have bred, both with each other and with autochthonous life forms such as your good self.'

Steadfastly ignoring him, Reágin reached the little bridge and stopped. Of course! The stream had to run out of the cavern somewhere! Maybe there would be just enough room for a slightly overweight scientist to squeeze through as well. He turned to follow the watercourse but then paused as a small and extremely furry animal pushed its way out of the nearby undergrowth and lolloped gently and appealingly towards him. It looked like a rabbit that hadn't bothered to visit its barber for a long, long time.

'Ah, now there we have one of our successes,' boomed Meiosin. 'We call it a *rabbion*.'

Ignoring the impulse to turn round and make an obscene gesture in the direction of the observation booth, Reágin bent down and held out his hand to the little creature. It paused and stared at him with dark, trusting eyes, nostrils whiffling delicately, and was just stretching its head forward to sniff his fingers when Reágin suddenly became aware of a large, threatening shadow looming over him. He whirled round, and was nearly sick with terror at the sight of the reptilian beast that had emerged from the trees to tower menacingly over him.

Standing upright on its massive hind legs, it was virtually twice his height. Powerful muscles rippled under a hairless, grey, scaly hide, and a crest of horny skin ran from the back of its head down to the long, tapered tail that lashed from side to side behind it. Black beady eyes gleamed at him from above a wide gash of a mouth that was packed with rows of horribly sharp backward-pointing teeth, and a pair of weak vestigial forelimbs tipped with small, sharp talons pawed the air, as though impatient to get at him. It looked like a gigantic lizard that had been weight-training regularly for years.

Reágin's mouth worked, but no sound emerged. He wanted to run, but there seemed to be no power in his muscles, no air in his lungs. His legs trembled, threatening to collapse completely, and his breath came in short, panicky gasps. He stared paralysed at the knife-like teeth hovering a few feet away, and could feel the acid bite of half-digested beer rising at the back of his throat.

The creature snorted, sending a wave of hot, foul air blasting past him, and he closed his eyes in helpless resignation as the great mouth opened wider. And then he was almost knocked backwards as a large, sticky tongue slurped affectionately across his face. Dragging his eyes open, he stared in amazement as the great creature peered at him almost lovingly, and then it stretched its neck forward and tilted its head sideways in an unmistakable hint for him to tickle it under the chin. A metallic sigh echoed around the cavern from the distant speaking tube.

'Another one of our failures, I'm afraid,' boomed Meiosin. 'The *giguana*. When we bred it we were hoping for a predator even more lethal than a *cobrat*. Unfortunately, all that it seems to want to do with people is cuddle them. Very disappointing.'

Reágin stared incredulously at the *giguana*, and then reached his hand out hesitantly and started rubbing the rough, dry skin of its throat. The huge reptile closed its eyes in rapture and began to make a deep but unmistakable purring noise. And that was when the *rabbion* at Reágin's feet stretched out its neck, opened its little mouth and fastened a pair of small but ever so sharp fangs into his calf.

'Ouch!' he yelped, for the bite had stung a bit. But then, in seconds, the sting had changed to an agonising, excruciating pain, as though his leg was being pumped full of white-hot molten metal, and he began to scream.

'I did warn you that the *rabbion* was one of our successes,' said Meiosin, from the safety of the observation booth. 'A rabbit with just a hint of scorpion, to make it lethally venomous. A most unpleasant death, I would imagine.'

'Horrible,' agreed Mitosin, beside him. 'Truly horrible.'

The two geneticists stood watching with interest for the few minutes that it took Reágin to die, and then, after the Chief Scientist's writhing, thrashing body had given one final violent convulsion, and the tormented screams had died away, Meiosin turned to his brother.

'Tell the other scientists that our beloved chief has met with an unfortunate accident,' he ordered. 'They need to select a new leader at once.'

He turned back to the window and stared out avidly at the small group of genetically altered abominations which had gathered around the still-twitching corpse of the Chief Scientist and were hungrily and bloodily ripping it into quivering fragments of dead meat. Beside him Mitosin grinned.

'And when they have selected you?' he enquired.

'Then we can begin our work in earnest. Tell our backers that we are nearly ready to carry out the first raid. It's time to find out just what our creations can do.'

In the boardroom of the Orcbane Sword Corporation offices in Ged, the board were meeting for the first time in several weeks. Wayta, the chairman, sat at the head of the table and surveyed the five men who were as close as he had ever got to having friends. They had been lean and hungry when they had started out, forty years before, but the years had not been kind to them. He had kept himself in trim: he worked out with Bownedd regularly, and his muscle tone wasn't too bad. But the others!

On his left sat Kaglav and Gahvanser, dark-haired Southrons from Iduin. Kaglav had always been plump, but latterly Gahvanser had outdone him in girth. Their hair had always been lank and greasy, but of late it had become streaked with silver, and Kaglav's was long and unkempt. Both were moon-faced, but Gahvanser had recently developed so many chins that he had grown a straggly beard to hide the fact.

Opposite them sat Missek and Mellial, who were brothers. They came originally from Baq d'Or, and had been the owners of flowing blond manes of hair when he had met them. They were now bald, with just a thin fringe of coarse white hairs around the back and sides of their skulls, and they too had put on weight. Indeed, Mellial had put on so much that he needed a specially constructed chair. Even the slightest effort these days caused him to puff and pant with exertion. Neither he nor his brother had ever come to terms with the southern heat, and their clothes were always sweat-stained and rumpled.

At the opposite end of the oval table sat the vice-chairman, Grole. He was a small, podgy man with little piggy eyes and a wet, slobbery mouth that was permanently open. He too was almost bald, but he tried to hide the fact by growing very long side-strands which he combed over the dome of his pink, flaking skull. He had been Wayta's right-hand man over the years, but he had changed a few weeks back when the witch, Shikara, had read the lustful thoughts in his mind and in revenge had inflicted some foul mental torture upon him. Somehow the spark had gone out.

Wayta looked round at the other five. He knew them well now. He knew their likes and dislikes, their fears, worries and vices. He knew of Missek and Mellial's devotion to some of the rarer drugs, and of Grole's unusual sexual appetites. He knew of the pain that Kaglav liked to have inflicted by his young mistresses, and of the pain that Gahvanser paid to inflict upon some of the city's poorer and more desperate gladiators. He could read their minds almost as well as he could read his own, and he could currently see the same thought behind each sheepish expression: *I guess we might have panicked just a little . . .*

'Gentlemen,' he began, 'welcome back. I sense that you feel we might have behaved a little precipitately in fleeing as we did. I'd like to reassure you that our assessment of the situation was correct.'

He paused as the door of the boardroom opened and a wizened, black-clad old hag wandered in, muttering and chortling to herself. The board ignored her as she shuffled across to the cauldron that was already bubbling away in the fireplace in one corner.

'If Ronan,' continued Wayta, 'and his female warrior friend Tyson had moved against us immediately, we would have been in severe danger. They had an entire army and some powerful magic-users at their backs. However, they appear to have been temporarily waylaid by the pleasures of the Perplec coastline, and their allies have dispersed. But their thoughts will again turn to revenge. And we are vulnerable . . .'

At this point he stood up and pulled out a square wooden box from under the table.

'In the past few weeks,' he continued, 'I have not been idle. I have been in contact with two separate organisations. One is the Guild of Assassins. The other is a tribe of dwarves, far to the north. I have been taking an interest in their scientific research for some years now. They have made fascinating strides in the new science of genetics, and have created some remarkable creatures. Allow me to show you through the eyes and ears of one of their scientists . . .'

Whilst talking, he had been pulling on a pair of stout leather gloves. Now he opened the wooden box, and instantly the room was filled with the miasmic stench of badly rotted flesh. The five others tried to refrain from gagging as the chairman reached in and, with an expression of distaste on his thin, pinched face, lifted out the severed head of a dwarf. It was blood-stained and eyeless, with much of the flesh eaten away, and the top of the skull had been hacked off so that the brain within bulged out.

He handed it to the hag, who cackled with delight, and then holding it high she screeched some garbled Words of Command and hurled it into the cauldron. A stream of flame erupted from the simmering surface, arcing upwards to lance into the white-painted wall nearby. The room darkened as the wall glowed a brilliant orange and then suddenly burst into life, and displayed upon its surface was a moving picture, an image of past events so realistic that it was as though they were looking through a hole in the wall into the room beyond.

It was a view of a scientific laboratory built apparently in an underground cavern. Dwarf scientists and troll technicians scurried busily about, and the six men could clearly hear the clink of glass test-tubes and the sound of someone humming.

'These are the last images seen by Purin, the erstwhile owner of the head,' Wayta told them. 'Now, watch.'

A young dwarf burst through the door of the lab, his face a mask of sheer terror.

'The *cobrats* have escaped!' he shrieked. For a moment it was as if the hag-magic had failed and the picture had frozen, so still were the occupants of the laboratory. Then a figure appeared in the doorway, a tall, lithe creature covered in dark fur, moving on its hind legs with a feline grace, its long tail swishing behind it. Its head moved from side to side as it surveyed the cowering occupants of the laboratory, and its eyes gleamed with a feral light. Then the mouth opened, and the rows of razor-sharp teeth glinted in a lethal grin.

'Sssssss,' it hissed. 'Fffood!'

It padded forward a few paces in a slightly crouched posture, as though ready to spring, and behind it three others prowled through the doorway. For a moment all four stood poised, their eyes flickering about the room as though trying to select a target, their tails twitching from side to side. Then suddenly they blurred into action, moving almost faster than the eye could follow.

Five of the board jerked backwards in their seats as the first *cobrat* leapt for Purin, seeming almost to burst out of the wall at them. The image blanked out for a moment as Purin's eyes closed in reflex action, and the boardroom was filled with angry snarling and agonised screaming. Then his eyes must have opened again, for the wall was filled with the *cobrat*'s grinning face. A taloned paw reached out to shove the dwarf's head backwards, and as the horrific teeth slashed downwards out of view at the exposed throat below, the screaming redoubled in intensity. Nearby they could see another dwarf pinned to the floor by a second *cobrat*, his arms and legs threshing about vainly as the creature bent its head to his abdomen, tore out his entrails and began to feed hungrily. And then the screams died away and the image faded . . .

The lights in the boardroom came on again, and Wayta looked round at the five pale, shocked faces, and smiled to himself with satisfaction.

'That will be all, Cartland,' he said, and the hag muttered something incomprehensible and shuffled out of the room. The other five stared at him, their faces gleaming with a faint sheen of perspiration.

'Those, gentlemen,' he told them, 'are *cobrats*. Without doubt the most lethal creatures you have ever seen. Fast, intelligent and venomous. There are only seven in existence. I am delighted to inform you that we now own all seven.'

He leant back in his chair and smiled to himself at the horrified reaction this statement had caused.

'But . . . they're dangerous! Incredibly dangerous!' gasped Grole, and the others chorused their agreement.

'Dangerous indeed,' answered Wayta, 'but not to us. They have been programmed to obey the one they regard as their master. Since I, ah . . . disposed of their previous master, an unimportant and expendable dwarf named Adenin, that is now me.' He smiled icily, and then leant forward and stabbed the table with a forefinger to emphasise his words. 'We must deal with this do-gooder warrior and his friends quickly. They are dangerous and could be a threat to our very lives, especially with the help of the Cydorian army or of magic-users such as Anthrax. Sooner or later they will seek vengeance, and I for one wish to keep my head firmly attached to my shoulders.

'Even now the first *cobrat* should be reaching Perplec. A single beast may be enough to finish off this interfering warrior and his friends. If not, the others will follow, and there is also the little matter of my contract with the Guild of Assassins . . .'

In a few quick words he outlined the plan he had made and the steps he had taken, and as he spoke, the other five men began to smile in admiration. It was plain to see that this time there would be no mistake. Ronan and his unfortunate friends were at the heart of a rapidly contracting trap of iron, and would shortly be snuffed out like a candle being plunged into a bucket of water.

CHAPTER FOUR

The Ilex Plain, in northern Cydor, is an area of rich, flat farmland noted for the excellence of its produce, and in particular for the large, sweet-tasting fruit known as the untah (from the elvish word for paradise). Now widely cultivated, these delectable red-skinned fruit originally grew wild throughout Cydor, and in his book Where Did We Come From? *the Sage of Welbug has put forward a theory that the first humans in Cydor were probably a tribe of nomadic untah-gatherers . . .*

Encyclopedia Midworldia

The rain had been coming down for a good hour now and was showing no signs of relenting. It hammered on the roof of the barn like an alcoholic trying to get into a pub that was having a lock-in after hours. The thick heads of barley that filled the fields all around were drooping sadly beneath the deluge, and great runnels of water were trickling off the soil and turning the surface of the track near the doorway into a muddy and glutinous morass.

'It looks like it's easing off,' said Tarl, hopefully.

Of course, the rain chose that moment to redouble its efforts. Lightning flashed in the distance to the east, shortly followed by a menacing growl of thunder, and all at once it was as though someone had dropped a curtain of water across the barn door.

'So you're a travelling soothsayer, are you?' muttered the farmer, doubtfully.

'Yeah, but I'm out of work.'

'Lost your job, did you? Can't say I'm surprised. What happened?'

'Unforeseen circumstances.'

'Ah.' The farmer turned to where Ronan and Tyson had hung their sodden cloaks on a wall manger, and were opening their backpacks. 'And you say you're his bodyguards?'

'Yeah,' replied Ronan. 'He'd be lost without us. He's upset a lot of people over the years.'

'I can believe that. Well, you're all welcome to spend the night in my barn. The roof's sound, so you'll be dry and warm enough.' The farmer paused to look at Puss, and shook his head dubiously. 'But I'm not so sure about yon animal staying in here. Not if it's anything like my donkey. I don't know as I should allow that. Goes against the grain, it does.'

'What does?' asked Tarl, whose mind had wandered on to the unopened wineskins in his bag.

'My donkey. We've had to throw half the grain away. Dirty beast.'

'Oh, you don't need to worry about Puss. He's well house-trained. He'll be okay.'

The farmer turned and watched the little donkey, who was sniffing around in between some bales of hay and the rear wall. Suddenly it froze, staring at something moving in the hay, and then it lunged. Its teeth snapped viciously together and there was a loud squeak, and then the donkey was backing out of the hay and trotting towards them with a large dead rat hanging from its jaws. It stopped in front of the farmer, looked at him for a moment, and then sucked the rat in like a piece of pasta and began to chew purposefully.

The farmer went pale.

'Calls it Puss, do you?' he cried. 'Poor little bugger, no wonder it's not right in the head! You wants to take it to see somebody, one of those folk what makes animals better. Oh, now, what do you call them?'

'Vet?'

'I said, you wants to take it to see someone,' the farmer repeated, louder. 'I don't know,' he added, shaking his head wearily, and then throwing the hood of his cape over his head he marched out into the rain, muttering something about the good old days, when you got a decent class of traveller in your barn.

Tarl watched him as he squelched off down the track. The torrential rain soon hid him from view, and Tarl turned back to the others. Tyson, having changed the bandage on her thigh, had spread out their weapons on a groundsheet in front of her. There were three swords, four knives, an elven bow, a quiver of slender arrows, the tiny crossbow that she called the Crow, and a small leather pouch of quarrels. She was examining them carefully, testing their edges for sharpness, and finding a knife blade that failed to measure up to her standards she took a small whetstone from her pack and began to hone its edge. Ronan, meanwhile, had cleared a wide space of stone floor, well away from the inflammable contents of the barn, and was building a small fireplace there. Puss, who had finished the rat, was sniffing around the back of the barn, looking for seconds.

Tarl sat down on a sack, grimacing at the soreness in his feet, and sniffed. The barn was redolent with the smells of fresh grain and new-mown hay, and felt strangely welcoming. Hauling the new wineskin from his bag, he broke the seal and took a deep swallow. The cheap, rough red slid down his throat as smoothly as a porcupine sliding down a cactus.

'By the gods!' he spluttered. 'I know I asked them for a wine with bollocks, but this one tastes as though it's been made out of old scrotums!'

Pulling a face, he wiped his mouth with the back of his hand and offered the skin to the others. Ronan shook his head without looking up, and Tyson waved the skin away.

'Not today,' she muttered. 'I think I'd rather feel well.'

Tarl took another swallow, and relaxed as the familiar warm glow spread through his stomach. Reaching into his pack, he began to pull out his food supplies.

'Okay,' he said brightly. 'You two have done the cooking for the last four days. Now it's my turn.'

Tyson looked up sharply.

'Oh, we don't mind,' she faltered. 'Why don't you sit back and let . . .'

'No, I insist,' interrupted Tarl, firmly. 'My turn.'

There was a sudden silence.

'I think I will have some wine,' said Tyson, gloomily, and with a happy smile Tarl tossed the skin to her and prepared to construct a meal in his own inimitable and unsavoury way.

When they had left the hotel complex, depressed and hungover, five days before, Tarl had been expecting that their journey back to Welbug would be a slow and leisurely affair. He had been looking forward to stopping in several cities on the way and sampling the varied delights that each had to offer. But Ronan and Tyson were in a hurry, and were determined to travel as inconspicuously and as speedily as possible, in case the Orcbane board had any other nasty surprises in store for them.

They had briefly considered travelling upstream by boat along the Errone River as far as Asposa before heading north through Behan, but had dismissed this idea on three counts. Firstly, they would travel faster on foot, secondly there were rumours of a horrifying and devastating outbreak of the Grey Plague in the city of Far Tibreth, and lastly, Tyson had said she would rather be dragged backwards through a lake of boiling pig's urine than ever set foot in Behan again. And so they had decided to travel through the fertile lands on the north bank of the Errone, skirting the Yaimos Desert and the Chrome Mountains, and then head north through the Ilex Plain to the Great River Leno.

They had stopped at Perplec so that Tyson could pick up the Orcbane GTI[6] sword that an armourer was adapting for her, and had then spent an hour sitting at a table outside The Frothblower's Arms, on Harbour Street, watching the hustle and bustle of the port area, and waiting for dusk to fall. As soon as it was dark they had stolen quietly down some quayside steps, borrowed a small, un-tended rowing boat, and had slipped quietly across the still, dark-velvet waters of the estuary, leaving the lights of the city behind them. One of the small collection of buildings on the north bank was an agency for the AEVIS Horse-hire Company (All Equines Verified Incredibly Safe), and a small pony had been waiting for them, tied to the railings outside. Then Ronan and Tyson had set off at a pace which, if he hadn't been on the pony, would have left Tarl trailing well behind.

For four days the weather had held good and the sun had shone on them as they travelled through the vineyards and olive groves of south Cydor. But on the fifth morning they had woken to find the sky obscured by thick, lowering clouds. As they had headed northwards, with the Chrome Mountains on their left, the clouds had gradually darkened, and by the time they had arrived at a trading post on the southern edge of the Ilex Plain, the sky was almost black. The trading post, a large, ramshackle stone building with a wooden stable block clinging drunkenly to the outside, was an AEVIS agent, and now that Ronan and Tyson felt safe enough to travel a little slower, they had decided to leave Tarl's pony there. It was also, according to the tatty wooden sign outside, 'the last off-licence for forty miles', and they had left with Tarl weighed down under the weight of two full wineskins. A steady drizzle had begun to fall, and by the time they reached the fertile farmlands of the Ilex Plain it was raining steadily. Ronan, experienced in such matters, had overruled Tarl's prediction that it was just a passing shower, and so they had sought shelter in the first farm that they had found. And thus it was

6 GTI – Goblin Throat-Impaler

that Ronan and Tyson were seated on bales of hay in a large stone barn, with Puss stretched out at their feet, watching Tarl's attempts at catering with horrified awe.

Tarl had two main methods of cooking over a campfire: boiling things fiercely in cheap red wine and frying things fiercely in cheap red wine. He was currently doing the former, and after chopping up all the vegetables, tubers and the dried meat that they had bought at the trading post into bite-sized pieces, he had placed them in the dixie, poured a good measure of wine over them, thrown in some leaves he had found which he claimed were herbs (but which had a pungent aroma reminiscent of stale urine), and had heated them over the fire until the resulting stew was boiling furiously. He'd often found in the past that putting everything into the can at once tended to result in the vegetables turning to mush by the time the meat was cooked, but what the hell, food was food, and anyway, he liked his vegetables that way. It saved you having to chew.

Tyson watched horrified as Tarl scratched his armpit, wiped his hand on the arse of his stained old trousers and then dipped his finger into the stew and tasted it. As a slightly worried look spread across his face, she turned to Ronan.

'Suddenly I don't feel hungry,' she whispered.

'Don't worry, Tarl's cooking always tastes better than it looks.'

'If it tasted like fresh cowpat, it would still taste better than it looks.'

'Yeah, I have to admit, he seems to have surpassed himself this time.'

'You'll have to eat it,' said Puss. 'Or he'll sulk for days. But you'll be all right, he takes his cooking seriously. Whenever he makes ratatouille, he always uses fresh rat.'

Unaware of this discussion on his talents as a chef, Tarl added some more wine to the simmering morass and tasted it a second time. Nodding happily to himself, he lifted the dixie from the flames and began to ladle out the stew. The pieces of meat rattled into the wooden bowls, and the vegetables landed with a splat that Tyson found remarkably apposite, considering her remark about cowpats. Smiling proudly, Tarl handed the bowls round with a flourish.

'Here you go,' he said. 'Casserole de dried meat avec loads of veg.'

Tyson looked apprehensively at her portion for a few moments, and then shutting her eyes she took a deep breath and spooned some into her mouth. To her surprise, it wasn't quite as appalling as she had expected. Admittedly, the meat was as hard and chewy as old shoes, and tasted remarkably similar, but if you ignored the occasional suspiciously short and curly black hair, it was almost edible. Almost, but not quite.

'What do you think?' asked Tarl, brightly.

'You'll make someone a *klatting* awful wife,' muttered Ronan, who was wondering if he'd broken a tooth on one of the pieces of meat.

'What?'

'Have you cooked for Guebral yet?'

'Yeah. Just the once.'

'So that's why she stayed in Yai'El, is it?'

'Here, don't you like my casserole?'

Ronan opened his mouth to give a full, frank and honest appraisal of the food, but then paused to remove a wiry little hair that had got stuck between two of his teeth, and Tyson stepped in hurriedly.

'It's remarkable,' she said, 'considering where we are, and how quickly you put it together.' *And*, she added silently to herself, *considering that you're a tasteless, untalented travesty of a chef with the culinary ability of a dead dog, but with even less connection with hygiene.*

'Ah,' said Tarl, quite touched. 'Thank you.'

'You're welcome.' Tyson realised that Ronan was staring at her with the horrified expression of someone who has just discovered that his loved one is totally insane, and hurriedly changed the subject.

'So, how was Guebral when you spoke to her last night?'

'Fine. Nothing's changed over the past five days. The mob has still got the Dead Boys trapped in the warehouse in Yai'El, but they're in no danger. Gueb's got far too much power for the besiegers, and they're beginning to realise it. She could drive them off now if she wasn't so soft-hearted, but she says it's not their fault, they're being *Controlled*, and she doesn't want to hurt anyone unless she has to. Still, she reckons she'll be able to slip away and join us in a few days. She doesn't want us to take on the Orcbane board without her.'

'We could do with her Power. Those sad old men are a tricky bunch.' Tyson paused, and looked at Tarl with her head on one side. 'You know, with your track record for fidelity, I'm surprised that Guebral let you out of her sight for a minute. She must trust you a lot.'

Tarl simpered horribly, and tried to hide it by taking a huge swig from the wineskin.

'She does,' he gasped, when he had finished coughing. 'Better than I trust myself.'

The donkey, which had been lying at their feet enjoying the exchanges, opened one lazy eye.

'She does too, you know,' it snorted. 'I was there. You should have heard them. It was sickening!'

'All right, all right!' muttered the embarrassed Tarl.

'Sweetheart this, lover that . . . And do you know what pranny boy here did?'

'Puss, shut it, will you?'

'Do you know what this grade-one, twenty-four-carat prize wol went and did?'

'Puss, I'll *klatting* well . . .'

'What did he do?' interrupted Tyson and Ronan, as one.

'He only begged her to cast a *Spell of Fidelity* on him, that's all. And she did.'

Tarl suddenly found that the other three were staring at him with big, smirking grins on their annoying faces. He stared fixedly down at his food.

'A *Spell of Fidelity*?' laughed Ronan. 'So, er, how does that work, then?'

'Never you mind!' muttered Tarl, who had gone the colour of an overripe *untah*.

'No, come on, we're your friends!' said Tyson, struggling to keep a straight face. 'We're interested.'

'I don't want to talk about it!'

'But we do. Does it stop you fancying other people, or does it stop you getting . . .'

'If you must know,' yelled Tarl, 'what happens is that it hurts really badly every time I get an . . . every time that it goes . . . well, when it, you know, my, er, my thingy gets . . .' He ground to a halt, unable to find words that wouldn't embarrass him even more, and gesticulated hopelessly.

'What you mean,' Tyson filled in for him, 'is that it hurts when you get an erection, right?'

Tarl nodded miserably.

'Unless I'm thinking about Gueb, it stings really badly. You've no idea.'

'Well, I wouldn't have, would I?' responded Tyson. She looked at him sitting there hunched up and almost literally squirming with embarrassment, and felt really sorry for him. She had teased him

56

enough. But then she looked down at the congealing sludge in her bowl, the mockery of an edible meal that Tarl had concocted, and she felt the harsh, bitter aftertaste at the back of her throat, as though she had been chewing up one of those white, circular, mint-like deodorants that you find swimming in a pool of urine in blocked urinals, and suddenly the feeling of sympathy vanished completely. What the hell was going on? She was tired and soaked, her wounded thigh was throbbing, and she was expected to eat something that tasted as though it had been scooped out of a swamp? She looked down at Puss, and the little donkey saw the glint in her eye and winked at her.

'Mind you, it's not really surprising that he's had to do something like that,' it said, innocently. 'I mean, women do tend to throw themselves at him, heaven knows why. There was this gorgeous girl who chatted him up in Dram Bewey's, when we were in Atro. Remember her, Tarl?'

'God, yes! You wouldn't believe what she said to me . . .'

'And what about Serena, back in Welbug?' Tyson interrupted. 'She really had the hots for you!'

'She was beautiful!' sighed Tarl, going a little dreamy-eyed.

'Do you remember the first time you saw her? She was wearing that short skirt, and she stood there smiling at you, and just gently moving her hips . . .'

'How could I forget? She was . . . ow! She looked . . . ouch!'

Tarl suddenly grimaced and clutched at himself uncomfortably, and Ronan, who had been staring at them a little puzzled by these exchanges, suddenly caught on.

'Remember when she was waiting for you in your room, wearing *that* outfit?' he grinned.

'Ouch! No, I don't want to think about it, Ronan! *Ouch!*'

'The horns and the fleece, the black rubber boots, and the little woolly tail hanging down over her bum . . .'

'OW! *Klatting* hell, that stings! Owwwww!'

'All that blonde hair hanging down round her shoulders . . .'

'Aargh! Ow! *Ouch!*'

'And you told me she had the nicest bum you'd ever bitten!'

'*Ow! Ow! Ouch!* You gang of bastards! *Aargh!*'

Tarl leapt to his feet, bent almost double, and with his hands clutching ineffectually at his stinging private parts he staggered to the door and disappeared into the rain, moaning with pain. Tyson felt a little guilty, for Tarl's reaction had been far more acute than she had expected, but the other two were chuckling happily to themselves.

'Do you know,' laughed the donkey. 'I never get tired of seeing that.'

'It's happened before?' asked Ronan.

'Oh, yeah. Just about every time a pretty girl walks past. He's a sad man, is Tarl.'

'I hope he's all right,' muttered Tyson. 'I don't think he should be running off by himself with the Orcbane board taking such an interest in us.'

'Don't worry,' said the donkey. 'I'll go and keep an eye on him.'

It stood up and ambled across to the door, and then flattening its ears to its neck and lowering its head against the rain it followed Tarl out into the late-afternoon gloom. Tyson watched it disappear, then dug into her backpack and hauled out a fresh loaf and some cheese. Breaking them in half she handed some to Ronan, and the two of them nestled down into the warm hay that was scattered about the floor and wolfed the food down before Tarl could return.

'Do you really think the board will have kept track of us?' Ronan mumbled through a mouthful of bread. 'We've been moving pretty fast.'

'No, I just wanted to get rid of Puss, so we could get some proper food inside us without Tarl finding out. You know the two of them are as thick as thieves. Puss would have blabbed, and then Tarl would have been all hurt.'

'You reckon we're safe, then?'

'Safe is a bit of a strong word when Tarl is doing the cooking, but I think so, don't you? As you said, we've been travelling fast, and we haven't left many clues as to where we're heading. I reckon we're okay. In fact, I don't think we've an enemy within fifty miles of us. I've got one of my gut feelings about it, and they're not often wrong.'

Ronan smiled, and relaxed back into the warmth of the hay. He'd learned from experience that Tyson's gut feelings were unerringly reliable. In fact, they had always been one hundred per cent accurate. It was a shame, then, that she should choose this occasion to be completely, utterly and totally wrong.

Slanved, Master of Assassins, was one of those people who could have been born to the profession which they take up in later life. His father, a mercer from the city of Asposa, had hoped that his son would follow him into the family business, but it became apparent at a very early age that his son's talents lay in a different field altogether.

As soon as he could walk, young Slanved would toddle round the house looking for insects to step on. At first, this seemed like a harmless little obsession (unless you happened to be an insect), but as he grew older he began experimenting, throwing ants into spider's webs or pulling the wings off flies. Soon there wasn't a spider in the neighbourhood with more than the odd leg left, and if any of the household flies wanted to nip out and examine that interesting bit of crap in the garden, they had to walk there.

Concerned by this apparent cruel streak and worried at the way he would sit and stare fixedly at the neighbour's cat through the window with his fingers flexing, his parents bought him his very first pet, a goldfish, in the hope that this would teach him to love and respect animals. Slanved sat and watched it swimming round and round its little bowl for two hours, but the moment his mother left the room, he pulled it out of the water and flattened it with her rolling pin. Lying in bed that evening, with the tears drying on his pillow and a pair of buttocks that still bore the marks of his father's belt, he came to the conclusion that perhaps a bit more subtlety was required.

A few weeks later another goldfish made its appearance in the bowl. Slanved sat and watched this one too, but when his parents left the room, he did nothing but continue to watch the fish. He had learned his first lesson. It was a few days later, when he was out shopping with his mother, that the new pet met a somewhat mysterious end. To his mother's consternation and to Slanved's (concealed) delight, when they returned home it was floating upside-down in the bowl, dead. This time his parents put it down to bad luck, but after three more goldfish, two kittens, a couple of hamsters and a puppy had all met with inexplicable deaths whilst Slanved was out of the house, they began to get suspicious. And when his father crept upstairs to his bedroom and found him mixing ground glass into the latest puppy's dinner, those suspicions became certainty. Slanved spent another painful night crying into his pillow, and the stream of pets came to an abrupt end (as, it must be said, had the pets themselves).

Soon afterwards, he started school. At first, although he showed no inclination to make friends or even mix with the other children, nothing untoward occurred. But then, shortly after an incident in which several of his classmates chased him round the playground

59

calling him names and throwing stones at him, a series of mysterious accidents and ailments began which killed two of them and laid low or injured another nine. His form teacher, her suspicions raised, visited his parents, and Slanved spent a third tearful and painful night in bed. Three days later, his teacher was found dead in her home. Her doctor said that she appeared to have all the symptoms of someone who had accidentally eaten ground glass.

Within an hour of hearing this news, Slanved's parents had packed up all his belongings and had marched him unceremoniously down to the Guild of Assassins and left him there as an indentured apprentice. Returning home, they breathed a sigh of relief that they had managed to jettison their murderous offspring before he turned his attention to them. Unfortunately, when they celebrated their narrow escape that evening, they chose the bottle of Cydorian brandy that he had carefully and undetectably doctored with rat poison a few weeks previously, and as a result Slanved unknowingly became an orphan.

His new home, the Asposa Guildhall, was also home to four Master Assassins, eight Brother Assassins, nine trainees, and fifteen apprentices, but despite the fact that he was now living amongst like-minded boys of a similar age, he still treated them with suspicion and kept himself to himself. For the first few weeks he was as good as gold, working hard at his lessons, being respectfully polite to his elders and doing his tasks and errands as efficiently as possible. But then, one day, after Worshipful Brother Praline had given him a bawling out and a beating for a prank that had been played by another apprentice, his old habits reasserted themselves, and he decided to take his revenge.

This time, however, he'd met his match. His tutors had been keeping an eye out for some such move, as the one thing that all the apprentices in the Guild of Assassins had in common was a penchant for killing people in devious and subtle ways. Attempts to kill their fellow apprentices or tutors were expected. In fact, they were essential, and Slanved's personal tutor (Brother Praline) had been getting so worried about the little angel who had been entrusted to his care that he had pushed matters a bit by punishing him for something he hadn't done. When, that evening, Brother Praline found rather a lot of ground glass in his dinner, it was a cause for general rejoicing, although this didn't include Slanved himself, who spent yet another painful evening crying into his pillow.

However, now that he had proved his credentials, as it were, he was taken aside next morning by Tim the Impaler, one of the Master Assassins, and given an hour-long briefing on the history, rules and beliefs of the Guild. It was pointed out to him that trying to kill a member of such a closely knit organisation of experienced and practised killers was not a particularly good idea if he wanted to remain alive himself. He was then introduced to the Prime Law of the Assassins' Guild: *No Assassin may kill, attempt to kill or purposefully cause the death of another member of the Guild.* He was also warned that transgressing any of the ten laws of the Guild's Constitution would result in immediate expulsion. The advantages of Guild membership were pointed out, not least of which was being paid large amounts of money to kill people in devious and mysterious ways. The top men were making a fortune, apparently. In fact (he was told), you could say they were making a killing . . . Of course, it would be perfectly possible to go round slaughtering people without being in the Guild, but the authorities did rather class that as murder, and it usually resulted in being on the receiving end of one of those messy public executions.

Once again, Slanved learned his lesson. From that moment on he threw himself wholeheartedly into the life of the Guild, and it soon became apparent that he had a rare talent. He made his first official kill at the age of fourteen, using a poison of his own invention to remove an overzealous tax collector who was bothering the merchants of Vabyus. As the years passed and the kills mounted, he rose through the ranks, eventually becoming a Master Assassin at the unprecedented age of twenty, and his notoriety grew until the mere mention of his name was enough to unsettle even the bravest of warriors.

And so, when some years later the chairman of the board of the Orcbane Sword Corporation commissioned an Open Contract on Ronan, it was Slanved who was the obvious choice to fulfil such a tough and challenging contract. Wayta had provided the Guild with a slim dossier on the target, and Slanved had studied this carefully for some days. He'd heard of Ronan, and the fact that he had teamed up with Tyson of Welbug made things very difficult. However, according to the dossier, the chairman had taken measures that would sting them into action at a specific time, and his guess was that they would then travel from Perplec to Welbug, possibly with a couple of friends, to meet with the wizard, Anthrax. However, their exact route was a matter of conjecture, and they would be moving stealthily but fast.

Slanved thought about this for a while. They wouldn't travel by boat – it was too slow, upriver. They wouldn't go near Far Tibreth, on account of the plague. They wouldn't cross the Chrome Mountains as they were in a hurry, so they would have to pass them on the east, and that narrowed it down to an area some five or six miles across. Unfortunately, it was an area of orchards, vineyards and olive groves, and fifty people could have passed through it without being discovered. However, if they carried on heading north to the Ilex Plain, they would have to travel across a place where concealment was next to impossible . . .

Several weeks previously, Shikara's orc army had cut a swath through the fertile farmland of Cydor, burning, trampling and destroying the crops and leaving a half-mile-wide trail of devastation. This strip of countryside was so ravaged and flattened that a flea couldn't hop across it without attracting attention, and if Slanved was to stake it out with watchers stationed maybe a mile apart, no one could get across without being seen. He would need at least six men, but then if he was going to tackle a pair of warriors with reputations like Ronan and Tyson's, he'd probably need six other assassins to pull the job off anyway. This was the same Ronan who had killed Karth, a Master of Assassins, in Welbug some months before. In fact, come to think of it, eight might be better . . .

And so it was that Slanved came to be crouched in a clump of scorched hay on the northern edge of the trail of desolation that had been left by the orc army, with eight of his fellow Assassins spread out in a cordon to the east at intervals of a mile. He had warned the others that they could be there for several days, waiting for a target that might not show up at all. It wouldn't be the first time that he had spent nearly a week on such a stake-out, doing without sleep and only daring to stretch his legs and relieve himself in the cover of the night. Assassin training had prepared them all for this and it was just another part of the job, but even so it was desperately tiring and monotonous work, checking the ground to the east for movement, then the ground to the west, then checking the sky for smoke-sign (the signalling method favoured by the Guild), then resting your eyes for a moment, then doing it again, and again, and again . . .

Still, it had to be done, and so Slanved lay there stock-still in the hay like the rest of his team, ignoring cramped and tortured muscles that longed for movement, and unaware that his estimate of their target's likely route had been so accurate that Ronan and his friends had spent the night camped in a barn just a few miles to the south, and were at that moment heading straight towards them.

As they strode along in the bright afternoon sunshine, Ronan and Tyson were feeling just a little guilty about the way they had teased Tarl. And to judge by his ramrod-straight back, his insistence on walking ten yards ahead of them and his refusal to acknowledge any of their attempts at rapprochement, he was still in the mother of all huffs.

When the little donkey had eventually escorted him back to the barn the previous night, Tarl had been soaked to the skin and extremely pissed off. He had ignored Tyson's apologies and Ronan's protestations of how much they had really enjoyed his stew, and marching pointedly past them he had stripped his wet clothes off, wrapped himself in the malodorous woollen rag that he claimed was a blanket, and gone to sleep in a corner behind a pile of hay.

Usually he would have woken up next morning and found that he was in a better, more forgiving mood, but this time he had woken up and found that he was in a small pool of discarded stew. Or, more accurately, his face was. Ronan and Tyson had been forced to admit that they had surreptitiously emptied their bowls out behind the hay while he had been gone, and when he had curled up to go to sleep in the dark, soaked to the skin, he hadn't noticed. The stew had been bad enough when hot, but stone cold it smelt appalling and had a sticky, greasy consistency that made it cling like a limpet with severe halitosis. Tarl had been hurt and upset, not only because they hadn't appreciated his cooking, but also because he had a sneaking feeling that when Ronan had described it as tasting like *lenkat* dung gone bad, he wasn't being insulting, just accurate. And so Tarl was stalking along ahead of the others in a furious sulk, and Puss wasn't improving the situation by making jokes about Shit Kebabs and Crap Suzettes, and occasionally referring to him as 'Masterchef' in an ostentatiously loud voice.

They were still travelling through rich, flat farmland, following tracks that wound between fields of waist-high corn and groves of tightly packed olive trees, when Puss began to tell the story of The Evening That Tarl Cooked Dinner For Guebral. Tarl, feeling highly uncomfortable, put on speed so that he wouldn't have to listen to the embarrassing denouement. Behind him, Ronan and Tyson were riveted to the donkey's highly embroidered narration and slowed down to listen properly. Thus it was that when they suddenly found themselves on the edge of a wide strip of devastation that ran from east to west through the farmland like a gaping wound, Tarl was fifty yards ahead of them and was marching across the bare, scorched earth as blatant and as easy to spot as a spider in a white enamel bath.

'Tarl!' hissed Ronan. 'Get down! You can be seen from miles away!'

But either Tarl didn't hear him, or else he was in the sort of mood where he was *klatted* if he was going to do anything that some muscle-bound lump-head warrior told him to do, and he just marched stiffly on.

'The pranny!' muttered Ronan. 'We've kept our heads down all this way, and he goes marching straight across a great wide-open space like that!'

'I wouldn't worry,' said Tyson. 'We're probably fifty miles away from the nearest enemy. Tarl's being a careless pranny, all right, but there isn't anyone around to see him.'

Ronan nodded slowly, and smiled. But then he didn't know that when it came to predictions, Tyson was having a particularly bad run that week.

Apprentice Assassin Marwood woke up with a start and peered blearily around, struggling to remember who and where he was. By the gods, he must have fallen asleep! Slimy Slanved would kill him if he found out! Guiltily he rubbed his eyes and began to sit up, but then froze. He could hear voices, or, more accurately, a voice. Someone was muttering indignantly to themselves nearby. Gingerly he eased back a few of the scorched stems at the edge of the clump of hay that hid him, and peered out.

A small, seedy-looking man was striding stiffly across the bare, burned landscape some fifty yards away, and was being followed at a distance by three other figures: a large black warrior, a smaller woman warrior and a scruffy little donkey. As Marwood watched, the donkey peered round at the blackened, ash-covered ground and called out a question to the leading figure as to whether he had been trying to cook the countryside this time.

Marwood ducked down hurriedly, his heart in his mouth. A talking donkey? Seven shades of shite, it was them! The target and his companions! There couldn't be a second disparate group like them wandering around northern Cydor! He lay there hidden in the hay, not daring to move, and it was only when the sounds of their

64

passing had completely faded and he was sure that they were well out of sight that he crept out from his hiding-place.

With trembling hands he took his pack of kindling from his backpack and prepared to send the smoke-sign that would tell the other Assassins that their target had been sighted and that the kill could go ahead. And it was he, Marwood, who had spotted them! At last he had done something right! And this time, he swore to himself, he would get the lighting of the fire correct. There would be no more jokes from the other apprentices about Marwood's Special Signal, a dense, black stream of billowing smoke that could be seen ten miles away and that meant, 'Oh, *klat*, I've set the whole bloody wheatfield on fire by mistake!' This time he would be careful.

Slanved was both pleased and surprised when he saw the thin plume of smoke drifting up to the sky a couple of miles to the east. He lay watching carefully to read the signal and saw it die abruptly, only to start again after a minute or so with a couple of small puffs and then a steady plume, followed by several thicker, blackish puffs and a thick grey stream.

Well, okay, he thought. *According to that message, five carrots and a vulture have just sailed across the bay in a chamberpot, heading downwards. Either something very strange is happening, or else it's Marwood who has spotted the target, and he's trying to let us know in his own, inimitable way.*

He scrambled to his feet, stretching to ease his cramped muscles, and shook his head as the distant stream of smoke turned into dense, black, billowing clouds. *Looks like another field of wheat is going up in flames,* he thought. *I don't suppose I could be lucky enough for Marwood to incinerate himself this time. Still, at least it doesn't look anything like smoke-sign, so it won't arouse the targets' suspicions. That means we can trail them for a while, then overtake them tonight, while they're resting, and ambush them in the morning. It's all flat grassland north of here, so we'll take them totally by surprise. Poison arrows from short range, I reckon, but we'll see when we get there. They won't know what's hit them, the poor bastards. I could almost feel sorry for them . . .*

And with a grin on his face that looked about as sympathetic as a Brannian crocodile surveying the remnants of its lunch, he stamped on a small beetle that had been scurrying along nearby and then set off to meet up with the rest of his murderous team.

*

The Tarl who marched alongside Ronan next day was a far happier, chirpier, more lovable version than the miserable sod who had spent the whole of the previous day in a giant sulk. The contents of the second winesack had done much to pour oil on troubled waters when they had made camp in the evening, and after several drinks and a meal of wild duck roasted whole over the campfire by Tyson, he had apologised sincerely for being such a pain in the backside, and the others had apologised (much less sincerely) for winding him up by setting off Guebral's *Spell of Fidelity*.

After a lazy night spent sleeping under the stars, they had breakfasted and set off in the warm, early-morning sunshine. After an hour they came to the end of the cultivated lands and found themselves walking across open grassland dotted with wild flowers. In the far distance to the north-west they could see the small range of low hills that hid the city of Ilex, but here the ground was flat and even, and the goat track that they were following headed north like an arrow. Insects hummed and buzzed busily about the flowers, and the only other sounds were the joyful singing of the Grassland Larks and the mournful cry of the Rudducks. Tarl, with the warm sun on his back and the sweet-scented breeze on his face, felt a song coming on.

'La-la-la-la-la la-la!' he carolled, giving his throat a practice run, and the larks, sensing some serious competition, decided to can it for a while and see what the opposition had to offer.

Ronan winced. He knew that Tarl's voice was a pleasant light baritone that could hold a tune quite well . . . in Tarl's own, sadly deluded mind. In the real world, however, his voice was very loud and very flat, and tended to miss the higher notes by a large margin.

'Hey,' began Ronan, turning to Tyson, 'weren't you . . .'

'There's an elven song,' interrupted Tarl, happily, 'that sums up my feelings on such a morning, when the sun is in the sky and the air is full of the scent of flowers. It goes something like this.'

He paused to clear his throat with a noise that sounded like an orc vomiting, then began to sing, and the whole plain seemed to reverberate with the noise.

> '*E bethíl hal regothílen*
> *Lemiri penna virsílen . . .*'

'You poser!' cut in Puss. 'You know damn well none of us speak elvish. You could be making the whole thing up.'

'Okay, okay, I'll translate it as I go along. Roughly, it goes like this . . .

> *'I once knew a girl from old Baq d'Or*
> *Who said she'd never been kissed before,*
> *So we kissed and cuddled and kissed some more,*
> *And two weeks later I found a big sore*
> *On my . . .'*

'By the gods, Tarl!' interrupted Ronan. 'Don't you know any clean songs?'

'It's not my fault,' moaned Tarl. 'It's the elves. They wrote the words. I'm just loosely translating them.'

'Very loosely,' muttered Ronan, and Tarl turned away, grinning. Seconds later his voice rose in song again.

> *'I met a young maid from Nevin way,*
> *As sweet and pretty as a summer's day,*
> *And I tell you it fair took my breath away*
> *When she kissed my chest and began to play*
> *With my . . .'*

'Hush!' hissed Puss, fiercely, and Tarl was just about to unleash a salvo about unmusical Philistines who kept interrupting before he could get to the good bits when he realised that Puss had stopped dead and was staring ahead fixedly.

'I can smell humans,' whispered the donkey.

The others followed its gaze, but could see nothing untoward. There was no movement, save for the insects that buzzed tirelessly about the flowers, and a couple of goats ambling aimlessly along half a mile away. Ahead of them stretched the flat, even ground of the plain, with nothing for a man to hide behind, not even a small bush. Even the longest grass was barely six inches tall and couldn't have hidden an anorexic hobbit.

'Where?' whispered Ronan.

The donkey's nostrils whiffled gently as it tried to analyse the smells wafting towards it on the light northern breeze.

'Maybe fifty yards ahead. Five or six men, at least. Maybe more.'

Ronan peered at the open ground before them. There was nowhere for a mouse to hide, let alone six grown men, unless they were masters of camouflage . . .

'Tyson,' whispered Ronan, 'could that have been Assassin smoke-sign that we saw yesterday?'

Tyson nodded slowly. Her gaze was fixed on the ground ahead of them, a little to the left.

'Look,' she hissed. 'Over there, by that little clutch of *sarhafilas*. See?'

Ronan followed her directions, and saw what she had spotted. A small wedge of turf was sticking up like the corner of an old doormat. It was just the effect you might get if someone had cut out a square of turf and had then replaced it a touch carelessly.

'It's an ambush,' he breathed. 'Assassins, using pit-hides! We'd better spring the trap!'

'Okay. Tarl, how's the magic?'

'I guess I could conjure up a *Fireball* or two,' came the nervous reply.

'Right.' Tyson paused, and quietly slipped her bow from her shoulders. 'They'll be judging this by sound, so we'd better keep moving. I'll cover our rear. Tarl, you'd better give us another verse. But be ready for action.'

They moved forward again with Tarl in the centre, Puss on his right and Ronan on his left, drawn sword in one hand, knife in the other. Behind them came Tyson, with an arrow notched to the bow.

Tarl's arms and hands were tingling, and looking down at his trembling fingers he saw that the familiar coruscating pinpoints of light were scudding around his hands and darting up and down his forearms. He took a deep breath and launched into the third verse of the elven song, and fear added an odd timbre to his voice, so that he was eerily in tune.

> 'In Brannan I met with a witch so old
> And wrinkled it fair made my blood run cold.
> She said, Young man, there's a pot of gold
> For you, if you'll just let me have a hold
> Of yer . . .'

But then his voice was interrupted by a blood-curdling yell, and black-clad bowmen were erupting out of the ground all around them.

Slanved had picked his ground very carefully indeed. He'd expected the targets to follow the goat track, as it was human nature to stick to a path. The spot he had selected for the ambush was so flat and level that no one could expect people to be hidden there, and yet the grass was just long enough to hide the rough edges where a lid of turf fitted into each of the nine pits that they had dug before dawn. With an Assassin hidden in each pit, it had just been a matter of staying alert for the time it took until the targets arrived.

In fact, it was only three hours before Slanved heard the sounds of the targets' approach. He had been listening very carefully, expecting soft footsteps and maybe the low hum of conversation, but someone was singing, if that was the word, in a voice that could probably have been heard in Ilex. There was a brief moment when the singing and the footsteps stopped, and he wondered if something could possibly have given them away, but then the voice launched itself into song again. Slanved waited until he was sure that the targets were in the very centre of the circle of ambushers, and then he screamed the order to attack at the top of his voice and thrust himself upright. And found, to his horror, that the targets weren't standing rooted to the spot by surprise, as he had expected, but were very much in motion . . .

Tyson was drawing her bow almost before the Assassin leader's yell had died away, and as he erupted from a pit to their rear she targeted him first. Her arrow had pierced Slanved's throat before he was fully upright, and he sagged tiredly downwards into a crumpled heap in the pit. A second Assassin to their rear managed to fit an arrow to his bow and was drawing it when Tyson's next arrow took him through the heart. His arms drooped, and his arrow thumped into the rim of his pit at an angle, like the gnomon of a sundial, as he toppled back.

Ronan too had been moving the instant he had a target. Two Assassins had sprouted from the ground on their right and were notching dark-tipped poison arrows to the strings of their bows. His thrown knife thumped obscenely home into the mouth of the elder, and the younger and less experienced one yammered with fear as Ronan pounded towards him, and loosed his arrow wildly. It whistled harmlessly past and the Assassin screamed in terror, a scream that was cut horribly short as the vast sword scythed through the air to crunch through flesh and bone, carving a diagonal path from neck to hip and cleaving him almost in two.

Tarl had hesitated, temporarily paralysed by fear, as two Assassins had risen in front of him, but the sight of a pair of arrows pointing straight at him suddenly concentrated his mind wonderfully, and yelling in panic he threw up his arms in a stabbing motion. Two brilliant red fireballs rocketed out of his fingertips, driven by small amounts of Power and a vast amount of panic, and fairly fizzed at the unfortunate bowmen, slamming home with an audible *whump* and turning the two men instantaneously into screaming, writhing columns of flame.

Unchallenged by threatening humans, the pair of Assassins on the left had lined their arrows up on Ronan and were in the act of drawing their bowstrings back before they realised that the tatty little donkey charging towards them might be a problem. And then Puss was leaping at the first, and its razor-sharp teeth slammed together like steel blades. The second bowman twitched in surprise as a horrendous scream burst from his confederate, and his arrow whistled away, harmlessly high. He turned and stared, aghast, and his jaw sagged to his chest, for all of a sudden his fellow Assassin had no face left, just a ragged, torn mask of blood. Quickly he fitted another arrow to his bow and lined it up on the donkey, thankful that he had ample time to fire before the foul beast could reach him with its lethal teeth. But as he pulled back the bowstring, Tyson's third arrow slammed into his back and burst through his heart, and he was dead before the pain could even register.

Ronan hauled his sword free from the cloven corpse at his feet and snapped his head round, looking for another target, but in vain. He could see five dead Assassins, and a couple more that were wreathed in flames and smoke, and giving off a smell of incinerated meat that reminded him of the time Tarl had done a barbecue. There was just the one near Puss who was still alive, but he was rolling around on the ground screaming, with his hands pressed to his face, and as Ronan watched, Tyson strode across and finished him off with her knife.

Jamming his sword point-first into the ground, Ronan wiped his brow with the back of his hand. *That was a little close,* he thought. *But for Puss's sense of smell, we'd have walked right into the ambush, and I'd be a writhing pincushion by now.* He looked across to where Tarl was watching the two burning bodies with a look of sick horror on his face, and he was just going to call out some words of encouragement when Tyson caught his eye. She was gesturing to him with an upright finger pressed to her lips in the signal for silence, and as he looked at her quizzically she pointed at a segment of the ground nearby and mouthed something at him. Ronan followed her finger and realised that she was pointing to the wedge of turf that stuck up like the corner of a doormat. The ground beside it was undisturbed, and Ronan realised what Tyson was trying to tell him. There must be an Assassin still hidden in a pit there!

He grabbed his sword and whirled round, half expecting a dozen more to burst from the ground, but there was no movement to be seen, and so he stalked warily across to the others. Tyson was standing with an arrow notched to her bow, waiting, and the donkey was inching forward, nostrils whiffling delicately.

'I reckon there's just the one of them left, in a hole here,' it whispered out of the side of its mouth. 'And either it's wearing Eau de Piddle aftershave, or else it's peed its trousers.'

An ashen-faced Tarl had by now joined them as well, and the four of them stood around the hidden pit. Now that they were close, they could see the rough edge of bare earth where the rectangle of turf had been replaced.

'Okay, we know you're in there,' said Tyson, raising her voice.

'No I'm not,' came a muffled answer.

'Well, where are you, then?'

'Er . . . um . . . *Klat*, I guess that was a bit of a giveaway, huh?'

'We're heavily armed, so come out with your hands up.'

'I think I'd rather stay here, thank you very much.'

'If you don't come out,' said Ronan, 'I'm going to stick my sword straight through the lid of that hole and poke it around a bit.'

'Ah, don't do that.'

'Why not?'

''Cos you might kill me.' The unseen Assassin sounded highly indignant at the thought.

'So?'

'But that would be, like, really heavy, you know?'

There was a short pause.

'I don't think this guy is going to give us too much of a problem,' whispered Tyson to the others, with a grin, as she slung her bow over her shoulder.

'And it would be a bit, like, final,' the voice wittered on. 'And it would probably hurt quite a lot.'

'Good grief, you're an Assassin, aren't you?' raved Ronan. 'Death is your middle name!'

'No, actually, my middle name is Clarence. Only, like, don't tell anyone, okay, 'cos the other Assassins will give me a really heavy time!'

'What's your first name?' asked Tyson.

'Er . . . Marwood, actually,' answered Marwood.

'Well, Marwoodactually, you'd better come out. You can't stay in there for ever, and if you're not holding a weapon we won't hurt you.'

71

'Are you sure?'

'Yes.'

'Promise?'

'Yes.'

There was a pause that dragged on rather a long time.

'Cross your heart?'

'MARWOOD, GET OUT OF THAT *KLATTING* HOLE BEFORE I KILL YOU!'

The ground at their feet heaved, and they stepped backwards as an ungainly, gangling figure rose doubtfully from out of his pit and stood there blinking in the sunlight and making vaguely apologetic gestures with his hands. Anxious eyes peered out from under long, gentle lashes in a thin face that was almost unhealthily pale and was stained with streaks of soil. Long black hair hung almost to the slim shoulders, and the rectangle of turf balanced precariously on top of his head like a large hat designed by one of those sad lunatics who are, apparently, top milliners. He was dressed in the black and silver uniform of the Assassins' Guild, but its usual intimidating effect was somewhat marred by the peace medallion hanging round his thin, oddly elegant neck, and by the bare feet that were clad not in the supple black leather boots normally favoured by Assassins, but in open-toed sandals. The overall effect was of a hippy dressed for Hallowe'en.'

'Hi, Marwood,' said Tyson, brightly, and then suddenly her tone changed and her unsheathed sword was waving menacingly under his nose. 'What's the big idea of the ambush then, eh, Killer?' she snarled.

'Hey, look, it was nothing to do with me!' Even though he was surrounded, Marwood somehow managed to give the impression that he was backing away from all four of them at once. 'I mean, it was old Slanved who planned it all,' he continued. 'Once they'd picked me as part of the team, I had no choice. I mean, you wouldn't believe the really heavy stuff that those Guild guys come at you with if you don't do what they tell you!'

'But you're one of them,' interjected Tarl. 'You're an Assassin. A Killer.'

'No, I'm not! I never killed anyone! I'm only an apprentice, and I didn't want to be that, but I had no choice.'

'How come?' asked Tarl.

'Well, I was doing a sociology degree at Drolic University, right, but it wasn't much fun, 'cos the work kept getting in the way of the parties, so I, like, dropped out.'

Tarl nodded. This all made perfect sense so far.

'But my dad is a really heavy bread-head, see, and he got really angry and said that he wasn't going to pay my grant any more. And then he fixed up this apprenticeship with a mate of his, who's a Worshipful Master in the Asposa Guildhall, and when I said I'd rather die, my dad said fine, that was the alternative, as if I didn't join the Guild of Assassins, he would send them after me. And so I joined.'

'Hey, hey, hey,' cut in Tyson, waving her sword under his nose again. 'We're straying a little off the point here.'

Marwood jerked back slightly, and the rectangle of turf slipped forward and slid down his face. He grabbed it and stood there twisting it nervously in his hands.

'The point *is*,' continued Tyson, 'we want to know why nine Assassins should be ambushing us.'

'Well,' said Marwood, indicating Ronan with his thumb, 'because of the Open Contract on your friend here, Slanved said that we should . . . er . . .'

His voice died away uncertainly, and he looked nervously from Tyson to Ronan. Both were staring at him with horrified expressions.

'An Open Contract?' Tyson repeated, aghast.

'Yeah. Look, I'm really sorry,' Marwood muttered, and sat down miserably in his pit.

Tyson turned to Ronan and lifted one hand to stroke his cheek, and he raised his own great hand and cupped hers against the side of his face.

'I don't want any arguments,' she whispered. 'We go together, and we go fighting.' Ronan opened his mouth to argue, but she moved her hand to cover his lips and hold them shut. 'I mean it,' she added, and Ronan gazed into her eyes for a few moments before nodding resignedly.

Tarl was staring from one to the other, bewildered.

'What's wrong? What is it?' he asked.

'An Open Contract . . .' answered Ronan, matter-of-factly.

'What's that?'

'A sentence of death.'

'Eh?'

'Tell him,' Tyson ordered Marwood, and taking Ronan's arm she led him quietly away from the others. Tarl crouched down in front of the reluctant Assassin and Puss sat down next to him, and Marwood suddenly became uncomfortably aware that the donkey had the most chilling eyes he had ever seen, even worse than Slanved's.

'Okay, then, what's this Open Contract?' Tarl asked him.

'Well, it's a contract that the Guild vows to fulfil, whatever the cost and no matter how many Assassins it takes. Once signed, the deal is irrevocable – even if the contractor dies, or changes his mind. They cost a fortune, that's why this is only the sixth there's ever been.'

'What happened to the other five targets?'

'All dead.'

'And we can't buy or frighten the Guild off? I mean, we've just killed eight of your guys. Won't the rest think twice?'

'No, man, those guys are dedicated! They'll just keep coming until they've got him.'

'*Klat!* So what you're saying is, we have to kill every Assassin in Midworld, right?'

'Yeah, I guess so.'

'How many are there?'

'About five hundred.'

'Oh.'

'And over a thousand apprentices.'

'Ah.'

Tarl pursed his lips thoughtfully as the severity of Ronan's position hit him, and looked across to where he and Tyson were standing with their arms wrapped around one another. All at once he realised with horror that they were basically saying goodbye. Their love affair had suddenly turned into a hopeless, pointless suicide pact.

'There must be something we can do!' he raged, but Marwood shook his head pessimistically.

'The Guild just can't be stopped. We pride ourselves . . .'

Marwood stopped dead as the donkey bared a set of horribly sharp teeth that were smeared with what looked unpleasantly like fresh blood.

'Er, I mean, *they* pride themselves on their professionalism,' he continued, more diplomatically. 'Once an Assassin takes on a job, he finishes it. There's no one in the whole of Midworld who he wouldn't target, apart from another Assassin, of course. And it becomes a matter of pride. Personally I don't get it. Make love, not war, that's what I reckon. I don't mean we have to get cuddly with everyone we meet. There's some pretty unattractive dudes out there, you know? All I am saying is, give peace a chance . . .'

Once again Marwood ground to a halt. Tarl was staring at him like a dragon eyeing half a ton of best anthracite, and he began to worry that Tarl might have got the wrong idea about this peace and love thing.

'Er . . .' he began.

'What did you say?' asked Tarl.

'I said er.'

'No. Before that.'

'Well, I was talking about peace and love, but only in general terms. I didn't mean that you and I should be having a f . . .'

'No, before that! Something about Assassins not targeting other Assassins.'

'Oh, right! Phew! Yeah, it's the most important rule of the Guild. No Assassin may kill, attempt to kill or purposefully cause the death of another member of the Guild.'

'So if Ronan became an Assassin they couldn't touch him?'

'Well, yeah, but it isn't that easy. You have to be accepted as an apprentice and spend years learning the trade, training in poisons and weaponcraft, and helping to fabricate plots and designs. Then you have to make your first kill. And after all that there's a written exam and an oral.'

'And there's no other way?'

'Not really. Unless . . .'

'Unless what?'

'Well . . . I did hear something . . .' Marwood looked across to Ronan thoughtfully. 'Your friend looks like a qualified warrior. I heard there's a postgraduate course at Gudmornen University, way up in the north. It's a one-year MA degree, but you need to be a graduate warrior.'

'An MA degree?'

'Mainstream Assassination. If he completed the course and passed the exam, he'd be a proper, fully qualified Assassin, and a member of the Guild.'

'When does the course begin?'

'Term will have started by now. But they might accept a late applicant, especially one who has a letter of recommendation signed and sealed by the great Master of Assassins, Slanved himself.'

'Who?'

'The guy over there with the arrow through his throat. We could write the letter for him.' Marwood paused, and a slow smile spread over his face. 'I can forge his signature, and as for the seal, I think you'll find that the ring on his right finger is his signet ring.'

Tarl thought about this idea for a while, but he couldn't find many flaws. They would have to give Ronan a new identity, for his Assassin tutors would simply carry out the contract if they found out who he really was. Otherwise the plan seemed pretty sound. As far as Tarl was concerned, spending a year on a university campus would give him a chance to find out if the rumours about students were true. He'd heard a lot about the drinking, the drugs and the parties, and he'd been truly envious . . .

'Sounds good to me,' he ventured at last, and the donkey gave him the sort of look that an orc would give someone who had just suggested not going out tonight, but staying in and having a cup of tea and an early night instead.

'Are you seriously suggesting,' it asked, incredulously, 'that we spend a whole year in Gudmornen? A town so far north that the inhabitants put ice in their drinks to warm them up?'

'If it's the only way we can save Ronan, yes. Look, they're coming back. Let's tell them the good news.'

Ronan and Tyson were walking purposefully back towards them, wearing the sort of set expressions that people adopt when they have made a decision and are determined to railroad it past everyone else, but are expecting a lot of argument. Tarl opened his mouth to speak, but Ronan held up an imperious hand to stop him, and launched into his own announcement.

'I've decided that this ambush makes no difference. I'm still going after the Orcbane board. They're only interested in me; you and Puss don't figure in their plans, and you're only in danger when you're with me. So I want you to go back to Perplec or Yai'El.'

'What about you?' Tarl asked Tyson.

'I'm going with Ronan.'

'But you'll both end up dead.'

'We know. But what's the alternative?'

Tarl told them. When he had finished they looked at each other with a burgeoning hope, and Tyson turned to Marwood.

'Are you sure about this?'

Marwood nodded.

'How can we trust you?' Tyson went on, doubtfully. Marwood looked round at the scattered Assassin corpses.

'I can give you eight good reasons,' he said. 'And anyway, I don't want to spend my life killing people, you know? I'm already well and truly *klatted* with the Guild. If Ronan becomes an Assassin, he can make me his official apprentice, and they can't touch me. And if he then orders me to go home and spend the rest of my life partying, it will be my duty as a Guild apprentice to obey him.'

'You mean you want us to take you with us?' Tyson said, incredulously. Marwood nodded again, quite vigorously, and Tyson studied him dubiously. There was a blatant honesty in his face that tended to make her believe him.

'Well, okay,' she said, and then she bent down until she was staring into his eyes from a range of about six inches and patted her sword. 'But I warn you, if you double-cross us, you'll end up wearing your rectum as a woolly hat.'

Marwood swallowed nervously. They could probably have heard the noise in Ilex. Tyson patted him on the cheek and straightened up, and she and Ronan began removing all signs of the ambush: gathering up the bodies, dumping them in the ready-dug pits and covering them over with turf. Marwood watched them for a while, taking in the smooth play of their muscles and the casual and practised ease with which they hefted the bodies about. Then he switched his attention to Tarl and Puss, who were having an argument nearby about whether Tarl should hack an arm off one of the bodies for the donkey to have as its supper.

Marwood swallowed nervously a second time, and this time they could probably have heard it in Perplec. All of a sudden he had the unpleasant feeling that he had fallen out of a red-hot saucepan only to land in a white-hot furnace . . .

Thirty minutes later, there were no traces of the ambush remaining that would be visible to the casual observer, and they were on the move again. Ronan and Tyson set a rapid pace, and Tarl struggled to stay with them. He was both surprised and a little ashamed to see that Marwood kept up effortlessly, his long legs covering the ground with deceptive ease and his sandals flapping as he strode along.

After a couple of hours they crossed the Ilex to Far Tibreth road and the ground began to slope gently upwards. They could see a low ridge of hills ahead of them to the north. The vegetation was changing, and the grassland was slowly giving way to low-lying clumps of heather and small patches of gorse. Tarl was lagging some fifty yards behind now, and the donkey had slowed down to keep him company. His feet were sore and blistered and his legs ached, but for some reason he didn't dare suggest stopping. He had an uneasy feeling of impending danger which had been growing for a while now, and the telltale pinpoints of light were once more beginning to seep out from his fingers.

On they trudged, until the ridge was no longer distant but rose in front of them, a long, narrow rocky spine that divided the Ilex Plain from the wide valley of the Great River Leno. Behind them, far off to the south-east, they could see the snow-capped peaks of the Chrome Mountains. Some miles to their left was the brooding bulk of Carn Jonnald, the highest point of the ridge, and they could just make out the famous Sentinel Statue on its summit. The slope of the ridge was steep in many places, sometimes sheer, but in front of them the rise was more gradual, and the track wound gently up towards the top.

As they climbed, Tarl's uneasy feeling grew, until the conviction that danger was imminent became overpowering. Picking up his weary feet, he broke into a staggering run, lurching up the scree of the slope with loose rocks and pebbles sliding beneath his boots, until he had caught the others up.

'How much farther are we going?' he gasped.

'As far as the Great River,' answered Ronan. 'Once we've crossed the Jonnald Ridge it's downhill all the way. A couple of hours, maybe.' He looked down at the iridescent sparks that were beginning to seep from Tarl's fingers to fall skittering amongst the stones of the scree. 'Oh-oh,' he muttered. 'Danger, right?'

'I've just got this feeling,' Tarl began unhappily, but then he stopped dead and thrust out a panicky finger. 'There's someone at the top of the ridge!' he yelled, and a ball of blue fire burst out of his shaking digit and went blasting up the slope.

The others stared after it and saw a figure outlined against the sky on the crest of the hill. It seemed to be waving, but as Tarl's fireball shot towards it they heard a distant despairing wail, and it dived for cover.

'That looks like Posner!' gasped Tyson. 'He's meant to be managing the Dragon's Claw in Welbug for me. What the *klat* is he doing here?'

'Getting his head blown off, by the look of it!' answered Ronan, and with a muttered aside of 'You pranny!' to Tarl, he went leaping up the hill, with Tyson beside him.

Tarl looked from Puss to Marwood and back again, but somehow they couldn't meet his eyes.

'All right, so I panicked,' he mumbled sheepishly. 'But I still reckon we're walking into trouble.' And with that he turned and followed the two warriors up the hill, and Puss and Marwood, trying not to laugh, went with him.

At the top of the ridge they found Tyson and Ronan helping up the mysterious figure. It was indeed Posner, and luckily the fireball had missed him, but he was in a shocking state. His face was grimy and bruised, and his usually neatly oiled hair hung lank and ragged about his head. He still wore his habitual smart clothes, but his tuxedo and his white shirt were ripped and dirty, his patent-leather shoes were muddied and his wing collar gaped open at his neck like a drunken albino bat.

'Oh, ma'am!' he kept gasping. 'Oh, ma'am!'

'Look, calm down,' advised Tyson. 'You're safe now. Tell me what's happened.'

'Oh, ma'am! It all went wrong about four days ago! Rumours suddenly began circulating saying that you're involved in bribery, corruption and treachery, and then, one night, La Maison du Bonque was burned to the ground!'

'That was our biggest rival,' Tyson explained to Ronan. 'It was a pretty classy cat-house, but not quite in the same league as the Claw. I wonder who burnt it down.'

'The rumours said that a huge, black-skinned warrior was behind it,' Posner rushed on. 'Everyone thought it must have been Ronan! And then Anthrax was assassinated by the same warrior!'

'Anthrax is dead?' gasped Tyson. '*Klat!* What happened?'

'Some sort of explosion, I don't know how. He was in one of the rooms with Takuma at the time.'

'Poor guy,' muttered Ronan. 'So he went out with a bang. In more ways than one.'

'The people of Welbug think that you and Ronan are behind it all, ma'am! Yesterday the Claw was attacked and looted by an angry mob, and I barely escaped in one piece. And warrants for the arrest of you both have been issued by the City Council! If you set foot in Welbug, they'll sling you straight into gaol. That is, if the mob don't lynch you first!'

Ronan swore viciously.

'We know who's behind all this,' he ground out. 'The *klatting* Orcbane board! They're going to suffer when I get my hands on them!'

Tyson laid a calming hand on his arm. 'Thank you for coming to warn us,' she told Posner. 'But one thing baffles me. How did you know where to find us?'

'Anthrax told me with his dying breath. He planned to come himself. He said it was vital that I warn you that there are six more, and that they will not stop until they've made their kill.'

'Six more what?'

'I couldn't make it out properly, ma'am, but it sounded like six more *cobrats*.'

'*Cobrats*? What the *klat* are they?'

'They're lethal killing machines like the one which ran amok at Thongs,' burst out Tarl, who was standing staring out over the Ilex Plain behind them. The others turned to him in surprise.

'What makes you think that?' asked Ronan.

'I don't just think it, I know it!' muttered Tarl. 'Look!'

They followed his pointing finger and saw, in the distance, six familiar, sinuous shapes gliding across the plain, following the track that they had taken less than an hour before.

'*Klat!* Run for it,' gasped Ronan, but he needn't have bothered. The others were already running for their very lives.

They had barely covered a couple of miles after scrambling down the northern slope of the Jonnald Ridge when Tarl's legs began to give out. The others were already well ahead of him, but seeing him beginning to stagger, all but Posner stopped and waited for him to catch up. The donkey snarled to him to leap on its back, and then they set off again at a rapid trot. Ronan and Tyson were setting a fast pace and Puss was only small, but Tarl was no great weight and they were easily able to keep up. Marwood too was going at a surprisingly fast pace, but Posner was overweight and out of condition, and they had all soon caught him up again.

'Only . . . another . . . half . . . mile!' he gasped, as they fell into place beside him.

'Where are we going?' yelled Tarl.

'River . . .' came the breathless reply. 'Oupase . . . the ferry-man . . . has his boat moored . . . waiting for us!'

'We'd better run ahead and warn him to be ready,' suggested Tarl, and at Ronan's nod of agreement Puss put on a spurt and moved ahead.

After a while the track plunged into a belt of forest, snaking through undergrowth so thick that they were forced to run in single file. Troll-briar and snare-thorn clutched and ripped at their legs, and they had to duck and dodge past the hanging *festa* vines. Tarl and Puss had disappeared in front, but Ronan, Tyson and Marwood stayed with the labouring Posner, encouraging him. They could hear a distant clamour gaining on them, an excited sort of reptilian baying, like a pack of alligators trying to impersonate foxhounds.

Tyson turned her head as she ran and yelled back to Ronan, who was bringing up the rear.

'We should be out in the clear soon, and the river is only a few hundred yards away. When we get to the riverbank I'm going to try a few arrows. If I take a couple of these creatures out we might be able to . . .'

THUD! The side of her head smashed into a low overhanging branch, and she fell to the ground as though she had just drunk ten of Tarl's best cocktails in one go. Posner stumbled to a halt beside her, his face a mask of horror, but Ronan shoved him past her and, stooping, picked up her limp body and flung it across his shoulder.

'Move it!' he yelled, and Posner turned and lumbered away after Marwood, with Ronan behind him. For what seemed an age they staggered along the track, and even Ronan could feel the muscles of his legs groaning and protesting at the strain. Then suddenly they burst out of the trees into the clear. In front of them the ground sloped gently down to the broad, slow river, and Ronan could see the ferryman's boat, which was drawn up on the bank about four hundred yards ahead. Puss and Tarl had almost reached it, and he could hear Tarl's panic-stricken voice drifting back as he yelled frantic instructions to Oupase, urging him to get the *klatting* boat back in the river, sharpish.

With the sound of the pursuing *cobrats* getting ever closer, Tyson's dead weight across his shoulders, and with Marwood easily outdistancing him, it felt to Ronan that he was covering the ground barely faster than a snail. However, he was easily outpacing Posner, whose laboured breathing and florid complexion showed that he was almost at the end of his tether. Even so, Ronan thought that they were going to make it to the boat with ease, but then a blood-curdling chorus of sibilant howls broke out behind him, and casting a quick look back, he saw that the six *cobrats* had burst out of the edge of the forest, and were streaking after them.

'Run, Posner! Run for your life!' he cried, redoubling his own efforts. He could feel the panic rising in his gorge, for he knew that with Tyson unconscious he would stand no chance against the six lethal pursuers. The thought of his own death, even such a painful one, held little fear for Ronan, but the knowledge that Tyson would die as well terrified him and lent wings to his feet, and he fairly flew down the slope.

Ahead he could see the boat sliding into the river, with Oupase holding the stern. Puss and Tarl were already on board, but Tarl leapt back on to the bank and raised an arm towards Ronan. From this distance the points of light that whirled about his hands looked like a nebulous cloud of light, and then suddenly a fireball burst from his fingers and came whooshing up the slope. Ronan threw another quick glance backwards and was horrified to see that the leading *cobrat* dodged the fireball with ease. It was already just yards behind the labouring Posner, and after a couple of lithe, ground-devouring paces it hurled itself forwards, hissing with blood-lust, and landed four-square on his back. With a screech of terror Posner fell forwards, and then three others threw themselves into the mêlée, and all that could be seen was a writhing mass of dark, greasy fur and slashing talons, beneath which something red threshed and screamed.

Ronan put his head down and ran as he had never run before. He only had fifty yards to go now, but two of the fell creatures had ignored Posner to chase after him, and one of them was so close that he could hear the hissing of its breath. Ahead of him Marwood was almost at the boat, and Tarl had scrambled back inside it next to Puss and Oupase, who had his oar poised against the bank, ready to thrust them out into the river. Forty yards to go, then thirty, but Ronan could tell from the look of horror on the others' faces that he wasn't going to make it. Again he snapped a quick glance backwards and found himself staring into the glowing red eyes of the *cobrat*, mere feet behind him. He realised with a pang of despair that he had no time to draw a weapon, and that anyway, Tyson was across his sword arm. The creature's eyes glinted cruelly and its mouth opened in a vicious grin as it tensed itself to spring on its helpless prey, and then suddenly there was a flash of silver as something whirled inches past Ronan's ear and buried itself up to the hilt in the fur of the *cobrat*'s throat.

Ronan snapped his head back and saw Marwood crouched on the bank, still frozen in the follow-through from throwing the knife. The thought flashed through Ronan's mind that either it had been one hell of a fluke, or else one of the best knife-throws he had ever seen, and then he was dropping Tyson over the stern of the boat and leaping in after her, with Marwood beside him. They cannoned into each other and fell sideways, sprawling against the gunwales as Oupase gave an almighty heave of his broad shoulders and thrust them out into the leaden waters. Then seating himself hurriedly on the bench between the two rowlocks, the ferryman slipped an oar into each with practised ease and began to row them strongly out towards the centre of the Great River, where the powerful current caught them and began to sweep them down towards the distant sea.

Behind them, the first of the *cobrats* reached the water's edge, and seeing its quarry speeding out of reach it threw back its head and gave a howl of anger that reverberated across the surface of the water and sent a shiver down their spines. It was joined moments later by its four surviving companions, and they too sent terrifying howls of rage skywards from muzzles now drenched with blood. And then the five of them set off along the riverbank at a steady, loping run, pursuing the now-distant boat with a single-minded dedication that would have brought approval from Slanved himself, had he still been alive to see it.

CHAPTER FIVE

There have been a lot of entry-level armours coming on to the market in recent years, but surely the cheapest are those produced by the Brannan BaNaNa Company. Set up five years ago by three entrepreneurial dwarves, Balin, Narvi and Nain, specifically to manufacture 'affordable armour', this company has produced some of the shoddiest and nastiest goods we have ever tested.

For example, the BaNaNa Helm (which is made from a cheap metal alloy that shatters if you sit on it) might just provide five minutes of protection against a chocolate sword, but any other weapon would shear straight through it. And the BaNaNa Breastplate, made from a silver-painted material that feels suspiciously like cardboard, went all soggy and fell apart after a few minutes in heavy rain.

Overall, our tests showed that the company really does merit its appalling reputation. So there you have it. BaNaNa Armour – the biggest load of crap we've ever seen . . .

What Weapon? *magazine*

In the second of his metaphysical treatises, *Where Are We Going To?*, the Sage of Welbug points out that all sentient races have their own particular version of an afterlife, and that these all divide neatly into two main versions: a paradise for those who have been good, honest, or valorous in this life, and a hell for those who have not.[7] However, the details of these beliefs vary widely from race to race.

Dwarves, for example, believe hell to be a wide-open grassy plain where evil dwarves are tied to the ground for all eternity by demonic, elf-like spirits, and then little chirruping birds come and pull their beards out bit by bit to use as nesting material. Orcs, on the other

---

[7] In his third and final book, *Who Gives a Klat Anyway?*, the Sage reaches the conclusion that, as we know bugger all about why we're here or where we're going, we might as well enjoy the ride, and goes on to advise his readers that if they really want to enjoy a ride, then the Dragon's Claw in Welbug is undoubtedly one of the best places in Midworld to do so.

hand, believe that hell is a place of hundreds of tiny rooms, where cowardly orcs will be made to sit in chintz-covered armchairs with dainty napkins on their knees, and will be force-fed endless cups of tea, soft drinks and tiny home-made cakes by evil spirits in the guise of little white-haired old ladies, who will talk endlessly to them of crochet and the weather.

This orcish version of hell is surprisingly close to the hobbit idea of paradise; a place of endless conversations and boundless meals (usually involving sticky buns and ice cream). Hobbit hell, however, is a place where lots of very tall people make tasteless jokes about hairy feet and short arses, and poke fun at harmless, normal names like Bilbo and Dongo. This goes a long way to explaining why humans don't see very much of hobbits any more . . .

Wayta was firmly of the opinion that hell was other people. More specifically, it was the succession of hags, witches and wizards of all varieties who the Orcbane Sword Corporation had employed for their magical powers over the past few years. From the very beginning, the members of the board had been unanimous in the opinion that use of magic would be vital if they were going to achieve the level of control and influence that they desired, but as none of them had the slightest vestige of the Power themselves, it was obvious that they were going to have to employ some magic-users. However, it soon became apparent that male wizards were far more trouble than they were worth. Highly egotistical, they tended to look down on anyone lacking the Power and were very difficult to control. Wayta had always found it a little tricky trying to discipline someone who, if upset, could turn him into a frog just for the hell of it. And so they had settled on witchcraft and hag-magic for the day-to-day running of their empire, occasionally employing wizards on a freelance basis when something a little stronger was required.

Unfortunately, as they had employed a large number of different hags and witches over the years, they had slowly discovered for themselves the three basic laws of witchcraft:

1. Magical ability increases with the age and experience of the practitioner.
2. Magical ability increases with the ugliness and bitterness of the practitioner.
3. As magical ability increases, the practitioner's grasp of reality decreases proportionally.

In other words, if you want strong witchcraft, you have to employ an ancient and hideously ugly hag who is going to be completely barking mad. And the board had wanted some very strong witchcraft at times . . .

Wayta thought back to the worst of the hags, and his fingers beat a tattoo on the polished surface of the boardroom table. There had been that appalling old biddy, Venna, who had turned out to have a thing about the colour purple, and had turned everything inside the Orcbane offices a revolting shade of heliotrope, including the staff. There had been Amliv, a wrinkled old crone with a face like a rotting prune who had slung *fireballs* at anyone who got her name wrong. Unfortunately, being several loaves short of a sandwich, she never had the slightest idea who or what she really was, and Wayta himself had only just managed to avoid being blown to pieces when he had called her by her real name on a day when she was convinced that she was a hatstand called Pauline. And there had been that horrifyingly bossy madwoman with the strange hair who had seemed to believe that the board members worked for her, and who had followed them around, lecturing them shrilly and shouting out orders until she got her own way. Wayta winced at the memory. His mind seemed to have completely erased her name, and all he could recall was that she had been married to a thatcher called Donald or Derek or something.

Still, when Shikara had briefly entered their employ, these problems had soon vanished. As, indeed, had the hags. Shikara had been in the habit of exploding people whenever peeved, annoyed or even just plain bored, and as she disliked anything that remotely threatened to rival her, and her magic was much stronger than theirs, the poor old hags had received short shrift. Orcbane had gone through nine of them in the space of a couple of weeks before the supply had virtually dried up. They had been reduced to using quite young, inexperienced and pretty witches in order to keep their stuttering communications network on its feet.

But then, after Shikara's demise, they'd advertised the post of Company Hag in *Witch* magazine, and there had been one or two rather promising applicants. Cartland had seemed like the perfect choice, as she was old and ugly but had appeared to be fairly sane. Unfortunately, as Wayta had now come to realise, her grasp on her sanity was tenuous in the extreme.

For a start, she talked to herself endlessly. This was a common trait in hags, but Cartland frequently disagreed with herself quite strongly, and on one occasion she'd had a raging argument with herself that had ended with her sulking childishly and refusing to talk to herself for three hours. And then there was her familiar. Wayta was used to witches having cats, dogs, ravens or other such creatures, but Cartland was the first one who had a cabbage as an attendant spirit. It was called John, apparently, and was supposed to help her with the trickier spells. But the final straw, as far as Wayta was concerned, was that for the past two days she had refused point blank to carry out any of his commands unless he addressed her as 'honeybunch'.

He leant back in his executive chair and watched her as she fiddled around with her cauldron, occasionally pausing to mutter something to the cabbage, which was resting on a chair beside her. He had come to the conclusion recently that the company was far too magic-dependent for its own good, and that was one reason why he was so excited by the huge strides in the field of science that the Dark Dwarves were making. Meiosin had talked about the possibility of a widespread instant communication network that would be quick, reliable, and above all, NOT powered by magic. Indeed, the dwarf had promised to bring the board up to date that very afternoon, which was why Wayta had a bottle of the very best vintage Trollinger champagne cooling in an ice bucket on the drinks cabinet behind him. He was desperately hoping that they would have something to celebrate.

When he had set the board meeting for that afternoon, he had expected to be able to announce the death of the meddling warrior, Ronan. The *cobrats* should have driven him and his friends into the Assassins' ambush. Unfortunately, the Guild reported that they had lost touch with Slanved and his unit, and Wayta was starting to get a little worried. *What if Ronan has somehow dodged out of the way, and the* cobrats *have run into Slanved's group?* he thought. *Those creatures could be traced back to me. If they've butchered a batch of Assassins, then I'm going to have the rest of the Guild after me for vengeance!* The thought sent a shiver down his spine, and all of a sudden he felt that maybe he could do with a glass or two of Trolly now, before the others got here.

'Cartland, open that champagne, would you?' he asked, without thinking.

'Buggeroff!'

Wayta winced, and eyed the old witch malevolently. He really couldn't put up with her any longer.

'Right, well then, that will be all, Cartland. I don't think we'll be needing you this afternoon.'

'Arr, ye greet gobbit slangy-gumble!' The old witch's voice sank to an almost inaudible mumbling as she took a huge spoon from a hook on the wall and began to stir the foul brew that was congealing in the cauldron. Wayta swallowed and gritted his teeth to do what had to be done.

'Er, you can leave the boardroom now, please . . . honeybunch.'

Cartland threw him a leer that would have curdled milk from fifty paces and shuffled towards the door. As she passed she grinned coyly and blew him a kiss on a waft of foul and miasmic breath. Then the door shut behind her, and with a hand that was shaking like a leaf Wayta grabbed the bottle and fumbled with the cork. It popped out and champagne frothed out of the neck, missing the trousers of his ultra-expensive suit by inches. Quickly he poured some into a glass and raised it to his lips, and then suddenly, without any noise or fuss whatsoever, there was a dwarf standing right in front of him. Wayta twitched violently and managed to spill the glass of champagne all over the crotch of his trousers.

'I'm sorry if I startled you,' said Mitosin, calmly.

'What . . . I mean how . . . How did you . . .?'

'How did I appear in the middle of your office without the use of your hag-magic?'

Wayta nodded dumbly, and then slumped back into his chair and took a careful swig of Trolly straight out of the bottle.

'Simple. The Physicks Department have at last perfected the Matter Transmitter which they, Necromancy, and Machines and Contrivances have been working on. We can pass instantly to any location we desire, using very low-grade magic indeed. But enough of that. My brother wishes you to know that our plans are proceeding exactly as expected. He has been voted in as the new chief scientist, and we start our Expanded Research Programme this very afternoon.'

'Good. Good. Excellent! That's the, er, the out-and-about stuff, isn't it?'

'The testing of various inventions, devices and magenetical creations in a field environment, and the collecting of suitable subjects for experimentation and research.' Mitosin paused and grinned humourlessly. 'So if you have friends in any of the towns or villages between the Northern and the Frozen Mountains, I would advise them to get out now.'

At that moment a strange beeping noise began, and a tiny red dot of light started flashing above the dwarf's head.

'Ah, time to be going,' he said. 'We'll report again a week from today. Oh, and my brother asked me to tell you that the whole Orcbane board are welcome to visit our research centre in a few . . .'

The beeping stopped, and suddenly Mitosin just wasn't there. Wayta stared in amazement at the space where he had been, and then very carefully poured himself another glass of Trolly and tried to contain his burgeoning excitement. Heaven knows what else these dwarves might produce, but a transportation device that could take someone hundreds of miles in an instant could make an absolute fortune in the right hands! Maybe it was time for Orcbane to diversify a little. The Orcbane Travel Agency, perhaps. Or how about Orcbane Unlimited Travel. Yes, that had possibilities. Get OUT and get about! He could see the adverts already . . .

With a happy smile on his lips, Wayta crossed to the drinks cabinet, took out a second bottle of Trollinger and pushed it into the ice bucket. He had a feeling that the other board members would shortly be wanting to celebrate as well.

Now that Meiosin had been elected chief scientist, the previously hidden magenetics section had been revealed to all the other dwarves, and every scientist in the Research Centre had visited to gawp in wonder at the Vivarium and pay their respects to Reágin at the place of his death. They had been warned of the dangerous creatures that dwelt there, and much had been made of Reágin's bravery and courage in regularly venturing therein without a thought to his own safety, to help with vital research. (Now that the old fool was dead, Meiosin had decided, it did no harm to promote the idea that he had known and approved of the new venture.) There had been vast excitement at the huge strides that the mageneticists were making, and when Meiosin had called for volunteers for 'field trips', he had been deluged.

Inside the vast new magenetics lecture theatre, preparations for the first of these 'field trips' were well under way. The place was awash with dwarf scientists struggling to get into the most outlandish armour that most of them had ever seen. There was an air of suppressed excitement as they examined the strange helmets and hefted the fearsome battleaxes experimentally, and some of them were even smiling.

Dwarves, unlike most other races, don't have a separate warrior élite. When the call to arms occurs, they all respond. It seems to be something in the blood: give a dwarf scientist or goldsmith a battleaxe and an enemy to fight and he's as happy as an orc in a brewery. Usually they don't bother with much in the way of armour. An iron helm, a chain-mail corselet and a shield is about it. But Meiosin had other ideas, and had purchased more than two hundred suits of matching plate armour. And none of your cheap rubbish either. With Orcbane's money behind him he had been able to buy the best, made by the Valdar Company.

Each suit was jet black in colour, with clusters of sharp spikes along the vambraces, greaves and cuisses. A single long spike protruded from each poleyn and cowter, enabling both knees and elbows to become potentially lethal weapons. The breastplate was painted with blood-red runes of death, and yet the most fearsome thing about the whole outfit was undoubtedly the helmet. It was cast in the image of a devilish head with slavering jaws, fanged teeth and huge, pointed ears. Although none of the dwarves was taller than five foot, wearing these suits of armour they looked like a tribe of demonic monsters from some foul netherworld.

Meiosin surveyed them with satisfaction. This was even better than he had expected! With the other small surprises that Alchemy and Necromancy were planning, they were going to provide a truly formidable spectacle . . .

He rapped on the hard stone of the lecture podium to attract everyone's attention, but no one heard him over the excited hubbub that was going on. He tried clearing his throat, then shouting, and then shouting very loud, but still no one heard him. It was only when he lost his temper, grabbed the nearest battleaxe and smashed it into the podium, sending a shower of stone fragments ricocheting across the room, that he succeeded in getting their attention at last.

'You have all had your instructions,' he began. 'There are eight raiding parties, going to eight separate destinations. Within each party are scientists from specific departments who will be testing various creations and devices on the indigenous inhabitants of these destinations. The rest of you are acting as fighters, and your role is to put fear and dismay into those inhabitants and to capture some and bring them back so that further experiments can be carried out in the laboratories. The armour is specifically designed to put fear into our targets, as are some of the effects our alchemists will be unleashing. However, it will also help if you abandon our habitual dwarvish silence when fighting, and shout and yell as fearsomely as you are able. Some form of war-cry or chanting would be most beneficial.'

'You mean chants would be a fine thing!' shouted someone at the back of the theatre. Meiosin stared angrily around, trying to identify the barracker, but with everyone covered head to toe in armour it was virtually impossible. Still, he was pretty sure it must have been Beneltin. It always was. That young dwarf was getting a bit of a reputation for never taking anything seriously, and Meiosin made a mental note to discipline him later.

'It only remains for me to wish you good luck. May your axes stay sharp and your enemies quail!' he finished, using the traditional dwarvish phrase.

At these words the two massive stone doors in the left-hand wall swung open. Beyond them was the Transmitter Room, a large chamber with eight cylindrical metal booths at one end. Each one was some seven feet in height, with a thick steel door at the front and a control panel covered in levers, dials and switches to one side. Scientists from the Physicks and Necromancy Departments were fussing and scurrying about, adjusting the levers and checking readings on the dials. As the armour-clad dwarves began lining up in eight columns in front of the booths, the scientists started flicking the rows of switches into the on position. Lights flashed, and a pulsating humming noise began.

Beneltin peered forwards from his position near the back of one of the columns, trying to see the transmitter machines, but he was small even for a dwarf, and he couldn't see much over the serried ranks of black metal helms in front of him. He turned to his immediate neighbour.

'This Valdar armour is the business, eh?'

The other dwarf growled something that his helmet rendered all but unintelligible. Beneltin carried on regardless.

'Knowing my luck, I'll come up against the only orc in the whole of Mahon who's armed with a giant tin-opener!'

There was another muted growl.

'But that would be uncanny . . .'

The other dwarf emitted something that sounded like a groan and stared at Beneltin balefully. He grinned happily back, then realised that this was a waste of time inside the thick, intimidating helmet. No one could tell if you were frowning or laughing. In fact, the other dwarf probably couldn't even tell who he was. Reaching out a metal-gauntleted fist, he rapped sharply on the other's helmet.

'What's up?' he asked, solicitously. 'A sudden metallic ringing in the ears? Must be tin-itus!'

The other dwarf raised his axe threateningly.

'If you want to cure it, try taking some iron tablets . . .'

The dwarf groaned and drew his axe right back, but Beneltin was saved from having his helmet severely dented, for at that very moment Meiosin shouted out the order for transmission to start, and a hum of excitement began.

The first dwarf in each column moved forward, opened the door of a booth and stepped inside. All the others watched anxiously, craning their necks to see as scientists threw more switches, and a green light flashed on top of each booth. Then all the doors opened, and the watching dwarves let out a collective gasp, half of surprise and half of relief, for every booth was now empty.

The next dwarf in each line moved forward and stepped into the transmitter, and then the next, until, in less than five minutes, more than two hundred dwarves had been transported instantly and successfully to their destinations, dozens of miles away, and eight innocent, unsuspecting and widely separated communities were about to receive a lethally rude awakening.

Chaz the Morose sat huddled at the top of the watchtower and peered unhappily at the drifting sea-fog. Great banks of the stuff had been rolling steadily ashore for a couple of hours now, wrapping itself around the rickety legs of the tower like a dank, chilly blanket, and the only signs of the little fishing village that he could still see were a few depressed chimneys poking through at varying angles like pieces of straw randomly stuck into candy floss. Chaz sighed. His rheumatic knee was aching, his eyes stung, condensation was dripping from the ends of his moustache and the chill seemed to be seeping right into his very bones. Then his fingers tightened on the safety rail as a gentle whisper of breeze caused the watchtower to sway alarmingly. Quietly but fervently he cursed to himself. Not for the first time, Chaz was regretting his rash, impetuous nature.

Mind you, it wasn't really his fault. Compared with the average person, Chaz was laid-back to the point of being horizontal. But compared with the other inhabitants of the little community of Vil, he was positively frenetic, as, over the years, his neighbours had turned idleness and indolence into an art form. Hundreds of years ago, when Chaz's tribe had been simple nomads, Mahon had been a pretty dangerous place. Having to compete for food with such savage creatures as *alaxls, lenkats* and *megoceri* meant that hunting parties were frequently completely wiped out. The only guys who survived to pass on their genes were the lazy buggers – the ones who didn't get to go hunting because they'd overslept, or couldn't be bothered, or had found a nice grassy knoll before they'd gone fifty paces and nodded off in the sunshine. And so the indolence gene became dominant.

In most places the tribe would have died of starvation, but the folk of Vil were luckier. They had built their settlement on the west coast of Mahon, where the warm currents swept north through a narrow channel between the mainland and the island of Near Kinnel. It was the best fishing in the world. All they had to do was drift out in their boats with a few baited hooks trailing behind them, and by the time the prevailing north-westerly wind had blown them back to land they had caught more fish than they could shake a stick at, and had had a nice forty winks as well.

The people had called their settlement The Village, as no one could be bothered to think of a name, and this was later shortened to Vil (well, why use three syllables when you can get away with one?). Life had stayed much the same for hundreds of years. Folk slept a lot, caught some fish and sold a few badly made pots to traders (Vil pottery was highly prized amongst the upper classes of the richer cities such as Port Raid who, burdened with little taste and lots of pretension, believed it to be classically primitive rather than thrown together in five minutes between naps).

Despite the dominant indolence gene, there were still occasional throw-backs like Chaz. The rest of the tribe viewed him with mistrust (when they could keep their eyes open). Ever since he was a child he had kept wanting to *do* things, and when he decided to do something, it was normally only a matter of months before he got round to doing it. Take the example of those sea-raiders, for instance. The Vagens. When rumours of their raids on southern coastal villages first reached Vil it had been Chaz who had nagged and nagged until something was done. And so reluctantly the men of the village had straggled round and built a watchtower. After cutting down and dragging across three tree-trunks, they had flatly refused to go to the bother of fetching a fourth, and so the tower only had three legs – and three very thin, bendy, easily portable ones at that. In fact, they had wanted to make do with two legs at first, but the tower had kept falling over, and Chaz had nagged at them until they added the third. Now, although the slightest breath of air caused it to sway alarmingly, at least the tower stood upright. Yet Chaz still hadn't been happy, but kept insisting that someone had to sit up in the top of the thing to keep watch. Well, said the rest of the tribe, if it's so important to you, then *you* can sit up there. But as far as we're concerned, it's cold, it's foggy, and we could all do with a nice lie-in by the fire.

And so Chaz found himself thirty foot up in the air, watching the fog rolling in, and slowly going numb with cold. He could hardly feel his hands any more. He swore to himself and fumbled clumsily for the guard-rail as the watchtower swung sideways again. The ever-freshening on-shore breeze was beginning to clear the morning fog away, but it was making the tower sway around like a watchtower that has had several pints more than it should have done, and Chaz was starting to feel decidedly queasy. He clung tightly to the guard-rail, closed his eyes and concentrated hard on keeping hold of his last meal. And below him, unnoticed in the eddying fog, eighteen demonic black figures materialised one by one in the small village square . . .

Mitosin surveyed the other seventeen dwarves and barely suppressed a shiver. In the evil black armour, with the last remnants of fog drifting about them, they looked like some malignant tribe of devils. It would be interesting to see what effect they had on the sleeping villagers. Silently he gave the signal, and the others spread out unnoticed through the small village, moving along the narrow, filth-strewn tracks that wound between the rough, tumbledown huts.

Vil had been chosen as a place where it would be easy to take captives, and where they could carry out a couple of interesting experiments into the effects of the new explosive chemical, Vnayalite, that Alchemy had developed from nitre, saltpetre and palm oil from the *vnaya* tree. Each dwarf was carrying a bomb equipped with the tiny timing mechanisms constructed by Machines and Contrivances. These were to be placed in huts and would, if the timers worked as hoped, detonate at the same instant. The effect on both the huts and their occupants could then be observed.

Mitosin looked round for a suitable target for the bomb that he was carrying, and his eyes fell on the watchtower. Perfect! He strode forward and began to strap it to one of the spindly legs, but it was difficult to see what he was doing from inside the confines of the black helmet. His fingers fumbled with the minute controls of the delicate timer, and sweat broke out on his brow as he realised he'd almost set it to zero, which would have made it blow up instantly. Swearing, he stepped back a pace, and looked round. There were still no villagers around to see him, and so he undid the retaining clip of his devil's-head helmet and pulled it off, then stepped forward again, ready to set the timer.

Up in the watchtower, Chaz was still stoically trying to keep hold of last night's dinner, but the whole edifice was now swaying about alarmingly in the freshening breeze. Realising that he was about to lose the fight, he opened his eyes, grabbed for the guard-rail and leant over. To his amazement, a black and gleaming demon was fiddling with one of the tower's legs, and as he stared at it, aghast, it stepped back and took off its head. Chaz was so surprised at this that he almost forgot to be sick.

Almost. But not quite.

Now that Mitosin had taken his helmet off he could see quite clearly, and it only took him a couple of seconds to set the timer. He was just about to step back and admire his handiwork when all of a sudden there was a retching sound in the air above him, and then a veritable torrent of something hot, sticky and carroty scored a direct hit on the back of his head and fountained down his neck into the suit of armour. He stood there for some moments, rooted to the spot, unable to believe that someone had actually been sick on him, while the stuff seeped down through his breastplate and began to drip down his leg. Looking up, he saw a horrified face peering at him from the top of the tower, and grabbing the leg he shook it hard, as though trying to shake down the perpetrator. But then the dial of the timer caught his eye, and Mitosin realised he only had seconds before the bomb went off.

Grabbing his helmet, he turned and squelched hastily away. The sour stench of vomit and the lumpy bits squishing beneath his right foot made him heave, and he paused to bend over, convinced he was about to throw up. And that was when every single bomb went off within two seconds of each other. Seventeen huts exploded in brilliant yellow balls of flame, and the eighteenth bomb vaporised one leg of the watchtower and ripped apart a second. For a moment the tower stood there, poised on its single remaining leg, and then with the sound of rending wood the whole edifice slowly toppled backwards and crashed to the ground.

Mitosin picked himself slowly up from the patch of weeds where the explosion had blown him and looked around in awe. The Vnayalite bombs, like the timers, had been far more effective than he had expected, and the shattered wrecks of seventeen huts were blazing fiercely, giving off a dense black smoke that was heavy with the distinctive aromatic scent of burning palm oil. As he watched, those few villagers who had survived the blasts came staggering out of the wreckage in a state of shock. Most fell to their knees and crossed themselves at the sight of the armour-clad dwarves, and were easily made captive. Three men wielded swords, but they were so disorientated that they could hardly put up a fight, falling prey in seconds to the razor-sharp battleaxes.

Mitosin watched with satisfaction. They had brought a number of other devices with them to test, but there seemed little point in utilising them as there wasn't much of the village or its inhabitants left to test them on, and so Mitosin gave the signal for everyone to prepare for transmitting back to the Research Centre.

This is going to make Meiosin sit up, he thought as he seated himself on a stone bollard on the quayside, and then he sniffed the aromatic smoke that was drifting heavily down from the burning huts. *Ah*, he thought contentedly, *I love the smell of* vnaya-*palm in the morning . . .*

Chaz had had quite a nasty fall. Indeed, he could have been seriously injured if his landing hadn't been cushioned by plunging straight into the village midden. As he sat there, up to his neck in steaming ordure and surrounded by fragments of watchtower, his brain at first refused to function. In front of him was what appeared to be a scene from hell. A tribe of dark demons seemed to have blown up every hut in the village, and were now massacring the survivors! Well, he had always had a bit of a reputation as being a man of action. If ever there was a time when action was called for, it was now . . .

But he'd better get a move on if he wanted to take a few of them with him! They had started vanishing, winking out of existence one by one until there were only five or six left. Dragging his sword free, Chaz stood up, roared out a challenge, waded forwards, stepped on something revoltingly slithery, and disappeared into the midden's steaming bowels a second time.

It took him quite a while to retrieve his sword from the noxious morass into which it had vanished, and by the time he had managed to find it and had extricated himself from the midden, every single demon had vanished. And though Chaz strode about the burning village, yelling threats and challenges, waving his sword and scattering fragments of crap everywhere, it was to no avail. There wasn't a demon or a living villager to be seen. They had all vanished into thin air, and Chaz was left with only charred and bloody corpses for company.

And thus it was in seven other locations across Mahon and Kahdor. All of a sudden, black figures like demons appeared, bringing with them fire and explosions, and killing, burning and looting before vanishing into thin air in front of the very eyes of the dazed and terrified defenders. In some places they also brought with them foul and loathsome creatures, the like of which had never been seen before, and even though a few brave and determined folk fought back, nothing could harm these demons, for they were clad in a dark and fearsome armour, and people fled in terror for their lives.

However, not quite all the demonic figures seemed to be bent on death and destruction. In Gudmornen, where some forty of them materialised in the city centre, a terrified newspaper-seller was cowering behind the counter of his kiosk whilst fireballs exploded and buildings burst into flames all around when he saw one of the demons stalking purposefully towards him. Flattening himself on the floor, he buried his head in his arms, praying to his gods to somehow save him, but when he risked a quick glance up he saw that the demon was leaning across the counter, looking down at him. As he opened his mouth to scream, it spoke.

'You wouldn't happen to have a copy of *Time Off* magazine, by any chance? You know, the listings magazine. The one with all the adverts for theatres and nightclubs.'

The newspaper-seller raised a shaking hand and pointed at the requested item.

'Ah, yes. Wonderful. Thank you,' said the demon, and pulling off one of its metal gauntlets to reveal a short and rather stubby hand, it took a copy. The newspaper-seller stared at the hand, confused.

'What do you want *Time Off* for?'

'Good behaviour,' said Beneltin. 'I think I'm the only one who hasn't killed anybody yet.'

Pulling off the second metal gauntlet he shook a few coins out of

97

it, dropped a couple to the grovelling newspaper-seller and began leafing through the adverts until he found the one he wanted.

'Ah, here it is,' he muttered contentedly. 'The Stand and Deliver Club, 19 Cur's Tea Alley...' He looked down again at the newspaper-seller. 'Er, you couldn't possibly tell me where Cur's Tea Alley is, could you?'

The kiosk-owner peered up fearfully from his supine position, thinking to himself that demons were awfully polite these days.

'What? Oh... It's off Dog Street, down there,' he said, pointing back over his shoulder.

'Thank you.'

The newspaper-seller was about to mutter something about not mentioning it when a tiny red dot of light appeared above the demon's head and began flashing. Then suddenly the demon just vanished into nothingness, and the kiosk-owner lay there, thanking his own personal gods for protecting him.

But most were not so lucky that night. Many people were wounded or killed, and others were stolen away from their families. Much property was burnt, looted or destroyed. And so began a reign of terror that would never be forgotten in Midworld's northern lands, and that would blacken for ever the dwarven name in the eyes of other races...

CHAPTER SIX

Most orcs have no understanding whatsoever of the human phrase 'girlfriend'. To an orc, a friend is someone with whom you spend several weeks at a time on a drinking spree, while a girl is a female who stays at home and has the babies, and the two are mutually exclusive. Unfortunately, it has to be admitted that a surprising number of human girlfriends have found, on becoming wives, that their husbands seem to share this sad view . . .

Morris the Bald, Orcwatching

Oupase shipped the oars and the ferry-boat drifted the last few yards before coming gently to rest on a stretch of shingle against the north bank of the Great River Leno. Ronan stepped carefully out and took hold of the prow to steady the boat, and one by one the others joined him until only Oupase was left. Then Ronan released the prow, and with a dispirited 'Farewell!' Oupase turned the ferry about and began the long, hard journey back upstream towards Welbug.

Ronan stood and watched him for a few moments, but the night was dark and moonless, and the small boat soon disappeared against the inky blackness of the water. Turning, he followed the others as they wandered disconsolately away from the riverbank in search of somewhere sheltered to camp. Tarl had cast an *illuminate* spell, and by the dim light of the radiant glow that surrounded him they managed to find a hollow sheltered by rocks which provided some respite from the west wind that had sprung up.

They had all been very quiet during the eight-hour journey downriver. When Tyson had come round, Ronan had told her quickly about Posner's death at the hands of the *cobrats*. Her face had set like stone and she hadn't spoken a single word since, just nodding curtly when he had asked if she was feeling all right. Ronan thought he understood why, and he could hardly blame her. It was because of him that she had lost everything and that Posner had died such a horrible death. She must be totally pissed off with him . . .

As Tyson gathered some wood and began to build a campfire,

Ronan had a quiet word with the others, asking them to leave him alone with her for a few minutes. Tarl didn't even have the heart to make any prurient comments about the reason for this, but just muttered something about contacting Guebral, and wandered off behind the rocks, with Puss and Marwood following. Then Ronan took a deep breath and prepared himself for the bitter onslaught that would follow the apology that he felt he had to make.

'Tyson . . .'

'What?'

She hadn't even looked at him, and the snapped retort came in a voice so laden with hatred that Ronan actually took a step backwards.

'Er . . . I'm really sorry. About everything. I know that it's all my fault, and that you must . . .'

But at that point she swung round and interrupted him in a voice that was thick with emotion, staring up at him wild-eyed, and he was stunned to see that tears were streaming down her face.

'Don't you dare! Don't you *dare* try taking the blame for this! If it hadn't been for you I would have died weeks ago, back in Welbug! You saved me, you prat, can't you see it? And now you're the only thing I have left, and those bastards want to take you away from me as well! *Klat!* I hate those evil old men! They aren't going to get away with this. We're going to find them and kill them somehow, I swear it! I am *not* going to lose you, Ronan!'

And suddenly she was in his arms, kissing him, and he could feel her warm body pressing against him . . .

It must have been about five minutes later that Tarl came dashing into the hollow, shouting excitedly.

'Ronan! Tyson! I've contacted Guebral and she . . . oh, *klat!* Sorry! I didn't know you were . . . I mean, I . . . that is . . .'

Giggling like naughty schoolchildren, Ronan and Tyson broke apart and hastily rearranged those bits of clothing that had somehow got disarranged.

'It's okay, Tarl,' smiled Tyson. 'We're decent.'

'Don't you two ever stop?' complained Tarl, trying to hide a smile. 'You're always at it! You make me . . . ow!' Quickly, he changed the subject. 'Listen, I've talked to Guebral. She can leave Yai'El now, things have calmed down a bit. She says there's a Vagen boat called in to see them, with Klaer and Kamila on board. She's going to join them and sail up to Unch Haven, and they can meet us there tomorrow night. If we head off southwards with them, anyone trying to track us is going to think we're making for the Maelvanta Islands. Then when we're out at sea we can swing round and head north. They'll put us ashore on the coast of Mahon, and we'll have lost those *cobrats* completely. They'll never find us! Good, eh?'

He grinned happily, then pointed one finger at the small pile of driftwood that Tyson had gathered, and a tiny blue fireball rocketed out of his fingertip, exploded into the wood and set the campfire burning merrily.

'Don't ya just love being in control?' he burbled happily, before dashing off into the night, and they could hear him calling to Puss and Marwood.

Shaking her head, Tyson smiled to herself and bent to take some bread and dried meat from her backpack. It was amazing how a little contact with your loved one could restore your spirits. But then, the prospect of having Guebral alongside them was a fillip for all of them. Although she looked young and frail, she had more ability with magic than just about anyone Tyson had met. Indeed, it had been Guebral who had held the sorceress Shikara at bay during those vital seconds at the end of the Battle of Grey Sea Fields. What with both *cobrats* and the Guild of Assassins on their trail, she would be more than welcome as a travelling companion . . .

Beside her, Ronan was also burrowing in his backpack for food, and Tyson could see that his spirits too had lifted. The pair of them were well used to violent death by now; each of them had lost friends and companions before. Posner's death was not forgotten, but life had to go on, and the time for revenge would eventually come.

Chewing on a strip of dried meat, Tyson sat down by the fire and stared thoughtfully up at the clear night sky. Above her she could see the beautiful scattering of stars that made up the constellation of Agnus Complexis, and beside it was the smaller cluster of Catellus Parvulus.[8] Nearby she could hear the sounds of two people larking about, throwing stones into the water and taking the mickey out of a companion who, being lumbered with hooves, couldn't throw anything further than about six inches. This was followed shortly by the unmistakable sound of a donkey galloping into someone at full tilt and knocking them into a river.

'What do you reckon on Marwood, then?' asked Ronan, as he sat down beside her. 'Can we trust him?'

'I reckon so. He saved your life back there, and I can't think of any

8 The Tiny Little Puppy-dog. Honestly, those elven astronomers need shooting.

reason why he'd do that if he was still interested in carrying out the contract.'

'I agree. He can come with us if he still wants to, I think I owe him that.'

Once again there was the sound of galloping hooves, followed this time by a startled cry from Marwood and a second splash.

'Sounds as though the kids are enjoying the holiday,' said Tyson. 'So, how long to Unch Haven, do you reckon?'

'No more than three hours by the Great West Road. Longer if we want to stay in cover, though.'

'I've been thinking about that. We must be well clear of the *cobrats*, and they're on the other side of a river that is almost two miles wide. The Assassins' Guild won't have the faintest idea where we are, and probably expect us to be dead. If we walk into Unch Haven tomorrow in plain view it will be at least twenty-four hours before the local branch manages to organise anything. We can take care of any individual Assassins who have a go, as long as we're watchful.'

'So we walk in openly.'

'Yeah. In fact, the more people who remember seeing us leave on the Vagen ship, the better. We want to make sure the trail leads south.'

Ronan sat quietly for a moment, breathing in the cool night air. They were less than ten miles from the sea here, and he could smell the faint salt tang on the westerly breeze. There was a lot of laughter coming out of the darkness now, and a fair bit of splashing going on, but it was underpinned by the deep, incessant murmur of the Great River Leno. He too looked up at the stars strewn across the sky like diamonds scattered across a black velvet cloth, and he was just thinking how indescribably beautiful it all was when every other sound was suddenly drowned out by the longest, loudest and ripest fart that he had ever heard, followed by two voices raised in complaint and the maniacal braying of a highly amused donkey.

'I don't think we're going to have any difficulty in getting people to notice us,' he whispered to Tyson. Then reaching out his hand he took hers, and the two of them sat by the fire, eating their supper companionably together and staring up in wonder at the cold beauty of the northern night sky.

Unch Haven was, in the eyes of the average human, rather an ugly and depressing place. Situated on the northern bank of the Leno estuary, it was the only city that had ever been built above ground in the whole of the Dwarf Lands, the mountainous area in the south-west of Frundor that was home to the majority of the dwarven race. Although built by men, the architecture was of dwarven influence, with long, low, dark-stone buildings crammed and clustered together, their second storeys and roofs stretching out over the narrow streets as though to hide the threatening vastness of the sky.

The city was surrounded by thick and lengthy walls, pierced by three great gates: the North, through which ran the ancient road that passed amidst the heart of the Dwarf Lands to the lost underground city of Samoth; the East, to which the Great West Road led, all the way from Welbug; and the South, which gave on to the quayside area, and through which all ship-borne passengers arrived. Never had the walls been breached, although once the city had fallen, let down by a grievous and costly mistake by one of the defenders, Gareth of the South Gate.

Like most great cities, Unch Haven was a melting pot for many races and nations, although few elves could tolerate the claustrophobic streets or the nearness of the sea. Dwarves and men, orcs and even the occasional troll mixed in the bars and cafés of the teeming thoroughfares. The City Gate Guards were a tough and hardy breed of folk, used to the strange and outlandish, and few things surprised them. But the group of people who came strolling along the Great West Road late that morning caused them to stop and stare with utter amazement.

In the lead was a small and seedy man who would have been totally unnoticeable were it not for two factors. Firstly, he was singing a remarkably obscene song in a truly awful voice, and secondly, a little ball of whirling yellow fire danced and twirled around his fingers and hands. The youth who walked beside him was, to judge by his black and silver garment, an apprentice Assassin. However, unlike every other Assassin they had ever seen, this one had open-toed sandals, long hair held back with a headband, a flower behind one ear, a happy smile on his face, and he too was singing. In between them strolled a small brown donkey, totally unremarkable save for the fact that it too was singing, and its voice was one hell of a lot better than the other two.

Close behind these three strolled two others. Both were clearly warriors, but they were as different as could be. One was male, tall, black and very muscular, with a seething mass of snake-like dreadlocks jostling around his head and shoulders and a massive sword slung, southern fashion, down the centre of his back. The other was female, small and lithe, with good muscle tone and a face to die for. Her hair was cut elven-fashion and had been bleached by the sun, and she carried a bow slung over one shoulder.

The Sergeant of the Guard, an older man who had travelled much, peered at them in wonder.

'That's Tyson!' he muttered. 'Tyson of Welbug! And that must be Ronan at her side!'

The word flew from guard to guard, and thence around the crowd of people who were gathered at the stalls and booths lining both sides of the road in front of the gate. No agents of the Orcbane board had been busy in Unch Haven, and word of the recent events in Welbug had not reached this far, but the townsfolk still talked of the orc army that had rampaged through Behan and Cydor, and of the Battle of Grey Sea Fields.

'Tyson and Ronan! 'Tis said they each killed a hundred orcs in the battle!' whispered a hawker to his neighbour.

'That must be the wizard who travels with them! I had heard that his familiar takes the guise of a donkey!' muttered an elderly fishmonger.

'It was Tyson who killed Shikara!' the Sergeant told the other guards. 'Rord Stryk himself told me!'

As the five strolled unconcernedly along towards the gate, all eyes followed them. Someone called a word of congratulation, and then someone else, then others, and this ran through the crowd as a low murmur, almost inaudible at first, but growing gradually, an eager wave of acclamation that became louder and louder until every single bystander was cheering and waving joyously.

Ronan and Tyson slowed slightly, completely taken aback by this reception and unsure how best to respond, but in front of them Tarl was smiling and waving back at the crowd.

'Don't you get it?' he hissed over his shoulder. 'Everybody loves stories of heroes, but they hardly ever get a chance to meet one! Folk are already singing songs and telling tales about you. You're superstars! Play up to it! Enjoy it while you can!'

And as if to demonstrate, he raised his arms, forefingers pointing at the sky, and sent a pair of brilliant white fireballs rocketing upwards and over the city walls. The crowd roared their approval, and with a happy smile Tarl led the others through the East Gate.

Inside the city the word had spread, and they found that the streets were filling up with shouting, cheering people. They couldn't have made a more obvious entrance to a town if they had brought twenty thousand orcs with them. As they walked along the narrow streets, waves of acclamation greeted them, and a crowd of exuberant townsfolk followed at a respectful distance.

'What are we going to do?' Ronan asked Tyson. 'I'd expected that we'd just wander quietly in and sit at a tavern until Gueb arrives, but with all these people following us . . .'

'I dunno.' Tyson shook her head, still dazed by their reception. She had been used to a bit of hero-worship back at Welbug, but this was something else. 'Tarl, Marwood, any ideas?'

'There's only one fitting place we can go,' grinned Tarl. 'I've been to Unch Haven just the once before, but if I remember correctly, I think it's along here somewhere.'

He led them down a narrow street that ran between dark, lowering houses, and the crowd followed them, still cheering and applauding. At the far end the street opened out on to a market square, and Tarl paused.

'There you go!' he said.

On the far side of the bustling square was one of the chain of themed restaurants founded some years before by three of the most famous warriors that Midworld had ever known: Arnold Blackplough, Drax the Strange and Sten Bloodeye. Decorated with memorabilia and souvenirs of some of the toughest fighters in history, the Rock Hard Café had become a very popular place to wine and dine, and was probably the best-known restaurant chain in the world.

As they crossed the square, pushing past the produce-laden stalls and barrows, the word still ran ahead of them, and they could hear the whispered exclamations. *It's Tyson! Ronan! The heroes of Grey Sea Fields!* A sea of faces turned towards them, and a pathway through the throng appeared in front of them almost miraculously. In the midst of the people the din was almost deafening, and daring hands reached out to pat them on the shoulder or back as they passed. They climbed the three broad stairs that led to the patio in front of the Rock Hard Café and Ronan turned to face the crowd, thinking that he should acknowledge their reception. As he did so, they fell respectfully silent.

'Thank you!' he said, and then paused. The crowd was waiting expectantly, and he suddenly realised he didn't have the faintest idea what to say next. The silent seconds stretched out, and as he stared at the mass of faces in front of him, Ronan could feel a sudden rush of embarrassment so acute that he thought he was going to faint. But then Tarl stepped forward, raised one hand and sent another shimmering white fireball sailing out over the roofs of the houses.

'We love you!' he shouted. 'We love you all!' and the crowd roared its approval.

Tarl grinned delightedly. *I could take to this like an orc to drinking*, he thought. He had already noticed that there were quite a lot of attractive women amongst the adulatory crowd, and some of the prettiest were smiling at him. But then he got a sudden quick reminder from the stabbing pain in the privates that was becoming all too familiar of late, and turning, he hastily shepherded Ronan and the others through the door of the restaurant.

Inside, the walls and ceiling of the long, low room were covered in weaponry and martial memorabilia of all kinds. There were dwarven axes, troll clubs, human spears and pikes, and, in a display case over the bar, an orcish Astral sword made by Amtus himself. A fire roared in a grate in the left-hand wall, and driven through the chimney breast above it was the biggest broadsword that any of them had ever seen. The place was empty of customers, as it had only just opened for the day, but even so the appetising smell of char-grilled steaks and fried onions hung heavy on the air and set their mouths watering.

The staff were clustered in an awe-struck group near the bar, staring wide-eyed at their illustrious customers. To judge by his size and musculature, the manager had once been a warrior, but even he was looking a bit star-struck. As he stepped hesitantly forwards to greet them, Tarl took one look at his face and accurately assessed the situation.

'Listen, guys,' he whispered to the others, 'we won't have to pay for a thing. Just leave the talking to me. Okay?'

And pasting his best cheesy grin in place, he switched on the charm, extended his hand and advanced to greet the overawed staff.

An hour later, after one of the biggest free meals he had ever eaten in his life, Tarl slipped quietly out of the restaurant, leaving the others slumped around the plate- and glass-covered, debris-strewn table. Ronan and Tyson were still talking shop with the captivated manager, and as he left Tarl heard the ex-warrior enquire whether Tyson had the famous Crow with her, and whether she would possibly consider presenting the Rock Hard Café with one of the tiny quarrels for them to display in a position of honour. He would have loved to have stayed there, yarning and drinking with the others for hours until they had all got hungry again, but for once in his life he had something more important to do, and so he had arranged to meet them all two hours later in a quayside pub called The Appalling Miss, by South Gate, and now he was slipping quietly off without even Puss for company.

He didn't expect that the deed would take him two hours, but it was something that was new to him, and he wasn't too sure how to go about it. He knew other people did it frequently, and were quite open and above board about it, but it made him feel uncomfortable, almost ashamed, and he didn't want any of the others to see him doing it. He knew they would find out sooner or later, and he would have to cope with their reaction then, but for them to actually watch him in the act would just be too embarrassing. For Tarl was about to go and do something that made him feel very, very vulnerable indeed. He was going to buy flowers for his girlfriend.

It was several weeks since he had seen Guebral in the flesh, so to speak, and in that time he had missed her dreadfully. He had always supposed that when people talked about missing their girlfriend, what they really meant was that they were missing their jollies, and he had always been a little puzzled to find that his usual piece of well-meaning advice (why don't you find a nice cheap whore and have a quick shag, you'll feel much better) didn't go down too well with folk. But now, all of a sudden, he understood. The things he missed about Gueb were her smile, her voice, the way she looked at him out of those huge, serious eyes – in fact, he missed just being with her. And now that he was only hours from seeing her again, he found he was getting dreadfully excited, and was consumed by an almost overwhelming urge to buy her something to show how much he had missed her, something that would surprise her and make her happy, and sod what the others said or thought. And the only thing he could think of was a bunch of flowers.

Tarl wandered along the streets, peering into the brightly lit windows of the shops and hoping for inspiration, for some gift that would be less embarrassing, but with no success. He walked past bakers, butchers, fishmongers, hardware stores, tailors and clothiers, past an axe suppliers called T. J. Hews and a Hobbit carpentry outlet called Little Woods. Coming to a shop selling underwear for dwarves he paused to stare into the window, and he was just thinking that this must be where they bought their smalls when he realised that the dark and gloomy window of the shop next door was full of vases containing masses of darker, gloomier flowers.

He took a couple of paces backwards and peered up at the sign above the shop front. It read *Orcadian Florists* in large, unevenly painted letters, and underneath that, in an almost illegible white scrawl, *Bouquets, wreaths, and nosegays. Floral tributes, warnings or threats.*

Tarl pushed open the door and walked in. The shop was dark and cramped, and nearly all of the available floor space was taken up with more vases full of cut flowers and plants, most of which were in dark and sombre colours, although some were violently, almost threateningly, bright. There were bunches of nettles and thistles, and Tarl also recognised poison ivy, deadly nightshade, wolf-bane, stinking hell-weed and giant pig-wort. He looked around in some confusion. This was the first time in his life that he had bought flowers for a woman (although he had once stolen a bunch for someone). He was just staring doubtfully at a rather unpleasant-looking plant with a ragged, reddish-purple flower that looked like an exploded nose when he noticed a small, scowling orc sitting on a stool in a shadowy corner of the shop, picking its nose with great concentration.

'Erm, I'd like some flowers for my girlfriend, please,' ventured Tarl, rather hesitantly.

The orc assistant studied him scornfully, and then pulled its finger out of its nose and replied in a sneering whine.

'We don't do swaps.'

'No, I mean I want to give them to her. As a present.'

'You're joking! Why?'

'Well, erm.' Tarl waved his hands vaguely in the air. 'She likes flowers . . .'

'And you don't think that's a problem?'

'Look . . . what would you recommend?'

'Getting a new girlfriend.'

'Listen, I want some *klatting* flowers, okay?'

The orc shrugged indifferently and swept one filthy clawed hand round in an expansive gesture to indicate the wide selection available. Tarl looked about him at the vast array, but found himself unable to come to a decision. Everything looked either menacing, ugly or downright horrible. He tried to remember what Guebral's favourite colour was.

'Have you got anything pink?'

'Only me haemorrhoids, and I'm not wrapping them up for you.'

Resisting the urge to ram the orc head-first into one of its vases, Tarl thought back to what Guebral had said about liking flowers. He had a vague memory of her sniffing at a bunch of desert roses and commenting on the beautiful scent.

'I think I'd better have something scented.'

'Where to?'

'No, I mean I want flowers that smell.'

'Oh, right, well then, these would probably do the job,' said the orc, plucking a thick bunch of dark-brown blooms from a vase. 'They're called Babeophila, or gipsy's breath.'

It thrust them without warning into Tarl's face. Tarl inhaled deeply and instantly recoiled, gagging at the noxious stench that met his nose. It was like rotten eggs mixed with fresh sewage, and with a fair helping of gladiator's armpit thrown in for good measure. He shook his head and rubbed his watering eyes with the back of his hands to clear them.

The orc watched with a look of scornful pity on its face, and tutted audibly. Next second it found itself hauled forward by the dirty lapel of its jerkin so that its face was hovering inches away from the bunch of stinging nettles which Tarl had snatched from a nearby vase.

'Listen, you poxy little piece of nasal waste,' he snarled at the orc, 'I do not want flowers that look as though the petals are made out of orc dung! Nor do I want flowers that smell as though you've kept them in your codpiece for six months! I want my girlfriend to cheer up, not throw up! Human women like flowers that are pretty colours, whites and pinks and reds and stuff. They like ones that have a sweet scent, like roses and things. Now, are you going to sell me a nice bunch of suitable flowers, or am I going to shove these nettles down your throat and give you a matching bunch of thistles up the other end?'

A couple of minutes later, Tarl walked out of the shop carrying a large bunch of tropic roses, luscious red blooms with a very strong, sweet smell. They looked absolutely lovely (he hoped), although they were wrapped in jet-black paper covered in stylised images of dismembered and bloody bodies. It was all that the orc assistant had, but Tarl wasn't too worried. He still had an hour and a half before he was due to meet the others, plenty of time to find a shop that sold a nicer, more romantic line in wrapping paper. And then he could settle in the tavern, have a few drinks with the others and wait for Guebral to arrive.

With a song in his heart, a smile on his face and a pleasant anticipatory tingling in his groin area, Tarl wandered off down the narrow street and disappeared into the crowds.

An hour later, as he stalked through the South Gate, he was in a very different mood indeed. He had discovered whilst shopping that the roses weren't just strongly scented, they were very, very strongly scented. In fact, every shop and street in which he had spent more than a few seconds had become filled with the cloying aroma, and everyone had turned and stared. All the men had made insulting or suggestive comments, and Tarl had felt too embarrassed to defend himself. Most of the women he had met had smiled at him, but when a woman smiled at Tarl it tended to produce a standard result which, at the moment, stung very nastily, and he had resolved to ask Guebral to lift the *Spell of Fidelity* as soon as he possibly could.

He stopped on the quayside in front of the Appalling Miss and looked up at the pub sign swinging above the door. It depicted a young girl with her face screwed up angrily in a temper-tantrum. Shaking his head and praying that this wasn't an omen of Guebral's reaction, he pushed open the solid wooden door and entered the tavern.

Inside it was warm and welcoming. The place was quiet, for it was mid-afternoon and most folk were still working. Tarl bought himself a pint of Low In Brow, his favourite dwarven beer, and settled himself in a comfortable window-seat on the first floor, where he had a clear view of the bustling port area outside and the river beyond.

Unch Haven harbour was protected by two long stone groynes that swept out into the estuary from either end of the quay, curving like the prongs of a short, stumpy horseshoe and sheltering craft from the strength of the river and the on-shore winds. Tarl could see the fishing boats coming home, sailing into the wide estuary with the prevailing westerly wind behind them and swinging into the mouth of the harbour.

On the other side of the river, some three miles distant, was the headland that formed the southern lip of the estuary mouth. Tarl could see the white-stone towers of the city of Dol Dupp shimmering in the sunshine, and he thought back to a weekend long before, when he had fallen in with a group of seamen in this very same tavern, and had gone across to Dol Dupp for a couple of days. They'd been drunk for the whole weekend, and he had ended up in a strange little back-street fetish club called Elf or Leather. What a weekend that had been! He really had needed to keep his hand on his holiday money.

All of a sudden he was brought back to the present by a burst of laughter, and looking round he saw that a group of builders by the bar were staring at him and sniggering. He became uncomfortably aware that the *klatting* bunch of flowers, which was lying on the table in front of him, had once again filled the room with an overpowering scent.

'Hey, darling,' called one of the builders, a large, muscular, tattooed man who was stripped to the waist. 'Can I buy you a drink?'

'Yes, okay,' replied Tarl, absently, and then his brain, which had responded automatically to the last six words of the man's question, belatedly registered the first two. *Darling?* he thought, as he took in the sneering grin on the man's face. *Oh-oh, he's taking the piss. Now I'm in trouble . . .*

The man hauled himself away from the bar, mug of beer in one hand, and began to swagger towards Tarl. His friends sniggered as he called back over his shoulder to the barman.

'Hey, Danny, give us a glass of shandy for the girlie in the window-seat. With a couple of nice pink straws.'

Tarl fixed a friendly grin on his face, but one look at the guy's malicious expression told him that he wasn't going to slide out of this one too easily. The man stopped by Tarl's table, looked down at the flowers and sniffed ostentatiously.

'Something round here smells worse than a Perplec whore,' he mocked. 'Is it you, or is it your sweet little flowers?' And with that he reached out, snapped the head off one of the roses and threw it scornfully into Tarl's beer.

For a couple of seconds Tarl could feel the anger surging up and threatening to engulf him, not because of the insult, strangely enough, but because this prat of a thug had dared to lay his filthy hands on Gueb's flowers. He had carefully kept his own hands below the tabletop, but he could feel the telltale sparks prickling about his fingers as the rage grew, and he knew that if this great slob touched the flowers again, he would be powerless to stop himself reacting.

The man sneered down at him and scratched his muscle-bound chest thoughtfully. Then he stretched out his hand a second time and snapped off another flower, and Tarl's rage flooded through him, completely swamping his self-control. He was within an ace of raising his hands and letting the guy have a fireball right between the

111

pecs when the red mist of anger cleared, leaving an ice-cold rage. Whether it was inspired by the memory of the Sentinel Statue that he had seen in the distance the day before, he couldn't say, but all of a sudden, the words of one of the spells he had used during his run-in with Nekros the Black[9] were crystal-clear in his mind.

Hauling back the Power that was threatening to burst out of his fingertips, Tarl instantly moulded it into a whirling ball of mental energy and focused this on the sneering builder as he began to mutter the words of the spell, softly at first, but rising in a crescendo.

'. . . *ergo pecti sam vulpum habe, faeces-cerebris*,' he finished, and the very air about him crackled with static.

'What are you muttering about, girlie?' teased the man. 'Don't be shy. Speak up.'

'You're calling *me* a girl?' asked Tarl, staring disparagingly at the other's chest.

The man frowned and looked down, then dropped his mug in shock, for all of a sudden he had developed a large, firm, shapely pair of extremely female bosoms. Aghast, he half turned to his friends at the bar, but the clamour of whistles and cat-calls that greeted him caused him to turn back, his arms crossed in a surprisingly feminine manner to cover his modesty.

'Nice nipps,' murmured Tarl, then instantly regretted it, as for a moment it looked as though the man would grab him by the throat and throttle him.

'Listen, mate,' he hissed quickly, as a pair of furious hands reached out towards his neck. 'I've given you tits and I can take them away again. Surely even you must have worked out by now that I'm pretty good with the magic, right? So if you don't piss off back to your mates at the bar right now, I'll take away a different part of your anatomy, and finish the transformation from he-male to female. Get me?'

The builder stared at him with the baffled look of an orc that has just made it through the doors of a pub seconds before closing time, only to see the shutters come rattling down on to the bar just as it is getting its money out. His right hand reached up to rub his stubbly chin, and then he looked down at his new, eye-catching bosom, and his hand moved down almost reluctantly and cupped his right breast.

'So we're agreed then,' said Tarl, trying not to grin. 'No more smart-arse comments about flowers, okay?'

[9] See *Ronan the Barbarian*.

The man nodded absently as his hand continued its slow exploration, and then he jumped as his fingers brushed across the nipple.

'Ooh!' he gasped.

'Look, I'd better change you back the way you were . . .' Tarl began, but his voice ground to an embarrassed halt, for the man's nipples were becoming disturbingly erect, and the guy was staring down at his new chest with a strange fascination. Making a visible effort, he dragged his gaze away and looked at Tarl. His face was flushed, and he was breathing heavily.

'Er . . . listen, could you wait ten minutes or so?' he muttered, and then, turning, he stumbled across the room and disappeared through the door that led to the toilets. Tarl watched him go with a horrified fascination, and he was still staring at the door when a familiar voice broke into his thoughts.

'Cor, you'll chat up anything, won't you?' it said with revulsion, and Tarl swung round to find Puss standing at the top of the stairs, with Ronan, Tyson and Marwood behind it. Tarl sat back, smiling, and a wave of relief washed through him. After a lifetime spent on his own, looking after himself, he hadn't realised how dependent on his friends he had become of late, and it felt oddly reassuring to hear the donkey's cynical drawl again.

Puss wandered up to the table, sniffed at the bunch of tropic roses and sneezed violently.

'Told you so,' it muttered to the others, as its eyes began to stream. 'The sad old slaphead has been buying flowers for his girlfriend! That's a steak you all owe me.'

Tyson and Ronan followed the donkey across, while Marwood wandered over to the bar, and the builders, who had gone strangely quiet, parted respectfully at the sight of the Assassin's robes to let him through.

'So who was the guy with the great pair of Mackers?'[10] asked Tyson, as she sat down. In a few well-chosen words Tarl told them what had happened, and they laughed as he described the builder's response.

'Anyway, I'll reverse the spell in a while,' he finished. 'I'm sure it will be a weight off his chest . . .'

The others groaned, and then as Marwood came over from the bar carrying a tray laden with eight brimming mugs of beer (and a large bowl for Puss), they fell to chatting. Tarl told them of the last time he had visited the city, and of the nightclubs and taverns he had found.

[10] Mackers – short for MacVities (Welbug rhyming slang).

'If you like, I could show you some of them when Gueb and the others get here,' he suggested. 'We could always set sail tomorrow.'

Marwood agreed eagerly, but Ronan and Tyson looked at each other doubtfully.

'I dunno,' muttered Ronan. 'I don't feel at ease. On the way here from the Rock Hard Café I was followed by two different Assassins. They looked as though they were working as a team.'

'Really?' Marwood sounded concerned. 'I didn't spot them, so they must have been determined to stay unseen. That's a bad sign.'

'How long before they try something?' asked Tyson.

'Soon. Could be a few hours,' answered Marwood.

'That's settled then,' said Tyson. 'We stay here until the Vagen boat arrives, and then we sail straight off.'

'Well, we won't be here long, then,' said Tarl. 'Look.'

They all followed his gaze and saw a familiarly shaped boat gliding up the river beneath the walls of Dol Dupp. Although it was over two miles away and was little more than a dot, there was no mistaking the sleek lines of a Vagen vessel.

'Well, we've just got time for another drink,' said Ronan. 'Same again?'

'Yes, please,' chorused Tyson, Marwood and Puss.

'Er, a mineral water for me,' said Tarl, who was staring longingly at the distant ship that carried Guebral.

There was a stunned silence that must have lasted a good thirty seconds, and when Tarl dragged his gaze away he found four pairs of horrified eyes staring at him in disbelief.

'Oh, all right,' he muttered, 'I'll have a beer.'

Ronan leant forwards and felt Tarl's forehead with his hand, as though checking for fever.

'Listen,' he said, 'don't ever do that again. I'm not prepared for the world to end, okay?'

Shaking his head sadly, he picked up the tray and headed off to the bar, and Tarl turned back, deaf to the ribald comments of the others, and watched the distant ship as it inched maddeningly slowly towards the harbour below.

Half an hour later, the five of them were standing at the end of a wooden pier that jutted out for some fifty yards from the quayside. Marwood and Tyson were facing the shore with bows unslung, watching for any hint at an attempt on Ronan's life by the Assassins' Guild, whilst Ronan and Puss stood patiently waiting for the Vagen ship, and Tarl hopped, skipped and leapt about in a paroxysm of impatience.

As they waited, they became aware of the sound of distant laughter, just one or two people at first, but spreading. It was coming from the fishermen who were mending nets on the western groyne. They had stopped their work and were nudging each other, grinning and pointing to something in the river that was out of sight from the harbour, hidden behind the vast stone bulk of the groyne. The laughter was taken up by fishermen on the boats moored out near the harbour entrance, and then, as the Vagen ship swept around the end of the groyne and turned towards the quayside, it spread to everyone else in the harbour. Even Ronan and Tyson couldn't stop themselves from grinning, whilst Puss just sat down and brayed with laughter.

It wasn't the way the Vagen longship was handled by its all-woman crew that was amusing everyone, for no one could have sailed the ship better. Nor was it the fact that the ship was crewed by women, for the exploits of Klaer and her crew during the Battle of Grey Sea Fields had become well known. The problem was the look of the ship itself, for the distinctive dragon-headed prow, the symbol of the Vagen sea-raiders that had struck fear and terror into folk the length of the western coastline, had been replaced. And not by an effigy of some other savage or frightening beast either, but by the carved head of a small, furry rodent with pop eyes, buck teeth and a decidedly goofy grin.

Hastily rearranging their expressions into ones of friendly welcome, Ronan and Tyson lifted their hands to greet Klaer and her crew. Beside them Tarl was leaping up and down, desperately trying to spot Guebral. For a few moments he thought that she must not have come, and his face didn't so much fall as plummet, but then he saw her standing in the stern, her slight figure almost hidden by the taller Vagens, and he gave a yell of greeting that could have been heard in Dol Dupp.

Despite their laughter, the local fishermen nodded with approval at the way the ship's sail was furled at just the right moment, so that it glided slowly up to the end of the pier and came to rest beside it with the merest of bumps. Tarl leapt down on to the long, low deck and was hugging Guebral almost before the ship had stopped moving, and Klaer scrambled up on to the pier's wooden planking and advanced to meet Ronan and the others, her hand outstretched.

'Hi,' she greeted them, as she gripped Ronan's wrist and they shook hands, warrior-fashion. 'Guebral tells me you could do with a lift.'

'Damn right!'

'Well, let's not hang about, then. Get on board.'

Ronan studied Klaer's face. She was smiling, but it looked strained. Her whole body language was stiff and embarrassed, and she was studiously ignoring the nearby fishermen, who were still pointing to the figurehead and laughing. Ronan was dying to ask her about it, but something told him that this wouldn't be a welcome topic.

'So, how's Martin getting on?'

Klaer flushed at the mention of the Vagen hero of the Battle of Grey Sea Fields.

'Badly. Very badly. We're supposed to be getting married, but I tell you now, it will all be off if he listens to any more of that pillock Dene's stupid ideas!'

She cast a furious look sideways at the furry figurehead, and at that moment one of the fishermen yelled across to her.

'Hey, darling! What's that meant to be on the front of your ship, then?'

Klaer ignored him, but the look of naked anger on her face was so strong that Ronan almost took a step backwards.

'I'll tell you what it is,' the fisherman yelled, as his friends grinned. 'It looks to me like a beav . . .'

'It's a *klatting* hamster, okay?' roared Klaer. 'It's meant to be friendly and disarming, and the first person who says a single word about beavers is going to get his *klatting* tongue ripped out! All right?'

She stared across at the fisherman, her head jutting out aggressively as though daring him to say another word, and then she swung round to leap back down to the deck.

'This hasn't been a good voyage,' she muttered to Ronan. 'What with . . .'

'Oh, oh,' cut in Marwood, who was still scanning the quayside. 'Here come the boys!'

The others turned back and saw that a cluster of some twenty men in Assassin's garb had come charging through South Gate and were now pounding along the quay towards the pier.

'I don't like the look of this,' muttered Tyson. 'They've all got bows. We'd better move it, sharpish!'

116

'We're not going to be able to get the ship away in time,' warned Klaer, as her crew grabbed their oars and ran to their positions. 'Can you hold them off?'

'No, but I guess we'll have to try!' answered Tyson. 'Oh, *klat*! Ronan, Marwood, get on board! Keep down behind that gunwale, or else they'll just pick us off!'

She knelt hurriedly behind a bollard and was just notching an arrow to her bow when a quiet voice spoke up from the deck of the longship behind her.

'It's okay,' said Guebral, 'I can take care of them.'

Tyson glanced quickly at the pale, serious face framed by dark-brown curls of hair, then switched her gaze to Tarl, who was standing with his arm around the waif-like girl.

'Go on,' he grinned proudly at Guebral, 'use that spell I told you about. The first one I ever cast.'

'Oh, no, Tarl, I can't! This is serious!'

'Go on! It means no one will get hurt, and it will be fun!'

'For *klat*'s sake, do something!' interrupted Tyson. 'They're almost on us!'

'Okay, okay.'

Guebral stared at the Assassins as they reached the quayside end of the pier and began charging along the wooden planking, and whispered a few words. It was as if the twenty men had suddenly run full-tilt into deep mud. All at once they slowed to a virtual crawl, moving their legs in a kind of bandy-legged slow-motion stagger, and a look of surprise mixed with horror crossed each of their faces.

'What on earth have you done?' asked Tyson.

'It's the spell I used on the gate guard at Carn Betw,' laughed Tarl. 'But Gueb does it much better than I could. It causes, er, shall we say, an immediate liquefaction of the bowels, and a total loss of control of the sphincter.'

'Oh, you nasty little sod! You mean they've messed their pants? All of them?'

Tarl nodded and hugged Guebral proudly, and Tyson gazed along the pier to where the twenty crestfallen Assassins were now standing in an uncomfortable group, holding the seats of their trousers away from themselves with one hand, and looking at each other in confusion. Nearby, some vociferously complaining fishermen were pinching their noses and flapping their hands from side to side in an unsuccessful attempt to alleviate what was obviously a pretty overpowering smell.

Tyson watched them with an unbelieving grin on her face for a few moments and then hopped down into the longship next to Ronan, who was holding an oar against the end of the pier.

'Aren't you glad she's on our side?' he laughed, and then flexing his muscles he shoved them powerfully away from the pier. At Klaer's shouted command the Vagen women hauled on their oars as one, and the longship swept round in a graceful arc to head out of the harbour into the powerful current of the river.

Tyson slipped an arm through Ronan's, and surveyed the ship. There were eighteen oarswomen, many of whom she recognised from their last trip in a Vagen vessel. Nearby, Tarl was shamefacedly telling Guebral that he had bought her a massive bunch of flowers but that he had gone and left them in the pub, and beside them, Puss was telling Marwood something that was making the ex-Assassin laugh uproariously. At the stern, Klaer stood in the traditional position of a Vagen leader, holding the steering oar.

'Guebral said you want to head south until we're out of sight of land,' she called. 'Is that right?'

'Yeah,' answered Tyson. 'We really need to cover our tracks.'

Klaer nodded in acknowledgement, and Tyson looked past her at the rapidly receding harbour. The fishermen seemed to have ganged up on the group of malodorous Assassins and were busily hurling them one by one off the pier into the harbour waters, presumably in an attempt to improve their smell. Grinning yet again, she turned back to Ronan and leant her head against his shoulder.

'We're still in with a shout, babe,' she murmured. The two of them stood side by side as the longship swept out of the estuary and veered south into the wide channel between the mainland and Isle B'Ibaq, and as they sped towards the open waters of the Grey Sea, the sun sank gradually down towards the distant horizon until the whole of the western sky was the colour of freshly spilt blood.

In a barn some miles to the east of Dol Dupp, the five remaining *cobrats* were sheltering for the night. Despite the heavy rain that had started falling after sunset, they were snug and warm curled up in the hay. They also had full stomachs, thanks to the farmer, who had provided them with a very large supper. Mainly because he had been a very large man . . .

They were still south of the Great River Leno, but they hadn't lost the trail of their prey. Although they found it much easier to track by scent, the *cobrats* had been specially bred with a unique ability: a sixth sense like a mental compass that always pointed in the direction of their target. So when their prey had lost them by taking a boat downstream, they had followed, instinctively knowing that they were heading in the right direction.

Shortly before they arrived at the barn, they had felt their target starting to move to the south, and that movement had continued into the night. But now the pack leader lifted its head from the shattered thigh bone that it had been chewing and moved it gently from side to side, its eyes closed, probing. The target had changed direction again, and was now heading north . . .

The lethal creature opened its eyes again and turned its attention back to the remnants of the farmer's thigh bone. It was in no hurry. Whichever direction their prey fled, the *cobrats* would know. Sooner or later they would catch up, and it would die beneath their flailing talons. Nothing would deflect them, not hunger, not cold, not wide rivers or snow-covered mountains, for they were programmed by their manipulated genes to pursue, and to keep on pursuing, following their master's orders until either they or their target lay dying on the ground . . .

CHAPTER SEVEN

Folk in cities such as Gudmornen are as cosmopolitan as any in Midworld, but the Mahon countryside is a totally different matter. Isolation and inbreeding have resulted in a peasant populace that ranges from the backward to the completely deranged.

As an example, arriving at one small village we were greeted by a group of men who were convinced we were demons, and who tried to scare us off by throwing chickens at us. Having introduced ourselves, we asked to be taken to talk with the village elders. They took us to meet a clump of trees . . .

The Rough Chronicle to . . . Mahon

As the Vagen longship sailed north through the night, the weather slowly deteriorated, until, by the morning, they were battling through the teeth of a gale. The strong south-westerly wind wrenched at the sail, driving the ship through the waves at a phenomenal speed. The torrential rain was coming down in curtains, and the deck was awash with water. There was no way of keeping dry, but Ronan and the other passengers crouched in the lee of the larboard gunwale, which at least kept the worst of the weather off them, and suffered in silence.

Ronan thought that he had never been so wet and cold. His clothes were saturated and felt as though they were freezing to his skin. He had gone beyond shivering now; a leaden numbness was sinking into his limbs, and he could no longer feel his fingers or toes. He gazed admiringly at Klaer. Since relieving Fjonë two hours earlier she had been battling non-stop with the steering oar, fighting to keep the ship from being blown off course. She had no shelter from the elements, and despite the thick cloak that was wrapped about her, she was drenched. Her hair whipped and lashed about her shoulders in the wind and her face was pinched and white with cold. Eight others of the crew were stationed at intervals up the centre of the boat, forming a line of communication to Kamila, who stood behind the new figurehead, peering into the murk ahead and watching out for hidden shoals and reefs.

120

Dragging himself to his feet, Ronan staggered across to Klaer, stumbling as the ship pitched and yawed.

'Can I help?' he called, but the wind grabbed his words and whipped them away into the distance, and he had to repeat them, shouting at the top of his voice to be heard.

Klaer nodded tiredly and he thrust his weight against the steering oar, adding his strength to her own.

'Shouldn't we head for land and find somewhere to ride out the storm?' he called.

'No,' she answered, and despite the fact she was shouting at him from three feet away, he could only just hear her. 'It's dying down a bit. We'll be clear of it in an hour.'

Ronan braced himself against the oar and peered forwards into the gloom. As the rain lashed viciously at him and the wind whipped his dreadlocks about his shoulders, he couldn't help thinking that Klaer was being rather optimistic. However, she was the captain of the ship, and the sea was her field of expertise. With the discipline of his warrior training, Ronan couldn't bring himself to argue, and so he just concentrated on helping her keep the ship on a straight course.

A while later, it became clear that she had been right. The power of the wind lessened and the rain began to ease off and then stopped completely. Slowly the visibility improved, and the clouds above them lightened. One by one the bedraggled passengers hauled themselves upright and stretched, beating their arms around their chests and stamping their feet in desperate attempts to get warm.

Now that the wind had quietened, Klaer could clearly hear any warnings from Fjonë, the lookout, without the need for them to be passed from person to person along the ship, and so the other crew members were set to baling out water, breaking out dry clothes from the waterproof lockers amidships, checking the kegs of fresh water for damage, and myriad other tasks. Two of them began unstowing the cooking equipment and setting dry wood in the square, stone-lined firebox that was set in a hole in the deck midway between the mast and the stern. Usually, making fire was a complicated and dangerous business at sea, but with a magic-user of Guebral's ability on board things were a lot easier. The others watched as she muttered a couple of words and the small pile of logs in the firebox burst into a steady flame, burning strongly beneath the cooking cauldron which hung from a tripod above it.

Tarl wandered across and crouched as close to the fire as he could get. He was shivering violently, and his teeth were chattering so much that he could hardly speak.

'I d-d-don't know why w-w-we d-d-don't have a b-b-bigger fire,' he stammered. 'W-w-we need w-w-warming up!'

The donkey, which was sitting nearby, gave him a look of withering contempt.

'Oh, brilliant!' it muttered. 'A huge, roaring log fire on board a ship made of wood. What a brain! And I suppose if we need any water you'd want us to dig a hole in the bottom of the ship, would you?'

Tarl frowned crossly and opened his mouth to reply, but at that moment sunshine broke through the clouds, turning the sea all around them from a threatening leaden colour to shimmering, sparkling gold. Although the air was still cold, suddenly they could feel the heat of the sun on their backs, and almost as one everyone turned to face it, letting the warmth soak into their faces.

Keeping one hand on the steering oar, Ronan unwound his sodden cloak and wrenched off his wet shirt, sighing with contentment as the sun seeped into his chilled muscles, causing the dampness on his bare torso to evaporate like steam. All around him Klaer's crew were following suit, and Tyson, who had been rummaging in his backpack, wandered across to him and held out his spare dry shirt.

'Here we are,' she smiled, 'put this on. Oh, and keep your roving eyes to yourself!'

Ronan grinned at her and glanced at the other two male members of their little group. Marwood, who was huddled against the larboard gunwale wrapped in his thick, waterproof cloak, stared in wide-eyed amazement at the female Vagens who were now going about their tasks stripped to the waist. Nearby, Tarl was crouched next to Guebral by the firebox, and was keeping his eyes studiously on the flames.

'Gueb,' Ronan heard him mutter, 'I need – ow! – to talk to you about – *ouch!* – about this *Spell of Fidelity*. OUCH! *Klatting* hell! OUCH!!'

Fascinated, Ronan strained his ears to listen in, but Guebral's reply was drowned out by Fjonë, who was still in the lookout's position behind the figurehead.

'Land ahoy! Land on the starboard side!' she called.

Immediately, all eyes turned to gaze on the welcome sight of the distant coastline. It was the first time that they had seen it since sunset the previous day. They had stayed far enough out to sea to make sure that no prying eyes would catch sight of a Vagen ship sailing north, and Frundor was a distant purple line on the horizon. Ahead on the right they could see the snow-covered slopes of the Northern Mountains, their peaks hidden in the dense clouds that had not yet cleared from the skies to the east and north.

'How far north do you want to go?' asked Klaer, tiredly. She was still clinging to the steering oar, and looked as though she would collapse without it to support her.

'Well . . . I don't really know,' Ronan admitted. 'None of us have ever been further north than the mountains there. We want to travel east to Gudmornen.'

'But we don't want to land near a city,' Tyson added. 'We'd prefer somewhere quiet.'

'Okay.' Klaer gestured to Kamila to take over the steering, and began to strip off her wet clothing. 'Well, we'd better keep out to sea and avoid Iheirano Bay. Iheirano's a busy little port. We'll come back in towards land north of Serreudta Point. It's very quiet up there, we can land you at one of the little fishing villages tomorrow morning at first light. Now, if you'll excuse me, I'm going to sleep for a week.'

Pulling off her soaking undervest she grabbed the blanket proffered by Kait, and then paused to stare curiously at Tarl, who had his eyes tight shut and was bent double, moaning with pain.

'Is he okay?' she asked Tyson.

'Him? Oh, yeah, he's all right. He's just finding things a little hard, that's all.'

Ronan sniggered, then tried to pretend it was a cough, and Klaer looked at him, a little mystified, and shrugged her naked shoulders. Wrapping herself in the blanket, she threw herself down in the lee of the starboard gunwale and was asleep in seconds.

Tyson linked arms with Ronan and stared across at the distant mountains. She too had changed into dry clothing.

'It's going to be a long, cold trek to Gudmornen,' she told him. 'According to Klaer, the weather north of the mountains isn't good at this time of the year. There could be snow on the ground.'

'Oh, wonderful! My beach sandals and swimming costume are going to come in really useful.'

'Don't worry, I've talked to Kamila. They're going to lend us some warm clothing.'

'That's all right then. I'll just wear one of Fjonë's wool shirts.'

Tyson smiled. The massive warrior would have had difficulty in getting any of the Vagen women's shirts over his head, but he wouldn't be able to get a single bicep into one of the petite Fjonë's.

'I'm sure we'll find a cloak that will fit you,' she said. 'Anyway, we'll manage. Klaer's probably being a bit pessimistic. I reckon we'll be too early for snow; in fact, I'm sure of it. I've got one of my gut feelings.'

It was to be Tyson's hat-trick of really crap predictions . . .

By evening the wind was light enough for the crew of the Vagen ship to be able to rig up the tent-like awning beneath which they slept in cold or wet weather. The sunshine had dried out most of their wet clothing and blankets, and they spent a night that was comparatively snug and warm. Klaer, who had woken as dusk fell and resumed her duties at the steering oar, had kept them well out to sea, and had been confident enough to keep sailing through the night instead of hoving to. And so, when Ronan awoke next morning, it was to find that they had left the Northern Mountains far behind them, and that way off to the north-east he could see the towering, snow-covered peaks of the Frozen Mountains.

As Ronan stretched to ease his stiffened muscles, Klaer hauled the steering oar across and swung the ship towards the distant Mahon shore. Although the newly risen sun was shining brightly, she kept looking over her left shoulder at a huge bank of lowering black clouds that was edging slowly towards them across the sea from the north-west. Ronan wandered across towards her, picking his way through the blanket-shrouded bodies of still-sleeping crew members.

'Good morning,' he greeted her. 'Everything all right?'

'I don't like the look of that lot,' she answered him, casting yet another look over her shoulder at the storm-clouds. 'I think we'd better get you dropped off quickly, and then we can get the hell out of here.'

As they sped towards the shore Ronan woke the others. By the time they were up and had packed their bed-rolls away, the details of the coastline could clearly be seen. Steep cliffs ran away as far as the eye could see to both north and south, but directly ahead of the ship they dipped to form a small sandy bay. In the centre of this was a tiny jetty with a few dilapidated fishing boats moored alongside it, and beyond was a scattering of tumbledown huts.

'Right,' said Klaer, as Ronan and the others gathered around her. 'Sorry to be dropping you off so abruptly, but that weather front behind us is going to be no joke, and if we're going to outrun it we need to be away from here sharpish. We'll drop you at that fishing village over there. Don't worry about the villagers passing on news about you: they're completely isolated around here, and so backward that if you use a knife and fork they think you're in league with the devil. Head a little south of east, and when you come to a river, it will be the Reudi. Follow it south-east and you'll come to Gudmornen. You can't go wrong.'

The rest of the crew crowded round to say their farewells, then scrambled to take up their rowing positions. Klaer shouted the order for the sail to be furled, and once again brought the longship round so skilfully that it eased up to the end of the jetty with barely a bump. Ronan and the others hopped on to the rickety planking, and almost at once the Vagen women bent over their oars and began to row, and the ship went surging out into the bay.

Ronan watched them for a few moments and then turned his attention to his companions. Guebral and Tarl were muttering together, and seemed lost in each other's company. Marwood and Puss, who had got very matey in the past few days, had wandered along to the end of the jetty, chatting. And Tyson, her sword half drawn, was carefully surveying the village, a look of puzzlement on her face.

Following her gaze, Ronan looked at the nearest of the dilapidated huts, and he too became aware of a feeling that something wasn't quite right. There was a stillness about the place, a complete lack of movement, a silence that suggested abandonment. He sniffed the air. Despite the on-shore breeze, there was a faint hint of smoke and burnt wood, and of something else as well, something that was too tenuous to place.

Drawing his sword he paced slowly forwards with Tyson beside him. At the end of the jetty a path climbed up the short sandy slope to pass between the first of the huts, and they followed this cautiously, their swords at the ready. As they climbed, the smell became stronger, until suddenly Ronan recognised the second, fainter aroma. It was of seared, charred flesh.

They reached the top of the path and crept warily between the two huts, and then stopped and stared aghast at the sight that met their eyes. Most of the other huts seemed to have been burnt, but not by a normal fire. They looked as though some infernal flame had blasted them apart, so little remained. Even the stone foundations of the biggest huts were cracked and charred. Blackened debris was strewn about the small square, and the burnt, twisted corpses of the incinerated villagers were all but unrecognisable as human remains.

Despite being accustomed to the sight of sudden death, Ronan could feel the bile rising in his gorge at such a hideous spectacle. He could almost hear the tortured screams of the burning villagers and see their death throes as they died in agony beside their blazing homes.

'No one should have to die like this,' he muttered. 'What happened here?'

'Demons,' said a cracked, shaky voice. 'Demons came from out of the night and destroyed our village.'

Ronan turned to find a strange figure advancing on him from out of one of the few undamaged huts. It was tall and thin, with wild eyes and a droopy moustache, and it was covered head to toe in a dried-on brown encrustation that made it look and smell as though it had been rolling in concentrated cow dung. It was holding a notched and battered sword in one trembling hand.

'Demons?' said Ronan. 'What sort of demons?'

The figure paused for a moment and considered.

'Well . . . demonic ones,' it said doubtfully. 'You know. Sort of black, and deadly. You must know what demons are like. They brought a lot of hellfire with them, and then they vanished before I could get at them. I've been waiting for them to come back.'

The figure stared at Ronan suspiciously, and a crafty look crossed its crazed face.

'The trouble with demons,' it continued, 'is that you can never be sure what guise they'll come in . . .' And waggling its sword purposefully, it started advancing again.

Ronan backed cautiously away across the little square. It wasn't the threat of the wavering sword that worried him, it was the overpowering smell of sewage, which was making him want to heave.

'Listen. My name's Ronan. And this is Tyson. We're warriors. Human warriors.'

'I'm Chaz. Chaz the Morose, they call me. Well, called me, before they all got burned to a crisp. So you're not demons then?'

'No.'

'Are you sure?'

'Positive.'

'Oh. Shame.'

Chaz lowered his sword, then looked across to Guebral, Tarl, Marwood and Puss, who had just wandered into the square and were standing looking about them with horrified expressions.

126

'What about you lot, are you demons?'

'No,' said Guebral.

'Not me,' said Marwood.

'Not when I'm sober, at any rate,' said Tarl.

'Of course not, you prat,' said the donkey.

Chaz looked at it in amazement and an admiring grin spread across his face.

'Wonderful disguise!' he said. 'Truly brilliant! I'm really impressed, honestly I am. You demons can be so clever at times!'

And with that he launched himself at the little donkey, his sword whirling round in a huge arc to come smashing down on its unprotected head. The attack was so sudden that Ronan and Tyson were taken totally by surprise. They stood rooted to the spot as Chaz's sword hissed down . . . and came to a sudden stop mere inches from the donkey's skull.

Marwood had reacted like lightning, jerking his dagger from his belt and intercepting the sword-stroke. His thin frame belied his strength, for he was able to absorb the power of the stroke, stopping the sword dead, and then with a deft twist he flicked it sideways and thrust his dagger upwards to slam home into Chaz's unprotected throat. For several seconds the only movement was the stream of blood that gushed forth from the resulting wound and fell past Marwood's arm like a crimson waterfall, and then with an almost inaudible sigh Chaz's legs folded and he collapsed to the ground, a blood-soaked, lifeless hulk.

Marwood gazed at his flaccid corpse, a look of total horror on his face, and then he flung down the dagger and fell to his knees, his face ashen.

'I didn't mean to do that!' he stammered to the others, who were staring at him open-mouthed, like shepherds gawping at a mild, retiring sheep which has just ripped the throat out of an attacking wolf. 'My training took over, and I just reacted. I really didn't mean to do that!'

The donkey reached its head forwards and prodded at the corpse with its muzzle, as though making sure that Chaz was dead.

'Some people,' it said, 'might say you overreacted. Personally, I would say that the vicious bastard had it coming.'

It paused and gave the other four a baleful look.

'And what,' it continued, 'were you lot doing? I'm just about to get my ears moved three feet apart by some nutter with a dirty great sword, and you're all standing there motionless, like blocks of wood! I've seen moss with quicker reactions than you gang of half-wits!'

It wandered off across the square, muttering to itself, and Tarl and Guebral exchanged guilty glances before scurrying after it, apologising profusely. Marwood stood up, his gaze still riveted by the corpse at his feet, and then tearing his eyes away he turned and lurched blindly after the others. Tyson and Ronan watched him go, and looked doubtfully at each other.

'That's the second time he's saved one of us,' said Tyson. 'I've never seen reactions that fast before. I hope we're right about him.'

'No, we can trust him,' replied Ronan. 'I'm sure we can. I'd stake my life on it.'

'I think that's just what you may be doing, babe . . .'

Ronan shrugged nonchalantly, then looked up at the sky. The massive bank of dark, lowering clouds was now directly overhead, and even as he watched, the advance guards crept across the face of the sun. In an instant the daylight darkened, as though someone had pulled curtains across a window, and then the first few snowflakes began to drift diffidently down from the sky.

'Oh-oh,' he said. 'I don't like the look of this. Do you think maybe we should stay where there's some shelter?'

'I reckon we should get moving,' said Tyson. 'I wouldn't worry about the weather. The clouds will soon blow over, and it isn't cold enough for the snow to stick.'

She was getting very close to the world record for the Most Crap Predictions in a Five Day Period.

By late afternoon they had travelled some fifteen miles inland across country. The snow had eased off at noon, and they had been able to see a spur of the Northern Mountains running towards them from the south-east. But then the snow had started again, redoubling its efforts, and visibility had been cut drastically. There was a good six inches on the ground now, and Marwood in particular had been finding the going tough with his open-toed sandals. As the blizzard began to intensify, Ronan and Tyson conferred, and then suggested to the others that they find a suitable place to make camp for the night.

Half a mile further they found somewhere. It was a small, boulder-strewn valley, with a straggle of stunted conifers growing by the side of the small stream that ran northwards along the valley bottom. Several of the trees were dead, and Ronan dragged the trunks of the three smallest across to six large boulders that were clustered together in a flattened horseshoe shape. With his knife he stripped away the side branches, and then with the help of the others he hauled the tree-trunks up on to the boulders, bridging the gap between them like rafters. Then Tyson and Guebral stretched three ground-sheets across them as a roof, anchoring them with smaller stones. Ronan, Tarl and Marwood rolled and trundled other boulders across, piling them up to fill the spaces between the boulders and leaving just one gap as a doorway, and then they scooped snow over them to seal any holes. The snow was already covering the ground-sheet roof in a white blanket, and they now had a refuge in which they could all fit comfortably, and which was comparatively warm and dry.

By the time they had finished, a veritable blizzard was falling, and visibility was down to a few feet. They crawled one at a time into their lair, and Ronan hung his cloak across the doorway to seal out the cold. Then they huddled together for warmth, rubbing and blowing into their chapped, frozen hands to restore the circulation, and making desultory conversation. Whilst building their shelter, they had all secretly thought that they would be so cold that sleep would be impossible, but within ten minutes the temperature inside had risen so much that they felt positively comfortable. All of them were bone-weary, and it wasn't long before they were beginning to doze off. Ronan had suggested that he remain awake on watch, but Tyson had convinced him that no one and nothing would be abroad on such a bad night, and so he let sleep gradually steal over him. The last thing of which he was aware was Tarl telling the donkey that if it farted even once in the confined space of the shelter it would spend the rest of the night outside, and then his eyes closed and he knew no more.

When Ronan awoke, daylight was creeping round the edges of the cloak that hung across the door. It was still warm inside the shelter, but his muscles ached a little from sleeping sitting upright on the hard ground. Tyson was leaning against him, still asleep, and Guebral was lying curled up beside them, her head resting on the donkey's side. But of Tarl and Marwood there was no sign.

Then Ronan heard the sound of laughter coming from outside. He leant forwards to twitch his cloak away from the doorway, and beside him Tyson stirred, opening her eyes and stretching. Daylight flooded in, and they looked out on a world that was more than a foot deep in snow.

With the doorway uncovered the laughter was louder, but Ronan could see no sign of the other two. However, the snow in front of the shelter was churned up and uneven, with long, continuous furrows a foot or more wide in which the bare ground showed through in places. There was something very familiar about them, and a childhood memory clicked into place in Ronan's brain. They were the sort of furrows produced when one pushed a ball of snow along the ground and it picked up more snow, getting bigger and bigger . . .

'Oh, I don't believe it!' he muttered. Unwrapping himself from his blanket he crawled outside and stood up, looking round.

There was snow as far as the eye could see, covering the ground in a smooth white blanket, although it was no longer falling from the sky. The only break was the thin dark line of the stream that still trickled along the foot of the valley. Slightly further up the hillside on one side of the shelter, Tarl and Marwood were bounding around in the snow, putting the finishing touches to a couple of large snowmen and laughing and giggling like children.

Ronan shook his head in disbelief as Tyson emerged from the doorway of the shelter.

'Look at that pair!' he said to her as she stood up and wrapped her blanket about her shoulders.

'By the gods!' she laughed. 'If the Orcbane board could see the crack team of lethal killers that's after them, they wouldn't be able to sleep at night. For laughing.'

They started to wade up the hill through the snow, and as they neared the others they realised that only one of the two snow sculptures could be called a snowman. The other was most definitely a snow-woman – and a very well-developed one at that.

'Hey, Marwood!' Tyson called. 'Is that based on anyone you know?'

Marwood turned and stared at them guiltily.

'Ah, sorry,' he mumbled, looking a little shamefacedly at the snow-woman's impressive bust. 'I got a bit carried away.'

Ronan and Tyson reached the snowman that Tarl was still working on and came to a halt, staring at it in disbelief.

'Tarl, you sad creature, what is *that* meant to be?' asked Tyson.

'A snowman.'

'I can see it's a snowman. It's very obviously male. But did you have to make it so . . . aroused?'

'It's frozen stiff.'

'And what are those two lumps underneath meant to be?' asked Tyson.

'Haven't you ever heard of snow balls?'

Tyson grimaced and scooped up a double handful of snow, which she compacted quickly into a sphere and hurled with great accuracy at Tarl. It exploded on the point of his chin, showering him with feathery fragments. He swore good-naturedly as the others burst out laughing, then reached down and grabbed a handful himself, and things were about to deteriorate into an old-fashioned snow fight when Ronan suddenly grabbed Tyson's arm.

'Wait!' he yelled. There was a sudden silence as the others stared at him, and he stared up at the sky. A huge bank of dark cloud was once again rolling almost imperceptibly across from the north-west. Almost as they watched it was getting darker, and then large, fat snowflakes began to drift lazily down, settling heavily on to the ground like elderly, overweight merchants lowering themselves into a couch after a nine-course banquet.

'We'd better get moving,' he continued. 'If it's going to keep on snowing, we've got to find proper shelter, or we could freeze to death this far north.'

Somewhat crestfallen, the others subsided, and they all trooped soberly back to the shelter just as Guebral and Puss emerged, yawning and bleary-eyed. They began to strike camp, clearing the snow off the roof of the shelter to retrieve the ground-sheets, and within ten minutes they were packed up and ready to set off again.

Although the snow was by now thick and heavy, it seemed warmer than the previous day, for the wind had abated completely. Ronan took the lead, picking a path up the side of the valley and heading due east across the gently rolling countryside. He could hear no sound save for the gentle crunching of the snow as it compacted beneath his feet, and his breath rasped softly in his own ears, contained and magnified as it was by the cloak that was wrapped tightly about his face and head.

After a couple of hours he realised that the countryside had levelled out into a flat plain. He couldn't see more than a few yards in any direction – the falling snow was thicker than anything he had ever before experienced and was showing no signs of abating – but the ground was now monotonously flat, with not even a ditch to be found. Ronan was by now wading through the lying snow instead of walking on it, and the others were in single file behind him, taking advantage of the path that his powerful legs were clearing. First came the donkey, with a blanket draped over its back to ward off the cold. It was followed by Marwood, and then came Tarl, Guebral and Tyson. No one had spoken for over an hour, as they were all saving their breath for walking. The realisation had come to each that this was not the friendly, picturesque snowfall of winter in Frundor or Baq d'Or. Nor were they experiencing the thick, heavy fall of one of the mountain skiing resorts near High Meneal or Goblin City, where when it got unpleasantly cold you could nip into your hotel for a hot bath, dinner and a few drinks. This was the wilds of the north, where in the winter the snow was heavy, the climate freezing and the hotels nonexistent. They were on their own, and if the snow persisted they would need to find shelter quickly, or they would not survive.

By mid-afternoon it had gone decidedly colder, and a freezing wind had sprung up which cut through their clothes like a knife. The snow was still falling. Hunger was gnawing at them, but Ronan kept them moving, for there was nowhere to stop. Their world consisted of the few square yards of featureless, snow-covered land which was all that was still visible through the tumult of whirling flakes. They ate as they walked, chewing pieces of dried meat cut from their supplies by knives held in fingers that shook almost uncontrollably with cold.

As the afternoon faded towards evening, exhaustion was beginning to set in. Guebral and Tarl were staggering and looked as though they were about to collapse. Ronan peered round desperately, looking for somewhere that might give a vestige of shelter, but in vain. Visibility was too poor. Eventually he stopped to confer with the others and waited for them to straggle round him in a circle. Tyson, like himself, was tired and breathing hard, but was fit enough to keep going through the night if necessary. The little donkey was wet and cold, but an indomitable fire was burning in its eyes, and it looked as though it could plod along in Ronan's footsteps for ever. Marwood, too, was not yet at the end of his tether, for his Assassin training had made him much tougher and stronger than he looked, although his feet were suffering, even though he had tied a couple of leather vests about them on top of his habitual sandals. But both Guebral and Tarl were suffering badly from the cold and from exhaustion, and seemed on the point of collapse.

'Listen,' Ronan shouted. 'We've got to find somewhere to shelter. Any ideas?'

Tyson and Marwood shook their heads wearily, but the others just stared blankly at him.

'Where do you suppose we are?' asked Tyson.

'Dunno. We haven't reached the Reudi yet, but I've never seen a map of this area. It could be twenty yards ahead, or twenty miles. I'd have asked a few more questions if I'd known we were going to get all this snow so early in the winter.'

'Is there anything you can do with your magic, Gueb?' asked Tyson.

Guebral blinked at the sound of her name, and then her eyes focused on Tyson and she shook her head almost imperceptibly. Her face was whiter than the landscape, and she was shivering uncontrollably.

'Nothing at all?'

'Look, magic spells use up a lot of energy,' cut in Tarl, and the others had to strain to make out his words, so distorted were they by the chattering of his teeth. 'Gueb could probably make a roaring fire here in the middle of the snow in front of us, but it would use so much of her reserves that she would freeze to death a few minutes later. Then the fire would go out, and we'd be no better off.'

'Wait . . .' muttered Guebral. 'I could . . .' But then her eyes rolled up and she sagged lifelessly against Tarl, who only just managed to keep her from sprawling headlong in the snow.

'Gueb! No!' Tarl's cry of distress was whirled away by the wind, but before he could utter another word Guebral's eyelids fluttered, and her hands clawed feebly at his arm.

'Sorry . . .' she gasped. 'Back now . . .'

'What happened?'

'*Mindsweep* . . . There's a building . . . a big one . . . a mile northeast . . . didn't have energy to find out more . . .'

Once again she sagged in Tarl's arms, but this time he was ready for her.

'A mile?' said Ronan sharply. 'Can you make that, Tarl?'

'If there's a drink at the end of it.'

'Tyson?'

'No problem.'

'Marwood?'

'I'm with you.'

'Puss?'

'No, I think I'd rather stay here and sunbathe a bit.'

There's always one, thought Ronan, trying not to smile, *and it's*

133

always that sodding animal. Sweeping Guebral up in his arms he turned to face what he hoped was the right direction, and muttering an invocation to Ovuk, he began ploughing through the deepening drifts, with the others following. The wind was almost directly in his face now, and the snow had turned harsh and gritty, whipping against him and stinging the exposed skin around his eyes. On he trudged, his feet numb and his leg muscles aching, his mind full of self-condemnation for bringing the others to such a perilous place with so little forethought.

'A bit further left,' mumbled Guebral from the folds of her cloak, and Ronan realised with a sudden start that he had been nearly asleep on his feet, ploughing along automatically without seeing where he was going. He half turned and checked that there were still four snow-covered figures staggering through the gloom behind him, and then veering slightly more to the north, he trudged on.

Once again he lost all track of time, but it was probably only a quarter of an hour later when Ronan became vaguely aware that there was hardly any snow falling in front of him any more. He stopped, feeling vaguely puzzled, and then all at once his frozen brain lurched into motion, and he realised that he was staring at a stone wall. Built from large grey rectangular blocks, it stretched up for at least fifteen feet, running away from him at an angle to disappear into the darkness on either side. Turning, he plodded northwards along it, struggling through the drifted snow that lay heaped against it, until suddenly he found himself stumbling over a single stone step, and realised that he was beside a large double door of dark, gnarled wood studded with black metal bolts. The wall had merged seamlessly with a large building of the same stone, and on either side of the door two rows of shuttered windows stared blindly out on to the night.

Relief flooded through him. Gently lowering Guebral to her feet, Ronan waited for the others to catch up, studying the building as he did so. Not a single ray of light escaped from the cracks in the window shutters, and not a solitary footstep marked the snow in front of the door. He listened intently but could hear nothing above the sound of his own laboured breathing. The place appeared totally deserted.

The donkey was the first of the others. Somewhere during the journey it had lost its blanket, and it was shivering as though fevered. Its hair had become soaked and matted with water and had

134

then frozen in little spikes, and the snow had stuck to it so that it looked like a large iced hedgehog.

'Puss! Are you okay?' Ronan asked, concerned.

'I keep seeing these visions,' the donkey shivered, 'of a huge, steaming bowl of meat stew. And I mean huge. Troll-sized. I warn you, if anyone in this place offers me a carrot, I will bite their *klatting* leg off.'

Ronan's face muscles tried to produce a smile, but found that the skin covering them seemed to have frozen solid, and gave up the attempt. Then Marwood trudged up. He too was shivering violently. Behind him, Tyson was helping Tarl, who had almost collapsed. He and Guebral fell together, somehow propping each other up, and Ronan reached out to caress Tyson's cloak-covered head briefly. Then he reached behind him and drew his sword, and stepping forward he hammered as loudly and heavily as he could on the doors with the hilt.

They waited for a good while, but nothing happened. Not a sound could be heard; silence covered everything with a blanket as deep and suffocating as the snow. The same frightening thought passed through every mind . . . *What if the place is deserted? What if we can't get in?* Ronan hammered on the door a second time and stepped back. Again nothing happened for what seemed like an age, but just as a creeping despair was settling over them, the judas window in the door slid open, and a shaft of yellow light flooded out. A face appeared in the aperture and studied them briefly, and then there was a muffled exclamation and the judas slammed shut again. They could hear the sound of huge bolts being thrust back, and then the right-hand door creaked open and they were stumbling inside.

The room in which they found themselves was a large, empty, stone-flagged entrance hall, unfurnished save for a roughly carved wooden settle along the left-hand wall. It was deathly cold, almost as cold as outside, and the only light came from the single candlestick held by the man who had let them in.

He was dressed in a dark-green habit made from some rough, coarse material, and had plain sandals on his feet. He looked to be about forty, but his hair was silver and had a tonsure, and there was an air of weariness about him. He watched them with patient concern as they brushed the snow and ice from their clothes, and then when they had all finally turned their attention to him, he spoke.

135

'Welcome, travellers. Welcome to the Monastery of Ceaseless Exertion. We are the Brothers of Perpetual Toil, and I am Brother Grindstone. We have little, for we are an order dedicated to a life of hard manual labour, but what little we have you are welcome to share.'

Everyone stared at him with sinking hearts, even though they had found shelter. When the door had opened to let them in, their spirits had soared, and visions of roaring fires, hot food and warm, comfortable beds had flashed through their minds, but the reality of the dark, gloomy room and the chill which emanated from the dank stone walls was instantly deflating.

'I thank you, Brother,' replied Ronan. 'We are travellers on our way to Gudmornen, but we mislaid our way in the blizzard. If we could shelter here until it has abated we would be deeply in your debt. Then perhaps you could direct us to our destination.'

The monk looked doubtful and shook his head.

'I know not the way, for 'tis twenty years since I set foot outside the monastery. But perchance Brother Drudgery or Brother Strenuous might know. Come, follow me.'

Holding the candlestick up, he opened a plain wooden door in the far wall and led them along a dark, narrow corridor. Ronan strode along next to him, and the others followed, hobbling along on the freezing stone floor as quickly as their exhausted bodies would allow.

'Maybe one of your fellows could guide us tomorrow,' ventured Ronan, but Brother Grindstone looked dubious and pursed his lips.

'I doubt if they will have the time,' he replied. 'For tomorrow is the Day of Unending Travail, and there is much to be done. And then the next day is the Day of Back-breaking Labour, and then comes the Day of Arduous Chores.'

He led them through the door at the end of the corridor into what appeared to be a large refectory. It was, if anything, even gloomier and colder than the passageway. A line of plain trestle tables ran along the centre, on each side of which were hard wooden benches. Through the windows of the far wall they could see that the blizzard had not relented, although half of each window was obscured by the snow piled on the ledge outside. The wind whistled under an ill-fitting door at one end, bringing with it small eddies of snow which lay unmelting on the stone floor like a white doormat.

'You see,' he continued, leading them towards a door at the opposite end of the refectory, 'hard work is our vocation, and so we have renamed the days of our week more fittingly. But come. You are obviously in need of some refreshment.'

He paused in front of the door and surveyed the five chilled, exhausted and thoroughly dejected travellers. He could have sworn that someone had muttered something about sticking his carrots where the sun don't shine, but only their donkey was watching him. The travellers seemed lost in their own depressed, pessimistic thoughts.

'And so,' he added, 'perhaps it is just as well that you have arrived here on the Day of a Little Light Dusting, when we relax after our week's labours. Welcome to the Common Room.' And he smiled and opened the door. Heat and light flooded out, bathing the travellers in warmth, and they stared open-mouthed at the scene within.

The room was some thirty feet long, and was brightly lit by a couple of huge candelabras at each end. Thick velvet curtains hid the windows, and the stone floors were covered in deep, soft carpets. A gigantic log fire roared in a large hearth in the left-hand wall, and at the other end of the room was a vast metal Aga, on which a number of pots and pans were bubbling. A whole pig was rotating on a spit above the fire. The fat ran off it to drip sizzling and spluttering into the flames, and the smell of roasting pork set their mouths watering. There must have been a dozen monks lounging about on couches and chairs, and all of them seemed to be holding flagons and mugs of what looked suspiciously like beer. The hum of conversation was in the air, as was the smell of pipe tobacco and the scent of hot cooking oil.

They stumbled forwards into the room and then paused, staring round awkwardly and feeling strangely out of place.

'Come,' said Brother Grindstone, 'Brother Treadmill yonder will provide you all with mugs of mulled ale. Food will be ready in half an hour, for the pig is nearly done, and Brother Cholesterol is as I speak readying the vegetables.'

They turned and stared at a fat, cheerful monk who was standing by the Aga, testing the temperature of a huge, oil-filled pan that was sitting on top of it. As they watched, almost hypnotised, he poured in a bucketful of sliced-up potatoes. The oil hissed and bubbled, and the smell of frying chips mingled irresistibly with the roasting pork.

'Is he the Head Friar?' asked Tarl, with a lopsided grin on his face.

Brother Grindstone turned and gave him a huge, friendly smile.

'Oh, no,' he said. 'He's the Chip Monk.'

And all of a sudden they all felt completely and totally at home.

Far to the south, on the bank of the River Betw, a filthy old ferryman was just untying the mooring rope of his battered little boat before crossing to go home for the night when an unearthly hissing howl from behind him froze him to the spot. Jerking his head round, the ferryman saw five tall, sinuous creatures gliding down the slope towards him. Their dark fur gleamed in the late-afternoon sun, and their long tails twitched behind them as they flowed upright across the grass, running almost like humans, but far, far faster. For a few moments he stood rooted to the spot, and then the leading creature threw back its head, and another hissing howl burst forth from a mouth that seemed to be unnecessarily crammed with sharp teeth.

Yammering with fear, the ferryman thrust his boat out into the river and hurled himself into it, sprawling in a tangle of legs and oars in the bottom. Scrambling to his seat, he fumbled the oars into position and began to row desperately upriver, his arms aching with the effort. Behind him, the creatures reached the bank and leapt into the river without pausing, but to his relief they ignored him, swimming strongly for the north bank instead. He leant on his oars, panting, and watched them as they reached the bank and scrambled effortlessly out. For a moment they paused and shook themselves like dogs, and the sun's rays glittered on the fine spray of water droplets. And then they were off, running northwards across the flat plain of Frundor towards the distant peaks of the Northern Mountains, and the ferryman buried his head in his hands and, with deep sincerity, thanked the gods that it was not he who was the prey that the terrifying creatures were tracking.

CHAPTER EIGHT

Yesterday was semi-finals day in the Gladiators' Cup at Ged Arena. The first match featured the favourite, Rabak the Southron, against Grold One-eye. It ended surprisingly quickly when Rabak sliced his opponent's leg off and he slipped from his saddle and was dragged around the arena by his horse. Grold is now trailing, with the second leg to come. In the other semi-final, Sargal of Atro quickly overcame Frango the Elder, and then, in a gesture that was warmly received by the sell-out crowd, he sliced his dead opponent's head off and carried it round the arena stuck on the end of his trident. Frango is currently just a head on points . . .

South Iduin Gazette

Wayta stared down at the victorious gladiator as he strode around the scorching-hot sands of Ged Arena, then turned away from the shaded window. After the glaring sunshine outside, it was almost dark in the comfortably cool marble-floored room that was the Orcbane Sword Corporation's corporate hospitality box.

'An impressive fighter, that Sargal,' he remarked to Bownedd, who stood at his side. 'Tell Acquisitions to look into recruiting him.' He paused to glance back at the other three members of the Orcbane board who were currently sharing the box. 'I think you'd better get our carriages brought round to the door,' he added. 'It's time we were leaving.'

Bownedd nodded briefly and marched briskly out of the door, and Wayta seated himself in one of the comfortable leather chairs and stared glumly at his companions. In recent years he had grown so used to making all the major decisions and looking to the other five merely for their backing that he had failed to notice the gradual erosion of the qualities that had brought them on to the board. But now that his plans had gone badly wrong and he was looking to them for help and support, they had nothing to offer him. It felt like walking up the stairs in the dark and miscounting the number of steps. You put your foot down expecting something to be there, but there's nothing . . .

Grole and Kaglav were standing together at one end of the long window, staring blank-eyed down at the arena, and Wayta could tell that in their minds they were re-enacting the defeat and decapitation of the losing gladiator, savouring and relishing the bloodshed. Behind them, Gahvanser had hauled his vast bulk away from the window and was now patrolling the buffet table. Wayta watched with distaste as the obese figure crammed handfuls of vol-au-vents and pastries into his capacious mouth, all the time conducting an unlistened-to monologue about the promises and practices of his latest dietician.

Gahvanser had developed this fad for dieticians a few weeks previously when, after months of searching, he had at last found someone who had sworn to him that he could lose weight without actually cutting down on his food intake. It was called the T-Plan Diet, apparently. It had been weeks later that they had found out that the T stood for tapeworm. What the charlatan had done, Wayta discovered afterwards, was to feed Gahvanser some pieces of semi-raw pork, so that after a few weeks he had a fully developed tapeworm residing in his bowels and living off his surplus calories. Unfortunately for the dietician, Gahvanser's food intake was so high in cholesterol and saturated fats that the tapeworm was unable to keep up and died shortly afterwards from severely clogged-up arteries. This being the first time that the T-Plan Diet had failed, the dietician had been forced to come up with a second idea really quickly. What he had invented was something that he called the Twenty-Stone Diet. He persuaded Gahvanser to swallow twenty large pebbles, with the idea that they would fill his capacious stomach, and he would want to eat less. Unfortunately, Gahvanser had developed acute food poisoning from eating infected semi-raw pork. Right at the end of what turned out to be his final consultation he had projectile-vomited, and the dietician had been stoned to death. And serve him right, Wayta thought. He had come to the conclusion that -tician at the end of someone's job description meant that they were a total bullshitter. Dietician, politician, beautician, they were all a complete waste of space.

He was just wondering if he should add musician to the list, and was thinking that after the performance of the lutist who had 'entertained' them earlier he probably should, when Bownedd came hurrying back in with a worried look on his face. Wayta crossed to meet him.

'The carriages will be here directly, lord,' he muttered. 'And a

140

messenger has arrived with news from one of our spies in Unch Haven.'

'Yes?' prompted Wayta, after looking round to make sure the others wouldn't overhear.

'Ronan, Tyson and two others entered the city four days ago. Twenty members of the Assassins' Guild attacked them as they boarded a Vagen vessel, but were held off by some friend of Ronan's who had, to quote our Guild agent, more *klatting* magical power than you could shake a shitty stick at. I'm sorry, but he's a little excitable, our Guild agent. Anyway, Ronan sailed south on the Vagen ship.'

'South, you say? *Klat!* The Vagen islands are no more than a day away from my estates! Was Slanved one of the Assassins?'

'No, my lord, they were all members of the Unch Haven lodge. There has been no word of him – but one of the two men with Ronan was dressed in Assassin's garb, although it was not Slanved himself.'

Wayta sat down and began to gnaw at one of his knuckles. So he was heading this way. That was very worrying news indeed. Although the *cobrats* or the Assassins' Guild were certain to catch up with Ronan sooner or later, it wasn't going to do the Orcbane board much good if the troublesome warrior had already killed the lot of them. And what the *klat* had happened to Slanved? Wayta offered a quick invocation up to any of the gods that might be prepared to listen, praying that the Master Assassin hadn't bumped into the *cobrats* . . .

'Bownedd,' he muttered, 'I think it would be wise for the members of the board to, er, disappear for a little while. Contact Missek and Mellial, and tell them there is to be a board meeting tomorrow at three. I think it is time that we took up Meiosin's kind offer of a visit to the Dark Dwarves' laboratories . . .

At the Deforzh Research Establishment, Meiosin had been rapidly discovering that being the chief scientist wasn't quite the straightforward job he had expected. When he had engineered the demise of Reágin, he had assumed that this would bring about an end to all his problems; he would be free to initiate a lot of experiments into fascinating (and previously forbidden) areas of research, and would be able to ensure that these could be carried out unfettered by such dubious and unscientific constraints as safety, decency or morality.

Unfortunately, the job of chief scientist entailed a lot more than just overseeing the research. Whenever people had a problem they came to him to have it put right, and for the past few days he seemed to have spent the vast majority of his time running around in circles, trying to sort out the kind of minor hiccups that he would have thought beneath him when he was a mere head of department.

Take now, for example. Just when he thought he might at last be able to spend a few minutes in the Magenetics laboratory, checking on the results of a particularly interesting cross-breeding programme,[11] three different problems had been brought to him. Firstly, the Physicks Department were complaining that they urgently needed a load more copper wire and Alchemy were refusing to let them have any, whilst Alchemy were saying that copper wire didn't grow on trees, and anyway, Physicks had been saying nasty things about them to the other departments behind their backs and they could go whistle for their wire, so there. And then secondly, some of the Magenetics lab technicians had delivered an ultimatum, saying that they were refusing to enter the Vivarium until something was done about the biting insects. Although this might have seemed a bit of a trivial complaint to an outsider, Meiosin had to take it seriously, for he knew that the biting insects in question were the product of the Magenetics Department. Some of them were over five foot long, with teeth to match, and they could take an entire arm off if you weren't careful.

However, the biggest and most baffling complaint had come from a deputation of scientists who had wanted to voice the disquiet they were apparently feeling about carrying out research on living, sentient beings. Since the raiding parties had been far more successful than anticipated in capturing prisoners, the creature holding pens were full of humans, orcs and even the odd elf. Meiosin had issued all departments involved in priority projects with orders to ensure that the effects of their project on sentient beings were fully understood. In other words, the captured humans and orcs were available for experimentation. In the eyes of Meiosin and his immediate circle, this was a logical necessity. The priority projects were being funded by backers who were interested in utilising the results in the field of warfare and weaponry, and as weapons were meant to be used on

11 Between a Golden Retriever and a Brannian elephant. Meiosin had hoped to produce a golden-haired elephant, but what they eventually ended up with was a dog that brought back a lot of memories.

sentient beings, it made sense to conduct their experiments on such beings rather than on laboratory animals. But a surprising number of the dwarf scientists seemed to think that this was wrong, and had been bandying about words such as 'moral' and 'ethical'. Meiosin, who thought that a moral was a type of fungus, was having a great deal of difficulty in even comprehending their grievance, let alone sympathising with it.

Tiredly, he pushed open the door of his new office and shuffled across to his desk, noting that since he had last been in here, half an hour earlier, someone had dumped another thick load of papers into his in-tray. He pulled the top one towards him and saw that it was a request from the Medicaments Department for a new coffee-maker, as Machines and Contrivances had borrowed their last one and were refusing to return it. Attached to it was a note from Machines and Contrivances, saying that they would return the coffee-maker when Medicaments replaced the barrel of beer that they had borrowed six months previously. Across the bottom of this someone had scrawled in pencil that they could have their *klatting* beer when they brought back the *klatting* kitchen scales that they had borrowed two *klatting* years ago, all *klatting* right?

Shaking his head, he slumped into his chair. He was just pulling open the bottom drawer where he kept his precious bottle of *vlatzhkan gûl* when there was a knock on the door and Mitosin stuck his head round it.

'You busy?' he asked, not realising how close he was to having his head caved in by a carved quartz bottle.

'No. Oh, no. Not at all. Why, has one of our top scientists had his new rattle stolen?'

'No, it's our backers. The Orcbane board. They want to come and see our laboratories as soon as possible, and they'd like to stay a while. Can you come and talk to them?'

Sighing, Meiosin slammed shut the drawer and stood up.

'Why not?' he snarled, forgetting that he had issued the invite in the first place. 'Let's ask them to bring their families and friends as well. Why don't we make a house-party out of it, eh? Give everyone a day off. No, make that a week off. Nobody does a stroke around here most of the time anyway except for me, so it won't make the slightest bit of difference!'

And with that he stormed out, leaving his brother staring after him with the surprised look of a messenger-pigeon which, after faithfully delivering the little container of paper strapped to its leg, has just had that container forcibly inserted into an unpleasant part of its anatomy by the disappointed recipient.

Meiosin was not the only annoyed and disgruntled dwarf in Deforzh that day. If there had been a competition for Seething with Discontent, he would have walked off with the silver medal virtually unchallenged, but he would have been forced to concede that when it came to the gold, there was one dwarf who was even less gruntled than he was, and that was Beneltin. The latter had been simmering with resentment ever since he had arrived back from the first raid on Gudmornen only to be hauled up before a disciplinary committee on charges of Insubordination, Being Disrespectful to Superiors, Disobeying Orders and Shaving Off His Beard. He had been expecting to be in a bit of trouble, for he knew that shaving off his beard had been an act of rebellion almost unprecedented since Fundin the Peculiar had outraged dwarf society by his actions three generations before. But he had not undertaken this deed lightly; it was all part of a plan, for Beneltin was a dwarf with a Purpose.

From his childhood years, he had been completely fascinated by comedy. His earliest memory was of a joke he had made which had caused his parents to stare at him with complete bewilderment, but which had made his Uncle Francarsin roar with laughter. Francarsin was a plump, permanently laughing dwarf with a long white beard that hid a multitude of chins, and everything he said (and he never seemed to stop talking) was a joke. Whenever he had arrived on a visit, Beneltin could tell from his parents' set expressions and exasperated sighs that, somehow, they disapproved of him. He would take the young Beneltin down to the Seam of Gold every Saturday night he could, and they would sit at the front, watching whichever comedian was playing that week and laughing their heads off together, while all the other dwarves sat silent and stone-faced behind them.

They had seen some of the great acts together. Thomas the Cooper, a hysterically funny human who was just about the worst magician Beneltin had ever seen; Max the Miller, most of whose jokes the young Beneltin didn't understand, but who caused an enormous amount of embarrassed coughing and foot-shuffling amongst the other dwarves and who made Francarsin literally fall off his seat, weeping with laughter; and the double-act of Ernest the Wise and Eric the Balding, who Beneltin thought were the funniest thing he had ever seen in his life.

144

But then, one awful day, a serious-faced Francarsin had sat Beneltin down beside him with his parents watching and told him that they wouldn't be going to the Seam of Gold together any more. The problem was that Beneltin had started telling his parents that he didn't want to be a scientist like his father, and that he was going to leave school at the earliest opportunity and become a stand-up comedian. Faced with a son who seemed set on a career which they regarded as being even less alluring than that of latrine cleaner, they had decided that the time had come to put their feet down and discourage this worrying interest in 'humour'.

'You can forget this stupid comedy stuff!' his father had told him. 'This is a scientific research establishment we live in, and you are going to be a scientist like me and my father, and his father before him.'

'But I don't want to be a scientist!' Beneltin had wailed. 'I hate science! Every time we have a science lesson I start sneezing. I'm allergic to it!'

'Listen, you got an allergy, you're a scientist,' Francarsin had told him, but his smile had been forced, and Beneltin had been able to tell he hadn't really meant it. However, his parents had been adamant, and when Francarsin had shuffled sadly off a while later, Beneltin's father had told the poor dwarf that he was a bad influence, and not to bother coming back again. He never had.

Eighteen months later Francarsin had died, and as Beneltin had stood paying his respects with his parents, he had looked down at the familiar, much-loved face in the stone coffin and had made a solemn and secret vow. Even though his parents had given him no choice but to become a scientist, he had sworn silently to his uncle's spirit that one day he would rebel. One day he would stand on the stage of one of Midworld's famous comedy clubs and deliver a routine that he himself had written.

Since then he had taken his exams, qualified, left school and taken up a minor research post in the Alchemy Department. His father had been reasonably pleased with him, but then he hadn't known that for the past two years Beneltin had been secretly scribbling jokes down, trying them out on a few close friends or in the privacy of his own room, and honing them into what he hoped would be a good routine. And every Saturday, when yet another comedian walked off the stage in the Seam of Gold to the sound of his own feet, Beneltin would be in one of the front seats, mentally comparing what he had just heard with his own (still untried) script.

When Meiosin had asked for volunteers for the raids, Beneltin had been one of the first to stick his hand up. He hadn't been able to believe his luck when he had been assigned to the group targeting Gudmornen, the home of the famous Stand and Deliver Club, as he'd expected that he would have to talk someone into changing groups. But he had taken his chance as best he could. Limited to just a few minutes in the town, he had managed to find the club's address in a listings magazine, and had tracked it down by asking directions from a newspaper-seller. As he returned to Deforzh via the new Matter Transmitter, Beneltin had been bubbling with excitement, for he knew that more raids were scheduled for the next few nights, and with a bit of luck he would be able to return to Gudmornen on one of the Stand and Deliver Club's Amateur Nights. But the instant he arrived back home, his hopes were dashed.

One thing that he had always noticed about the best acts that he had seen was that they all had a trademark of some sort. A bright suit or a silly red hat, a pair of glasses, or maybe a cigar. It was always something distinctive, something that the audience associated with that particular act. He had spent a while thinking about one for himself, and had eventually come up with the idea of shaving off his beard. He would become Beneltin, the Bare-faced Dwarf. No other adult dwarf would dream of appearing beardless and so it would really make him stand out, and was also a way of sticking a finger up at his parents and his superiors.

Thinking that he might get a chance to get to the club during the very first raid, he had cut it off half an hour before he was due in the Magenetics lecture room, and had immediately panicked, realising that he wouldn't be allowed on the raid without it. However, after a little bit of work with some glue, paper and cotton, he had managed to re-affix the old beard to his chin well enough not to attract attention until he had struggled into his suit of armour, after which it hadn't mattered when it had fallen off and slipped down one leg. But when he had returned from the raid only to be immediately arrested for Insubordination and Being Disrespectful, he had not been able to re-affix it, and at the sight of his naked chin, the judge had thrown the book at him. Beneltin had found himself put on fatigues for two months. And, almost as an afterthought, the judge barred him from setting foot outside Deforzh until his beard had regrown to a suitable length, a process that would take at least two years . . .

With a snarl, Beneltin gave the latrine floor one last vicious scrub, and then knelt upright. His back was aching, his knees were aflame, but with an almost savage defiance his brain kept coming up with jokes for the stage act that seemed to have been indefinitely postponed. Through the open door he saw Meiosin stalk by, his face like thunder, his brother Mitosin trotting deferentially behind him. *Did you hear about the two dwarf brothers who got pushed down the latrines?* he thought to himself. *It was a horrible death, but at least they were in turd together* . . .

Tiredly he hauled himself to his feet, and then scratching the thin stubble on his chin he picked up his bucket and brush and trooped wearily to the door. *I'm not going to let them do it to me, Francarsin,* he thought. *I'm not going to let the buggers grind me down. I'm going to do that act, one day. I promise you* . . . And with a steely determination in his mind, he stalked out and set off along the dark stone corridor towards the next filthy latrine.

'Of course you can visit our establishment.' The image of Meiosin's face, ten times larger than life, stared out of the boardroom wall at the six members of the Orcbane board. 'We'll be delighted to bring you up to date with our research. In a couple of days' time we'll set up the transmitters to whisk you straight here.'

'A couple of days?' exclaimed Wayta, with concern.

'Yes. The transmitters are currently undergoing an overhaul. They've been in almost constant use for over a week.'

'Ah. Well, okay. And, er, have you had any success with the, er, the *other devices* that Mitosin mentioned?'

Meiosin looked mystified.

'What other devices?'

Wayta cast a quick glance sideways to where Cartland was babbling away to herself beside her cauldron, and lowered his voice.

'The non-magical communications,' he hissed.

'They're coming along. You can see when you visit. Look, how long do you want to spend here?'

'Oh, a week or two,' answered Wayta, feigning nonchalance, and then seeing that Meiosin's face had suddenly changed to a choleric puce colour and his eyes had almost bulged out on stalks, he continued, 'Well, Orcbane has invested large sums of money in your research. There must be a vast amount for us to see, and we need to have a thorough understanding of things so that we can make an accurate and informed decision on how much future investment is merited . . .'

147

Wayta left this veiled hint dangling in the air like a fishing lure, and was gratified to read from Meiosin's sudden change of expression that the Chief Scientist had swallowed it whole. All at once, with the prospect of more money that might be forthcoming, his demeanour had changed from a polite indifference to a gruff joviality.

'Of course, of course,' he chuckled. 'Let me see. Now, if you give us three days, to be absolutely sure, we can arrange everything. Proper accommodation, plenty of demonstrations, a few lectures and of course a banquet or two in your honour. So if you are gathered there at four o'clock on Thursday afternoon? Wonderful. I look forward to seeing you then.'

As the dwarf's image faded from the wall, the other five board members began talking volubly and excitedly amongst themselves, but Wayta took no part. He was lost in his own thoughts. Three days was not as soon as he had hoped, and he prayed that it would not be too late. And it wasn't just the threat of Ronan that worried him, either. No, there was something else looming on Wayta's horizon which was causing him almost as much fear . . .

He cast another surreptitious glance sideways at Cartland, and to his horror she noticed and leered back at him, then blew him a kiss. She was wearing a vast amount of make-up, inexpertly but zestfully applied so that her face looked like something drawn on by an enthusiastic six-year-old with a brand new set of day-glo crayons. She had also used heated rollers in her hair. Wayta could tell because four of them had been overlooked and were still hanging from the straggly grey mass at the back. She was wearing a mini-skirt, and her thin, knobbly legs had the colour, texture and veining of blue cheese.

Wayta shuddered. He was getting the awful feeling that the old hag had formed a romantic attachment to him, and the very idea of it was making him feel quite queasy. All of a sudden the trip to the safety of Tor Deforzh in three days' time seemed a horrifyingly long way away. He would not have thought it possible, but he had suddenly discovered that there was a prospect even more horrifying than a painful death at the hands of the vengeful Ronan, and to judge from the expression of simpering lust on Cartland's face, that prospect was frighteningly imminent.

CHAPTER NINE

The Stand and Deliver Club in Gudmornen! It's where bad acts go to die. What a hard audience! They send you hate mail – and that's before they've even seen your act.

I saw the legendary magician Salemon the Shite have one of his really bad nights there. The audience invented a new trick for him: forcibly making a whole string of coloured hand-kerchiefs disappear up a crap magician's backside. I've never forgotten the look on his face as he waddled painfully off that stage with the last couple of hankies trailing dismally behind him . . .

The Sad Life of Tarbuk the Ancient

Tyson stood on the front step of the Monastery of Ceaseless Exertion with Puss beside her, and surveyed the Mahon countryside. The ground was still covered with snow, but the sky was clear and blue, and the sun was low in the western sky, bathing the land in a rich yellowish glow and turning the snow the colour of clotted cream. Now that the weather was clear, she could see that the monastery was built near the edge of a slight plateau, and that to the north-east the ground sloped gently away towards a river that meandered slowly off into the distance. Brother Drudgery had told her that this was the River Reudi, and that if she followed it to the south-east, Gudmornen was merely a brisk day's march away.

She turned to thank Brother Grindstone, who was hovering in the doorway behind them. Even though the monks worked hard for six days of the week in austere conditions, only repairing to the warmth of the Common Room in the evenings, their guests had been well looked after. The guest rooms had been warm and comfortable, and they had been able to rest and recuperate, spending a whole day sitting near the fire and making plans.

It was obvious from their reception on arriving at Unch Haven that they made too recognisable a group, and so they had decided to split into three pairs and to head for Gudmornen separately. Ronan had left before dawn that morning with Guebral, who with her strong magical powers would be the best able to help him should he be recognised. (However, this seemed unlikely. He had taken the irretrievable step of cutting off his beloved dreadlocks and shaving his skull to a gleaming baldness, and Tarl and Guebral had spent a couple of hours in the Scriptorium and emerged with a set of lovingly prepared false documents that proclaimed him to be a Brannian warrior named Rhand ib Uggah, which had set Tyson laughing fit to burst.) Tarl and Marwood had followed them a few hours afterwards, dressed in a borrowed pair of habits. If questioned, their cover story was that they were monks from some obscure religious brotherhood of sad old hippies, similar to the Seventh Day Hedonists. Tyson, however, had still been troubled by the wound in her thigh that she had sustained during the fight with the *cobrat*, and so she had decided to rest it for an extra day, and had stayed behind with the donkey for company.

It had been pleasant to spend a second day at ease, but now she was raring to be on her way, and she couldn't wait to set out next morning. She could see the footprints of the other four leading off towards the river, and she wondered how they were faring in Gudmornen. Although she knew that nothing disastrous could have happened or else Gueb or Tarl would surely have been in touch via one of their strange little magical spells, she was still worried. The previous night, she had dreamt that Ronan was lying dead in the snow with one of the *cobrats* ripping at his flesh, and Anthrax's final warning was hammering at her brain. *They will not stop until they've made their kill. They will not stop . . .*

She shook her head as if to rid her mind of the message. Nothing could have followed them across the sea, and no one knew where they had gone. The *cobrats* must be scores of miles away by now! But for some reason she felt convinced that the five fell creatures were still following them, and were a huge danger. In fact, she would go so far as to say that she had one of her feelings about it. She just hoped that this one was no more accurate than the last four had been . . .

In fact, Ronan and Guebral's journey to Gudmornen had been completely uneventful. They had followed the river south-east for several hours, and the going had been easy, for down beside the river the snow was only a few inches deep. Gradually, the foothills of the Northern Mountains had risen on either side of them, and although the hills were white with snow, none seemed to have fallen in this part of the wide Reudi Valley, and they had soft green grass underfoot as they walked.

By late afternoon they had realised that they were nearing civilisation, for they had begun to pass the occasional farm or cottage, and there was now a broad track snaking along the riverbank for them to follow. It had twisted and turned, diving into the thickets of alder and the copses of fir trees that dotted the valley floor, and although the only sound that they had been able to hear was the song of countless birds hidden in the trees and the ceaseless turmoil of the river, they had known that the city must be near, for there were many footprints and cartwheel ruts in the muddier sections, and the track had been lined with the litter and detritus casually jettisoned by those too lazy or ignorant to take their rubbish home with them. At one point the track had left the bank of the river to wind up the side of a long, bare, rocky outcrop that all but blocked the valley, and as they had reached the top of this they had seen Gudmornen for the first time, spread out before them and filling the valley ahead.

Ronan had been quite taken aback by the sheer size of the place, as this far north he had been expecting nothing more than a large village. The town walls, he later discovered, were reputed to be the longest in Midworld, but even so there were so many buildings constrained inside their limits that the city looked squashed and uncomfortable, as though it had bought itself a set of walls that were several sizes too small but had been determined to get into the damn things, no matter how uncomfortable they were, just to prove that it hadn't really put on that much weight. There was a huddle of houses and shacks around the outside of the walls that made it look as though the city had burst as a result, spilling its residue untidily across the valley floor to the surrounding foothills and along the river and the track towards Ronan and Guebral.

They had wandered through the wide-open city gates well before dark and, after asking for directions from an elderly woman, had found their way to the student quarter without too much difficulty, although Ronan had been a little taken aback by the doubt and suspicion manifest on her face at the mere mention of the University. Then they had rented rooms in a tavern obviously frequented by students, and after Guebral had run a quick *Scan* to contact Tarl and had found that he and Marwood had reached the city quite safely, the two of them had left the tavern for a short stroll to familiarise themselves with the lay-out of the Gudmornen campus.

The University was built in a loop of the river, and was the oldest part of the city. The original buildings were clustered around a small central piazza, but as the University had expanded over the years it had gradually spread outwards, taking over adjacent houses and buildings until it was as constrained as the city, squeezed in on three sides by the river, and with its premises reaching out along the streets and alleys of the fourth side like the tentacles of a squid.

It took them a while to find the Faculty of Assassination, and by the time they did so night had fallen, and the converted stone warehouse hidden in a narrow alley called Tannery Mead was dark and deserted. Ronan felt very uneasy, half expecting that any passing stranger might turn out to be an Assassin stalking him, and so they decided that it would be better to return to the safety of their tavern, and retraced their steps.

The only other occupants of the tavern were a large gang of students and they were so busy playing a drinking game called 'Bunny-rabbits' and getting extremely pissed that they didn't even notice the large, shaven-headed young warrior and the quiet, slim girl who slid into a corner seat with a couple of mugs of beer. Ronan and Guebral sat there for a while, sipping their beers, talking about Tyson and Tarl, and keeping a very careful eye out for anyone who looked as though they might be taking more than a cursory interest in them.

However, the night turned out to be completely uneventful, and no one took the slightest notice of them. Even so, Ronan went up to his room feeling physically sick with the constant strain. Guebral carefully set a *Trespass* spell about the room so that anyone entering would be instantly rendered unconscious, but Ronan still found sleep desperately difficult. Every time he was close to nodding off some little noise would penetrate his consciousness, causing him to jerk upright, his nerves jangling, and the sky was beginning to lighten in the west before he eventually managed to fall into a troubled, restless sleep.

Tarl and Marwood had reached Gudmornen soon after darkness had fallen, only a couple of hours after Ronan and Guebral, and both had felt an instant affinity with the town. In many Midworld cities the pulse of life faded with the light of day, as shops, restaurants and even some taverns closed and people spent the night-time hours behind their own locked doors. But Gudmornen, with its high numbers of students, was plainly different. As they had wandered along the main shopping streets, they had been delighted to find that the thoroughfares were lit by large, flickering torches wedged into metal sconces on the walls, and that every bar, tavern and restaurant was still crowded with people. Even some of the shops had still been open, their goods displayed in the windows by the light of oil lamps and candles.

As they strolled along in their borrowed habits, absorbing the atmosphere, Tarl had been deeply impressed by the fact that passers-by tended to smile amicably or nod respectfully to them. He was far more used to people snarling or scowling, or even throwing things, but he was level-headed enough to realise that it was the religious garb they were wearing that was attracting this unaccustomed respect. He was just starting to wonder whether all this would place any sort of restraint on the serious fun he was expecting to have over the next few days when his eye was caught by an item in the window of a shop called Brothers in Alms, which to judge by the items on display sold religious clothing.

He ambled across and stood staring, open-mouthed. Most of the clothes in the shop looked pretty dull and nondescript (although there was an intriguing dummy in one corner dressed in some of the garments favoured by the Holy Sisterhood of Carnal Enlightenment, which seemed to consist mainly of strategically placed holes connected by sheer black silk), but the item that was the centrepiece of the window display stood out like a sore thumb. It was one of the robes worn by the Seventh Day Hedonists, a bright-orange habit with distinctive lime-green swirls, and Tarl found it fascinating. Here was an item of clothing that certainly didn't suggest chastity, humility, abstinence or any of the traditional virtues of the average religious brotherhood. Instead, it suggested in the strongest possible terms that its wearer was someone who wanted to PARTY, very long and very loud.

'Check that out,' he whispered in awed tones to Marwood, who had come to stand beside him.

'Mmm. A restrained little number.'

'I want one.'

'You're joking! Have you seen how much it is?'

Tarl switched his attention to the discreet price label and nearly swallowed his tongue.

'*Klat!* That's more than the whole shop is worth!' He stared in disbelief at the brilliantly coloured habit, and then noticed the tiny green *alaxl* motif embroidered on the left breast that showed it was designed by Christian the Cross.[12]

'Come on,' said Marwood. 'We need to find the student quarter and sort out somewhere to stay tonight.'

They wandered off past street stalls and pavement bars where, despite the chill of the northern climate, throngs of laughing, chattering people congregated to drink beer and gossip. The acrid smell of the smoke from the burning torches mixed with the alluring aroma of char-grilling kebabs and barbecuing meats. They stopped briefly at a stall to buy a couple of *velakis*, small, succulent goat-meat kebabs wrapped in soft, flat bread, and then leant on the counter of a pavement bar called DT's Choose 'n' Booze to have a glass of beer and to ask the way. Marwood too was a little surprised to see the hostile looks they got at the mention of the University, but Tarl, who had spent most of his life attracting such looks, thought nothing of it.

The beer, an orcish brew called Old Organs, was remarkably good, and the two of them decided that the first thing they ought to do in the student quarter was to find a decent inn and check out its beer before booking rooms. They set off down the side street indicated by the bar-tender and found that it brought them out beside the river. Ahead of them, a gently arching footbridge spanned the dark, fast-flowing waters. They ambled across it to the other side and Tarl paused, seeming to Marwood to be almost sniffing the air.

'What are you doing?' he asked, puzzled.

'Just checking the vibes,' answered Tarl. He grinned up at the tall ex-Assassin. 'Good pubs put out an aura. They almost call to you. I'm just . . .' He paused, his head tilted delicately to one side. 'Ah, now I think we might have something here. Come on.'

The ground sloped steeply up from the river, and dark, silent buildings crowded the slope, looming up into the night sky above them. A tree-lined road ran from left to right along the river embankment, and a side street ran away from it up the hill between the buildings, but Tarl led Marwood to a narrow alley that led off the embankment at an angle, snaking between two dark, shuttered houses to become a steep flight of steps that led up the hill. These they climbed, their footsteps echoing eerily back off the stone walls. Cats hissed and yowled at each other behind a rickety wooden

12 Christian the Cross was a talented but short-tempered fashion designer from Ilex who created what was known as the Christian Look (something between a grimace and a snarl).

gate as they passed, and when Marwood accidentally kicked a bottle lying on the ground it spun away from his feet with what seemed like enough noise to wake the whole town. After more than two hundred steps the alley levelled out, curving around the back of a circular building that might have been a small temple, and then it emerged on to a dark street that was lit by a single torch on a wall some thirty yards to their left. Marwood paused uncertainly, but Tarl turned left without the slightest hesitation and strode confidently down the street, so Marwood followed him.

The buildings around them were silent and unlit, but they could hear a distant hum of voices. A few yards beyond the torch another street branched off to the right, and as they turned along it they saw the noise was coming from a brightly lit tavern some fifty yards away on the right. Tarl grinned happily.

'That's the place,' he said. 'Come on.'

Unusually, there was no pub sign hanging outside the tavern, but a roughly painted board above the door told them that they were about to enter Intoxy Kate's, the Home of Good Hooch. As they opened the door, light, sound and warmth flooded out, and they found themselves engulfed in a jostling sea of laughing, shouting revellers.

The tavern was a large single room with a wide bar running almost the entire length of the back wall. Down one side ran a spearboard alley, and both end walls had large stone fireplaces in which log fires roared. Tables and chairs were randomly dotted about, although these appeared to be used purely for placing drinks on (the tables) or standing on (the tables *and* the chairs). Marwood breathed in and instantly caught the distinctive aromatic smell of elfweed. He grinned happily. The place seemed just about perfect.

Then a discordant but recognisable noise started up over to their right. In between the fireplace and the end of the bar was a battered old piano, and someone was plonking out a happy rhythm that was so out of tune it could have harmonised perfectly with Tarl on one of his less melodious days.

Marwood and Tarl pushed their way through the crowd to the bar and ordered a couple of tankards of Old Organs. It was only when the barman trotted away to get their drinks that Tarl realised he was a centaur. He stared, incredulous, for he had only once before seen a member of this rare, shy race, who mainly inhabited the eastern plains beyond the Irridic Mountains. Then he realised that the group of people next to them were grinning at his reaction.

There were three young men and a couple of girls, and Tarl guessed from their ages that they were students.

'Hey,' smiled one of them, a girl of about twenty, 'what do you think of our Garresh, then?'

'Garresh?' said Tarl. 'Is he the barman? I'm impressed!'

'But I'm surprised to find a centaur doing bar work,' added Marwood. 'I wouldn't have thought he was suited.'

'You'd better believe it!' she responded. 'He's the best. The cocktail king. The Head Hooch Honcho.'

One of her companions, a long-haired youth who had busily been building an elfweed cigarette, looked up.

'S'right,' he told them. 'You should see him on a busy night. He's got two hands and four hooves, see. He can mix your cocktail and kick the shit out of troublemakers at the same time!'

He gave the cigarette paper one last lick and rolled the spliff firmly between his fingers before handing it to the girl. Tarl leant forwards.

'*Fiat ignis*,' he said. A small blue flame sprang into life on the end of his thumb, and he reached out and lit the end of the cigarette for her.

'Hey,' she said, obviously impressed, 'can you actually speak Magic language?'

'*Ursa in silvis defaecetatet?*' replied Tarl, smirking horribly. Then he added, 'Ow! Ouch!' and turned away from the girl's laughing blue eyes rather hurriedly, to talk to the maker of the cigarette.

The night became a little confused after that. Tarl and Marwood merged with the group of students, who appeared to know nearly everyone in the tavern. There seemed to be a large number of drinks being bought, and Tarl was enjoying himself so much that he even bought his round. Some time around midnight there was a mass exodus, and everyone drifted along to a party in a nearby house. And so it was that at about two in the morning, Tarl and Marwood found themselves sitting cross-legged on a carpeted floor together, leaning back against the wall.

Marwood was building a very large elfweed cigarette, and Tarl was watching, fascinated, because it seemed to involve the use of an awful lot of cigarette papers and concentration.

'What on earth are you making?' he asked, carefully.

Marwood gave one last twirl to the thick, cone-shaped construction and held it up for the impressed Tarl to inspect.

'That,' he said proudly, 'is what is known to the cognoscenti as a Welbug Wizard's Hat.'

'Why,' asked Tarl very carefully, to make sure that he got it right, 'why do the cog-that's-empty call it a Welbug Wizard's Hat?'

Marwood lit the fat end and carefully inhaled a lungful of the aromatic smoke.

'Because,' he gasped, when he had finally finished coughing, 'I invented it in Welbug, and it looks like a wizard's hat.'

He took another drag and offered it to Tarl, but the latter didn't seem to notice. He was staring at a group of students on the other side of the room like a hobbit staring at a plate of cream buns. Marwood followed his gaze, but he could see nothing unusual about them. They just appeared to be five students sitting there playing cards . . .

'Oh, wow!' breathed Tarl. 'Wow. Oh, wow!'

'What is it?'

'It's a gift from the gods, that's what it is. A game of cards. With students! And they're using an elven deck! I think I'll join them.'

'What do you want to be playing cards for?'

Tarl thought back to the bright-orange robe he had seen in the window of Brothers in Alms. 'Because I have a very expensive habit to fund,' he replied. 'Look, I'll see you later, okay?'

With the smile of a *lenkat* closing in on a flock of sheep, Tarl stood up and strolled across the floor towards the card-players, and Marwood leant back against the wall, took another inhalation and concentrated on trying to stop the room from spinning around his head quite so fast.

The sun was well above the horizon when Ronan was awakened by a sudden gasp and sat bolt upright in bed to find that Guebral's spell had worked perfectly. The cleaning maid was lying flat-out unconscious by the door, a large bundle of clean bed-linen beside her. Sighing, Ronan got up and gave his face a desultory wash. He was feeling tired, lonely and miserable, and although he was desperate to get down to the University and find out whether he would be accepted on the MA course, he was also apprehensive about sticking his head into the dragon's lair quite so blatantly. Assassins had the unfortunate habit of cutting off heads without the slightest warning.

After a preoccupied, brief and untasted breakfast during which he said precisely three words to Guebral ('What?', 'Eh?' and 'Huh?'), they set out together for Tannery Mead. Even though his fears had lessened in the bright light of day, Ronan still felt acutely vulnerable in the crowded streets. As part of his disguise he had abandoned the broadsword that he always wore slung down his back, southern fashion, and was carrying a lighter sword in a sheath hanging from his belt. It seemed like a toothpick in comparison and he felt grossly under-armed, but now he looked no different from most of the other students who scurried hither and thither, and nobody seemed to give him a second glance.

They arrived at the Faculty of Assassination without mishap, and spent almost an hour waiting for someone to see them, but once they had been allowed in to see the Admissions Secretary things moved a lot faster. Ronan explained that he was a late applicant for the MA course, Guebral exerted the lightest amount of pressure through an *Acquiesce* spell, and half an hour, a session of form-filling and three more quick interviews later they found themselves being ushered into the Dean's office.

Ronan was by now almost shaking with nerves. He was used to the straightforward dangers of battle, but this slow, creeping fear of being recognised was a different matter, and he almost felt that he would welcome the moment when his anonymity was torn from him and he could get down to the normal, everyday business of fighting for his life. However, he need not have worried. His disguise, aided by a subtle and undetectable *Blurring* from Guebral, appeared to work perfectly, and the Dean, although a Master of Assassins and a member of the Guild, didn't seem in the least suspicious.

Dean Blackwell was, in fact, rather preoccupied, and was staring out of his office window as they entered. He was a tall, thin, gloomy man with a stooped posture and an almost apologetic air. He was wearing academic rather than Assassin dress (although his black gown had the silver tracery around the neck that was peculiar to the Assassins' Guild), and his office was so cluttered with books, scrolls and parchments that there was hardly space to move, let alone sit down.

'Mm, yes, come, come,' he muttered absently, as they paused in the doorway, and then turned his attention back to the window. 'Look at that!' he added. 'Dean Holdsworth shouldn't allow it, he really shouldn't!'

Ronan hovered nervously in front of the desk, scared to go too close lest he be recognised, but Guebral picked her way between the piles of books to stand next to the Dean and peered out of the window. They were on the second floor, and she found that she was gazing across a small, neat garden towards another lower but wider building. It looked considerably older, and its ancient red-tiled roof had four gaping holes in it. Three of them had obviously been there a while, but the fourth was plainly recent, for the broken tiles and splintered timbers had fresh, raw edges. Smoke was eddying out of this hole, and Guebral could see people hopping around outside the building and pointing.

'It's the Faculty of Alchemy,' said the Dean, by way of explanation. 'They carry out far too much dangerous research there. That's the third large explosion this year. Holdsworth says that it's a matter of finance, and that unless they can find a way of transmuting base metal into gold they will be forced to close down the Faculty. Waste of time, I call it. They've been searching for twenty years now, and all they've managed to do is find a way of transmuting base metal into a dirty great hole in the roof!'

'Can't the Faculty of Magic help them?' asked Guebral, who had spent the time in the waiting room reading the University prospectus, and had been quite impressed by its claims for that particular department.

'Probably, if we could only find it.' The Dean turned away from the window and fixed her with a baleful stare. 'Trouble is, they're a clannish lot, Dean Saunders and those wizards of his. They made the whole flaming faculty building vanish three years ago, after a row about overspending. We know it must be round here somewhere, because they keep turning up in the Student Union Bar wearing those smug bloody smiles of theirs, but can we find it? Can we hell! Dean Sturridge of Sociology reckons they've hidden it inside his faculty building because his students keep on mysteriously vanishing, but you know what sociology students are like. I mean, if you'd been going to sociology lectures for two years, wouldn't you be tempted to slip quietly away?'

Guebral shrugged, and Ronan, who had never even heard of sociology but thought it might be something to do with darning, nodded uncertainly. Dean Blackwell threw one more sour glance at the roof of the Faculty of Alchemy, then turned and began to go through some papers on his desk.

'So,' he mumbled, 'you want to join our MA course, do you, er . . . um . . .' His voice trailed away, but then he pounced with an exclamation of triumph on a form that had been on top of all the other papers. 'Ah, here we are! Er, Rhand, that's it. So, you want to become an Assassin, do you, Rhand?'

He looked up from the form and studied Guebral doubtfully, and she smiled back at him and pointed to Ronan.

'That's Rhand. I'm just a friend.'

'Ah, right. Yes. Exactly.' He switched his attention to Ronan and smiled benignly. 'So, Rhand, tell me. Why do you want to become an Assassin?'

'Well . . .' Ronan paused. He felt he ought to talk to a Master of Assassins about the joy of killing or some such thing, but Marwood had coached him carefully in what he claimed would be the right answer to this question, and so he took a deep breath and launched into his rehearsed reply.

'As a warrior, I'm used to plain, simple killing, and I find it unsatisfying. I want more than that. I want to study the myriad ways and means of the professional assassin, to delve into the, er, the psychology of the killer, to investigate the interrelationship between the hunter and his prey. I want to research in depth the history of assassination, and to see if I cannot, in my own small way, add something to the sum total of human knowledge of the subject . . .'

He paused, hoping that he hadn't got it wrong, but he needn't have worried. The Dean was smiling broadly.

'Excellent!' he said. 'A theorist! Do you know, we get so many people applying who just want an excuse to go round massacring folk. You're just what we're looking for. You are a little late, though. The course started a couple of weeks ago.'

'Yes, I'm sorry about that. I was on my way here when the Shikara wars broke out down south. The Iduinian Guard needed every mercenary they could get, so I thought I ought to do my bit. But I was wounded at the Battle of Grey Sea Fields. It's only just healed.'

Ronan was uncomfortable with lying and his unease clearly showed, but the Dean appeared to misread it as simple heroic modesty.

'Capital, capital.' He smiled, and glanced briefly at Ronan's forged papers. 'Well, your references are excellent. I'm sure we can find room for you . . .'

He was interrupted by a knock on the door, which swung open before he could answer to reveal a small boy of about four standing there, his big eyes roaming round the room to settle wonderingly on Ronan before swinging back to the Dean.

'Are you busy, Grandpa?' he asked. The Dean smiled fondly at him.

'No, these people are just going, Jack,' he answered. 'You can come in.' He smiled fondly as the little boy toddled across the floor towards him. 'My grandson,' he added, by way of explanation. 'I

160

promised I'd take him to the canteen for lunch. He just loves their chips. But yes, if you'd care to be at the Faculty Office tomorrow at eight, I'll make all the necessary arrangements. Now, if you'll excuse me . . .'

Ronan and Guebral thanked him and quietly made their way out, closing the door behind them. The Dean sat down in his chair on top of a number of papers and allowed the little boy to scramble happily on to his knee. He smiled at his grandson absently, but then the smile left his face and he gazed thoughtfully at the door that had just closed behind his visitors.

'Well, well,' he murmured. 'How interesting. How very interesting. I wonder. I think maybe we'd better find someone else to look after you tomorrow morning, Jack. Grandpa might have proper work to do . . .'

And if Ronan had been able to see the cold and calculating look on the Dean's face, he would have had second thoughts about coming anywhere near the Faculty of Assassination ever again . . .

Marwood was awakened by something digging him insistently in the ribs, and woke up to find that Tarl was prodding him with his foot. Squinting to minimise the amount of painfully bright daylight that his poor eyes had to deal with, he peered blearily round. He was lying propped against the wall in a sea of cigarette ends, empty bottles and mugs, and crashed-out people. He began to shake his head to clear it but stopped immediately, as it felt as though someone had gone and nailed the ceiling to the floor. Picking up the mug of beer that he had been drinking from the previous night he took a swig of the dregs to try and get rid of the foul taste in his mouth, then spat it straight out again, as four stubbed-out cigarette ends were floating in it. To his horror, only three came back out of his mouth.

Squeezing his eyes shut for a moment and ignoring the appalling pain in his head, he tried to work out what it was about the room that was bothering him. Something had changed. Then the realisation hit him and he sat up and rubbed his eyes in disbelief. Tarl was now wearing a bright-orange habit with lime-green swirls and a little green *alaxl* embroidered on the left breast.

'*Klat!* Where did you get that?'

'Won it. From him,' smirked Tarl, jerking his thumb over his shoulder to indicate a body that had crashed out by the couch and was flat on his back, snoring loudly. He was a short-haired individual with long tapered sideburns, and was wearing Tarl's old habit. One hand still clutched a beer bottle and the other rested on his chest with a burnt-out cigarette between the fingers that had a fragile, two-inch tower of ash still somehow attached.

'Who is he?'

'A Seventh Day Hedonist, at a guess. Anyway, he sure likes to party. He joined the card game at about three o'clock, lost most of his money, then got a really good hand – a prile of kittens.[13] His habit was all he had left to bet with. Sadly for him, I had a prile of bunnies. But I have to admire the guy. I would have run away or cheated or something, but he just swapped clothes without a murmur, opened another beer and tried to chat up this gorgeous blonde girl.'

'So you won, then?'

Tarl smiled and drew his hand out from the recesses of the habit. He was holding a leather pouch which was stuffed to bursting with coins.

'I love students, they're always eager to learn. I taught them how to play Guts. Great game, but you need to know what you're doing, and they didn't. If they hadn't all passed out by five o'clock I'd probably own this house by now.'

Marwood tried to focus on Tarl's garish habit, but his eyes weren't having any. It was far too vivid for them to cope with in their current state, so they simply closed and refused to open again. Tarl sighed, took hold of Marwood's shoulder and shook him roughly.

'Listen, bollocks, it's after midday and we have to be going.' Tarl paused and waited until his friend had finished groaning, before continuing. 'I've been in touch with Gueb, and she and Ronan are going to meet us at a restaurant in an hour. I don't know about you, but I need something to eat.' He paused again, and a mischievous smile crept over his face. 'Snails in garlic butter, perhaps, and a raw oyster or two.'

One of Marwood's hands flew up to clutch at his mouth, and his eyes opened and stared beseechingly at Tarl.

'Some liver, and a couple of lightly poached kidneys . . .'

Marwood made a noise like a bullfrog with heavy catarrh clearing its throat.

'. . . or perhaps some sweetbreads on a bed of tripe . . .'

Tarl paused again and stared after the ex-Assassin as he vanished into the toilet, making strange heaving noises. *Marwood's an okay*

13 *For the details of elven cards, see Appendix Two.*

162

guy, he thought, *but he's going to have to do a bit better than this if he's going to keep up over the next few weeks. There's a lot of serious fun to be had in this town.* And he tossed the pouch of coins nonchalantly up and down, and thought happily about seeing Guebral again.

The maître d'hôtel of Le Bâtard Gros stared suspiciously at the two men who had just walked through the front doors of what was generally accepted to be Gudmornen's top restaurant, like someone staring at an unpleasant stain. One was small and balding, and was wearing a Seventh Day Hedonist habit which was a couple of sizes too big, and the other was tall and pale, looked extremely ill and was clad in a plain brown hessian habit which appeared to have been slept in and which had something down the front that looked suspiciously like vomit. As they wandered towards a window table, he intercepted them quickly.

'Yes?' he said, in a voice that could have frozen oxygen.

'We'd like a table, please,' said Tarl. 'Well, not just a table, we want some food as well.'

'Do you have reservations?' he asked haughtily.

'Not half,' answered Tarl, 'but when you're as hungry as we are, you'll eat anywhere.'

The maître d'hôtel was just about to politely request them to remove their shitty little carcasses from his restaurant when the taller one lifted his hand tiredly and showed him a glimpse of a card that was discreetly hidden in the cupped palm. The maître d'hôtel swallowed nervously. It was an ImEx card, jet black with silver writing on it, and he didn't need to read it to know that the bearer must be a member of the Guild of Assassins. ImEx stood for Imminent Execution, and the card was usually produced as a warning that if you didn't stop *klatting* about very quickly indeed, you were likely to suffer an extremely rapid demise.

One minute later Marwood and Tarl were in a window-seat with a carafe of red wine (compliments of the house) on the table. Marwood was slumped forward with his hands covering his face. Tarl waved the hovering waiter away, poured himself a large glass and then leant forward conspiratorially.

'Marwood, you in there?'

Marwood's whole body seemed to tremble, and then his fingers parted slowly and two bloodshot eyes peered out from behind them. Tarl splashed a little wine into his glass as well and tried not to grin.

163

'Come on, drink it. It will do you good, honest.'

Marwood put out a shaking hand, grasped the glass and threw the wine back with all the eagerness of someone plunging a dagger into their own stomach.

'Right,' said Tarl. 'Now, when Guebral and Ronan get here, we don't acknowledge them, okay? Gueb told me that they've been to the Faculty of Assassination, and your stuff worked. Ronan's on the course. But just in case, they want to make sure that he hasn't been recognised, and so they're going to eat here. We watch to see if anyone is following them, and when they leave, we check again to see if they're still clean. You're our trump card when it comes to recognising undercover Assassins, and we need you functioning. So how are you feeling? Here, you haven't half gone a funny colour . . .'

Marwood's face had changed from an unhealthy white to a greyish yellow, like a three-month-old rice pudding, and his voice when he spoke sounded as though it was coming out of the soles of his feet.

'I'll be all right. Don't get me any food, but if the waiter could find me a couple of dozen aspirin, I wouldn't mind.'

Tarl smiled, then picking up the menu he gave it his undivided attention for a while before ordering a starter of grilled *velakis*, and a large helping of *mulampos*, the lethally hot meat dish, to follow. Then he sat back, leisurely sipping his wine, and watched the passers-by in the street outside whilst Marwood fell asleep with his head resting in the bread basket.

Three-quarters of an hour passed, and Tarl was just mopping up the last of the *mulampos* with a rather hairy piece of bread, when Marwood woke up again. The short sleep seemed to have helped, for he now looked if not quite like a human being, at least as though he might once have been one. He lifted his head and cleared his throat so loudly and thoroughly that diners at nearby tables grimaced and pushed their plates away, suddenly not hungry. A waiter, fearful that something unpleasant might be about to occur, came dashing across, and Marwood grabbed hold of his sleeve.

'Eggs,' he ordered, hoarsely. Then he shook his head, showering the waiter with breadcrumbs. 'And bacon. And aspirins. And sausages. And more bacon, and some mushrooms, and plenty of toast. And bacon. Oh, and a large pot of tea.'

'Tea?' queried the waiter.

'Oh, well, wine, then, if you insist. Just don't forget the bacon, okay?'

Marwood released the waiter's sleeve, turned him to face the kitchens and gave him a gentle shove to help him on his way. Then he gave Tarl what might just, by a large stretch of the imagination, have been a smile.

'When your stomach is in revolt,' he muttered, 'I believe in letting it know just who's the boss.'

'I'm impressed!'

'Yeah, sure. This from a man who appears to have eaten a large bowl of *mulampos*, and at three o'clock in the afternoon, too. By the gods, your bowels must hate you!'

Marwood was about to expand on this theme when he realised that Tarl's face had gone blank and preoccupied in a way that he was coming to realise meant that Guebral was in touch through one of their magical communication spells. Tarl nodded absently a couple of times, as though agreeing with something, and then his eyes suddenly focused again and he looked at Marwood.

'They're almost here. Don't forget, we don't take the slightest bit of notice of them, but we keep our eyes open for anyone else who might be, okay? And when they leave, we follow them, but a long way behind.'

A minute later, Ronan and Guebral entered, and wandered across to a table near the rear of the restaurant, apparently without even noticing the scruffy pair seated by the window. Tarl and Marwood were poised and ready for any eventuality, but they needn't have bothered. No one took the slightest bit of notice as the other two entered, and no one followed them in. No one even walked along the street outside. They sat quietly at their table and ordered some food, and shortly afterwards, Marwood's late breakfast arrived. He made short work of it, clearing his plate completely, and then he and Tarl finished the wine while the waiter took the plates away. The others were still eating, and so Tarl and Marwood chatted desultorily and stared out of the window.

After a while, the maître d'hôtel appeared again and began to hover near their table, obviously hoping that they were about to leave.

'Anything wrong?' Tarl asked him in his politest voice.

'Oh, no, sir. I was just wondering, er, if, er . . . if sir would like pudding.'

'Ooh, I don't know. I've never been pudded.' Tarl grinned as this riposte had its desired effect and the maître d'hôtel retired, shrugging fatalistically to the cowering waiter and leaving them alone.

Half an hour later, after another mental message from Guebral, Tarl called the tremulous waiter across and settled the bill. He and

Marwood waited whilst the other two left, but once again no one appeared to be taking the slightest notice of them, and so after giving them a two-minute start and leaving a tip so sizeable that the waiter's eyebrows disappeared over the top of his head, Tarl led the way out into the street.

'Now what?' asked Marwood, who had improved so much that he just looked ill, instead of looking as though he had died two months previously.

'We follow them for a while and keep our eyes open. Then we head down to wherever the Merchants' Guildhall is. Tyson and Puss should be here by six, and that's where we said we'd meet them.'

'And then?'

'And then,' said Tarl, looking at Marwood's pale face and still-shaking hands, and trying unsuccessfully to hide a grin, 'and then we head back to Intoxy Kate's for another night of fun. Hey, are you all right? Was it something I said . . .?'

Tyson and Puss had made good time travelling to Gudmornen, arriving in mid-afternoon. They too were in disguise. Tyson had borrowed yet another of the monks' habits, and was wrapped up in a voluminous black cloak that Brother Bursitis had given her. Puss the donkey just looked like any other small brown donkey, but it was its usual behaviour that was the dead giveaway, and so it was under strict instructions to act differently. Tyson had told it that it was not to say a word to anyone, even under extreme provocation, and that if someone gave it a carrot or some hay it was to eat the proffered gift with every appearance of enjoyment. If it failed to follow these simple instructions, she told it, she would go to a health-food shop, buy a month's supply of tofu and force-feed it to the donkey, with a large side helping of miso. The donkey had no idea what tofu or miso were, but they sounded truly appalling, and so it had been on its best behaviour, following Tyson docilely into the city and standing patiently outside the front of a coffee shop while she sat inside drinking a quick cappuccino and absorbing the atmosphere.

Tyson had always found this to be one of the best ways of finding out what was happening in a town. An hour spent just sitting and listening to the surrounding gossip was never wasted. Frequently you just picked up a few scurrilous rumours, but if anything serious was happening in town you heard about it. And today, there seemed to be one main subject that each little group of customers got on to, sooner or later, and that was the University.

166

The coffee bar she had chosen was a small place near the main gate, and was apparently a fair way from the student quarter. Its customers were simple townsfolk, and they all seemed a little in awe of the University and its denizens. However, there seemed to be three things that everyone was agreed on. Firstly, they were a strange lot, these University folk, and not to be trusted. Secondly, they were probably responsible for all the recent goings-on, and that something ought to be done about it. And thirdly, that if there were any more of these goings-on, then the rest of the town would just have to march up there and show them that they wouldn't stand for it.

By the time Tyson left the coffee shop, she had come to the conclusion that whatever had been happening in the town recently, the average person thought it was something to do with the scientists up at the University. It was fairly clear that they were pretty aggrieved about this, and it seemed that a lynch-mob was highly likely to march up to the University and exact a strong revenge if anything further occurred.

Wondering exactly what it was that had been happening, Tyson set off down the road with Puss behind her, following the path that she had been told would take her to the Merchants' Guildhall, where she had arranged to make contact with the others. It was beginning to get dark now, and the City Torch-lighters were out, dragging their cartloads of fresh street-torches around their habitual routes and replacing the previous night's burnt-out remains with new, freshly lit ones. The streets were crowded with people and she began to hurry, worried that she might have tarried in the coffee shop too long and would be late.

However, it didn't take more than a few minutes before they came to a large cobbled square and saw in front of them the imposing red-stone building that was the headquarters of the Merchants' Guild. Flags bearing the coats of arms of the three main merchant families of Gudmornen hung above the vast double doors, and richly dressed Guild members scurried up and down the broad steps leading up to the colonnaded front, or lingered in gossiping groups nearby. Four men-at-arms stood at the foot of the steps, keeping the beggars, street-walkers, life insurance salesmen and other riff-raff well clear of the richest businessmen as they braved the pavement between the safety of the hall and the opulent luxury of their private carriages.

Tyson found a spot by the foot of the steps, near one corner of the Guildhall, where she could see what was going on throughout the square, and lowered the hood of her cloak so that the others would be able to recognise her. At first, no one took any notice of her, but it wasn't long before she began to get the feeling that she was being watched. She looked around casually and found that one of the merchants gossiping on the steps nearby was leering at her. He was younger than his companions and was expensively dressed, with thick gold jewellery around his neck and fingers, and the hilt of his sword was encrusted with silver and gemstones. His face, however, was thick-lipped and fleshy, and his gaze looked cruel and cold. His eyes met hers and he grinned, and she suddenly realised that, dressed as she was and with her head uncovered, he was not seeing a warrior, but a young, attractive and, above all, unaccompanied woman.

He whispered something to his friends, who looked in her direction and laughed coarsely, and then, to her disgust, he began to walk towards her. *Klat,* she thought, *just what I need. If Ronan turns up now he'll kill this guy . . .*

The merchant walked up to her and made a deep bow that was apparently meant to impress but which just made her want to squirm. He reached out one podgy, gold-laden hand to take her arm, and his dark, slicked-back hair glistened in the light of nearby street-torches.

'Good evening, milady,' he oozed. 'Perhaps you would care to walk with me a while?'

'No, thank you,' replied Tyson, removing his hand gently but firmly from her elbow, but he ignored the hint. Smiling humourlessly he moved closer to her, crowding her a little, and she could smell the sweet aroma of expensive hair-oil. There was something unpleasantly greasy about him that set her nerves on edge. It was like being hemmed in by an oil-slick.

'Perhaps I can change your mind. Surely you can spend an hour or two with me – if I make it worth your while?'

He took hold of her elbow again, more insistently, and Tyson suddenly realised that he had no intention of taking no for an answer. Angrily, she shook his hand off a second time.

'I said no thank you,' she said firmly, but she could tell from the half-amused, half-annoyed expression on his face that mere words were not going to be enough.

'But I'm sure you didn't really mean it,' he said, and he was about to grab her again when something took hold of his hand. Looking down he saw that a small brown donkey with angry red eyes had fastened its rather sharp-looking teeth gently but firmly around his fingers.

'Listen, pal,' it said through clenched teeth, 'if you don't *klat* off right now and stop bothering my friend, I'll bite off all the fingers of your right hand and ruin your sex life for you.'

The merchant stared at Puss with a mixture of anger and amazement.

'Or would you rather I bit your minuscule dick off?' added the donkey, before he could speak, and then it increased the pressure of its jaws ever so slightly.

'Ow! All right!' he gasped, and the donkey relaxed its grip enough for him to pull his fingers free. He backed away a couple of steps, rubbing them and looking daggers first at Puss and then at Tyson. 'Foul witch!' he spat out. 'Get gone from here before I set the guards on you!' And, turning, he strode up the steps to the Guildhall doors.

Tyson sighed with relief, then turned angrily on the donkey.

'I told you to keep silent!' she hissed.

'Look, you were going to have to fight him off,' it replied, 'and then you'd have been recognised. You're too distinctive. And where Tyson is, people will look for Ronan. This way, he thinks you're a witch, so we haven't broken our cover. And no one else is going to guess. He's not going to go round telling people he was frightened by a donkey. It won't fit nicely with his macho image of himself . . .'

Tyson was going to argue further, but at that moment she caught sight of a familiar face on the other side of the square. It was Ronan, and at the sight of him, her heart did its usual little skip and flutter. He was standing talking to Guebral, but his face was towards Tyson, and as she looked across he gave her the faintest of winks. A few seconds later, she saw Tarl and Marwood wander past him, deep in conversation. In fact she could hardly have missed Tarl, for the brilliant-orange habit that he was wearing stuck out like a boil on a nun's neck. They strolled across the square and exited along a street on the eastern side, and Ronan and Guebral turned and followed them at a distance.

Tyson bent down and scratched the donkey's ears.

'Come on,' she said. 'It looks as though Tarl is going to lead us somewhere where we can all get together in safety.'

'Bet it's a pub,' muttered the donkey under its breath, but it followed Tyson quietly as she set off at a rapid pace, eager to meet up with the others again.

Beneltin finished cleaning the last of the latrine floors that he had been assigned to for that day, and clambered wearily to his feet. It had been a long, tiring and infinitely depressing day, and he was glad that it was almost over. He would be able to wander down to the Seam of Gold and have a few beers, although he'd be virtually on his own down there, as most of the other dwarf scientists were busy. For tonight they were carrying out the largest raid so far.

By the gods, it was so unfair! If he hadn't been arrested, he'd be going on the raid to Gudmornen, and it was the Stand and Deliver Club's Amateur Night! The raid was planned to last a full thirty minutes, and he would have had plenty of time to find his way to the club, get on stage and try out his act. It might have been his last chance, as well, for Meiosin had hinted that if they got enough prisoners for experimentation, this would be the last of these raids for a good while.

Angrily, he threw his scrubbing brush into the bucket, picked up his mop and wandered across to the door. The corridor outside was deserted, for all the dwarves would have been in the Transmitter Room by now, and Beneltin began to slouch dispiritedly along it towards the cleaning stores. Then he paused. He could hear the rhythmic clanking sound of someone trying to move fast inside a suit of armour.

He turned and looked back as a figure came into view around a corner behind him. It was Mitosin, wearing the distinctive Valdar armour, and carrying his helmet under one arm. He had obviously got caught up in one of his experiments and failed to notice the time, and was now scurrying down to the Transmitter Room, late. Beneltin moved to the side to let him pass, and lifted his arm in the salute that a dwarf traditionally gave a superior dressed for battle. To his chagrin, Mitosin ignored him, trotting clumsily past without even giving him the slightest of acknowledgements, and all of a sudden Beneltin saw red. One moment he was standing respectfully to one side as Mitosin passed him, the next moment he was whirling his mop handle round in a vicious arc to thump home on the back of the dwarf's unprotected skull. There was a loud crack, and Mitosin collapsed with a clatter to the ground, unconscious.

For several seconds Beneltin stared at him, aghast at what he had done, and then reaching down he picked up Mitosin's helmet and looked at it. Like all the other helms, it had the clan's signature rune, $\angle\cap$, painted on the side, but Mitosin had also added his own distinguishing rune, $L_\equiv$, so that he could be clearly recognised when wearing it. At the sight of this, the plan that must have been rattling round in Beneltin's subconscious when he knocked Mitosin out suddenly leapt into the forefront of his brain, and with shaking hands he leant down and began to loosen the straps that held the other dwarf's armour in place.

Meiosin was fuming. This was the biggest raid he had planned so far, and there were a number of new items and inventions that needed to be tested under field conditions, in particular a new throwing explosive that Alchemy had come up with. He wanted good results to show to the Orcbane board when they arrived, and he needed a full stock of captives for the demonstrations that he had planned, but as soon as he had briefed his dwarf troops he had been faced with a virtual rebellion. Once again, there had been all this talk about the moral aspect of conducting experiments on sentient beings, and he had been forced to bully, cajole and threaten until at last his troops grudgingly filed into the Transmitter Room, ready to carry out his orders. And now they stood waiting, muttering discontentedly amongst themselves, because the raid leader, Meiosin's very own brother, was late.

Mind you, Meiosin wasn't a bit surprised. If you wanted a reliable assistant chief scientist, Mitosin was perfect: full of good ideas for new lines of research, painstaking in his attention to detail and dedicated to the job on hand. But take him out of the laboratory and put him in the real world, and he was hopeless. Meiosin had seen zombies with a better grip on reality. He was probably holed up in the lab right now, lost in that experiment he'd been conducting on the next-generation zygotic frequencies in a panmictic population of Black Teaser spiders. Either that, or he was off playing with himself again, the dirty little beggar . . .

But then an armour-clad figure clunked through the door, and Meiosin heaved a sigh of relief. He rapped on the lecture podium to attract attention, ready to deliver the rousing little speech he had prepared, but to his surprise Mitosin didn't come across to stand at his side, but clunked his way to the front of the lined-up warriors. Before Meiosin could say a word, his brother had opened one of the gently humming transmitters, stepped into the booth and closed the door behind him. The scientist beside the machine pulled a couple of switches, the humming increased, and then a green light on top of the booth began flashing and he was gone.

Taking this as the signal to proceed, the four-hundred-strong dwarf army began filing forward and entering the booths. Mitosin hammered at the podium, desperately trying to attract their attention, but to no avail. The humming from the transmitters was so loud that it completely drowned him out, and he was forced to stand there and watch, his painstakingly prepared speech clutched tightly in his hands, until the last warrior had gone and the last green light had flashed off.

As the scientists fussed about the transmitters, checking and readying them for the army's return in half an hour, the furious Meiosin turned and strode out of the room, mouthing dire threats and promises to himself.

'I'll kill him,' he muttered. 'When he gets back here, I will *klatting* well kill that brother of mine.'

'What have I done now?' said a voice, and Meiosin turned to see Mitosin staggering towards him down the corridor. He was dressed only in his dwarven underwear (vest and short-johns) and had a dazed look in his eyes. Blood was streaming down his neck from a wound on the back of his head. He slumped to his knees, and Meiosin ran forwards to help him. But as he assisted his dazed brother to his feet, the same thought kept pounding through his mind. If Mitosin was here, who the hell was leading the raid on Gudmornen?

Despite an almost overwhelming urge to go running up to Ronan and hug him, Tyson had hung well back as she followed him and Guebral along the streets. She and Puss had shadowed the others down a side alley, across a footbridge over the river, into a narrow alley and up a seemingly endless set of stairs. Coming out at the top there had been no sign of them, but Puss had sniffed the air and the ground, and unhesitatingly turned left. Some forty yards ahead another street branched off to the right, and they reached this just in time to see Ronan and Guebral entering a large tavern.

'Told you,' whispered the donkey.

They walked along the street and round to the tavern's rear yard, where they found a stable block. It was just beginning to spit with rain. Through the open door they could see the ostler grooming one of the horses that had been left there.

'You're not going to tell me to wait out here, are you?' asked the donkey, disbelievingly.

'Normal donkeys just don't go into pubs and eat platefuls of *mulampos*. It would blow our cover.'

'Well, all right. But I'm not eating hay.'

They wandered through the door and the ostler looked up from his grooming and smiled. He was a small, toothless man with a wrinkled brown face and gentle eyes.

'Hello,' he said, and Tyson realised that he was talking to the donkey. To her relief, Puss had the sense not to answer.

'Can you look after my donkey for a few hours?' she asked.

'Sure. Ah, now, you look a bit on the hungry side to me, he said, stroking Puss's neck. 'And I've a feeling you'll not be thanking me for carrots or straw for your tea.' He paused, his head on one side as he looked at the donkey thoughtfully. 'I'm thinking that you've probably shared some proper food in your lifetime,' he went on. 'How would it be if I slipped across to the kitchens and fetched you a plate of stew?'

Tyson had never, even seen a donkey grin quite so widely before. It was obvious that Puss was in safe hands, and so she turned and walked across the quiet, deserted yard through the rain to the tavern's rear door. From inside she could hear the sound of laughing and talking, and someone was playing an out-of-tune piano very badly. Although she had never been here before in her life, she knew that Ronan and the others were inside, and all of a sudden it felt as though she was coming home. With a happy glow inside her, she opened the door and went in.

The large single room of the tavern was packed from wall to wall with people, all intent on having a seriously good time. Nearby, Marwood and Tarl were talking to a group of what looked like students. It was plain that they had already met, for she could hear one of the boys warning the others not to play cards with Tarl, who was grinning and trying to look modest, but totally failing. She wondered what Guebral would make of this, for a couple of the girls were flirting with him.

'Is it true what Lanja was saying?' asked one. 'Can you really speak the magic language?'

Tarl shrugged, affecting nonchalance.

'Pontifex petasum comicum geratet!' he replied.

Tyson winced, but then she saw Ronan and Guebral over by the bar, and the wince turned into a gasp of astonishment. Gueb was watching Tarl with an amused grin, so she obviously didn't mind him flirting, but the thing that took Tyson's breath away was the fact that Ronan was talking to a couple of centaurs. She had never seen one of these creatures before, let alone two, and was unprepared for their sheer beauty. The male had long brown hair and a short beard. His bare chest was broad and well muscled, and his equine

173

body was a deep chestnut. One powerful arm was about the shoulder of his female companion, whose hair was long, thick and blonde. Her face was beautiful, perhaps more beautiful than any human female that Tyson had ever seen, and her green eyes sparkled. She was wearing a bodice of blue, washed-out cotton that was laced up the front and covered a bosom so shapely that it would have put most human women to shame. Her equine body was smaller and slimmer than her male companion's, and was a light palomino in colouring. The overall effect was stunning, and Tyson stared at the pair of them, lost in admiration.

'Shame you didn't bring Puss in with you,' muttered a voice beside her. 'He and Marwood could have tried for a threesome with that centaur girl.'

Tyson sighed, the spell irretrievably shattered.

'You're a really sad man, Tarl, you know that?' she hissed.

'I do my best.'

She looked round, worriedly, but no one seemed to be watching them, and she turned back to find Tarl pressing a glass into her hand. He had an open bottle of Pouilly Varicait in the other hand, and he sloshed some into her glass.

'Don't worry,' he told her, quietly. 'No one's watching us in here. We're safe. They've already found out that I talk to everyone who comes in, especially if they're female.'

'Is Ronan okay? Has he got on the course?'

'Yeah, yeah. Everything's cool. They've accepted him, and he hasn't been recognised. Apart from the few in the University, there aren't any Assassins in the city. And Marwood says that once Ronan has officially signed on to the course, the University guys wouldn't touch him even if they found out who he is. It would be dishonourable or something.'

'So when does he sign on?'

'Tomorrow morning.' Tarl looked casually round, a happy smile on his face, and made an expansive gesture with the wine bottle. 'Right, we're openly in contact. I'm going to go and talk to Garresh, the male centaur over there. He works as the barman, but it's his day off, so he's in here with his girlfriend. That'll get me talking to Ronan. And if you go across to the bar, Gueb is going to get chatting to you. Then we're all openly in contact. Not that anyone in here gives a *klat*, but all this secrecy is making Ronan feel a bit less threatened, so Gueb says. Now, everybody in here is dead friendly, so you can talk to anyone. All you need to know is that the big bloke in the make-up at the end of the bar is Intoxy Kate, and she owns the joint.'

Tyson looked across and saw a big, muscly guy with tattooed arms, a long blonde wig and loads of make-up. He was wearing a dress, high heels and pendant earrings, but despite the feminine accoutrements, he looked as hard as nails.

'If you talk to her, remember to call her Kate. If she hears you call her "he" or "him" she'll throw you out, and you'll be barred. Okay?'

He smiled at her and then wandered off, grinning and nodding at everyone he passed, the very soul of conviviality. Tyson cast a quick glance at Ronan, who was talking animatedly to Garresh, and then at Guebral, who was listening carefully to something the female centaur was saying. They were both holding beer mugs that were already nearly empty. Nearby, Marwood was deep in conversation with a group of students, and he, like Tarl, was gesticulating with a half-empty wine bottle.

Tyson sighed, and began to push her way over to the bar, a little apprehensively. It looked as though it was going to be a long night, and she had a feeling that, once again, she might be regretting it in the morning.

Beneltin strode along Dog Street, peering at the myriad side alleys that ran off it and trying to work out which one was the one he wanted. He was shivering slightly, partly from nerves, but mainly because he was lightly dressed for a northern winter evening. He had thought it best to abandon Mitosin's armour, for this was the third raid on Gudmornen, and anyone wearing Valdar armour was likely to be about as welcome to the locals as a *megoceros* with diarrhoea.

He stopped and peered up at another street sign anxiously. He reckoned that he ought to have plenty of time, for he had been told that the transmitters homed in on something in the armour, and if you took it off they wouldn't be able to bring you back to Tor Deforzh. But he didn't know for certain that this was true, and he wanted to make sure that he got up on the stage before the half-hour was up. Meiosin and the others would lock him up for the rest of his life after this little escapade, and he wanted to make damn sure that it was all worth while.

There it was! Above the darkened window of a butcher's shop was a street sign telling him that the wide, cobbled alleyway on the left was Cur's Tea Alley. It was more like a narrow street than an alley, and was lit by a couple of guttering torches, one at either end. About halfway along he could see a striped barber's pole sticking out above a shop called, accurately enough, the Alley Barber, and next to that was the entrance to the Stand and Deliver Club itself.

All of a sudden, a series of large explosions went off in the distance, and the night sky seemed to light up. *Whoops*, thought Beneltin, *it looks as though the boys have started. Better get off the streets.*

He swallowed nervously. The doorway in front of him was open, and bare wooden stairs led down to the basement below the barber's, where the club was situated. There was no doorman or bouncer to be seen, but a fading notice pasted on the wall by the door proclaimed that every Friday night was Amateur Night at the Stand and Deliver. The sound of voices and the clink of glasses floated up the stairs on a thick stream of cigarette smoke and stale beer fumes, but he couldn't hear any laughter. Maybe they were between acts, or maybe they hadn't started yet. Maybe Amateur Night had been cancelled. Or maybe they were a *klatting* tough audience . . .

With his heart in his mouth, and the contents of his stomach threatening to join it, Beneltin walked through the door and down the stairs that led to the nearest thing he would ever have to a destiny.

It was about five minutes after Garresh's centaur girlfriend had said good night to everyone and left the tavern that the first explosions went off. Tyson was sitting in a quiet corner talking to Ronan and Tarl, and Marwood and Guebral were standing nearby, in a group that included Garresh and Intoxy Kate. The explosions were so loud and close that the tavern actually shook, and everyone in the place stopped talking. Then, as the noise faded, the door of the tavern opened and a man staggered in, blood streaming from a cut on his forehead.

'They're back again,' he yelled. 'The demons are back again!'

Tyson stared at Ronan and Tarl blankly.

'Demons? What's he talking about?'

'Apparently Gudmornen has been attacked twice before,' shouted Tarl, and then jerked his thumb at a pale, long-haired youth who was slumped in a corner, dead to the world. 'Grimtif over there told me that demons in black armour came and killed or stole away a lot of people. But then he also told me that he could see tiny red dragons running up and down my arms, so I didn't take a lot of notice.'

'The nutter in the fishing village told us that demons had

destroyed his village,' said Ronan. 'We'd better find out what's happening.'

He pushed his way through the milling, frightened customers with Tyson and Tarl behind him, and as he got to the door a second series of explosions broke out.

'What the *klat* is going down here?' he muttered as he yanked the door open and strode outside, but then at the sight that met his eyes, he stopped dead.

Just a couple of hundred yards away, the University seemed to be on fire. Flames were licking skywards, and the night was lit with a lurid red glare that was drowned out every few seconds by the blinding white flashes of further explosions. Already the smell of smoke was in the air, and they could hear distant screams, shouts and yells.

'Come on,' yelled Ronan, and drawing his sword he dashed down the street towards the distant turmoil, Tyson at his side, and Marwood, Tarl and Guebral following. As they passed the entrance to the stable yard, there was the sound of clattering hooves, and Puss came skidding out to chase after them.

The street curved down to the left, slightly away from the uproar at the University, until it opened on to a wider road lined with shops. This was full of fleeing, screaming, terrified people, all pushing and trampling anything that was in their way in their determination to escape whatever was causing the explosions. Ronan and the others turned right, forcing their way past the fleeing people until the crowd thinned and they were able to run again, their feet sliding and slipping on the rain-dampened cobbles in their haste. After fifty yards, the road opened into a small square, and they skidded to a halt and stared, horrified, at the sight before them.

A group of twenty or so dark, metallic figures were spread around the square in the midst of rubble, bodies and eddying smoke. Crates and boxes were strewn about them, and some of them were fiddling with strange, indecipherable bits of machinery. One group of three were clustered behind a gleaming metal tube that was angled away from them. At regular intervals one of them would drop something round into the top of the tube, which would make a deep *whump* sound, and a few seconds later there would be a distant explosion in the direction the tube was pointing.

Beyond them, on the far side of the square, three more were hurling small, round metal balls through shop windows and timing how long it took until an explosion blasted out the front of the shop.

They were leaving behind them a trail of burning and devastated buildings.

In the centre of the square, near a small fountain, four more dark figures were standing beside a couple of large cage-like crates which had been opened to release a pair of creatures that looked like a cross between rabbits and wolves. They were at least four feet long, with the powerful hindquarters of rabbits, but they had massive, vaguely lupine heads and strong jaws lined with horribly sharp teeth. They were leaping up and down beside a twelve-foot-high marble statue of an old University dean, trying to grab the legs of three students who were clinging to the dean's head, yammering with fear. Before Ronan and the others could move, one of the creatures caught a flailing leg and hauled its screaming owner down. Both creatures pounced on the unfortunate student, who disappeared in a welter of fur, teeth and blood. His two companions screamed and howled in absolute terror, but the four dark figures ignored them. They were watching the rabbit/wolves with dispassionate interest, and one of them seemed to be making notes on a clipboard.

'What *are* those things?' whispered Tyson.

'Whatever they are, they're not demons,' muttered Marwood. 'I've never heard of a demon that could afford Valdar armour.'

'Is that what it is?' Ronan asked him.

'Yeah. Just look at the lines of those helms. That's top-class gear, that is. But they're a bit small for humans.'

'They're dwarves!' yelled Tarl. 'They must be! Look, most of them have got battleaxes!'

'Then let's get the bastards!' growled Ronan, and he leapt forwards with Tyson and Marwood at his heels.

Tarl was about to go with them, but Guebral grabbed his arm.

'Wait!' she hissed. 'Can't you feel it? The air is buzzing with Power. We've got to keep our magic for when it's needed. Watch and be ready!'

The two of them moved forward cautiously, feeling for the outbursts of magical power around them like snakes sensing the air with their tongues, and Puss paced slowly behind them. Tyson and Marwood were sprinting towards the dark figures near the statue, but Ronan had gone for the closest ones, who were firing the gleaming metal tube. He burst into their midst like a berserker, sword flailing, expecting to scythe them down despite their armour (for a skilled and experienced warrior can always find a seam or a weak point), but it was not to be. The air about them felt thick and

178

viscous beneath his blows, as though he was hacking at them through thick mud, and all he succeeded in doing was knocking them sideways. Tyson too found that she could not force her blows home with any power, but Marwood had more luck as he attacked the rabbit/wolves. Having ripped apart their first victim, they were intent on bringing down the other two students from the statue, and he was able to grab one by the scruff of the neck as it readied itself to leap, jerking it backwards and slicing its throat open with his knife before it could respond. The second hurled itself at him, growling fiercely, but he dodged calmly beneath it, ripping its stomach open with a casual slash so that it landed in a sprawling mass of its own entrails to scrabble its life away on the cold stone flags, howling.

Marwood watched as the two students leapt down and ran for their very lives, but then three dark figures came racing towards him, and he was forced to retreat, skipping nimbly behind the statue. The dwarves, startled at first by the ferocity of the attack, had recovered, and were launching an attack of their own. Both Ronan and Tyson suddenly found that they were trying to fight off what seemed like a horde of whirling battleaxes, and each was forced to give ground rapidly, fighting desperately to prevent the blades from slicing home.

Tarl, who was watching with dismay, nearly wet himself when Guebral suddenly gripped his arm tightly.

'Can you feel it?' she gasped. 'A surge in Power, every time Ronan or Tyson strike an attacking blow! The armour is imbued with some magical device. I've got to undo it, quickly. Guard us, love!'

And then she knelt down, eyes closed, her hands stretched forwards as though pushing something away, and Tarl stood above her, waiting to fend off whatever nameless horror should hurl itself at them, and feeling about as much use as a barbed wire codpiece.

Tyson was managing to hold off her assailants. They didn't dare to press home their attack too strongly, for Marwood was drifting about behind them like a balletic scarecrow, and they had all witnessed his attack on the rabbit/wolves. He was too fast for them to chase him, and despite the remarkable qualities of the armour, they couldn't bring themselves to ignore him either, and the resulting hesitancy was enough to enable Tyson to keep them at bay. But Ronan was hemmed in and was having severe difficulties. His sword was a whirl of metal in front of him, yet even so he was only just managing to deflect the axe-blows. His defence was as fast and skilled as it had ever been, but every time he saw an opening for a riposte, his blow was as slow as if someone had encased his arm in lead.

Twenty yards behind him, Guebral fell forwards with a gasp. Ronan was too engrossed to notice, but he did vaguely register that the dwarves' armour suddenly seemed to have lost some of its dark lustre. Another microsecond of opportunity presented itself and Ronan lunged forward once again, more in habit than in hope, but this time, to his surprise, his sword plunged home beneath his target's raised arm, in the gap between the vambrace and the breastplate. The dwarf staggered back and then collapsed on to the stone flags with a metallic clatter and lay there motionless, with dark-red blood seeping out from his armpit. His confederates paused for an instant, stunned at this unexpected setback, but then with a roar Ronan went back on the attack, and they were forced to defend. Now there seemed to be nothing holding back his blows, and his sword smashed violently against their helmets, carving great dents in the metal and knocking the dwarves half senseless.

Tyson too switched to the attack, her sword flickering in and out past the dwarves' desperate parries, leaving three of them wounded from stabbing blows that had penetrated the joins in the armour. Behind them, Marwood was still skipping round out of reach of the fearsome battleaxes, darting in when an opportunity presented itself to drive his dagger home through the eye-slit of a helmet with a sickening *thock*. A couple of the dwarves turned and tried to attack him, but he was far too nimble for them, and their axe-blows whistled harmlessly past him. It was like trying to hew mist.

Tarl watched from the edge of the square, one hand resting protectively on Guebral's shoulder. She was kneeling on all fours, her eyes shut, every muscle tightly tensed with effort as she strove to suppress the magical power of the armour long enough for the others to defeat the dwarves. It was working, too, for six of the armour-clad figures were now spread-eagled on the ground, and Ronan, Tyson and Marwood were chasing others across the square. But still more were arriving from side streets and alleys, and there were over thirty of them now. Tarl realised with a frisson of horror that someone must have released another of the rabbit/wolf creatures, for it was moving across the square towards them in a grotesque lollop. He threw a quick glance at Guebral, but she was concentrating so hard that she was oblivious to everything else, and he realised that it was up to him. Still, it should be no problem to a man of his ability.

He was just working up to a nice little *Fireball* when another dwarf emerged from an alley about twenty yards away on the right. It lobbed something towards Tarl, and before he had time to act, one of the explosive metal balls had come looping through the air to bounce off the cobbles and skitter beneath Guebral. Realising that he had about two seconds to act, Tarl grabbed at the first halfway-suitable spell he could think of.

'*Tempus ibi duce!*' he gasped. He must have got the spell off in time, because the silver ball didn't explode, but his hold was tenuous, and he knew that if he relaxed his concentration for a moment, the spell would waver and the ball would explode. Nor could he back a safe distance away and then release his hold, because the explosion would kill Guebral. And so he kept his gaze on the ball, concentrating on keeping the spell working, and all the time he could sense the rabbit/wolf getting nearer and nearer . . .

But then the little donkey trotted out from behind him and advanced to meet the creature.

'Hey, Bugs,' it called. 'Wanna rumble? Then hop over here!'

With a hungry snarl, the rabbit/wolf leapt at the donkey, and even in the position he was in, there was a small portion of Tarl's mind that was busily ruing the fact that there was no one here to have a quick bet with. It was only a few weeks since he had seen Puss get the better of a *lenkat* in Atro's Cumanceum, and he knew a good thing when he saw it. He watched out of the corner of his eye as the donkey dodged sideways, its teeth slashing out at the creature's hind leg to sever the hamstring, before darting back in and ripping open its throat as it lay sprawled on the ground.

Nice one, Puss, he thought, and then concentrated his full attention on holding the spell and stopping the silver ball from exploding.

In the square, sixteen of the dwarves were now down, and the rest were panicking. It was clear that Ronan, Tyson and Marwood were far too skilled and quick for them, and they were in too much disarray to bring any of their foul machines to bear. But then, just as Ronan had cornered one particularly stubborn dwarf against a wall and was trying to find a way past his defence, a small red spark suddenly started flashing in the air immediately above his head, and the next second he vanished into thin air.

Ronan stared, astonished, and then turned round and surveyed the square. Throughout, the dwarves were winking out one by one, even the dead ones, and their crates, boxes and equipment were vanishing too. Nearby, Guebral shook her head as if to clear it, and then peered at Tarl. He was staring rigidly at something beneath her as though hypnotised. His face was a mask of intense, desperate concentration, and was covered in a sheen of perspiration. Looking down, she saw the small silver ball. Quickly, she *Scanned* to see what was happening. *Klat!* He'd cast a *Delay Time* around the ball, but his hold was shaky. It could slip at any moment, and then the thing would explode!

Quickly she rapped out a *Hurl* incantation, and the ball rocketed away from her as though whacked with a bat, and went skittering across the square, fetching up against the base of the dean's statue. It exploded with a dull *boom*, and the statue toppled slowly forwards and fell face-down in the square (a position that the dean himself, when alive, had often achieved after a night on the Cydorian brandy).

Tarl let out a great sigh of relief and looked around. Ronan was trudging slowly towards them, one hand clutching a wound on his arm where the tip of an axe had gouged out a deep slice of flesh. Tyson and Marwood were walking dejectedly alongside him. But the dwarves and their equipment had completely vanished; even the corpses of the rabbit/wolves had gone, leaving only a few bloodstains behind. In fact, if it hadn't been for the bodies of students littering the square, the burning buildings, the distant screams and wails, the smoke-filled, brimstone-scented air and the row of shops with their fronts blasted out, you wouldn't even have known that they had been there at all.

He stood up and hugged Guebral.

'Are you okay?' she asked him, worriedly, for his face was whiter than Marwood's had been that morning.

'Yeah, no worries,' he told her. 'Piece of piss.' But then he started shaking like a leaf, and he didn't stop until they'd taken him back to Intoxy Kate's and had got four large brandies down him.

Beneltin couldn't believe what was happening. In fact, he had been in a total daze since he walked down the wooden stairs and found himself peering through the haze of smoke that cut visibility in the Stand and Deliver Club to about twenty feet. He had been expecting such a famous club to have a décor to match, but the bare brick walls, the sticky, beer-stained carpet, the small wooden stage and the cheap tables and chairs gave the place an air of squalor which the pervading smell of stale beer, smoke and mould did nothing to dispel.

The club had been pretty full when he entered, with well over a hundred people squeezed into the large main room. Most of them were sitting at the small round tables strewn in front of the stage, and the rest were crammed in a solid phalanx in front of the narrow bar that lined the rear wall. Beneltin had bought himself a pint of beer, and had stood and watched the man on stage, who was probably the worst comedian that he had ever seen. The guy had been trying to tell a story about coming home from the pub, but he was nervous, repetitive, and worst of all, the story just wasn't funny. After about thirty seconds, a couple of thrown coins had whizzed past his head, followed by a bottle, and he had given up in mid-story.

The club's owner and compère, an old man with bouffant blond hair, a white shirt and a bow tie, had got up on the stage, reminded the audience (as if they were in any doubt) that it was Amateur Night and that there was a prize of five silver *tablons* for the best comedian, and had introduced the next contestant. Beneltin had edged his way round to the compère, put his name forward, and had then stood and watched the next few appalling acts (and their even worse receptions) with mounting horror.

By the time the compère had announced that the next act was a dwarf all the way from Toddy Forge, so would they please put their hands together for Nell Benton, Beneltin had become a vibrating mass of nerves with a brain that seemed to have turned to mush. But then, as he had clambered up on to the stage and had stood looking out at the sea of hostile faces, he had suddenly seemed to hear Francarsin's infectious laugh in his ear. *This is it*, he'd thought. *This is what you've been wanting to do for all these years. Don't chicken out now. Go for them!*

He'd started with an old joke, but one that a surprising number of people had never heard.

'I went to see my analyst today. (PAUSE.) Apparently I'm ninety-four per cent water. With a bit of carbon.'

After a slight silence there had been a small waft of laughter near the front, as a few people got the joke. He'd stared at them, hands on hips, as he'd seen Tarbuk the Jester do.

'Come on, come on. Keep up.'

Another small laugh, but a quicker one. That was good – they'd responded to him. So he'd gone into the stuff he'd made up about crime, as it seemed the right gear for city-dwellers. He'd been right, it had got some good laughs.

'. . . and then I woke up the other night, and I'm lying there in the dark, and I can hear rustling downstairs in the hall. I went down next morning, and all my cattle had gone . . .'

Big laugh. Great! And suddenly the realisation hit him. He was standing on stage in a famous club, doing his own material, and the audience were laughing. He couldn't believe it! For a moment, everything seemed to sway, and he felt dizzy. Hastily he took a swig from his beer glass.

'Sorry! Almost passed out for a moment there.' The audience were staring at him. *Quick, think on your feet.* 'Thought I heard someone say it was my round . . .'

This reference to the dwarven reputation for stinginess got an instant laugh. *You can do it, just keep going!*

He switched to his stuff about orcs, and then decided to end with the routine about the difference between the sexes. They were laughing at every gag now.

'This new thing, bulimia. Eating loads of food and then chucking it straight back up again. We dwarves have had that for years. We call it going for a takeaway after fifteen pints . . .'

He thought about using his best gag, the one about the tissues. Highly dubious taste, but he went for it, and the audience exploded with laughter, especially the women. He rubbed it home.

'Look at them, all the men, sitting there saying to their girlfriends, "Not me, love. Dunno what he's talking about!" Don't believe them.'

He paused again and looked round confidently. The whole room was watching him, grins on their faces. Even the bar staff were watching. Time to quit while he was ahead.

'Okay, you've been a great audience. My name's Beneltin, good night.'

He stepped off the stage and the place erupted with applause. As he walked in a daze to the rear of the room, deafening applause rang out and hands reached over to pat him on the back. But he hardly noticed, for all he could see through the mist of tears that suddenly filled his eyes was the kindly face of Francarsin floating in front of him, mouthing, *Well done, kid! Well done!* at him over and over again.

CHAPTER TEN

According to elven myth, when Progenitin, the Father of All Elves, created dwarves, he fashioned them firstly from mud which he scooped from beside a river, drying his new creations in the warmth of the primeval sun. But later, when the first rain-storm fell, it softened and melted them, washing them clean away.

So then did Progenitin try again, and this time he fashioned the dwarves from a stout and sturdy branch taken from Kavasa, the Father of all Oak-trees. But these new dwarves were stiff and wooden, not lithe and agile like elves or humankind, and when the autumn came, all their hair fell out.

'Bollocks,' said Progenitin. 'Oh well, maybe I'd better make them from flesh and blood.' And so he took some muscle from his mighty buttock, fashioning them from that (although it left a wound that stung him nastily for days). And, the elves say, dwarves have been a pain in the arse ever since . . .

The Pink Book of Ulay

Meiosin was in an ugly mood before the raid on Gudmornen had even begun. By the time that everyone had returned and they had counted up the cost, he was in the foulest of tempers. Most of the groups raiding Gudmornen had carried out their tasks adequately, but the group that had been targeting the University area had screwed up badly. Not only had they allowed themselves to be taken apart by some *klatting* warrior and his friends, losing five dead and another nine wounded, but one of the wounded had dropped a throwing bomb whilst being brought home, and it had exploded inside the transmitter, blowing it and him to fragments, and damaging four adjacent transmitters, more than thirty dwarves and a lot of expensive equipment.

After screaming abuse at everybody who came within ten feet of him, Meiosin had stormed along to his office, and when a hesitant Mitosin poked his head round the door half an hour later, more than half of the contents of his bottle of *vlatzhkan gûl* had disappeared.

185

'Come in,' he told his brother, but Mitosin, who had experienced these moods before and had once taken an empty *vlatzhkan gûl* bottle right between the eyes, stayed where he was.

'The final count is six dead and forty-three wounded,' he said without preamble. 'And my armour came back empty. The only dwarf missing is Beneltin.'

'Beneltin, eh? I should have known it was that little turd.' Meiosin paused and thought for a few seconds. 'Well, we'll leave him for the moment. The next two *cobrats* will be grown in a few weeks. They can take care of him. What's the news on equipment?'

'One transmitter destroyed and four damaged. It will take a couple of weeks to repair them. A fifth is malfunctioning, but could be used if necessary.'

'Bugger!' swore Meiosin, reaching for the bottle. Mitosin ducked quickly out of sight, just in case, but his brother merely took a deep swallow of the fiery liquid, before continuing. 'We've got the Orcbane board turning up this afternoon, expecting to see all sorts of wonderful inventions. If they find us like this, they'll pull the plug on the financial backing.' He paused for another swallow. 'Get on to them, tell them we'll transport them tomorrow. Make up some excuse. And then get all the mess in the Transmitter Room cleared up. I want the dead entombed this evening, and all the wounded out of sight. Oh, and Mitosin?'

Mitosin stuck his head back round the door just in time to take the now-empty bottle smack between the eyes. He fell backwards and sprawled on the rocky floor of the corridor, stunned, a lump the size of a large nugget of gold rapidly forming on his forehead. Meiosin sauntered out of the door and looked down at him.

'Next time you're late for a raid briefing, I'll set the *cobrats* on you. Okay?'

And stepping over his comatose brother, the Chief Scientist strolled off down the corridor in search of another bottle of *vlatzhkan gûl*.

As the sun rose over Gudmornen, the city was still reeling from the events of the night before. After the dwarves had vanished, an angry mob had gathered in the market square and had marched on the University, believing that its scientists were behind the chaos, but the sight of burning University buildings and injured students had convinced them otherwise. Unable to find a target for their wrath, the mob had dispersed, but an air of simmering anger still hung over the town, as did the mingled smells of smoke, ash and brimstone.

Ronan, Tyson and the others had decided that something needed to be done about the dwarves that were carrying out these attacks, but their first priority was to get Ronan safely registered on the Assassins' course, and so, after arranging to meet his friends at Intoxy Kate's for lunch, he had set off for the Faculty of Assassination through the rubble-strewn streets. The extent of the devastation had surprised and horrified him, for there was hardly a street that didn't have at least one burnt-out building. He knew that the dwarves of the far north seldom came into contact with the human or elven races and regarded themselves as being superior, but these callous and pointless attacks seemed brutal even for them. By the time he reached the faculty he had decided that he was going to sort out these dwarves just as soon as he had dealt with the Orcbane board.

The faculty building was undamaged, and the receptionist smiled at Ronan and asked him to take a seat, for Dean Blackwell was expecting him. He sat there for a few minutes, idly thumbing through a recent copy of *Maim* magazine. Then the door of the Dean's office opened, and the Dean popped his head out and blinked at him short-sightedly.

'Erm, ah yes, Rhand,' he said. 'You've come to enrol. Capital, capital! Come in, my dear chap.'

He held the door open and Ronan walked past him and sat in the chair that was waiting in front of the Dean's desk. The desk was even more cluttered than the day before, and the papers on it gave the impression that they were only waiting for one of them to take the plunge and slide off on to the floor before they all joined in with a will.

'I'm so pleased you returned,' said the Dean from behind him, and there was a slight edge to his voice that triggered a warning in Ronan's brain. He was about to leap up and swing round when the merest prick at the right-hand side of his neck, just above the jugular, made him stop instantly. He sat there with his head absolutely motionless, his eyes squinting sideways and down, trying to confirm what his suddenly fearful mind was telling him.

The Dean laid a sympathetic hand on his left shoulder, and Ronan could just see the fingers of his other hand, rock-steady as it held a thin, pointed object against his skin.

'Yes, that is a *klaven*-blade that you feel at your neck,' said the

Dean softly, and his voice was no longer that of a hesitant, absent-minded university professor. 'The traditional poisoned knife of the Assassin. The slightest scratch, and you will be dead five seconds later. But then, you must have been expecting this for some time, eh, Ronan?'

At the use of his real name, Ronan felt despair flooding through him.

'But I'm . . .'

'Don't bother trying to keep up the pretence. I knew who you were the instant I set eyes on you. You're too famous, lad. Oh, you can shave your hair and carry a toothpick of a sword, but you can't hide the bearing of a top-class fighter. And any doubts I had were removed by the reports I've had of your performance against the dark invaders last night.'

Ronan closed his eyes. So this was it, then. Still, with him dead, they'd leave Tyson alone. But she wouldn't half be cross when she found out he'd got himself assassinated. She'd probably kill him . . .

'You must know by now that there is an open contract on you. I did hear that the Guild gave the job to Slanved. Did he find you?'

'I presume so. Nine men jumped us near Ilex. We . . . disposed of them.'

'You must be remarkably talented. But I knew that.' The Dean paused, and Ronan tensed himself, waiting for the blade to puncture his skin and wondering if five seconds was long enough to grab the old Assassin and break his neck. Then the Dean sighed, as though he had come to a decision.

'You're here because you know that becoming an Assassin yourself is the only way to negate an open contract. You are a brave, honourable and talented man. And that is why I have decided to deal with you in an honourable way . . .'

Then, to Ronan's amazement, the point of the knife lifted from his skin, and the Dean walked round to his chair and sat down facing him, placing the thin, ugly *klaven*-blade on the desk between them. Ronan felt relief flood through him like a tidal wave, followed immediately by a huge surge of anger, but somehow he managed to restrain himself from leaping up and throttling the old guy.

'But for the raid last night,' the Dean continued, staring down at the knife, 'you would now be dead. Instead, I grant you the gift of life. You wish to become a member of our Guild. Few people know this, but I am one of the five members of the Ruling Council of the Assassins' Guild. I have the power to grant you an honorary degree. It can be yours this minute, and the threat of the open contract will be gone for ever. But I want you to do something for me to return.'

'What is that?'

The Dean looked up at him, and Ronan was stunned to see that his eyes were full of unshed tears.

'Last night, the invaders burned and killed, but they also took with them living captives, to what end I hate to think. They took my grandson. I want you to get him back.'

Tyson and the others were holding a large council-of-war with some of the locals in Intoxy Kate's when Ronan returned. It was Marwood who realised the significance of the black-and-silver sash that he was now wearing. The others crowded round demanding to know how he had managed to become a Guild member, and Ronan told them about the Dean's grandson.

'A lot of folk have gone missing,' said Tarl. 'Remember Garresh's partner, Tragath? The female centaur? They've got her, too.'

'Well, we'll just have to get her back as well.'

'But how the hell are we going to do it?' asked Tyson. 'We know that these raiders are dwarves, but we don't know where they come from. Just appearing and vanishing like that, it could be anywhere in Midworld.'

'They had those runes on their helms,' Ronan reminded her. 'Maybe another dwarf might recognise them.' He turned to Intoxy Kate, who was wearing a fawn twin-set and a matching tweed skirt. 'Have you got any dwarf regulars, Kate?'

Kate shook his head and scratched his bristly chin, thoughtfully.

'Nah,' he growled. 'We ain't got a single dwarf in the whole of Gudmornen, as far as I knows.'

'There was one in the Stand and Deliver Club last night,' interjected a student. 'He was very funny. But I'd never seen him before. He just turned up out of the blue.'

'Out of the blue, you say,' responded Ronan, with interest. 'What happened to him?'

'I dunno. When I left he was lying propped in the corner, pissed as anything, and singing to himself.'

Ronan looked at the others.

'I reckon we should start with him,' he said. 'So. How do we get to this Stand and Deliver Club, then?'

Beneltin woke up to find that he was lying underneath a table on a carpet that was so beer-stained and tacky it stuck to his clothes like velcro. His head was hammering painfully, and his stomach felt as though it was about to climb up his throat and leap out of his mouth. He dragged himself out to find that he was still in the Stand and Deliver Club. To judge by the daylight that was flooding down the grimy steps into the cellar room, it was morning.

The club's owner was sitting at another table, counting the previous night's takings. His white shirt was crumpled now, and his bow tie was undone and hung limply round his neck. His tousled blond hair looked as though it was forty years younger than the tired old face beneath it.

Beneltin staggered across and launched into a stumbling apology for passing out in his club, but the owner waved this aside.

'A lot of the lesser acts do that,' he said. 'They're happy to perform just for food and a roof over their head for the night.'

'Oh.' Beneltin nodded, and immediately wished that he hadn't.

'Mind you, you're a lot better than they are,' added the owner. 'By the way, my name's Cordman. Was that really your first time on stage?'

'Yeah.'

'And you write all your own material?'

'Yeah.' Beneltin peered round, vaguely looking for something to drink. His mouth tasted as though a gang of orcs with dysentery had held a month-long party in it. Cordman, recognising the symptoms of a bad hangover from long years of practice, went to the bar and fetched him a pint of water. Beneltin drained it in one gulp.

'So . . . are you working?'

Beneltin hadn't really given any thought to the consequences of his actions. It didn't take a genius to work out that if he returned to Tor Deforzh, he'd probably end up in short-term employment as food for some of the more unpleasant creatures that Meiosin and his mageneticists had produced.

'No,' he answered.

'Fixed up somewhere to stay?'

'No.'

'Look, I need someone to work as compère at the club. Do you want to give it a try for a couple of weeks? It would give you the chance to work on your act. If it goes well, we can sort out something longer. What do you say?'

For a moment Beneltin said nothing at all, convinced he must be dreaming. But then he became aware of the five silver *tablons* nestling in his trouser pocket, the prize from last night. By the gods, he'd shown that he could do this, standing on his head!

'Yeah, okay,' he said casually. They spent the next twenty minutes talking about details and then shook hands, and Beneltin was just thinking that he should get out and stroll around town a bit when he heard the sound of footsteps on the stairs. A strangely assorted group of five people wandered into the cellar, led by a massive black warrior. They paused, blinking, as their eyes adjusted to the gloom after the bright sunlight outside.

'We're closed,' said Cordman, apprehensively, but the warrior lifted up a placatory hand.

'That's okay,' he said. 'We just want a quick word with your friend over there.' He crossed to Beneltin's table and looked down at him quizzically.

'So. You're a dwarf, right?' he said.

'Coo! Very little gets past you, does it?' answered Beneltin, with what he hoped was a friendly grin.

'That's right. And talking of very little gets, some of your dwarven brothers took this town apart last night.'

Oh-oh, thought Beneltin. *This could turn nasty . . .*

'Did they?'

'Yeah. They were clad in black Valdar armour, and the helms were marked with this symbol.'

The warrior took a pencil out of Cordman's shirt pocket, and drew a rough ∠⌒ rune on a beer mat.

'Have you any idea what it means?' he asked.

Beneltin hesitated, but only for a moment. This guy looked deadly serious and very capable, and as far as he was concerned, if the shit was about to hit the fan, he hoped that Meiosin and his cronies were standing right behind it. And there was something about the penetrating stare that the thin, big-eyed girl was giving him that convinced him to stick to the truth.

'Yeah. It's the symbol for Deforzh. That's the Dwarf Research Establishment beneath the mountain, Tor Deforzh. It's some-where to the north-east of here, but I don't know how to get there.'

'Thank you,' said the warrior. He looked genuinely pleased. 'You've been a big help.'

He nodded to Cordman, then led his friends back up the stairs towards the light. Beneltin sat for a moment, his brow creased in thought. Then he leant forward with a smile on his face.

191

'Can I borrow your pencil,' he asked Cordman. 'That guy has given me an idea for a routine about warriors . . .'

Ronan led the others out into Cur's Tea Alley, then stopped.

'Okay,' he said. 'It looks as though we're up against an army of dwarf scientists several hundred strong, holed out beneath a mountain in the wastelands of the north, and armed with magic, explosives and some really unpleasant creatures. So far, there's five of us. Six counting Puss. Any ideas?'

'Yeah, as it happens,' mused Tyson, slowly. 'But I need to look at some decent maps of the north.'

'They'll have some in the University library,' Ronan told her. 'The Dean said I could use any of their resources.'

'Right. I'll try there.'

'I think I'll go back and have a quiet word with that dwarf on my own,' mused Guebral, who had been looking back at the entrance to the Stand and Deliver. 'I have a feeling there's something he's not telling us. I'll see you back at the tavern.'

She turned and trotted back down the steps of the club.

'Okay,' said Tyson to Ronan, 'why don't you go back to Intoxy Kate's. Talk to the regulars, see if there's any chance of raising a few fighters or a local militia. Then relax for a couple of hours. Take it easy. Have a few drinks.'

Ronan nodded.

'And as for you two,' she continued to Marwood and Tarl, who had perked up at the sound of the magic words, *have a few drinks*.

'Yes,' they responded, brightly.

'You can come with me to the library. There's work for you to do . . .'

The library was housed in a large stone building that had once been a merchant's mansion. It was silent and virtually deserted, and the sound of their footsteps on the polished wooden floors echoed through the corridors. The librarian, a voluptuous forty-year-old woman who made both Tarl's and Marwood's jaws sag open, told them that the map room was on the top floor. And so Tyson left the two of them sitting at a table in a side room with a dozen encyclopedias, looking up references to Deforzh, and went in search of local maps by herself.

It took her half an hour before she found what she wanted. It was an old orcish map of the Northern Mountains, and it clearly showed not only Gudmornen and the Reudi Valley, but also Tor Deforzh, some forty miles to the north-east. And, even more importantly, it showed her just where the orc town of Weldis was. She made a quick sketch of the relevant points, did a few rapid calculations, and then went in search of the other two.

She found them sitting on the floor of the room where she'd left them. They were surrounded by huge encyclopedias, and there was a massive dictionary and a small pile of coins on the floor between them. They hadn't noticed her, and so she paused in the doorway and watched them.

'Cuisine,' said Tarl. Marwood grinned at him.

'You don't fool me,' he said. 'I know that begins with a cee, not a queue. But if we're playing like that, you can have pharynx.'

'Oh, you bugger. Come on then, open it.'

Marwood picked up the dictionary, inspected its closed pages, then inserted a fingernail and flicked it open.

'Page two fifty-four again,' he read out. 'Decalitre.' He turned back a few pages. 'Cuisine is on page two forty. Only fourteen out. Beat that.'

'Not bad,' said Tarl, taking the dictionary. 'Right, then. Pharynx. I reckon it's a pee aitch.'

'What the hell are you doing?' asked Tyson, and the pair of them jumped with surprise, and stared at her guiltily, like a couple of schoolboys found eating sweets in class.

'Er, it's a game that Tarl's made up,' said Marwood. 'It's called dictionary gambling. You each give the other a word, and whoever opens the dictionary at the nearest page to their word wins the stake.'

'You mean you've been sitting here gambling? You're supposed to be finding out everything you can about Deforzh!'

'It was on page two five four,' said Tarl. 'I was only six pages off that one.' He lowered his eyes and cleared his throat as she glowered at him. 'But all it says is that it's a mountain in Kahdor.'

'Never mind. I've found out what we need. Get all these books tidied away, and then let's head back to the tavern. I want a quick word with Guebral, and then I think we might just have something going . . .'

Tarl carried the tray across to the table, and set it down carefully. He passed round the five tankards of Old Organs, placed the bowl of beer on the floor under the table where Puss could reach it, and sat down.

'Right,' said Tyson, wiping froth from her mouth with the back of her hand. 'First things first. Ronan, any luck?'

Ronan shook his head ruefully.

'There hasn't been a sniff of a battle north of the mountains for over a hundred years,' he said. 'Gudmornen folk don't know the first thing about fighting. There are a few low-grade warriors acting as bodyguards for rich merchants, but that's about it. The City Militia is basically an excuse for its members to get out of the house, ponce about pretending to drill for a few minutes, and then get down to the pub for a skinful.'

At this news, Tarl, Marwood and Guebral looked downcast, but Tyson just nodded.

'I thought as much,' she said. 'Gueb, did you get anything more out of that dwarf?'

'Yes, rather a lot,' answered Guebral. She was sitting beside Tarl, holding his hand, and she was probably the only woman in the whole of Gudmornen who would have made Tarl look bulky. 'I used a *Truth* incantation on him, although he doesn't know it. He'll think that he just needed to talk about things.'

She paused and sipped her beer, then continued.

'He's from Tor Deforzh himself, although he's run away. He says that they have a new leader called Meiosin, who has organised all these raids, and that a lot of the dwarves are against it. The raids are apparently to test out all the new weapons and equipment that they have been developing, and to capture prisoners for more tests at Deforzh. Oh, and there's a rumour that some rich backers have been throwing gold at them.'

'So how many dwarves are there?'

'More than eight hundred.'

Ronan whistled and shook his head. As far as he could see, this project was a non-starter, but for some reason Tyson was smiling. He watched her, mystified, as she paused in thought for a moment.

'Hm,' she murmured. 'Gueb, are you sure you can do a *Teleport* spell on Tarl?'

'If his memories are strong enough.'

'Tarl?'

'Pint of bitter, please,' came the instinctive answer, before Tarl dragged himself back from daydreaming about getting those students to play cards again. 'Oh, er . . . what?'

'You've been to the orc city, Weldis, haven't you?'

'Yeah. What a shit-hole!'

'Do you remember it well? Think!'

There was a pause as Tarl thought back to the week he had spent there, some years before. Guebral concentrated for a moment, then nodded.

'His memories are strong,' she said. 'I can get him there.'

'Here, what are you . . .' Tarl began, but Tyson cut him short.

'We've got eight hundred dwarves to deal with. We're short of time, because we need to rescue those prisoners before the dwarves injure or kill them. We need an army, but we haven't got one. But I know someone who can raise one really quickly.'

Briefly she sketched out her plan, and Tarl's face grew more and more concerned.

'So what we need,' she finished, 'is a volunteer who can pass for an orc . . .'

'Eh?' said Tarl, now downright worried. 'What the . . .'

'. . . someone who can drink with orcs . . .'

'Here, I hope you're not thinking of . . .'

'. . . and someone who has the alcohol tolerance of an orc.'

'Oh *klat*! You *are* thinking of me!'

Tyson, Ronan and Guebral managed not to smile, but Marwood grinned openly.

'It has to be you, Tarl,' Tyson told him. 'You're the only one qualified.'

'Okay, okay! But I'm not going on my own.'

'You're the only one who can pass as an orc.'

'Doesn't matter. Orcs respect natural-born killers. If they can see straight away that someone is a lethal, sly and devious murderer from, for example, their black-and-silver Assassin's robes . . .'

Marwood, who was taking a deep swig of beer, suddenly choked and began to cough and splutter, shaking his head violently.

'Gueb,' said Tyson, 'can you get them both there?'

'No problem.'

'And I take it that you two are both keen to do your bit in helping to save the lives of a lot of people, including Garresh's girl-friend, the Dean's four-year-old grandson and your friend Ronan here.'

When Tyson put it like that, there was very little that Tarl and Marwood could say, so they busied themselves in draining their beer. Now it was Tarl who was smiling, whilst Marwood looked daggers at him.

'Right. Ronan, Gueb, Puss and I will head straight for Tor Deforzh.

It's no more than a couple of days away. You two do your bit and meet us there. Any more questions?'

'There is one thing,' said Ronan slowly. 'After seeing those creatures that the dwarves brought with them last night, the ones like wolves crossed with rabbits. They reminded me of the things that killed Posner, the *cobrats*. Do you reckon they could be anything to do with these dwarves as well?'

'I dunno,' shrugged Tyson. 'It's possible. But I wouldn't worry about them, they must be hundreds of miles away. Now, let's drink up and get moving, we've got a job to do . . .'

Brother Strenuous slammed shut the front door of the monastery and thrust the bolts home hard. Then, with shaking hands, he opened the judas hole and peered through. He had never seen creatures like the ones passing by outside before, but there was something about their loping, purposeful, upright gait and their sleek, powerful bodies that scared the life out of him. One of them glanced sideways at him and snarled, exposing masses of razor-sharp teeth, and he slammed shut the wooden shutter and ran for the safety of the refectory. But he need not have worried. The *cobrats* were hungry, for they had found little prey in the snowy wastes of the mountains, but they could sense that they were closing in on their quarry, and they knew that they would soon be feeding from Ronan's warm but lifeless flesh.

CHAPTER ELEVEN

*Orcs are almost impossible for humans to insult, unless you
know what you're doing. We humans tend to insult people by
calling them names that fit into one of three categories: other
animals (for example,* cow *or* pig*); sexual or excretory organs
and functions (*prick *or* turd*); or sexual proclivities (*wanker,
puff*). To orcs, these so-called insults are meaningless.*

*The reason for this is that, despite their permanent love affair
with alcohol, orcs are surprisingly well-balanced creatures.
They are not on some massive ego trip which insists that they
are head and shoulders above all the other animals, and so
being called the name of another creature does not bother
them. They are not screwed-up about or ashamed of their
bodies, and so calling them after body parts will not upset
them. And they have a very wide and tolerant sexuality.
Anything goes. Same sex, different sex, different species, it
makes no difference to an orc. If it has an orifice, it's fair game,
and so calling them a name based on some activity that they
probably find quite pleasurable will have little effect.*

*However, be warned. There are one or two things that orcs
find deeply offensive, and any hint that they take part in these
activities will produce a violent response. Never call an orc a
teetotaller, a vegetarian or a folk-singer . . .*

Morris the Bald, *Orcwatching*

Marwood had never experienced a mode of transportation anything
like it. One moment he was standing in the stable yard at Intoxy
Kate's, holding Tarl's hand and feeling a right wally as the others
grinned at them, and then Guebral had muttered something, and
whoosh! Everything seemed to blur, and all of a sudden he and Tarl
were standing outside a large, dingy and incredibly noisy pub in a
street of low, hemispherical stone houses that looked like over-
turned bowls. Vast mountains loomed up all around them in the
evening sky, and the street ran directly towards the nearest,
becoming a tunnel that disappeared beneath its craggy slopes.

'Welcome to Weldis,' muttered Tarl.

'*Klat!* It's not exactly scenic, is it?'

'Put it this way, if Midworld got piles, they'd be clustered around this place.'

That's a pretty apt simile, thought Marwood, for the pub they were standing outside was called The Troll's Haemorrhoids. He stared up at the inn sign with a curious mixture of horror and fascination. It wasn't that he was surprised it should illustrate the pub's name, it was just that he hadn't expected such a realistic portrayal, nor one executed in such vividly accurate colours. It made his own backside ache in sympathy.

'Come on,' said Tarl. 'Tyson reckoned our target told her that this was his local. Let's go and see if they've heard of him.'

He pushed open the door and led the way inside. The place was packed out with orcs, and the sheer volume of noise hit them like a physical blow. They ploughed their way in to the heaving mass of orckind, and Marwood was fascinated to see that as they did so, something in Tarl's demeanour and posture changed subtly, so that all of a sudden he looked more orcish than human. As a result, no one took any notice of him, but all eyes turned to watch Marwood as they pushed through to the bar. He met the gaze of one or two, and they slid quickly away from him, but there was no threat there, only interest or curiosity. Even orcs respected the black and silver of the Assassins' Guild.

They leaned on the bar, and Tarl gestured to the barman.

'Two pints of Spavin's Colonic Crustings,' he snarled. The barman nodded, and began drawing the beers.

Marwood picked up the bar menu and ran his eye down it. He was feeling quite hungry.

'We eating here?' he asked.

'I don't think so.'

'Shame. It sounds quite good. Quiche Lorraine, Steak Diane, Crêpes Suzette . . .'

The barman placed their beers on the bar top and Tarl dropped a couple of *tablons* into his clawed hand. Then he took a deep swig of the beer, wiped his mouth with his sleeve and squinted up at Marwood seriously.

'Look,' he said. 'I don't know who Diane was, but I don't want to eat a steak cut from her.'

He paused as Marwood stared at him, aghast. 'That's an orc menu,' he added, by way of explanation.

'*Klat!*' muttered Marwood. 'I forgot they eat humans.' He went through the menu again, reading it in a new light and wrinkling his nose in distaste at the descriptions of Navarin of Thigh and Forearm au Poivre.

'Here,' he muttered. 'What's human veal?'

'Calf.'

'Oh.'

The barman returned with Tarl's change and saw Marwood reading the menu. Correctly surmising that this human wasn't too taken with any of the orc dishes, he decided to draw his attention to the Special. They always had a fish dish on, in case any human customers dropped by.

'Perhaps you'd be more interested in our Sole Bonne Femme,' he suggested.

Marwood went white.

'Arsehole Bonne Femme?' he repeated in horror. It didn't paint a pretty picture in his mind. 'I don't think so . . .'

The barman decided not to pursue it, as the human was looking a little strange, and he'd heard that it didn't pay to upset an Assassin. He turned his attention to Tarl.

'You guys just passing through?'

'Nah. We've come here looking for an orc called Chigger. You heard of him?'

'Heard of him?' said the orc proudly. 'Course I have! He's a party hero, [14] isn't he! You've heard of that huge orc war-party that went storming all the way across Midworld to the shores of the Grey Sea, a few weeks ago? Well, Chigger went all the way with it! He's the only orc from these parts to make it home! Says he was standing right next to that Shikara when she was killed!'

'Damn right he was,' snarled Tarl. 'I was there.'

'That a fact!' said the barman, impressed.

'Yeah. So, do you know where we'll find him?'

'He was in here on his first night back . . .' The barman paused as a thought hit him and looked worriedly at Marwood. 'Here, the killer's not after him, is he?'

'Nah, we're just interested in a bit of action, that's all. Heard he might be leading another party.'

'Join the queue. That's why the pub's so full. Dozens of orcs have turned up expecting him to be off again, but he's keeping his head down for some reason. Haven't seen him all week.'

---

[14] For details of orc parties, see *Ronan's Rescue*.

199

'He's probably planning. Maybe his wife knows where he's gone. She live near here?'

'Yeah. They've got an overground lair on Shagrat Street. You can't miss it. It's got a *garden*.'

The barman shook his head despairingly as he passed on this piece of news, and Tarl nearly grinned, but turned it into a grimace. Most orcs didn't understand the human preoccupation with flowers and gardens. As far as they were concerned, if you couldn't eat it, drink it, smoke it or shag it, what was the point?

'Can I get you another drink?' continued the barman. 'On the house, seeing as you're a veteran of the Long Party to the Sea.'

'Nah, we've got to be going. But we'll be back later, with Chigger. And you can spread the word that there might be another serious party in the offing . . .'

Chigger was sitting in the snug room of his lair with his wife, Pellagra, and four of their like-minded friends. They were a close-knit group, for they had discovered years ago that they had several rather shameful interests in common. In everyday life they put on a pretence, acting like the rest of orcish society, the males getting drunk, the females staying quietly at home, cooking and looking after the orclings. But every now and then they would gather at one another's lairs for a Special Evening. With the door locked and the blinds drawn, they would eat human food and drink tea, coffee, or even (when they were feeling really daring) fruit juice. And then, after dinner and a civilised chat, they would continue their long-running game of F & F until the small hours.

F & F (or Family and Friends) was a role-playing game that Chigger had invented, and for orcs who disliked the everyday stress of a heavy-drinking, party-till-you-drop society, it was sheer, un-adulterated escapist fun. They took on the imaginary roles of human estate agents or bank clerks, and had to find their way through the everyday life of a human town that Chigger (who was the Town-master) had designed. They were doing pretty well in the current game, and had found their way to the shopping centre, although they were running short of time.

'Okay,' said Chigger, when Pellagra had passed around the cheesy nibbles and had made sure that everyone had a full glass of orange squash. 'You're standing outside the door of a very large shop, remember?'

'I think we're all agreed,' said Mellit, whose turn it was to be spokesman. 'We enter the door.'

'Right. The door opens, and you walk through. Inside is a massive supermarket. There is a single trolley on your right, and a big line of them on your left. An aisle leads straight ahead between racks of newspapers on the left and shelves of vegetables on the right.'

'Erm. Take the single trolley, and move forwards.'

'You get hold of the trolley and push it. It has one wheel that doesn't work. The trolley veers sideways, making a squeaking sound, and everyone looks at you.'

'Oh, you idiot!' exclaimed Sanies. 'We should have examined the trolley!'

'Too late now. Never mind, let's look at the vegetables, okay?'

The others all nodded, and they turned to Chigger.

'Right,' he said. 'Oh, by the way, you are beginning to run short of time. There is now exactly three hours before the Smiths arrive for dinner. Erm . . .' He consulted his F & F notes. 'Ah, yes. You examine the vegetables. There are peas, beans, cabbages and onions. Also some fruit: apples, grapes and some avocados.'

'Um. Well, let's keep on moving . . .'

'Wait!' squeaked Fishflaps in excitement. She was feverishly scrabbling through her notes. 'When we talked to Mr Smith at the squash club yesterday, didn't he say his wife just adores avocados?'

'Oh, yes!' chorused the others. 'You're right! Well done.'

'Great,' said Mellit. 'Then we'll take the avocados.'

Chigger smiled inwardly. You'd think they would have learned by now! They should have examined the avocados first. Now they were going to have to roll two dice later, and they had a fifty per cent chance of the avocados being unripe, which wouldn't impress Mrs Smith in the slightest!

He was about to describe the next supermarket options to them when there came the sound of someone hammering on the front door. Sighing, he put down his maps, notes and pencils, and stood up. He hated it when the real world intruded.

'I'll only be a moment,' he said. It was the most inaccurate statement of his life.

As the door opened, Tarl fixed his friendliest, cheesiest grin into place.

'Hi,' he said. 'Chigger, isn't it? Remember me?'

The orc in the doorway looked extremely worried, but no signs of recognition crossed his face.

'Well, I'm not surprised,' continued Tarl. 'It was after the Battle of Grey Sea Fields, but we didn't see much of each other, 'cos I was getting over taking an arrow in the shoulder. You spent a lot more time talking to my friend Tyson.'

At the mention of Tyson's name, Chigger looked even more worried and tried to shut the door, but Tarl's foot was somehow in the way.

'Don't worry, this isn't anything unpleasant,' he continued. 'We just need your help.'

'Sorry.' All of a sudden, Chigger found his voice. 'I'd love to help, but . . .'

'Oh, good. You see, we need an army. Several hundred orcs would do just fine. And we can't raise one. But you could.'

'No, I'm afraid I'm busy.'

'You're a party hero. There's a lot of orcs in the Troll's Haemorrhoids already, hoping you might be thinking of starting off a bit of fun . . .'

'Out of the question.'

' . . . and it won't take long. It's a matter of some unpleasant dwarves, and they're only a couple of days' march away. Once we've sorted them out . . .'

'No chance!'

' . . . you'll be free to come back here at the head of a victorious orc army. You'll be even more of a hero than you are now . . .'

'Forget it!'

'You'll have Ronan and Tyson to help you . . .'

'Look, will you sod off!'

'And if you do it, we'll never need to tell all the orcs in Weldis that Chigger, the hero of the Long Party to the Sea, shot Shikara, the war-party leader, in the back with an arrow . . .'

Chigger stared at him, speechless.

'But . . . but . . . the other orcs would kill me!' he eventually managed to gasp. 'They'd lynch me and barbecue me!'[15]

'Then it's a pretty straightforward choice,' Tarl told him. 'Come with us and be cheered on all sides, or stay here and be charred on both sides. It's up to you. What do you say?'

[15] Forming a lynching party and then eating the victim is a popular orc recreation, and a number of the more enlightened orc businesses often give their employees Lynching Vouchers.

202

Chigger said rather a lot, but very little of it was repeatable, although Marwood did pick up several interesting new words that he hadn't heard before. However, the orc was trapped, and he knew it, so comforting himself with Tarl's repeated assurance that this would only be a four- or five-day trip, he apologised to his guests, kissed his wife goodbye (which in itself was enough to get him lynched, as far as most orcs were concerned) and packed a few belongings in his party bag.

Half an hour later, the two humans escorted the reluctant orc into the Troll's Haemorrhoids. The place was even more crowded than before, and when the assembled orcs saw that it was Chigger, and he was carrying his party bag, they let out a roar of approval that could probably have been heard at Tor Deforzh. Tarl leapt up on the bar, waved for silence and then spoke.

'You may have been wondering why you haven't seen the great party hero, Chigger, all week. Well, he's been waiting for me to bring him the details of a little party we've been planning. Not a big affair, just a few days. But we're ready to go, and you're all invited . . .'

There was another roar of approval. Most of the orcs waved swords or spears enthusiastically, and a couple suffered quite nasty lacerations as a result.

'We'll be doing a bit of a pub crawl round Weldis tonight, to build the numbers up, but if any of you want to nip home for weapons, or let your friends know, you've got plenty of time, because firstly . . . we're going to have a few more drinks!'

Just to impress them, he sent a small *Fireball* rocketing out through the pub window, but his aim was slightly low and the *Fireball* grazed the head of a small orc, setting its hair alight, to the delight of the rest. There was a huge cheer, and Tarl jumped down and grinned at Marwood. Then the orcs besieged the bar, clamouring for more drinks, and many of them bought one for Chigger and his two friends. Marwood looked at the six pints of beer that were already lined up in front of him, and wondered if he had the slightest chance of surviving the next two days.

By the time the sun rose next morning, Marwood was so pissed he could hardly stand up. They had been to four more taverns, and now had an enthusiastic following of over five hundred orcs, most of whom had their weapons and war packs with them. Tarl had lasted the pace a bit better, although he was feeling it now. He wasn't at all sure if they had a big enough army, but they had run out of time.

They needed to get moving now, while he could still walk. In fact, they were only waiting here on the edge of town long enough to ensure that every orc had had the chance to buy enough booze to last for two days.

Leaving Marwood sitting slumped on the ground talking to a beetle, Tarl pushed the reluctant Chigger up on to a large rock and scrambled up after him. He staggered and nearly fell off, and then stared blearily at his army. There looked to be a thousand orcs out there staring at him, but then he could also see two Chiggers beside him and two Marwoods slumped at the foot of the rock, so it was probably his eyes. He hiccuped, belched loudly, then gestured dramatically for silence and nearly fell off the rock again. The orcs fell silent, and he drew breath to speak.

'Wally,' shouted someone near the back, and a few others took up the cry.

There's always one, thought Tarl.

'All right?' he yelled.

'All right,' the orcs yelled back. Tarl cupped his hand behind his ear.

'I can't hear you,' he yelled, and this time the sound waves nearly knocked him off the rock, and sent Marwood into a foetal position with his arms wrapped round his head.

'All right,' shouted Tarl. 'Chigger and I know of a dwarf town under a mountain called Tor Deforzh, two days' march away. The dwarves have got a lot of gold . . .'

He paused. There was a small cheer.

'. . . and they've got a lot of explosives and stuff . . .'

Another cheer, bigger this time.

'. . . and they've got a massive pub that brews its own beer.'

A huge, enthusiastic cheer, and a lot of sword and spear waving. He nudged Chigger in the ribs, to indicate it was time for his rehearsed lines.

'Are you with me?' yelled Chigger, eagerly. He was quite getting off on the idea that all these guys had come on the party because he was leading it.

'YEAH!!!' The roar was so deafening that Tarl had to thump the side of his head to get his eardrum working, and Marwood started trying to burrow underneath the rock.

'Okay,' yelled Chigger. 'What are we waiting for? Let's go!'

The orcs roared again as he leapt down, and Tarl waved a borrowed sword at them and fell off the rock. Luckily, he landed on Marwood, breaking his fall. Dragging his friend upright he shook him in an attempt to clear his fogged brain. Marwood's head lolled back and forth, and his eyes rolled round in their sockets like roulette balls before coming to rest. He stared at Tarl and then grinned at him as recognition dawned.

'Hic,' he said.

'Right,' said Tarl to Chigger. 'Let's move it.'

The two of them began to jog northwards, dragging Marwood with them, and the orc army parted to let them through, cheering and waving their weapons. Then they fell into step behind them, following as they ran towards the narrow pass that snaked round the bleak, crumbling grandeur of Tor Riepahti to the vast, open wastes of the Kahdor plain beyond.

Meiosin was dreaming that Reágin was digging out huge chunks of metal ore from a rock face, and was using him as a pickaxe. With every swing, his head would slam home into the seam with a force that sent a shaft of agony through his whole body and threatened to smash the top of his head off. And all of a sudden it did come off, and the enraged Reágin swore and shook him to and fro in fury . . .

And then Meiosin woke up to find that his head was throbbing with pain, and someone was indeed shaking him. It was a worried-looking Mitosin. Meiosin blinked, and stared round blearily. He appeared to have slept on his office floor. He stood up, grasping his head with one hand, and his foot sent an empty *vlatzhkan gûl* bottle skittering across the floor to collide with a second one by the door. Well, that explained the headache . . .

He suddenly became aware that Mitosin was babbling on about something and kept repeating, 'What are we going to do? What are we going to do?' Extending one hand in a peremptory signal for him to stop, he inched his way across to the small sink in the corner, ran a little cold water and splashed it over his face. Then, feeling a fraction better, he walked back to his desk, picked up the chair that was lying on its side and carefully seated himself.

'Right,' he said. 'Now, what's all this about?'

'Most of the scientists have walked out!'

'What do you mean, they've walked out?'

'They've gone! All of Reágin's old supporters, and a few others as well!'

'What? Why didn't you stop them?'

'It must have been during the night. They've left a letter. You'd better read it.'

Meiosin snatched the proffered paper from his brother and stared at it.

'What the *klat* does this mean? Undwarvish experiments? Cruel? Callous? Heartless? By the gods! We're scientists, aren't we? We're above all that!' He shook his head, baffled, and read on. 'So they're going back to Toltecel, are they? Good riddance. This weeds out the faint-hearted, that's all. How many have stayed?'

'Less than two hundred,' replied Mitosin.

'Hm.' Meiosin tossed the letter on to his desk. Then picking up one of the empty bottles, he toyed with it absently, his brow creased with thought.

'Have we heard from the Orcbane board this morning?' he asked.

'Yes,' answered Mitosin, getting ready to duck. 'They seem very eager indeed to visit us.'

'Fine. Now listen, this is what I want you to do. Close down the Biology and Necromancy Departments. Put all the biologists into Genetics and the magic meddlers into Machines and Contrivances. Use Medicaments for the injured, and run it with a skeleton staff. Spread the rest between Alchemy and Physicks.' He winced as his head started thumping with renewed vigour. 'If the Orcbane people say anything about the closed-down departments, we tell them we're understaffed through lack of money, and hint that we need twice as much. This could yet work in our favour. Now get moving. I want everything ready to fetch the board here in one hour.'

'Right away!' his brother said, and dashed eagerly out of the door.

'Oh, and Mitosin?'

There was a pause, and then Mitosin's right eye managed to peer round the door without any other part of his face coming into view.

'Yes?' he said doubtfully.

'Fetch me a couple of aspirin, would you? I seem to have a bit of a headache, for some reason . . .'

The Orcbane board had been gathered in the boardroom for two hours when they finally got the message that the dwarves at Deforzh were ready for them. They had been talking animatedly, even excitedly, about travelling to see the wonders that these dwarven scientists claimed to have invented. Or at least five of them had. Kaglav, Grole, Gahvanser, Missek and Mellial were sitting round the table eagerly discussing the reports they had received and the images of the *cobrats* that they had seen in this very room via Cartland's hag-magic. But Wayta sat separately, hunched up in his chair, shivering, with a blanket wrapped about his legs and another about his shoulders. For Wayta was suffering from the mother of all colds. His nose was streaming, his throat was sore, his eyes were watering and every joint ached. Currently, the only question he could raise any enthusiasm for was whether the dwarves' Medicaments Department might have invented anything that would ease his symptoms.

He was just thinking that it might be preferable to sit here and wait for Ronan to come and cut his head off, as at least his sinuses would stop hurting, when there was a faint chime like a very distant bell, and all at once an image of Mitosin's head appeared in the centre of the polished oaken table. The image revolved slowly, smiling and nodding respectfully to each of the men in turn.

'My apologies for the delay, gentlemen,' it said. 'We have been repairing and overhauling the transmitters, but we are ready to transport you now. Only three of the machines are currently operational, however, so three of you will have to wait a short while. Now, who's first?'

The others looked eagerly to Wayta, but he just shrugged indifferently, so Grole, Kaglav and Missek stood up quickly.

'This will only take a moment,' said Mitosin's head. The three waiting men looked at each other nervously, but then a flashing red light appeared in the air above their heads, and all of a sudden they vanished.

Gahvanser and Mellial gaped in astonishment.

'Incredible!' muttered Mellial. 'But are we sure that . . .'

'They have arrived safely,' interrupted Mitosin's head. The dwarf sounded a little irritated. 'However, we have a slight problem with another of the transmitters. For safety's sake, we're shutting it down, so this time we can only transport two of you.'

Wayta gestured wearily with one hand, indicating to the others to go ahead, then pulled his blanket closer around his shoulders and sniffed miserably. Gahvanser and Mellial hauled themselves upright and stared nervously at one another as red lights began to flash above them, and then they too vanished.

Wayta gazed curiously at the dwarf's head, which was now staring blankly at something he couldn't see with an expression of disbelief.

'Oh, bugger!' it muttered. Then it turned sideways and seemed to be arguing with someone out of sight, although Wayta couldn't hear anything more. He wiped his streaming eyes and peered blearily at it, wishing that it would go away and let him die in peace, instead of sitting there sticking out of the table like a ghostly bust. It was irritating him and so he pulled a face at it, sticking his tongue out. It turned and stared straight at him.

'We have a problem,' it told him, icily polite. 'Those last two fat bast . . . er, I mean, the last two board members are a little larger than we expected. You must remember that the Matter Transmitters were built for the use of dwarves.'

'Are they all right?' Wayta asked, interestedly.

'Oh, yes, they're fine. They're just a little wedged, is all. We're using goose-grease and leverage, and they should pop out eventually. We'll get back to you as soon as we have a free transmitter.'

Mitosin's head vanished, and Wayta was left sitting morosely alone in the boardroom. But not for long. There was a knock on the door behind him, and then he heard it open. Knowing that it could only be Cartland, he sat with his back resolutely towards it as her familiar footsteps shuffled in. He had problems with her at the best of times, and when he felt this wretched, she was about as welcome as a dragon with hiccoughs in a kindergarten.

'Agh, shame!' she cackled. 'Blaggum issy wargle got the flu, then?'

Wayta nodded, despite himself, although he still refused to acknowledge her by turning round. Any sympathy was welcome at the moment, although it worried him that he was beginning to be able to understand the mumbling cackle of her speech.

'Guddum addy potion, argle saggy feel better,' she mumbled, and a skinny hand extended over his shoulder and proffered a glass of hot, steaming liquid with a yellowish tint.

A hot lemon drink, he thought. *The mad old biddy has her moments, after all!* He took the glass with a muttered word of thanks and raised it to his lips.

'Gablanga munchy wangle glass of fresh piss,' she told him as he knocked it back, and the import of her words hit him at exactly the same time as the foul, acrid, nauseating taste of the liquid. His stomach went into immediate spasms, his throat contracted and he leant forward, retching violently time and time again until his body had rid itself of the liquid.

'You daft old biddy,' he yelled, as the last spasm subsided. 'What the *klat* do you think you're doing, giving me fresh urine to drink?'

He swung round accusingly, but at the sight of her his facial muscles froze in a mask of horror, and his jaw dropped so far he nearly swallowed his feet.

Cartland was wearing an expression of naked lust that was so blatant it scared the crap out of him. She was heavily but randomly made up, and was clad only in a calf-length négligé of some sheer, flimsy material that was semi see-through. Seeing him staring at her, she cackled with glee and went into a stomach-churning parody of a pirouette. Wayta swallowed. Something was wobbling behind the material just above her knees, and he had the horrid feeling that it was her breasts. Either that or her stomach . . .

'Lagga singy uggle bubber shag, then?' she asked, leaning towards him, and suddenly Wayta found he was standing on the opposite side of the table to her without any idea or memory of how he had got there, like a wounded animal fleeing to its lair.

'No!' he yelled. 'Go away. Cartland, go! If you don't leave this room now, I'll . . . I'll . . .'

But it was to no avail. Cartland was creeping round the table towards him with the expression of a hungry *lenkat* that has just spotted its breakfast bunny. With a wail of fear, Wayta made a dash for the door, which was still ajar. But then he heard a muttered incantation behind him, and it slammed firmly shut in his face and refused to yield to his desperate tugs. He turned, looking around frantically for some way out, but there was none. Cartland was advancing on him, almost drooling with lust. And then, at the very last moment, he had a brainwave . . .

Mitosin watched with mounting impatience as two groups of sweating, straining orcs struggled to extricate the pair of obese humans who were tightly wedged inside the two remaining working booths. Then a Machines and Contrivances technician came running across to him.

'We've sorted the problem with the other transmitter,' he said. 'Loose connection. It's working now, if you want to risk getting the last human stuck in it.'

'Oh, he's not as fat as the others,' said Mitosin. 'Let's bring him in.'

He followed the technician across to the repaired transmitter and watched as he pressed buttons and pulled levers. Lights winked and the machine hummed. Then a green light on top of the booth began flashing.

'We've got him,' said the technician.

Mitosin fixed a friendly grin in place and pulled open the door of the booth, but his words of greeting died silent on his lips, and he stared in astonishment at the man inside.

Wayta was standing facing them with a blanket loosely wrapped around his shoulders. His eyes were clamped tight shut and his face was taut with strain and fear. He was holding a knife in one hand and appeared to be about to plunge it into a large cabbage which he was clutching in the other.

'I mean it,' he screamed, without opening his eyes. 'If you come one step closer, you demented old crone, John the Cabbage gets it! And don't give me any more of that crap about your familiar crying his eyes out, because cabbages don't have eyes! That's potatoes, you mad old harpy!'

Then he opened his eyes and saw the mass of bemused dwarves staring at him. A lesser man might have been embarrassed at being caught in this strange behaviour, but Wayta actually appeared relieved to see them.

'About bloody time!' he snarled to Mitosin, jamming the knife back into its scabbard and stalking out of the booth. 'So, this is the rapid and reliable form of transport you told me about, is it? Quite remarkable! How did we ever manage without it?'

He looked angrily down at the cabbage, then jerked his knife back out and sliced the vegetable clean in half.

'Here,' he added, tossing the two halves to Mitosin. 'Send this back where I've just come from, will you?'

And then he stalked across to a bench, sat down, wrapped his blanket round his shoulders and started sneezing furiously.

When the two halves of cabbage rematerialised on the highly polished oaken table of the Orcbane boardroom, Cartland was still staring at the space where Wayta had been with the baffled look of a *lenkat* which, on being about to pounce upon its breakfast bunny, sees it disappear into the safety of a burrow. She stared at the pieces of cabbage unbelievingly for a few seconds, and then her face crumpled. Reaching out, she touched one of the halves, gently fondling its leaves.

But then the look of sorrow was replaced by one of fury. She glared fiercely at the table with an unblinking stare. After a few seconds, wisps of smoke began to rise from its surface. After a minute, flames were licking along it. She backed to the door, still staring at the table, and her voice rose in a bitter, hate-filled chant. The flames grew with the intensity of her voice until they were a column of fire that reached to the ceiling, and then they fanned out along it like fingers, groping hungrily for the curtains.

Cartland backed down the plushly carpeted corridor outside, still chanting, and only when a torrent of flames erupted through the boardroom door did she turn and hobble down the main stairs towards the street, a satisfied smile on her face at a job well done. That smug git of a chairman might have turned her love to ashes, but when he got back from wherever he'd been spirited off to, he'd find that she'd done exactly the same thing to his entire office block. It might smack a bit of overreaction, but what the hell, she was in a foul mood and her bunions were playing her up again. And, as she always liked to say, hell hath no fury like a woman's corns . . .

Ronan, Tyson, Guebral and Puss had made good progress. After seeing Tarl and Marwood off, they had gone to bed early and slept for seven hours. Then, rising, they had left Gudmornen in the middle of the night. It had been a clear night, and the full moon had made travelling easy. By dawn they had climbed out of the Reudi Valley and were picking their way through the foothills of the mountains towards the flat plains of western Kahdor.

The weather was fine but cold. This far north the sun didn't rise very high in the sky, and the thin, watery sunlight had little heat in it, but the exercise kept them warm. They ate on the move, keeping up a steady pace, and by noon they had left the hills behind them and were heading east across the undulating plain.

It was late in the afternoon when they first spotted the distant mountain. For almost a mile they had been walking up a gentle slope, and when they came to the top it was Ronan who noticed the orange glow low to the east. At first he thought it was a cloud low in the sky, but then he realised that it was the setting sun shining on the snow-covered peak of Tor Deforzh. They were making good time, and were more than halfway.

In front of them was a small valley through which a large stream ran northwards. A fair number of scrubby bushes and stunted conifers grew along its banks. They decided to camp here for the night, and set to work constructing a rough shelter, for there was plenty of dead wood to hand. They had also brought a stout bundle of firewood with them from town, and it wasn't long before they had a roaring fire going, and were contentedly sitting beside it, eating an evening meal of dried meat, bread, cheese and fruit.

Afterwards, Guebral did a quick *Scan* to check on Tarl, and the others watched, amused at the expression on her face as she contacted him.

'How is he?' asked Tyson, when she had finished.

'Pissed as a rat. But they're going well. We should meet up with them tomorrow evening.'

'It must be a strain for him.'

'No, he's enjoying it. I can tell from his thoughts. It's hard going, but he's having fun.'

'What about Marwood?' asked Ronan.

'Ah. Well. Tarl seems to get very amused when he thinks of Marwood, so I have a feeling that maybe the poor man's not having a very good time at all, at the moment . . .'

In fact, Marwood was having a truly awful time. He had a stitch in his side that hurt badly but was nothing compared to his aching lungs, which in turn were nothing compared to the pain in his feet. But even that was dwarfed by the pain in his head.

It wasn't the fact that they had been running all day that was bothering him, for his Assassin training had prepared him for sore feet and aching lungs. But he had never in his life experienced the onset of a hangover whilst awake. Hangovers were meant to arrive while you slept and be sitting there in your head when you woke up. This one had crept over him whilst they were running, slowly turning from a dull headache and a feeling of incipient nausea to a blinding pain that stabbed through his skull with every pace he took and gut-wrenching bouts of vomiting.

He had stopped to be sick several times, but hadn't fallen behind. An orc war party consists at any one time of eighty per cent running, while the other twenty per cent have stopped to empty their bladders, be ill or have another drink. And so, rather than marching in exact formation, an orc war party moves in a continuous streaming motion. Half the army may jog past you while you've stopped to be ill, but sooner or later you'll pass them while they've stopped to have a quick beer or nip on to a handy rock for a pee.[16] Marwood was somewhere in the mid-section, and both Tarl and Chigger had slowed down to stay with him.

In fact, Tarl was beginning to get a little worried about him. His face had gone grey again, and his eyes were a strange mixture of red, white and yellow, like half-cooked fried eggs set in the middle of two raw steaks. The problem was that the poor guy didn't have Tarl's

16 Orcs don't nip *behind* rocks to urinate. They like to climb on top of them with the aim of soaking as many people as possible.

experience of matching the orcs by taking in a slow but steady flow of alcohol so that you didn't sober up, but stayed just nicely drunk. He'd got far too pissed and had suffered accordingly.

Still, he'd be able to have a rest in a minute. Tarl had let the war party keep running, even though his own feet were killing him, for he wasn't too sure how much time they had. But now that Guebral had been in touch, he knew they could afford to rest up for several hours, and so he'd passed the word forward that they were going to stop for a decent drink. This would have another advantage as well, in that the orcs would probably finish off all the available booze, and that meant that by the time they reached Tor Deforzh tomorrow, they'd be feeling as dry as a bone, and would fight like demons to take possession of the dwarves' supplies of alcohol.

Yes, the orcs ahead were stopping. As they broke up into shouting, laughing groups and began broaching the main body of booze, Tarl grabbed Marwood's sleeve to stop him, for he was tottering along like an automaton, and dragged him to a halt.

'We're going to make camp,' he told the dazed ex-Assassin. 'Why don't you get some sleep before we eat. You'll feel much better.'

But before he'd even finished speaking, Marwood's eyes had closed, and he had folded up like an accordion and slumped to the ground. Worried, Tarl bent down to shake him, but a gentle snoring told him that he was fine. Tarl sighed enviously and stood up again. He would have liked to catch a bit of sleep himself, but he didn't dare. Someone had to keep an eye on the war party and make sure that it didn't suddenly decide to march off somewhere else, just for the hell of it. And so, with heavy eyes and aching feet, Tarl wandered off to see if any of the orcs had brought a pack of cards with them.

CHAPTER TWELVE

Although it was a comparatively minor skirmish, the Battle Beneath the Mountain became renowned in orc history, mainly because it was the subject of a song by their most famous female singer, Bjorc. An art-school drop-out from Goblin City, Bjorc is an unfamiliar name to many humans, although most would recognise the wonderful songs she crafted around minor incidents in her life. Her most famous song was based on the events that caused her to abandon art school, when she lost her whole portfolio one night after leaving it in a discothèque owned by a friend, and few indeed are the humans who would fail to recognise the melody of 'I Left My Art In Some Friend's Disco' . . .

The Pink Book of Ulay

Ronan lay flat behind the rocky outcrop, peering around the side of it towards Tor Deforzh. Behind him was a small gully in which Guebral, Tyson and Puss were resting. Ahead of him lay almost a mile of open grassland before the craggy slopes of the single, cone-shaped mountain rose skywards. Had he been a geologist, Ronan might have recognised its volcanic origins, but the snow-covered, cratered peak and the now-quiescent fumaroles held little import for him. He was examining the nearest slope of the mountain, where it rose sheer from the plain for two hundred feet, as in the centre of this cliff face was something of far greater interest – the main gate of the dwarves' city.

It was mid-afternoon, and he could clearly see the two great stone doors standing ajar. In front of them, four sentries stood and gossiped. It looked to Ronan like something of an insurmountable obstacle, for the gate was some thirty feet above the level of the plain, and was reached by a sloping earthen ramp. Creeping up on it would be an impossibility, and charging it openly would give the sentries ample time to shut and bar the gates. Nor would attacking after dark be of any use, for the dwarves' routine was likely to be the same as every other dwarf city he had visited, where the gates were closed as twilight fell. No, he couldn't see how Tarl's orc army were going to get in without a long and pointless siege . . .

Wriggling backwards until he was out of sight of the mountain, he stood up and scrambled down to the others. Tyson and Guebral were taking their chance to have a bite to eat, and Puss was lapping up water from a tiny brook.

'Well, I can't see any way of taking the gates quickly,' he said, sitting down on a boulder next to Tyson.

'Don't worry,' she told him. 'Guebral reckons she knows how it can be done.'

Guebral nodded.

'I think I can *Teleport* inside the city. Beneltin gave me two strong memories, so I can target either of them. We can get the gates open for you.'

'*We* can?' echoed Ronan.

'Yes,' said Tyson. 'I need to go with her. You have to stay here with Puss and lead the orc army in at the right time.'

Ronan sighed. He was getting a little fed up with the number of times he was having to part from Tyson. During their sojourn at the hotel near Perplec, he had discovered how wondrous it was to spend time with your loved one, doing absolutely sod all except lie in the sun and enjoy yourself. Crouching in near-freezing gullies at the arse-end of the world and planning how to gatecrash cities full of pain-in-the-bum dwarf scientists was, for some reason, not nearly as much fun.

'Hold on,' said Tyson, suddenly. 'Can you hear something?'

They listened for a moment. Ronan could just make out a distant murmuring. It sounded like a massive pub brawl heard from a long way away.

'It's the orcs,' said Guebral, but Ronan was already scrambling up the side of the gully to his position behind the rock. He crawled forward on knees and elbows and peered out hopefully, but he could see straight away that the dwarf sentries had already heard the noise, for they were standing together peering southwards and pointing.

'So much for a guerrilla attack!' he muttered to himself as he scrambled back down to the others. He was going to ask Guebral to pass a message on to Tarl, but he could tell by the vacant look on her face that she was in contact with him already, so he squatted down and waited. Guebral frowned worriedly, then her eyes re-focused and she looked from Tyson to Ronan in concern.

'Tarl's none too sure that he can control the orcs,' she said. 'He and Marwood are on their last legs. It's been all they can do just to keep up with them.'

'How long have we got?'

'Fifteen minutes. Maybe less. The orcs are thirsty and sobering up. Now they've seen the mountains they've started sprinting.'

'*Klat!*' swore Ronan. 'We'd better get moving!' He reached behind his back to unsheathe the massive broadsword that Dean Blackwell had found for him in the Museum of Assassination, and Tyson reached out to take his other hand and squeeze it. All at once Ronan felt a strange prickling feeling in that hand, and at the same time Tyson shivered with apprehension.

'Take care, love,' she warned him. 'I have a bad feeling about all this.'

He grinned at her and squeezed her hand back, but he too had felt the sudden certainty that something was about to go badly wrong. Then Tyson released his hand and reached out to take Guebral's. She grinned uncertainly at him as Guebral closed her eyes and muttered something, and suddenly they just weren't there.

'Useful ability, that,' muttered a voice near Ronan's thigh, and he looked down to see Puss staring ruefully at the spot where the two women had been. 'Beats hooves, I can tell you. Not that I've got much left in the way of hooves, after all the walking I've had to do in the past few months.' It lifted its head and stared lugubriously up at him. 'Anyone ever tell you you're just an old stick-in-the-mud?' it asked, before starting to plod painfully up towards the top of the gully.

Tyson gasped slightly as they materialised in a pitch-dark room and dropped six inches to the floor.

'Sorry,' whispered Guebral. 'I was making allowances for a dwarf's-eye memory. I must have overcompensated.'

There was a brief pause, and then Tyson blinked as a soft white radiance lit the room in response to Guebral's *Light* spell. They were in a large, roughly hewn cave with a vast, brightly gleaming metal machine in the centre. It was sitting on a solid rock plinth, and was making a gentle humming sound. Thick metal cables snaked out of the top and looped to the wall, disappearing through pipe-like holes bored in the rock, and the air was thick with the smell of oil.

'Okay,' said Guebral. 'I need to put this out of action. Keep an eye on the door.'

Tyson padded across to the open arched portal behind them, and peered through. The bare stone passage outside was lit by a single wall-torch jammed into a sconce, underneath which was an unoccupied stool. She stood warily on guard, her sword in her right hand, listening for footsteps.

Behind her, Guebral was studying the machine, her head on one side. After a couple of minutes, she seemed to come to some sort of decision. Standing back, she raised one arm and pointed at the metal cables. Tyson, casting a quick look back, thought she could just make out a thin, shimmering, misty beam connecting them to Guebral's pointing finger, but whatever she was doing, it had an instant effect. The metal of one cable seemed to melt where it left the machine, flowing and dripping like water, until suddenly the cable snapped, hanging down from the hole and bouncing gently against the wall with flashing sparks spurting from it. Guebral moved her finger a fraction, and the next cable snapped, and then the next, until all were sagging from the wall, and none were still connected to the machine. Then she switched her gaze to the machine itself, and the humming sound faded and died.

At the doorway, Tyson heard the sound of approaching footsteps. She looked back to Guebral, who beckoned and held her hand out. Tyson hastened across, and Guebral caught her by the wrist. Once more they vanished, and seconds later a dwarf stomped into the cavern. He looked a little puzzled at the lack of noise, but when he saw the cables sagging loosely down the wall, his jaw sagged and he looked as dazed as if someone had just hit him on the back of the head with most of the mountain. For almost a minute he stared, his eyes bulging, his mouth moving wordlessly, and then he turned and ran from the room as fast as his legs would carry him.

As he strolled towards the gates, Ronan watched the dwarf sentries arguing and peering into the distance. They had seen him, but a single human strolling towards them with a small donkey appeared to offer little threat. They were ignoring him, as he had hoped, for he needed to reach the gate at the same time as the orcs, yet there was no cover to allow him to get closer without being seen.

He smiled to himself. They couldn't work out what was causing the noise, nor could they see. He was approaching them in plain view from the west, the direction in which the gate faced, but the orc war party was coming from the south, and was hidden by a low spur of the mountain. All they could see was a large dust cloud above the spur, the sort that would be caused by a stampede of wild horses or cattle. However, animals didn't make the sort of noise that accompanied the cloud. Ronan, who had seen a war party in action, recognised some of the distant chants, but to the dwarves, they would have been completely baffling.

Then, when he was a few hundred yards short of the gates, the orc vanguard came streaming round the spur of the mountain. Seeing their target, they let out a howl of excitement that sent a shiver down the spine, and this was echoed by the rest of the army still out of sight.

Ronan grinned, for he could clearly see the expressions on the faces of the sentries, and they didn't look at all happy. They backed through the gates, apparently unable to take their eyes off the orcs, and one of them reached out and pressed a large button on the wall just inside the right-hand door. Then he jabbed it again, and yet again, each time more frantically, but nothing happened. If the button was supposed to work the doors, it was failing miserably.

'Well done, girls,' Ronan breathed. 'Whatever you've done, it's worked.'

But then the dwarves grabbed hold of the edges of the doors and began to pull. To Ronan's amazement, the doors began to swing slowly shut. They must have been superbly balanced, for they were nine feet high, and over a foot thick. He began to run, fearful that they would yet be closed before Tarl's orcs could get there. But then the familiar figure of Tyson glided out of the gates, with Guebral close behind her. The dwarves grabbed their axes and turned towards the two women, but Guebral lifted a hand, and all four fell as though poleaxed.

Tyson beckoned to Ronan frantically, and he could just make out her distant yell above the clamour of the orcs.

'We've been seen! Hurry!'

She disappeared back inside with Guebral, and Ronan began to sprint, with Puss galloping beside him, desperate to follow her before the leading orcs got there. To his relief he reached the gates a good fifty yards ahead of them. The sentries had managed to half close one, but he leaned against it and pushed it fully open. Then, pulling his sword from its scabbard, he strode through into the gloom inside.

The six members of the Orcbane board followed Meiosin through the Transmitter Room into the main Magenetics lecture theatre, each lost in his own thoughts. All were deeply impressed by the sights they had seen and the information they had been given in the past twenty four hours. Wayta was thinking of the incredible weapons that Orcbane would be able to manufacture, once they could harness the new explosives that the dwarves had invented. Grole was wondering whether the Alchemy Department would succeed in finding a way to produce gold. Kaglav was wondering whether the dwarf would allow him to use that gorgeous female centaur they had just seen in the holding pens for the night, whilst Gahvanser was entertaining similar thoughts about a couple of the male captives. And Missek and Mellial were both wondering about some of the new drugs that the Medicaments and Alchemy Departments had produced, and what interesting side effects they might have. Behind them, Mitosin was wondering whether he would get a chance to nip down to the Seam of Gold for a couple of beers.

Meiosin climbed on to the lecture podium and gestured to the board to be seated. He paused, relishing the moment, for the visit had gone well and they had been fascinated by the scientific advances that had been demonstrated. It had already been made clear that there would be plenty more gold to fund further such advances. And now he was about to show them the Vivarium, and demonstrate some of the fascinating creatures that Magenetics had bred. This was going to knock their socks off . . .

He cleared his throat, but before he could speak a panting dwarf barged through the door and stood there gasping. It was Pylin. Meiosin stared at him crossly, and Mitosin, recognising a dwarf with bad news to impart, hastily grabbed Pylin by the arm and dragged him back into the Transmitter Room.

'What is it?' he hissed.

'The new generator!' gasped Pylin. 'All the cables have melted! The power is down in the whole city, apart from Magenetics!'

Mitosin swore under his breath. Building a second generator like the one in Magenetics, and introducing Electrycks to the rest of Deforzh had been one of the first things Meiosin had done after taking over from Reágin, and he was proud of the feat. If he found out about this, he was likely to start throwing bottles at people again.

'Okay,' Mitosin whispered, 'I'll come and have a look. Let's not bother the boss with it just now, eh?'

And he followed the other dwarf out into the passage, closing the Transmitter Room door behind him.

The vanguard of the orc war party came pounding up the earthen ramp and exploded through the gate of the city, a rampaging mass of thirsty revellers in urgent need of a drink. Inside, they found themselves in a vast hall lined with columns along both sides. A few yards inside the gate, three humans and a small brown donkey were besieged by a ring of attacking dwarves, and at the far end of the hall a score of others were streaming down a broad marble stairway to join in the attack.

The leading orcs were in no doubt what was happening. They had been briefed that morning by Chigger's two friends, the human killer and the half-orc. These must be the three humans they had been told would be joining the party: the huge black warrior, the woman warrior and the small magic-user. With a roar of excitement, the leading ranks threw themselves at the dwarves and swept them backwards by sheer momentum, leaving Ronan and the others free of their assailants.

With the donkey clearing a path by snapping viciously at anyone who got in the way, Ronan waded to the side of the hall through the excited, sword-waving orcs, and Guebral and Tyson followed. Leaning on his sword, he drew a deep breath of relief. For a few seconds, things had been a little bit frantic, but the war party had turned up in the nick of time. Dwarves are far more fearsome foes when defending their own territory, and they had really had their work cut out to hold the gates. But now the weight of numbers and the exuberance of the orcs was too much for the thirty or so defenders, and they were being forced into flight.

'According to Beneltin,' said Guebral, as the tide of cheering orcs swept up the stairs in pursuit, 'the gates and the first stairway are the main defensive points. Once the orcs have got past those, there's little to stop them. They'll just fan out along all the main passages. It's going to take the dwarves a while to get any sort of defence organised.'

'Then we'd better get moving before they do,' answered Ronan. 'We need to find where the dwarves keep their captives.'

The stream of orcs was thinning now, and the weaker, slower and drunker ones were staggering through the gates. And then, after the last orc had tottered in, two familiar figures brought up the rear.

'Tarl!' called Guebral, and dashing across she flung her arms around him. Marwood, who had been supporting Tarl, relinquished him into her arms, and then strolled across to the others. He was out of breath, but otherwise seemed fine. Tarl, however, was gasping like a fish out of water, and was making as much noise as an asthmatic dragon.

'Are you all right?' asked Guebral, worriedly.

'Oh, he'll be fine,' Marwood reassured her. 'He's just a bit out of breath, that's all. He could do with being fitter. And he can't hold his ale, poor bloke.'

Tarl began to splutter indignantly, but Ronan held up a hand to forestall any arguments.

'Listen,' he growled, 'you two can sort out your differences later. For now, we've got work to do. Tarl, Marwood, find Chigger and try to keep those orcs in order. We don't want them massacring anyone. Guebral, you reckon you can find your way to the captives?'

'Yes,' she answered, nodding. 'Beneltin told me where they're being held. We need to find our way up to the main living areas, then work our way down through the research levels to something called the Magenetics Department.'

'Okay. Lead on. Puss, you come with us. We don't want you ending up as an orc barbecue.'

And with that he led them along the stone-flagged hallway, and they began to pick their way up the marble staircase past the still-bleeding corpses of orcs and dwarves.

Mitosin stared at the dangling metal cables. There was nothing he could think of that could have caused the ends to melt like that apart from magic, and there was that same prickling feeling in the air that he always sensed whenever the Necromancy Department had pulled off one of their really big experiments. Some magic-user had done this. Either they had a renegade in Deforzh, or else there was an intruder!

He turned to Pylin.

'Get downstairs and tell the Chief Scientist that we've got a saboteur in the place. But don't blurt it out in front of the guests, all right? Tell him quietly.'

Pylin went scurrying out, and Mitosin scratched his head, then followed more sedately, wondering what was going on. He turned the corner just in time to see the other dwarf reach the end of the narrow corridor and run out into the main passage. Then something seemed to sprout from his neck and he toppled sideways with a scream of pain.

Mitosin stood rooted to the spot with fear. That had been an arrow! He pressed himself against the wall, and next moment a seemingly unending stream of orcs went charging past the end of the corridor. It was impossible to count numbers, but there must have been over fifty. He waited for more than a minute after they had gone past, listening intently until their howls and jeers had faded, and then he crept along the corridor. Reaching the end, he peered out.

Some thirty yards to the right, the wide passage ran into the main hall of the living-quarter levels. Here he could see seven dwarf corpses lying in a group where they had tried to make a stand, and there were five headless orc corpses in front of them. And then Mitosin froze, for a very strange little group of people were passing the end of the passage. There was a vast black human warrior, a couple of human women, one of whom was armed to the teeth, and a small brown donkey which appeared to be singing to itself.

Mitosin drew back into the passage and thought carefully. It rather looked as though they had been invaded, and if humans were involved, they were going to be extremely pissed off with the dwarves after the number of raids they had carried out recently, and might be out for revenge. In fact, it was highly likely that they wouldn't be taking many prisoners. It might be a good idea to slip out while the going was good, and try to catch up with the guys who left the other day. Yes, it could be time to look after number one. After all, he'd taken one bottle in the face too many to feel that he owed Meiosin anything.

With his mind made up, Mitosin slipped silently out into the passage, and crept towards the distant hall.

Throughout Deforzh, the orcs chased and harried the dwarves, pursuing them along passages and down stairs, hacking and slashing at them. It should have been a hard battle, for dwarves could be fearsome foes, but the defenders lacked the will to resist. The strong and the brave had left already, driven away by Meiosin's unpleasant regime. Those remaining included the cowardly, the weak and the selfish, and they were incapable or unwilling to fight to the death. Many surrendered, and the rest fled into the dark recesses of the city to hide, or sold their lives cheaply.

As they stalked wearily through the corridors and tunnels, their swords in their hands, Tarl and Marwood couldn't find a single living defender. There were corpses aplenty, though, and many of them were a sight that few people had seen before: dwarves with wounds in their backs.

Though he was near exhaustion, Tarl's pub compass was still functioning. They made their way to the Seam of Gold without any difficulty, although the noise from revelling orcs who had already found the place helped. They discovered that a chain of orcs had formed, stretching from the cellar to the bar, and they were passing barrels of beer from hand to hand. The word from those in the cellar was that there was at least a barrel for every orc.

Tarl and Marwood stood in the doorway and surveyed the wreckage. Already, most of the tables and chairs had been smashed. A group of orcs were playing Chicken with a dwarf barman in one corner, and another group were playing a dare game that they had just invented called Catch the Battleaxe. Already, several fingers were littering the floor.

'What do you reckon?' asked Tarl. 'Orc parties can be a dangerous place.'

'Yeah,' said Marwood. 'But then again, I'm thirsty.'

They looked at each other and grinned, and then stepped forwards into the chaos.

Guebral led the other three along the passage as it curved to the right, sloping gradually downwards past open-doored, empty rooms into the heart of the mountain. There were regular wall-torches and the passage was well lit. All of a sudden it bent sharply back to the left and ended abruptly. There were three doors here: one on either side and a large stone portal in the end wall.

'If I've remembered Beneltin's instructions correctly, it's through here,' she told them, laying her hand on the stone door. It swung quietly open at her touch, and they walked through. Beyond was a square passage some sixty feet long, with wooden doors on either side and a solid metal matt-black door at the far end. A bluish light seemed to seep out of the very stone of the walls, giving them an eerie metallic sheen.

Guebral opened the first door on the right, and led them into a brightly lit laboratory. They wrinkled their noses at the bitter, choking smell of chemicals as they crept past work-benches and sinks towards a door in the right-hand side of the far wall. Beyond this was a narrow, dimly lit corridor that ran for ten yards and then curved sharp left.

'This should be it,' said Guebral, and Ronan moved past her and inched along to the bend. He peered around it, but the corridor was deserted. It ran straight ahead, with doors every six feet on either side. Turning to look back at the others, he raised a finger to his lips, and then stood and listened hard. He could hear the faint sound of muffled sobbing: not just one voice, as he had thought at first, but several, softly and hopelessly weeping, and the sense of almost overwhelming despair wrenched at his heart. He turned and looked back at the others again.

'We've found them,' he whispered.

Mitosin padded softly down the stairs past orc and dwarf bodies, and crept along the deserted entrance hall. In front of him, the main gate was open and unguarded. He slipped through it and sighed with relief. He was out! It was dark now, and the chill of the night air bit home, but it was infinitely preferable to lying on a cold stone floor with an orc arrow through his neck.

He strode briskly forwards, and then gasped in surprise as a dark shape suddenly rose up from the darker ground in front of him. The gasp turned to a scream of horror as he realised that it was a *cobrat*. *By the gods*, he thought. *Where the klat has this nightmare come from!* He turned to run for the comparative safety of Deforzh, but there was suddenly another one behind him, and more on either side. Four, no, five of them surrounded him! *No*, he thought. *This can't be happening!* Terror flooded through his body, and he sank to the ground as though hoping to merge with it.

'Go away!' he tried to yell, but his larynx refused to function, and the sound came out as a hoarse whisper. 'I helped to create you. Leave me alone.'

But the *cobrats* closed on him greedily, and one of them reached out a forepaw and hoisted him clear of the ground.

'Meiosin!' he screamed. 'Brother! Help me!'

But then the scream rose through several octaves as lethal talons ripped through his clothes and tore open his stomach.

The *cobrats* watched with avid interest as the screams faded, the kicks subsided and the gouts of blood died away. There were an awful lot of hot, moist entrails hanging from the body cavity of the dwarf, and they were very hungry, but feeding could wait. The leading *cobrat* dropped Meiosin's still-twitching corpse to the ground, and the others ignored it, for they had scented the trail of their prey now, and it was very, very close. Eagerly, they stepped over the body and strode through the gate into the hallway beyond.

Meiosin was delighted. His little lecture had gone really well, and the Orcbane board had hung on his every word. He had told them about the history of the magenetical experiments, and their hopes and aims for the future. He had explained how they had created the *cobrats*, and had talked about the other fascinating creatures they had bred. Now it was time to show them the pride of his accomplishments, the Vivarium.

He quickly explained the dangers, and outlined the precautions to be taken inside the vast cavern. Then he waited patiently as they pulled on the protective boots. When they were ready, he gave them one final warning.

'Remember,' he told them. 'Do not go more than twenty feet from the door, and stay near me. You'll be quite safe, for all the animals are genetically programmed to look upon me as their master, and should not harm anyone who is with me.'

They all nodded seriously, and he wanted to laugh at their nervous expressions. But instead he cleared his throat, and then led them through the Transmitter Room and across to the door on the far side.

Ronan opened the tiny observation hatch in yet another of the solid metal doors and peered through. Inside the bare stone cell, three women were sitting cross-legged on the rocky floor, their shoulders slumped with despair, and between them, his head lying in the lap of one of them, lay Dean Blackwell's grandson. With a sigh of relief, Ronan closed the hatch and turned to Tyson.

'Found him!' he said.

She nodded thankfully and smiled, but inside she was burning with anger. They had counted thirty cells, and at the end of the corridor were steps leading to a second level. Guebral had gone up to check, but Tyson reckoned that if the cells up there were full, there might be almost two hundred captives.

Guebral came back down the steps and walked towards them.

'I can't find any keys,' she told them. 'Do you want me to unlock all the doors with a spell?'

Ronan looked at Tyson and shook his head.

'Not yet,' he said. 'Until we know what's happening between the orcs and dwarves, they might be safer where they are. Look, you stay here and keep guard over them. Tyson, Puss and I will find out if we've got control of the place. We'll be back shortly.'

He led Tyson back to the lab, where Puss was patiently keeping a look-out, and together, swords at the ready, they went through to the eerily lit main passage beyond. Ronan quietly shut the door behind them, but before they could move, a door at the other end of the passage opened, and six men and a dwarf filed out. Ronan stared at them, unable to believe his eyes.

'Hoy!' he yelled hoarsely. 'Stop!'

The six men took one look at Ronan and then ran as if for their lives down the corridor, to vanish through the matt-black metal door at the end, but the dwarf simply hopped nimbly back through the wooden door and slammed it behind him.

'I don't believe it!' gasped Ronan, and began to fumble in the money pouch at his waist.

'What is it?' asked Tyson. 'Do you know them?'

'Know them! It's the Orcbane board! Look!'

Ronan pulled a crumpled piece of paper from the pouch and handed it to Tyson. Quickly she unfolded it and found that it was a picture torn from a Perplec newspaper.

'See?' Ronan yelled, excitedly. Tyson peered at the picture. According to the caption, it was of the board members of the Orcbane Sword Corporation, and she recognised at least two of the faces as belonging to the group of men who had just vanished through the door.

'You were right, babe!' she breathed. 'The dwarves must have something to do with the *cobrats* if those sad old men are here.'

'We've got to get them,' gasped Ronan. 'Come on!'

He ran down the corridor with Tyson and Puss at his heels. Quickly they tried the wooden door through which the dwarf had bolted, but it was locked. However, the black metal door unlatched easily and swung back to reveal a second similar door ten yards beyond. Ronan held it open for the other two, and was about to follow them through when there was a ferocious hiss from behind him, and he turned to see five *cobrats* streaking down the passage towards him. Yelling with shock, he yanked the door closed behind him and hurtled to the second door past the startled Tyson. Jerking it open, he hustled Tyson and Puss through. There was no handle on the inside, and so taking hold of the edge, he slammed it shut as hard as he could.

'Did you see them?' he babbled. '*Cobrats! Klatting cobrats!* They've followed us all the way here!'

But then he realised that the other two were staring about them in amazement, and he turned to see what they were looking at.

'*Klat!* he gasped. 'What *is* this place?'

Although they knew they were still underground, they could have been outside in the open air. They couldn't see the roof of the cavern, for it was so far above them. It was hidden by a bright, diffuse light that shone down from some concealed source, giving the impression of a cloudy summer's day. They were standing on soft, lush grass above which insects buzzed lazily. Butterflies floated past, and a stream chuckled its way across maybe forty yards away. Beyond this was a forest of trees and shrubs, and they could hear birds singing in the branches.

'Look,' said Tyson, pointing, and Ronan saw the fattest two board members dodging into the trees. He turned and looked worriedly at the featureless metal door.

'How long before they work out how to open the door, do you reckon?' he asked Tyson.

'Not long,' she answered, and her voice was shaking. 'Let's skewer those sad old bastards quickly, and find another way out of here. Come on, Puss.'

She led the way quickly across the grass, with Puss following her. Ronan brought up the rear, walking crab-like, half turned to face backwards so that he would see the moment the *cobrats* got the door open. He was concentrating so hard on this that when Tyson screamed he bit his tongue, and he jerked round to find that she was flat out on the ground, with something that looked like an eight-foot snake with wings towering over her. It seemed to be about to bite her, and he roared with panic because he was too far away to reach it. Whirling his sword once round his head he threw it, but missed by a good foot.

But then, just as the creature began its strike, the little donkey threw itself at it, its teeth fastening in the snake/bird's tail. The creature hissed furiously and lashed its tail, sending the donkey flying through the air to crash into the ground several feet away, stunned. Then it turned back to its victim. But by then Ronan had launched himself after his sword, and the snake/bird turned just in time to find itself being seized by a pair of enraged hands. Ronan yanked it into the air, raised it high above his head and dashed it as hard as he could on to the ground. There was a crunching noise, and the creature gave a few convulsive twitches and lay still.

Ronan dropped to his knees beside Tyson, desperate to make sure she was all right. She was stunned, but to his relief, she was still breathing, and he smoothed her hair back from her forehead. And then, to his horror, the metal door of the cavern opened, and the five *cobrats* stalked through.

*

Wayta had had the shock of his life when he had seen Ronan at the other end of the passage. For the first time in a long while, he had panicked. It was only when he had reached the safety of the trees in the Vivarium that his brain began ticking over with its usual fluency. He stopped and watched the other five struggling across the grass like fat slugs as he tried to puzzle out what was happening.

For Ronan to be here, something dramatic must have gone wrong, or else the dwarves had double-crossed them. Somehow, he had the feeling that it wasn't the dwarves. Still, there was little he could do at the moment, so it was probably best to sit tight and see what happened. Meiosin had warned them about some of the lethal creatures that lived in the Vivarium, so he had better be prepared. He drew his sword, then sniffed as quietly as he could and wiped his streaming nose with the back of his sleeve, not daring to blow it on his silk kerchief lest he draw attention to himself.

He watched from cover as the others blundered into the trees and went crashing through the undergrowth. They had scattered quite widely, but Grole wasn't far away and he could hear him moaning with fear. Then the distant door opened, and Ronan and the woman entered with a tatty little donkey. Wayta watched as they sped across the grass, and he was as surprised as anyone when the snake/bird plummeted from the heights above and knocked the woman out only ten yards away from him. He stared, impressed despite himself, as the little donkey took on the creature, enabling Ronan to destroy it. But then as Ronan knelt over the woman, he realised that his chance had come, for the huge warrior was unarmed, and had his back to him . .

Tiptoeing out, Wayta crept across the small wooden bridge towards his deadly enemy. Five yards to go . . . then three . . . he was there! Ronan seemed to have tensed and was staring at something, but Wayta's every nerve was concentrated on the warrior, and he had eyes for nothing else. Hardly daring to breathe, he drew his sword right back, ready to bring it smashing down on Ronan's unprotected head.

Tarl drained the mug of beer to the last drop and watched happily as Marwood followed suit. He always felt a lot better after a couple of beers, let alone six, and he began to wonder what the others were doing. Whatever it was, they would probably feel a lot better as well if they had a beer or several inside them.

'I reckon we should find the others and give them a drink,' he said. Marwood thought about this, and then nodded.

'Damn right,' he said. 'They're probably dying for a beer. Dying for one.'

Picking up the wooden beer barrel that the others had given them, he slapped Tarl on the shoulder, and the two of them ambled through the debris and bodies, and went in search of their friends.

Ronan was staring at the *cobrats* and trying to fight down the rising tide of despair that threatened to engulf him, when there was a loud sneeze immediately behind him. He snatched his head round to find Wayta looming over him, his sword raised and ready to strike, his face still screwed up from the sneeze. They stared at one another for a microsecond that seemed to last for ever, and then the sword came hissing down. Ronan reacted instinctively, throwing up his left hand to block it, and the blade sliced into his wrist, carving through flesh and bone. Grunting from the force of the blow, Ronan grabbed Wayta's sword arm with his right hand, and then straightening, he shook it as though he was cracking a whip. There was a snapping sound, and Wayta screamed, the sword falling from his lifeless fingers to land beside an object on the floor that Ronan realised with shock was his left hand.

And then the pain hit home and he screamed, his cry of agony drowning out Wayta's moans. Out of the corner of his eye, he could see the *cobrats* gliding towards him. At his feet, Tyson groaned, and he could see Puss beginning to stir too. The *cobrats* would be upon them in seconds, and they had as much chance against them as a helpless swimmer against a shark. Lifting his left arm, he stared at the blood that fountained from the stump of his wrist. Rage flooded through him and he roared out loud with impotent fury, snarling at Wayta, the chairman of the board, who had caused all this to happen. Then, burying the stump in his right armpit and clamping his other arm over it, he seized Wayta by the throat. The chairman stared at him, then gasped in fear and pain as his grip tightened. Ronan's face shook with effort, the blood roaring in his ears as his right hand squeezed. Wayta's hands scrabbled at him, and his feet drummed on the ground. But all at once there was a sound like someone stamping on an apple, and Ronan's fingers crushed through cartilage. Wayta's head lolled backwards, his sightless eyes staring skywards, and Ronan lifted him by the throat and dashed his lifeless body to the ground.

Then he knelt beside Tyson and closed his eyes, squeezing his wrist as tightly as he could beneath his arm to stem the flow of blood, still instinctively seeking to cling to life, although he could sense the *cobrats* towering over him and smell the sourness of their breath. He waited for the pain of death, muscles tensed, too shocked and tired even to make a fight of it. But nothing happened, and opening his eyes again, he saw that the five *cobrats* were standing in a semicricle in front of him, peering from him to Wayta and back again. They seemed puzzled, almost baffled.

The largest leaned down to the dead man, prodded him with its taloned forepaw, then straightened and stared at Ronan.

'Our massster,' it hissed. 'You have killed our massster!'

Oh-oh, thought Ronan. *Now it will happen. Still, it was almost worth it to kill one of those murderous, power-mad old bastards.*

'Yes,' he said.

The large *cobrat* looked at him with its head tilted to one side.

'Iffff you have killed our massster, then you are our massster,' it hissed.

Ronan thought about this for a while. He was finding it very difficult to concentrate. Beneath him, Tyson shook her head and opened her eyes, then gasped with fear at the sight of the creatures standing above her.

'Are you sure?' Ronan finally asked the *cobrat*.

'Yesss,' it hissed. 'Our massster killed our lassst massster. That is why he was our massster. Now you have killed him. You were stronger than him. So you are our massster.'

The other four *cobrats* nodded their sleek, greasy heads in agreement.

Ronan gave a great sigh, hardly able to believe it. Then he turned to Tyson.

'I need your help here, love,' he said. 'My hand . . .'

Tyson stared at his blood-soaked side and at the stump of his wrist as he withdrew it from under his arm. Reaching out wordlessly, she tore a strip from Wayta's shirt, and tied it as a tourniquet about his forearm. She wasn't sure what was going on, but from the sight of Wayta's corpse beside them, and from what the *cobrat* had said in its travesty of a voice, Ronan seemed somehow to be in command of things.

'Puss!' said Ronan loudly. 'No! They're on our side now.'

Looking round, Tyson saw that the little donkey had been stiff-leggedly stalking towards the *cobrats*, ready to attack them, and despite everything, she found herself smiling.

230

Ronan squeezed her arm with his remaining hand, and stood up.

'Okay, guys,' he said to the *cobrats*. 'This is your master speaking. There are five other men in here. They came in with your ex-master here.' He stirred Wayta's body with his foot. 'Can you scent them?'

'Yesss!'

'Well, I am leaving this cavern now. I want you to wait until I have left, and then you are to hunt down and kill the five men. Then stay here. Do you understand?'

'Yesss!'

Ronan nodded, satisfied, then walked the few paces to where his sword lay in the grass. Picking it up, he limped back to Tyson, and she put her arm about his waist to support him. With Puss beside them, they trudged tiredly across towards the door. But when they were about ten yards short, a new wave of pain swept over him. The cavern seemed to whirl about his head, and he fell to his knees, gasping.

'Come on, love!' urged Tyson. 'We must get out of here! I don't trust those killing machines!'

'Ah, but it hurts!' he whispered. 'I wish I had something to take my mind off the pain!'

Tyson looked down at him, then glanced back at the *cobrats*, which were staring at them unblinkingly.

'If he dies, they'll be after us again,' remarked the donkey, brightly.

'He's not going to die!' she snapped. But looking at Ronan, she wasn't so sure. He had lost a lot of blood. His face was grey, and his skin felt cold and clammy. She needed to get him to Guebral, quickly, for she had seen the girl's near-miraculous healing powers before. *Ah, well,* she thought. *I've got to tell him sometime. It might as well be now, or he may never know.*

'Ronan,' she whispered. 'I'm pregnant.'

There was a sudden pause, and for a horrible moment she thought he had stopped breathing, but then he turned to stare at her, and at the expression of wonder and joy on his face she felt the tears start from her eyes.

'Ah, love!' he breathed. 'Is it . . . are you . . . is it mine?'

'You ever ask me a question like that again, and I'll cut your other hand off. Now come on!'

She helped him to his feet, but as they began to stagger towards the door, a disembodied voice rang out.

'A touching little scene,' it said, 'but I'm afraid you'll find that the door cannot be opened from your side.'

231

They stared round, then saw that they were being watched with interest by the dwarf who had dodged back through the wooden door. He was sitting inside a small enclosed observation booth hollowed out of the rock wall a few feet to the right of the door. It appeared to be sealed off from the cavern by a thick glass window.

'It has been most entertaining watching you,' his voice continued, and they saw that it was emanating from a small speaking tube above the window. 'But I'm afraid your time is at an end. The *cobrats* now regard you as their master, and the only way I can alter that is to have you killed. I think it is time to let the latest batch of *cobrats* in to the Vivarium. When they kill you, the others will then merge with the pack, and I will be master to all of them.'

Ronan saw with horror that the dwarf had his fingers on a small lever. He staggered across towards the booth, waving his sword.

'No!' he yelled. 'Wait!'

'The glass, by the way, is unbreakable,' the dwarf told him. 'Another of our little inventions. Well, goodbye. It's a shame about the Orcbane board, but then I'm sure I can find other backers for my plans . . .'

Ronan stared at Meiosin in disbelief. This smugly grinning dwarf was behind all the misery that had racked Mahon and Kahdor, the death and destruction that they had witnessed in Gudmornen. And now the *klatting* little sod was condemning not only him but Tyson to a horrible death. And not only her, but her child. His child. *Their* child . . .

Once again the rage of a berserker filled him. A red haze clouded his eyes, and with a roar of utter fury he drew back his sword and thrust it against the window with a power greater than the dwarves had ever expected the glass to have to withstand. It didn't break, but split like wood, and Ronan's sword speared through unchecked to plunge home into Meiosin's chest, skewering him to his chair. The dwarf gave one horrible shriek of pain then sagged back, lifeless, and Ronan watched with horror as the weight of the dwarf's arm dragged his dead fingers past the lever, pulling it with them.

Klat! Was that going to let more *cobrats* loose? He glanced back at the trees, terrified, then hammered on the window and dragged at his sword, trying to free it, but the glass clung to it, refusing to let go. All of a sudden he had no more strength left. He staggered across to where Tyson was beating on the door with the hilt of her sword, but then his head began to spin again, and he fell to his knees.

232

Tyson put her arms around his waist and managed to haul him to his feet. She stared around, desperately looking for a hint of some other way out. The five *cobrats* were still standing near the trees, watching them. But then she saw another movement, away to their right, near where the stream entered the vast cavern, and for a moment she thought her heart had stopped. Two more *cobrats* were stalking across the grass towards them, and there was no mistaking their intent.

Marwood and Tarl had been trying to track the others down using a *locate* spell, but it was taking a while as they kept stopping to have another swig from the beer barrel, which made Tarl lose track of the spell. They had just pushed open a large stone door and were staring interestedly at the long, eerily lit passage, when they heard what sounded like someone hammering on metal. It seemed to be coming from ahead of them, and so they ambled along to the black metal door at the end and opened it. In front of them was another similar door, but the sound had stopped now, and so they paused. Tarl was just going to suggest that, as they couldn't find the others, they have another beer themselves, when all at once the hammering began again. It was someone beating frantically on the other side of the second door.

'Okay,' called Tarl. 'Coming.'

He ambled forwards, lifted the latch, and the door rocketed open, smashing into him and sending him flying backwards into the wall. Puss shot through as though fired from a bow, followed by Ronan and Tyson. Marwood had a momentary glimpse of what looked like two *cobrats* charging at the door, but then Tyson slammed it shut just in time, and fell back, gasping.

'All right,' muttered Tarl sulkily as he picked himself up. 'There's plenty of booze for everyone, you don't have to rush.'

He paused as Tyson looked venomously at him.

'Here, what's wrong?' he asked her. 'Aren't you having fun? Have some beer.'

So Tyson told him exactly what he could do with his beer, and Tarl's face turned ashen with shock.

The five original *cobrats* watched as their new master staggered out of the door with his friends. The instant it slammed shut behind him, they turned and began the hunt, and the newcomers, deprived

233

of their prey, joined in. They knew that the five men were trapped, and so they took their time, toying with them like cats with mice.

Grole was the first to die, screaming as the razor-sharp talons ripped open his fat belly for the *cobrats* to feed. Kaglav was next, hunted and chivvied for ten terror-filled minutes before the creatures tired of their sport and finished him, ripping him apart in seconds. Mellial was already dead, for one of the sweet little *rabbions* had found him hiding in the bushes, and he, like Reágin before him, had died in agony from the venom.

Missek, fleeing through the undergrowth at the very rear of the cavern, stumbled into what seemed like a massive, sticky fishing net, and only when it clung to him so tightly that he couldn't free himself did he realise what it was. He struggled desperately, but his struggles alerted the giant spider that had spun the web. Five minutes later, when Missek was so entangled he couldn't even blink, it punctured the skin of his neck with its huge mandibles and began to feed.

The last to die was Gahvanser. It was almost an hour after the chase had started, an hour filled with such fear and horror that, when the *cobrats* trapped him against a wall, his weak, overtaxed heart gave way, and he was dead before they even touched him. But the *cobrats* bent over him, content that they had done as their new master ordered, and began to feed. Their job was complete, and they could now wait here where they had been born until their master had new tasks for them.

EPILOGUE

. . . and of all the folk saved from the Dark Dwarves by Ronan One-hand and his friends, most famous must be Tragath, the female centaur who went on to become one of Midworld's best-known models. She achieved notoriety some three years later, when a picture of her posing naked was splashed across two pages of the Gudmornen Herald, *and thus did she become Midworld's first nude centaur-fold . . .*

The Pink Book of Ulay

Tarl stood near the door of the room and stared at the eight cylindrical metal booths with their thick steel doors and their control panels covered in levers, dials and switches. Across the top of each booth was an inscription in dwarvish runes.

'Have we found out what these things are yet?' asked Tarl.

'According to the runes, they're Matter Transmitters,' replied Marwood, who was busy stacking large wooden boxes in front of them. 'Now, what do you suppose a Matter Transmitter does?'

'Er . . . gets rid of zits?' suggested Tarl.

Marwood broke open the side of one of the boxes, and looked at the contents doubtfully. To him they looked like large red candles, but he had been assured that they were a lot more dangerous than that.

'Okay,' he said, 'we're finished in here. Time for us to be leaving. We don't want to be around when this lot goes up . . .'

For three days, Tarl, Tyson, Guebral and Marwood had explored the city of Deforzh, whilst Ronan lay in bed in the Medicaments Department, his arm swathed in bandages, recovering. He had lost so much blood that by the time they got him to Guebral, he had lapsed into unconsciousness again. Gueb had used her powers to ease and restore him, but there was nothing she could do for his severed hand.

He had passed most of the time asleep, and Tyson had spent what time she could with him, sitting quietly by the bed whilst he slept, and talking with him when he woke. They had many plans to make, for now that the Orcbane board had been eliminated, their task was complete. Ronan was safe from the Assassins; thanks to Dean Blackwell, he was now an honorary MA, and he had fulfilled his side of the bargain. The Dean's grandson had been rescued safe and sound, as had Tragath and all the other captives. On the day after their release, they had all set out in well-provisioned and heavily armed groups to return to their homes.

The orcs had departed as soon as they had drunk the bar dry, which had taken a mere twenty-four hours. Tarl and Marwood, with Chigger's help, had kept them in some sort of order. Most of them were city orcs who had spent their lives drinking in pubs, talking about the old days and legendary party leaders like Gaz the Tall. For them, this was their first experience of a real live war party, and it had gone well. As a result, Chigger was a complete and utter hero to them, and they would have done virtually anything he demanded of them (as long as it didn't involve giving up drinking).

As for the dwarves, not many remained. The orcs had killed a lot, and others had fled the city. There were perhaps a hundred who had surrendered. All seemed truly contrite for the excesses of Meiosin's regime, and after talking to them, Guebral and Tyson had accepted their allegiance. The dwarves had shown them around the city, explaining the various inventions and discoveries, although Tyson had made damn sure that no one had been allowed through the doors into the Vivarium.

It was when Guebral was told about the properties of the various explosives, and discovered what vast quantities the dwarves had manufactured, that she came up with the idea of what to do with Deforzh. The remaining dwarves had no wish to stay there any longer, and were planning to join a large expedition that was being planned within the dwarf world to resettle Samoth, the abandoned dwarf city beneath the mountains of south-west Frundor. It was obviously too dangerous to leave Deforzh empty, and something had to be done about the lethal equipment and creatures that it still contained. Tyson for one was determined that the *cobrats* should never see the light of day again.

And so the dwarves had been put to the job of moving all the stored explosives into twelve strategically located places throughout the city. After three days the job had been completed, and the dwarves had been freed from their allegiance and had left the city to head for the dwarf-lands of the south-west. Tarl, Marwood and Guebral had then made the preparations necessary for the successful simultaneous detonation of all the explosives.

The plan was simple. Each of the twelve hordes of explosive had an opened box, in the middle of which was a single stick of TNT. Under the fuse of this stick was positioned one of twelve candles which Guebral had chosen. She reckoned that she could light these candles simultaneously with an *Ignite* spell from a distance. And in half an hour's time, that was what she was going to try to do.

The six of them stood on the featureless plain, a mile away from the mountain. It was mid-morning, and the grey skies threatened snow. A chill wind was blowing from the east, but they were all wrapped up in stout cloaks, and had full stomachs to help keep the cold at bay, for the dwarves had been well provisioned.

Guebral looked at the others, and one by one they nodded. She turned and stared at the mountain, then muttered a few words. At first, nothing seemed to have happened, but then they felt more than heard a distant deep rumbling. And then the ground really shook, so much that they staggered. The distant mountain trembled, and then bits of it seemed to sag and crumple inwards, as though undermined. That was all; there was no fire, no flames, just a gradual collapse, like a sandcastle when the waves of the sea lap round it.

'Ah, well,' said Marwood. 'That's that, then.'

They turned and began walking south-west towards the distant chain of mountains. In the front walked Ronan, Guebral and Puss, and behind them came Tarl, Tyson and Marwood.

'So, what now?' Tyson asked Marwood.

'I dunno. I'm not going back to the Assassins, that's for sure. What about you?'

'Gueb and I fancy heading for the dwarf city of Samoth,' said Tarl. 'That is, if they manage to get the place going again. There's a pub there that I wouldn't mind running ... But first we're going to Yai'El, as Gueb wants to say goodbye to her friends.'

'Ronan and I are going along as far as Yai'El,' added Tyson. 'Gueb has a friend that might be able to fix him up with a pretty neat false hand. Then we fancy a bit longer on the beaches of Perplec. I've had enough of cold weather. And I've had enough fighting for a while. We want to find somewhere we can bring up a kid in peace.'

'What's Puss going to do?'

'Ah, he'll tag along for the ride,' said Tarl. 'He's always welcome.'

There was a short pause.

'Want to come along?' asked Tarl.

'Yes,' said Marwood. 'I don't mind if I do.'

There was a sudden rumble like distant thunder behind them, followed by a loud explosion. Turning, they saw that a river of bright-red lava had burst from the side of Tor Deforzh and was inching its way down towards the plain.

'There,' said Ronan. 'Nothing is going to survive that.'

And he winced as a sudden burning pain shot through the hand that wasn't there any more. Tyson linked her arm through his.

'Come on, sweetheart,' she murmured. 'Let's go and enjoy life a little. After all, that's what it's for.'

And turning, they set their faces to the west and began the long, cold journey back to Gudmornen.

GLOSSARY

Carn Jonnald: a large hill in north Cydor overlooking the River Leno, famous for the Sentinel Statue. This huge stone effigy was commissioned by a powerful and warlike king of Cydor, Longvar the Bear, and was carved from the very rock of the summit of Carn Jonnald. It stood facing north, looking over the Great River Leno to Frundor beyond, and was intended to be an effigy of Longvar himself and a monument to his strength and popularity.

Unfortunately, the man chosen to carve the statue was Hardric, a talented but rather depraved sculptor whose unsavoury personal habits had left him quite deaf. Longvar the Bear issued him with instructions that included the phrase: 'I want to see fortitude in stone, the Bear our soldiers know and love.' Hardric misheard this as: 'I want to see four tits hewed in stone, the bare arse soldiers know and love.'

The resulting forty-foot-high statue was a sight to behold. Longvar's distinctive, bearded face stared forth proudly from on top of a naked and extremely buxom female body which was endowed with twice the usual number of bosoms. At the unveiling ceremony, performed in front of several detachments of the Cydorian Army, Longvar's hair is said to have turned pure white with shock, while the entire army were rendered helpless with laughter. Their howls of mirth are reputed to have been audible in the city of Ilex, several miles away.

The sight of his beloved army rolling about on the ground in paroxysms of mirth sent Longvar into something of a decline, and from that moment forth he gave up waging war, devoting the rest of his life to growing tomatoes (which he kept in large baskets by his throne and hurled with great force at any sculptors who came anywhere near him).

fire-skink: a small sand-lizard native to the tropical beaches of Iduin which has developed an unusual method of body-temperature regulation. Lacking sweat glands, the *fire-skink* will urinate over itself in extremely hot temperatures to cool down. Unsurprisingly, it is a solitary creature. It can be recognised by its bright-red colouration, which is caused more by acute embarrassment than anything else.

Fundin the Peculiar: a dwarf from Tor Deforzh who shocked and astounded polite dwarven society by suggesting that their obsession for gold was an evil thing, and that the wealth of the richest should be shared out amongst them all so that the poor and hungry were cared for. A member of one of the richest families, Fundin gave away much of his money, and used the rest to found a charity, Share Out Dwarven Wealth Amongst Needy Kindred. Because of the unfortunate acronym this was later shortened to SHARE and the charity began to attract a lot of interest.

However, everything changed when Fundin, who even by dwarven standards was several seams short of a gold mine, went a bit too far. Firstly, he shaved off his beard (which in dwarven society was as much of a social gaffe as if we were to ask the Queen for a snog) and took to wandering about Deforzh wearing only an old coal sack. And then, one fateful day, he attacked Thorin, one of the richest and most respected scientists in the colony, seriously injuring him.

Fundin spent the whole of his trial denouncing the dwarves of Deforzh for their greed and avarice, and no one was surprised when he was found guilty of treason and sentenced to immediate exile. And so he left the colony in disgrace, and was never heard of again. His charity, SHARE, which had been doing very good work until then, was sadly forced to close down shortly afterwards, owing to lack of Fundin . . .

giguana (**pronounced 'jy-gwanna'**): a nine-foot-high lizard with an upright posture and the most fearsome set of teeth imaginable. The *giguana* looks like a cold and lethal killing machine, which just goes to show that looks aren't everything, as it is actually sweetly good-natured, extremely charming and as daft as a brush. *Giguanas* were first bred during the Second Age by the Dark Dwarves of Tor Deforzh. They escaped from captivity by becoming friendly with their guards and getting invited home for tea. They can frequently be found in the wilder areas of northern Baq d'Or, where they latch on to travellers, following them around making polite conversation and begging for chocolate.

Guild of Assassins: one of the Seven Ancient Guilds and Brotherhoods, the Guild of Assassins is an august and venerable

240

body that was founded during the First Age by Anherr the Obnoxious, Hitman by Royal Appointment to Lardo the Psychotic, the last King of Iduin. Its headquarters are in the city of Tena, in the Azure Mountains, although it has a Guildhall in every major city in Midworld. The Guild's motto is *Erechím, meänomíl, a valan portíllo.* Translated from the elvish, this means *Knowledge, guile and the heart of a total bastard,* and is a fair summing-up of the average, run-of-the-mill psychopathic Guild member.

Kelvin: dwarven scientist of the First Age, creator of the science of Praecipitinfelicitology (the study of sheer bad luck), and founder of the dwarven scientific research centre at Deforzh. Kelvin was one of those unfortunate people for whom if anything can go wrong, it will. After a lifetime of appalling misfortune, he postulated a number of Laws of Bad Luck, based upon his own experiences. These are often irreverently referred to by less unlucky scientists as Kelvin's Laws for Losers. They include:

Boil's Law. On any day that you have an important date with an attractive member of the opposite sex, you will awake in the morning to discover that a large red boil has formed on your nose, and is glowing like a malignant beacon.

Hook's Law. Whenever you go fishing, no matter how careful you are, at least one fish-hook will embed itself in the back of your neck.

First Law of Mechanics. No matter how trivial the fault in the mechanical item with which you present him, the first thing a mechanic will do upon looking at it is shake his head doubtfully from side to side before saying, 'It's going to cost you, squire.'

Second Law of Mechanics. The bill you are presented with by a mechanic will bear no relation to the work done, but will be directly proportional to his estimation of your gullibility.

klat: if you haven't worked it out yet, you must have led a very sheltered life. Either that or it's way past your bedtime, so put Daddy's book down and go and have your bath right away.

magenetics: the science of genetically mutating and altering creatures by the use of magic. Whereas normal genetics only allows interaction between creatures of the same species, magenetics allows it between virtually any combination of known creatures. For example, in a notorious series of experiments in the laboratories beneath Tor Deforzh, a dwarf scientist named Mitochondrin attempted to cross a domesticated cat with a bird, aiming to produce a feline that could fly. Unfortunately, knowing very little about birds, he selected a Brannian Ostrich as the parent. The resulting offspring, although flightless, were very fast runners indeed, and proceeded to chase every dog in the neighbourhood and give them a right good kicking. Mitochondrin later attempted to market them as household pets, but failed miserably. No one was interested in a creature which, every time it excreted, attempted to bury its head in the shit.

Ovuk: the god of Imminent Death. Ovuk is usually invoked by those who find themselves in mortal peril or extreme danger. Ovuk is the second-busiest god in the pantheon, being invoked on average every minute or so by somebody or other who has just been scared crapless. The busiest god is undoubtedly Ogese, the god of Orgasm, who is beseeched on average approximately every 0.34 seconds. Ogese, a small, stooped, white-haired god, is so overworked that he is usually about twenty minutes late in replying to supplicants, by which time they are frequently fast asleep on their backs, snoring. However, this is normally just in time for their unsatisfied female partners, who have quietly locked themselves in the bathroom with just a cream bun and their imaginations for company . . .

praecipitinfelicitology: sorry, run out of space. See **Kelvin**.

rudduck: a small, nervous, twitchy bird that inhabits grasslands throughout Midworld. *Rudducks* build compact, well-hidden nests in the long grass, and lay a single egg, which quickly hatches. Inside this nest, the dun-coloured fledgling is extremely well camouflaged, and the adult birds spend half their time looking for food, and the other half trying to find where the hell their nest has got to. They can be recognised by their mournful cry of *Baby! Baby!* and after breeding, the adults develop pure white feathers (mainly through worry). The *rudduck* is the only bird that is known to bite its nails incessantly.

sarhafilas: a small, dainty white flower that grows wild on the plains and grasslands of Cydor and Behan. The name comes from the elvish *sarha filas*, which means 'little baby's toes', and just goes to show that you should not, under any circumstances, ask elves to name anything at all, ever.

Sentinel Statue: see **Carn Jonnald**.

Vnaya: an exotic tree similar to a palm, and native to western Brannan. It produces a large golden fruit with a rock-hard shell, inside which is soft, juicy flesh that tastes truly delicious and acts as a remarkably effective aphrodisiac. The fruit are produced inside large pods, several feet long. Each contains about forty fruit, and when ripe, these pods explode with such force that the fruit are violently ejected like small cannonballs, and can be thrown up to half a mile away. This is all very well for the trees, being quite an efficient way of spreading seed, but it makes life for *vnaya*-growers extremely hazardous. In fact, the mortality rate amongst the *vnaya*-gatherers is second only to that of the Orcville casinos' professional Gambling Chips.

Appendix Two

ELVEN CARDS

As is widely known, most elves have a sentimental streak a mile wide, and at times they can become embarrassingly soppy. As a result, elven playing-cards bear little resemblance to a standard pack of cards, and have more in common with a tarot pack.

To begin with, there are a hundred cards in an elven pack, divided into four suits (or guilds) of twenty-five cards: hearts, flowers, ribbons and little furry animals (yes, we know, but that's elves for you). Each suit contains one master card, and the other twenty-four cards are divided into six sub-groups, with four cards in each.

For example, the suit of ribbons is subdivided into cotton, silk, linen, paper, muslin and calico, each of which has four varieties: pink, grass green, snow white and baby blue (yes, baby blue. Well, we did warn you what elves are like). Thus you have cards called the grass-green paper ribbon, or the baby-blue silk ribbon. The suit of little furry animals is subdivided into kittens, bunnies, gerbils, baa-lambs, puppies and little bear cubs. These again have four varieties: happy, sad, sleeping and teeny-tiny (look, you don't have to read this if it makes you feel ill). Hearts are divided into kind, broken, loving, forgiving, generous and sweet, with the four varieties of man, woman, little boy and little girl.

This may sound confusing, but on inspecting an elven pack it all becomes clear. Numbers and symbols are not used to distinguish the cards. Like the major arcana of a tarot pack, each one is depicted by a picture. The artwork can at times be magnificent – the suit of flowers includes beautiful studies of some of Midworld's rarest flora. Unfortunately, the paintings can also be downright mawkish – for example, the pictures for the little boy with a broken heart, or the little girl with her sweetheart. But without doubt, the worst of all are found in the suit of little furry animals, and cards like the sleeping baa-lamb and the teeny-tiny bunny are capable of producing acute nausea.

Some of these packs are much prized by professional card-players, as with experience they are frequently able to tell who has got which cards simply by the expression on their face. Tarl of Welbug owned a pack that was so grossly sentimental, he claimed he could always tell who had the teeny-tiny kitten because when they looked at their hand, invariably their eyebrows would shoot up and a look of incredulous horror would cross their face, and then they would lay down their cards and either bury their head in their hands or knock back their remaining drink in a single gulp.